The Turning Point

THE ELI CHRONICLES
BOOK 3

Julia Ash

DEDICATION

*To two courageous, loving women
who have greatly influenced me:*

*Mary Brennan
(1939 – 2020)*

and

*Regine Dönges
(1959 – 2018)*

ഇ ങ ഇ ങ

What they're saying about

The Turning Point

ACCOLADES

Writer's Digest Honorable Mention
(2020 Self-Published E-Book Awards, Fantasy)

"An incredibly original story I escaped into easily!"
— Judge, 8th Annual Writer's Digest Self-Published E-Book Awards, 2020

BookLife Prize Semi-Finalist
(2020, Sci-Fi, Fantasy, & Horror)

"Ash plots a twisty, surprising course through this extravagantly inventive material, always guiding readers to what matters most in any of the crisp, tightly written chapters." — The BookLife Prize

REVIEWS

Kirkus Reviews

"Ash is a fearless author who holds little back in terms of imagination and worldbuilding." — Kirkus Reviews

Miranda Reads
#1 Best Reviewer on Goodreads

"Just when I think this series can't get any better - it does. Again. I am absolutely blown away by the direction of this book - so much fun, excitement, and mayhem. A perfect ending for this fabulous trilogy! What am I supposed to do now that it's over?"

Dita Daub
#3 Best Reviewer and Librarian on Goodreads

"Julia Ash's third installment in the ELI Chronicles is her best to date. Saying goodbye to beloved characters and bidding adieu to the magical world Julia has thoughtfully crafted would be much harder if I didn't believe we have many more amazing books coming from this author!"

Note: Reviewer rankings on Goodreads were at the time of publication.

The Planets

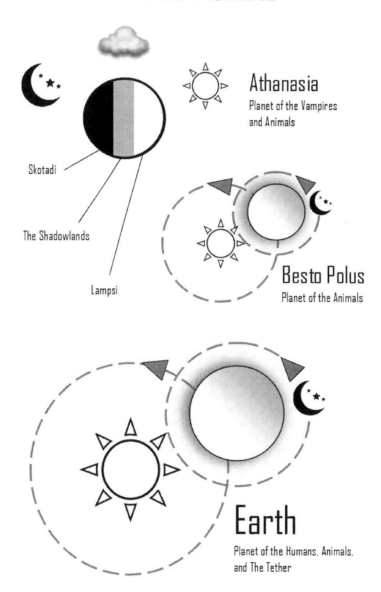

Athanasia
Planet of the Vampires
and Animals

Skotadi

The Shadowlands

Lampsi

Besto Polus
Planet of the Animals

Earth
Planet of the Humans, Animals,
and The Tether

NOTE: Pages featuring translations (of animal language), pronunciations,
and planet information are located in the back of the book.

The Turning Point

THE ELI CHRONICLES
BOOK 3

Julia Ash

THE ELI CHRONICLES SERIES
(ELI = Extinction Level Infection)

The One and Only

The Tether

The Turning Point

1

THE FIRST LADY of the United States occasionally hissed and grunted, but she had never chirped.

Ruby Spencer listened, standing in the master suite of the Executive Residence. Only a locked bathroom door separated her from the President's wife.

Concentrating, Ruby cognitively eavesdropped inside Irene Unger's mind to learn what she was thinking, what she was feeling. The effort was futile. Within the First Lady's brain, the repetitive chanting was more like gibberish.

Amadad ahoee, amadad ahoee, Irene droned, pausing every now and then to vent a few chirps or teeth clicks into the physical world.

The bathroom door rattled, threatening to break from its hinges.

Maybe the mental babble represented a dialect, but it wasn't one Ruby spoke. Surprising, since she was fluent in over two dozen languages, not to mention her added proficiency for countless regional variations. But Irene's garbling didn't resemble any of them.

Finally, the door stilled. Silence returned.

With wide eyes and an elevated pulse, President Unger stepped back as if his wife might burst through the door. He was pale. Dark circles dimmed his eyes. Perspiration beaded on his forehead, and fear soured the moisture staining his shirt's underarms.

"When did Irene lock herself in the bathroom?" Ruby asked him.

Using the heel of his hand, the POTUS wiped sweat collecting on his eyebrows. "Nine o'clock, last night."

"It's three-thirty in the afternoon, Will. She's been in there for over eighteen hours. Why didn't you call staff for help? Or her personal physician?"

"I promised not to let anyone see her," he admitted, lowering his gaze. "At least, not in her current…state. She made me swear."

"Explain."

"Before bed, she was brushing her hair. Whole swatches unrooted from her scalp. Irene panicked. *Your body's been through hell,* I said. *Hair loss is common in cancer patients.*" His eyes grew glassy. "Told her we'd buy a fancy wig, and no one would be the wiser. She'd be beautiful, as she's always been."

A tear escaped, running down his cheek.

There were legitimate reasons not to respond to a health crisis near someone's final days, like abiding by a terminally ill patient's advance healthcare directive. Ruby was also 100-percent sure that beauty (or the lack of it) did *not* constitute an incurable disease.

News media contributed to her confusion since White House correspondents claimed the First Lady had miraculously healed from her bout with cancer.

Yet, Irene Unger sounded far from well.

Which meant Clay's suspicions were spot-on.

Ruby's husband believed something sinister was behind Irene's full recovery from stage-four ovarian cancer. Something involving the notorious Emory Bradshaw.

The evidence was mounting. Whoever (or whatever) was on the other side of the bathroom door had to be a consequence of evil forces greater than cancer's lingering side effects.

After thoroughly assessing Irene's physical condition, Ruby would glamour the POTUS, applying a powerful hypnotic suggestion that forced him to tell the truth about the "remedy" he and Emory had conjured up for the First Lady. No doubt genetic tampering would be involved. Emory, her former college best friend, had evolved over the last 15 years into a dark science deviant.

At one time, the U.S. government had subsidized his unorthodox experiments. But Emory turned out to be a monster impersonating an innovator.

Unnerving, then, that the POTUS had pardoned him from a Virginia penitentiary despite Emory's heinous crimes against humanity. Pardoned him, as in yesterday.

With strange clucks and chirps emanating from the bathroom, Ruby predicted that a simple wig on Irene's head wouldn't be enough to conceal the mad scientist's handiwork. After all, Emory fancied himself as a maverick, creating DNA Frankensteins like his "frat," a genetic fusion between a frog and rat. He was a master at bioengineering the grotesque.

Why the government had ever funded him was almost as mind boggling as how she and Emory could've ever been friends. Clearly, his genius had sucked her in. But with every passing year since graduation, his projects had grown more inhumane and sadistic.

Ruby was one of Emory's first human experiments. *Non*-consensual, of course.

Evidently, Irene was the newest member of his hybrid freaks.

"How was your wife feeling before she entered the bathroom?" Ruby asked, trying to suppress her anger. "I mean, besides her panic over hair loss?"

"Light irritated her eyes. She retired to bed early. Around eight."

"How about dinner? Did she have an appetite?"

"None. Didn't even sip her wine. Said her teeth and jaws hurt."

"Anything else?" she asked.

He stared blankly for a moment, as if replaying her symptoms in his mind. "Irene was freezing—shivering and chattering her teeth. After bundling her in blankets, she was roasting. She didn't seem sick, per se. More like she couldn't regulate her body temperature. The slightest deviation in coldness or warmth affected her."

Without intending to display exasperation, Ruby realized a little too late that she was shaking her head in disbelief. Or was her reaction disapproval? Probably both.

"You're judging me?" he snapped. "I love my wife. Cherish her every breath and heartbeat. And I asked you. I asked *you* to heal her of cancer by giving her some of your blood. You refused, lecturing me that death was natural! So don't you dare judge my efforts to save her. Don't."

"You're right. I'm sorry." She nodded, feeling guilt rise to her throat. "It's just that Emory Bradshaw's test subjects usually end up dead. In a very *un*-natural way."

"You're alive."

"I'm a vampire. Technically, I'm undead—which mostly falls on the spectrum of the deceased. Don't get me wrong. After nine years, I've accepted my fate, but I didn't have a choice. No one asked me if I wanted to turn. Did you at least give Irene an option?"

"We both knew the risks," he said. "Em explained them all."

"Guess I better see what those risks yielded."

The quicker Ruby observed what they were dealing with, the quicker she could figure out how to help. *If* healing Irene was even possible at this point, since within Ruby's mind, the cognitive etchings on the First Lady's lifeline stone were no longer glowing. In fact, they were slowly dissolving. Soon, her stone would be blank.

Ruby deeply inhaled. The clock was ticking on another front as well. Though not critical by any means, she couldn't deny her heart longed to be with her family.

Clay and Gabby were waiting for her at their Cedar Lane property where they were rebuilding their home after the devastating housefire. She had promised her husband and daughter she'd only be an hour. Having been apart from Clay for 11 days, all she really wanted was to spend time with him. Not that she'd push aside her civic responsibilities; her duties ultimately came first.

The only reason she had rejoined the ranks of the immortal, as a vampire fueled with the most powerful blood and gifts, was to continue serving others more than herself. To help bring safety, balance, and harmony to every living thing in the world and universe. A tall order, for sure.

Fulfilling her duty as The Tether might be inconvenient at times. She had accepted that fact and would serve regardless. Truth was: danger never considered anyone's needs or wants. Danger had no timeclock, no schedule. It never abided by any civilized rules.

Her recent challenge to save humanity proved as much.

Danger had been cloaked in the unexpected. It had drained the innocent of blood, flown with bats and ravens, heated coins into flames, and traveled with dust.

Hard to believe that hours earlier, she and Gabby were in

Athanasia, the vampire planet, where they had successfully orchestrated a ruse, resulting in the intended death of danger's embodiment: Zagan, the King of Darkness. An unavoidable outcome, all because the immortal king had disregarded an oracle's warning 2.8 mega-annum ago. By eating forbidden berries from The Tree of Awareness, followed by a fig from The Tree of Immortality, Zagan had afflicted himself with a curse, locking evil inside his soul. Death was the only way to set his goodness free and destroy the evil that had corroded his conscience.

Even with regrets over Zagan's death, she couldn't deny that the universe was a safer place without him.

She wondered what kind of evil, what kind of danger, was manifesting itself within Irene.

"What are you going to do?" President Unger asked, his hands trembling.

"Travel inside the bathroom. Learn what freakish hybrid she's become. Albeit, cancer free."

The POTUS clenched his jaw. His face flushed crimson.

Before he could ease his guilt by blaming *her* for the horror she'd undoubtedly find on the other side of the door, Ruby turned to dust.

2

Friday, July 12, 2041
The White House Executive Residence: Washington, D.C.

RUBY MATERIALIZED IN the bathroom as a ghost, levitating near the shower.

Standing in front of the mirror, the President's wife shivered and raised her chin, stretching her neck like a howling wolf. She released a doleful cry with a stream of chilled mist.

Vonaig ahoee, Irene whimpered inside her mind. *Miangui ree.*

Her words were meaningless, except for the recognizable anguish coating each sound. Even with a language barrier, most people could easily interpret emotional torment.

Ruby's heart bled for her friend. Even at first glance, the First Lady's outward despair was obviously the tip of the iceberg.

Naked and bald, Irene looked as though she'd lost all her body fat, making her skin two sizes too large. Sporadic white whiskers, long and thick, had grown from enlarged pores, with clusters of hair concentrating between her fingers and toes.

Torn clothing, hair, and teeth lay scattered on the tiled floor.

The master bathroom reeked of feces. Only, the excrement wasn't *in* the bowl. Instead, feces covered the frosted window, as if to block the daylight from entering.

Ruby's eyes didn't widen in shock over the foul stench, however. No, Irene's mouth personified the overwhelming horror.

On average, human mouths could open about two inches wide, give or take. A vampire's, three and a half inches. Irene's was opening a smidge under six. Moreover, she brandished two sets of three-inch incisors: a curled pair protruded from her top jaw and the other rose up from the bottom. However, the beaver-like fangs had poked through the skin above and below her lips—which now resembled loose folds of skin.

The locked door separating the bathroom from the bedroom revealed fresh trenches in the hardwood. Irene had been gnawing.

Ruby squeezed her eyes shut.

She had to stop calling the monstrous aberration *Irene*. The beast's DNA undoubtedly represented remnants of the First Lady, but the hybrid standing by the door was predominantly another creature.

Scanning her memory banks to identify the genetically prepotent half of the hybrid, she filtered her search on animals who were cancer resistant. Results quickly narrowed to two: elephants, which rarely contracted cancer, and naked mole rats, which scientists had never documented with the disease. Not ever.

East Africa's cold-blooded naked mole rat was a match.

How she hated Emory's cruelness. Loathed him for his misuse of animals. For his gross interference with nature. With humanity.

"Is Irene okay?" the POTUS hollered to Ruby from the other side of the door. "What's happening in there?"

"Give me a minute," she answered, her voice sounding hollow in ghost form.

Irene, who still hadn't noticed Ruby's shadowy presence floating behind her, tilted her head toward her husband's voice before resuming her efforts with vigor. Scraping her teeth against the door, she fully extended her mouth and carved out wood shavings that curled and dropped to the floor. Deepening the trenches, she was minutes from penetrating the door.

Ruby's give-me-a-minute request to the President wasn't going to make a difference. Nor would three or five or thirty minutes more. No amount of time would change the inevitable.

What the mad scientist had done to Irene couldn't be undone.

Ruby's blood healed, but healing wouldn't reconstruct someone's genome. When her blood had healed Gabby after the housefire, the process didn't switch out genes or modify the genetic sequencing of her daughter's DNA. Ruby's blood merely repaired cell damage, enabling Gabby's heart to beat again.

Sculpting wouldn't restore the First Lady either. Although Ruby could manipulate matter, this competency also had limitations.

When she had rewound time so that The Tree of Awareness could return to its fruit bearing cycle on New Zealand's Great Island, she hadn't altered the tree's cellular composition; its carbon molecules remained the same. When she had sculpted doppelgängers as look-alikes, they were nothing more than fleshy figurines—external works of art using human biologics. None of the transformations were truly viable beings. And when she had altered her face to mask her identity, the process was more like reshaping clay, not changing the clay's cellular makeup.

Ruby was a healer and a sculptor, not a creator.

Vampire venom would also be ineffectual in returning Irene to her former self. Ruby's venom (a complex secretion of proteins, enzymes, and toxins) couldn't undo the genome of a hybrid. And turning the hybrid standing before her into an immortal version of itself would be an injustice. A risk to humanity, to say the least.

Would the POTUS agree? Or would he still believe that life in *any* form was more humane than death?

I'm so sorry, Irene, she whispered into her friend's mind. *I know you must be scared and trapped. Not knowing what to do next.*

This time, the First Lady turned in her direction. She raised her pink face to look at Ruby hovering near the shower. In a mental whisper, Irene repeated, *Vonaig ahoee. Miangui ree.*

Clearly, the repeated sounds weren't random. They were words that meant something.

Channeling the microfibers in the towels, Ruby sculpted a bathrobe to cover Irene's body. The creature received the gesture with an irritated squeal, followed by a few low grunts.

Since the POTUS was human, as well as the leader of the United States and the world's Federation of Independent Nations, Ruby needed to keep his safety top-of-mind. She sculpted pressure to move the hybrid's arms behind her back, before constructing invisible restraints around her wrists and ankles. To prevent Irene from biting her husband, she also sculpted an invisible mask on the First Lady's face.

"Stand back," Ruby ordered the POTUS.

Dust swirled around her. As Ruby's feet touched the tiled floor, she materialized in the flesh, positioned behind the creature.

Using her mind as her hands, Ruby unlocked the bathroom door and flung it open.

3

Friday, July 12, 2041
The White House Executive Residence: Washington, D.C.

WILLIAM UNGER FELT bile race up his throat, threatening to erupt. He swallowed hard, forcing the burning acid to retreat. If he had been alone, he would've dropped to the floor and vomited, spilling his guts. Purging the bitter agony of failure.

Although Will was no scientist, he understood that every action generated an equal and opposite reaction. His attempt to save Irene's life had been extreme. Went without saying that the extreme *reaction* could've gone either way: positive or negative.

He had his answer: a resounding *no*.

No, bioengineering a hybrid would not save his wife. *No*, the love of his life's unique DNA would not remain dominant when spliced with that of a naked mole rat's. And *no*, bastardizing Irene's genome would not give rise to a cancer free Cinderella.

The answer was more like *hell no*. Because the aberration emerging from the bathroom with Ruby was repulsive. And the stench that perfumed Irene's skin triggered yet another wave of nausea. This time, he gagged. Saliva flooded his mouth.

"You can't..." He swallowed again. "You can't heal her anymore, can you?" he asked, trying not to fall apart.

"No," she answered, releasing a blood tear that stained her cheek. "I'm so sorry, Will."

Imagine that: another fucking *no!*

Now was not the time for anger. He had to stick to the schedule.

Irene twisted her body. He assumed she was trying to free herself from some sort of invisible shackles. Her eyes were wild with frustration.

"I suspected as much," he said. "So I developed a Plan B. The medical examiner will arrive after I call him, after Irene's suffering has been permanently…mitigated."

His wife stopped fighting her restraints. Her shoulders drooped with an exhale through her nose. Maybe she understood his implication or the hopeless tone of his voice.

"What can I do?" Ruby asked.

At last, she wanted to help. Didn't she know that *better late than never* didn't always pan out? Sometimes late and never were equally negligent.

"First, let's have her lay down," he said.

Ruby walked Irene to their bed and lifted her body onto the mattress. After his wife rested on her back, the vampire fluffed the pillows in an attempt to make her more comfortable. What a joke. He doubted Irene cared about comfort and niceties any longer. For Christ's sake, she had shit caked on her hands. At least he couldn't see them tucked under her body.

The filth would've appalled his wife, his precious Irene.

Grief and irritation sloshed in his stomach.

"I'm hoping," he started, choking on the words and coughing to clear his throat. "I'm hoping you can stop her heart after I've said goodbye. Is that possible?"

She nodded.

"After Irene's no longer suffering," he continued, "Austin Tomb will examine her and determine she died of sudden cardiac death, occurring peacefully, while she slept last night. Every American knows how physically strained Irene's been during her valiant battle with cancer. A body can only take so much."

Hearing the words leave his lips made his emotions internally collide. Grief crashed into despair. Despair, into anger. Anger, into thoughts of revenge.

His inner firestorm would spare no one.

Take Austin. Five years ago, despite interviewing more qualified candidates, Will had elevated him to D.C.'s top medical examiner.

Back then, the POTUS had needed some record tweaking regarding a Congressman's messy suicide. Did the public really need to know the Congressman had blasted his temple with a nail gun after hackers threatened to expose that he preferred child pornography over legislation? No. Accidentally falling asleep in the garage, with the car idling after a heavy night of drinking, preserved the family's reputation. The Congressman had two kids for Christ's sake. And his cremation ashes protected the secret, since Will had made damn sure the hackers went PMIA—permanently missing in action.

Austin was eager to play along.

That was then.

Apparently now, his go-to medical examiner felt entitled to *more.*

At this point in Will's life, nothing surprised him. He had already lost faith in the living. Scumbags, all of them. Every. Single. One.

Sure, Austin would replace the current Secretary of Health and Human Services by the year's end, as promised. But somewhere down the not too distant road, the greedy bastard's new Cabinet appointment would earn him an equal and opposite reaction. Because everyone knew Austin liked to ride his Suzuki Hayabusa hard and fast. And no one would be suspicious if his appetite for weaving in and out of traffic on the Capital Beltway resulted in a lethal accident.

Cars had blind spots, after all.

Will sat on the mattress edge and locked eyes with Ruby. "Even though you can't heal her, can you...*sculpt* her to look like herself?"

"I can."

Staring blankly, Ruby's green irises briefly hid behind her opened eyelids and quivered. When her eyes refocused on Irene, his wife visually transformed into the woman whom he had adored for 30-years and two months. Her hair grew back shiny brown, with only a hint of gray peppering the outline of her face. Familiar freckles marked her rosy cheeks. Hazel eyes looked at him with yearning. Or was it regret?

Ruby's artistry had omitted the scar near Irene's temple, but that was okay. The vampire had remembered his wife well enough.

With his fingers, he touched her skin. How he'd miss the woman he affectionately called Sweet Tea. Born Irene Téa Smith, his Alabama beauty queen had never protested over his nickname, despite the fact that Téa was actually pronounced TAY-uh.

He and Irene had enjoyed a remarkable life together. A political powerhouse on the outside. A Hallmark love story on the inside.

As an undergrad at Harvard, everywhere he had turned, Irene Smith was there.

When he attended Citizens Against Ruining Ecosystems, Irene sat two rows in front of him. When he delivered the keynote speech for One World, One Planet, she was in the front row, studiously taking notes, hanging on his every word. And by the time they had joined Science Saves Society, Sweet Tea was by his side, pure southern charm.

Irene held an elected office first, as a county commissioner. He became a delegate, followed by a senator. She transitioned to a community organizer before President Newton appointed her as the Secretary of Climate Change. Together, he and his wife had cultivated relationships with every mover and shaker—the deep pocket donors with personal agendas.

In 2036, he was elected President in a landslide victory.

He and Irene were THE Ungers. A force to be reckoned with.

Now he'd have to journey alone. The thought terrified him.

Tears streamed down his cheeks.

"We tried. At least we tried," he said to his wife, his voice beginning to quiver. "You're so brave. You took on the Grim Reaper, Unger style—without fear."

He wiped his runny nose with the heel of his hand.

"Death can only separate us for a short while, Sweet Tea," he whispered. "I'll find you when I pass. Heaven or hell, I'll call out your name until we're reunited. I promise."

Irene was no longer resisting. No longer agitated. Instead, moisture escaped from her eyes, dripping onto the sky-blue pillowcase and darkening the fabric like storm clouds.

Could she understand his words? Or did she detect his sorrow?

"Don't take your eyes off mine," he urged. "I'll stay with you. See you off to your resting place. A place where your spirit can be free. Where it can soar with the eagles."

He turned toward Ruby, sniffling. "We're ready."

4

Friday, July 12, 2041
Cedar Lane Property: Annapolis, Maryland

FEELING ANTSY, CLAY sat on the lawn, observing his daughter playing with their dogs.

Construction workers had poured the slab foundation for his and Ruby's new home—their work in progress. The fresh concrete was setting. A few minutes earlier, the crew had wrapped up for the day and left the property.

A cool gust ruffled his golf shirt.

He glanced at his smartwatch.

Ruby had told him she'd return from the White House in one hour, and she was always spot-on punctual. Her four o'clock estimate was now 4:20 p.m. For someone cognizant of each passing nanosecond, she was on the verge of being significantly late. Not to mention, she could've whispered into his thoughts with an update or popped in and out, using her traveling dust. Even the old fashion way, like leaving a vext on his watch, could've communicated she was running late. But he wasn't getting anything.

Thunder rumbled. A dark cloud's irregular arm eclipsed the sun.

Rain on setting concrete. Figured.

A chill ran down his spine.

He never should've agreed to let Ruby go alone, despite her assurances that she could handle any crisis after what she'd been through on Athanasia. No doubt, the dire warning from Eyes (the Secretary of Defense whom they still referred to by his Navy SEAL call-sign) was valid: something sinister had happened at Pennsylvania Avenue.

Why, why, *why* had he accepted Ruby's downplay of the threat?

He took a deep breath. Worry was counterproductive. Instead, he needed to think positively, like she'd be back in a heartbeat.

Cupping his hands around his mouth, he hollered for Gabby to make her way to the SUV. A blustery wind scattered his words before they reached her. In a second effort, he motioned his arms above his head, crisscrossing them until he got her attention.

Gabby dashed across the lawn toward him.

The dogs didn't budge.

Mai froze in place, as if on point. She looked tense, staring into the wooded parcel beside their property. And the pup wasn't going anywhere without her mother.

"What's up, Dad?" His daughter bent at the waist, placing her hands on her knees. "Is Mom done?" she asked, in between rapid breaths. "Or is she going to be longer?"

"She'll be here any minute, I think." He glanced at the darkening sky. "At any rate, we'd better find shelter in the vehicle. A storm is coming."

Barking grabbed his attention.

Mai's curiosity in whatever lurked in the woods had turned to fur-raised alarm. The dog's muscles shivered as she barked in protest, warning something not to come any closer.

Zoe tucked herself by Mai's hindlegs.

"Go ahead and get in," he said to Gabby, nodding toward the passenger side. "I'll start the engine. Cool down while I get the dogs."

Wearing his khaki shorts, Clay jumped into the driver's seat and wished he had felt the leather before letting the back of his bare legs brush against it. "Wait," he warned, grabbing a cloth from the back seat. He draped it over his daughter's seat cushion. "Remind me to select a light-colored leather for our next vehicle."

"Or no leather at all," she huffed.

"I know. I know," he said, hoping to avert a recurring lecture from his nine-year-old. "At least we use every part of the cow. Very little is wasted."

Placing his thumb on the smooth disk-shaped sensor, he told the

SUV to start. The engine purred. Chilled air blasted through the vents. With more verbal directions, he instructed the onboard computer to lower the volume of the classic rock tune streaming through the speakers.

Looking through the opened door toward the dogs, he shook his head. Mai continued barking, moving closer to the edge of the woods. Was anything ever easy?

A wave of thunder vibrated the vehicle.

"Hang tight," he said. "I've got to get the dogs before the deluge."

Stepping out of the vehicle, he closed the driver-side door and traipsed across the lawn. With his luck, the dogs were carrying on about a skunk. Getting sprayed would most definitely put a kink in his family's reunion. After all, his wife's olfactory system was superhuman. Clearly, he'd be in the proverbial doghouse along with Mai and Zoe. Literally and figuratively, that would stink.

Ten feet away, though, Clay realized that whatever hid in the thick brush wasn't ankle or calf high. More like knee level, and he was six-foot-two.

His heart accelerated.

Barking wildly now, Mai took several steps back from the woods.

"Easy girl," he said. "Come, Mai."

His Brittany looked at him, seeming conflicted as to whether she should follow his order or offer protection. She retreated several more steps and resumed her verbal assault, perhaps thinking she had reached an acceptable compromise.

Clay inched toward her. He'd grab Mai's collar and end the ordeal.

Lightning lit the intensifying skies and he glanced upwards. An eerie green swirled amid the charcoal thunderheads. Oversized raindrops pelted the grass and smacked leaves on the trees and bushes. Mother nature was about to let loose.

Mai paused her barking tirade after the celestial flash and boom of thunder.

When Clay refocused on the scene, he gasped.

The large head of a coyote appeared within the brush. Its upper lip rose, exposing sharp fangs and pristine teeth. Releasing an ominous growl, the coyote took several more steps into the open, revealing muscular shoulders.

"Eeeasy," Clay said again.

Coyotes were skittish around humans, especially in daylight. Which meant there was a strong likelihood of rabies.

Mai must have sensed the escalation of danger because she continued to back away from the edge of the woods. They all did. At the same time.

Except for the coyote.

Having a pelt of rust and gray, the animal emerged from the dense thicket, ears straight up, baring its teeth. Beside the male emerged another, equally brazen. Their tongues licked at their raised lips, dripping with drool.

Clay's throat constricted. He couldn't even swallow. Or breathe.

The situation was about to turn dire.

He, Mai, and the puppy stood a chance against one crazed coyote. But two?

And what about Gabby?

No way did he want her to witness an attack.

He raised his hands and stomped his feet.

"Shoo!" he yelled, determined to shift the vibe in his favor, from prey to predator.

The coyotes countered.

Crouching, they showed no signs of retreat.

5

RUBY COULD NOT contain her tears as she watched the POTUS clutch his wife's hands.

Unexpectedly, Irene glanced at her with wide eyes. *Laa-tah ayuuloza,* she cognitively whispered, sounding frantic. *Ayuuloza!*

Ruby nodded, not knowing what the sounds meant, but wanting to affirm she had heard them.

"Keep your eyes on me," the POTUS urged. "I won't leave you."

To ensure the First Lady's passage was as painless as possible, Ruby fouled the sinoatrial node in Irene's right atrium, preventing the node from generating electrical current to make her heart contract and beat. Sculpting a blockage in Irene's aorta where it connected with her heart, she stopped oxygenated blood from leaving the left ventricle. At the same time, she cognitively pinched the pulmonary artery above the left atrium, so deoxygenated blood couldn't return to the lungs for replenishment.

Irene's eyes widened before closing.

"Safe travels, Sweet Tea," the President said, leaning over to kiss his wife's forehead. "Remember, I'll find you in paradise. Listen for my voice."

The First Lady's body released her spirit.

Thank God that Irene was free from the monstrous hybrid she'd become. At least Ruby had been able to conceal the visual horror by sculpting superficial features resembling the First Lady's former self.

Ruby wanted to remain emotionally in the moment—conveying sympathy and support to the President, but she couldn't stop the wheels turning inside her brain, cranking out relief. Relief because the natural order of Earth's physical world had been restored.

Since Emory's deviant tampering had only delayed what seemed inevitable on Irene's lifeline stone, he had forced friction and imbalance in the gap between what *should've* been and what finally occurred. Irene had been on borrowed time.

Humans weren't designed to live forever on Earth. Death was as natural as birth. Everyone entered life as a baby, and everyone exited life some 90-years later if sickness or injuries didn't take them sooner. The cycle was as expected as sunrise and sunset. As certain as the tides rising and ebbing with the moon's gravitational pull.

Emory's manipulations were unnatural. A bastardization, plain and simple. Not to mention, an utter misuse of the animals.

Vampires were a different species entirely, with their own set of natural laws. One could argue their laws were more palatable since the species was immune to disease and could heal their prey. That, and they were immortal. Then again, they needed blood as sustenance and could never procreate offspring.

Both species had their advantages. Both had their downsides.

She walked to the bedside, pushing her thoughts aside.

The President still held Irene's hands.

"I can only imagine your loss, Will. Irene was warmhearted. Courageous. A fierce advocate for society's vulnerable. Kind to everyone she encountered." Placing her palm on the President's back, she added, "I'll miss her. She was a friend."

The President shrugged, hard enough to make her hand slip from his back.

Dropping his clasp of Irene's fingers, he stood, towering over Ruby who was five-foot-seven compared to his lanky six-foot-four. His face flushed.

"Friend?" he snapped. "That's what I call irony."

Ruby took a step back. The President projected hostility and she needed to determine if his anger was grief induced or something else altogether.

She whispered into his mind to eavesdrop.

Bitch, he shouted in his thoughts. *A friend would've saved Irene right away, not forced me to take drastic measures. At least the vampire will learn how it feels trapped inside a useless body. Completely helpless.* He smiled. *What goes around, comes around.*

Trying to initiate distance between her and the POTUS, she retreated further.

Why had she insisted on coming alone? Clearly, President Unger still harbored resentment over her initial refusal to interfere with Irene's health.

Ruby's heart accelerated. Her eyes scanned the room, analyzing the environment.

She gasped. Her lifeline stone was fading. She was at risk.

Sniffing the air, she detected familiar scents that hadn't been present before.

Alarmed, Ruby decided to travel.

Her body hummed, ready to turn to dust.

And that's when she felt a prick in her back.

6

GABBY WATCHED AS her Dad stretched his arms above his head, stomping his feet, trying to look bigger and meaner than the coyotes. He had always told her to look like Sasquatch if a bear ever approached while they were on vacation in the mountains.

Maybe coyotes weren't afraid of Bigfoot because they didn't seem to mind her Dad's angry dance. They still looked ready to attack.

Her heart pounded like the drums on the radio.

Gabby had to do *something.* What would her Mom do?

Noise. Noise might help.

She commanded the SUV to blare its horn. Again. And again.

The coyotes didn't even turn their heads. Their eyes stayed locked on Mai and Zoe. And her Dad.

He glanced at her from across the yard, while stepping backwards. She could see that her Dad's lips were thin and clamped shut. His whole face looked different. Worried. Maybe even afraid.

Her Dad's expression made *her* scared.

Stay inside the vehicle, he repeated several times in his thoughts, probably knowing she'd whisper into his mind. *If something happens, call nine-one-one.*

The music made it hard to concentrate.

As she was about to order the radio to turn off, she remembered her other gift. Not only could she whisper into people's minds, she was also a sculptor. She could change stuff; make things happen. If she could heal her Mom's hand during the fake wedding to King Zagan, she was more powerful than nasty coyotes.

Allowing her eyes to hide behind her open eyelids, she gathered the music within her mind, cranking up the volume to a deafening pitch. She pictured blasting the music inside the coyotes' brains. And when she opened her eyes, her thoughts became reality.

The coyotes cowered, tucking their tails in between their hind legs. They ran back into the woods like scaredy cats.

"Take that, bastards," she said victoriously, hoping to sound in charge like her Mom and knowing no one could hear her to disapprove of her language.

After the coyotes fled, her Dad scooped up Zoe and ran toward the SUV. This time, Mai followed, or Gabby would've visited her thoughts to tell her she'd better listen.

The sky blazed with lightning. The kind that looked like old crooked fingers.

Rain poured from the clouds in buckets.

Her Dad threw open the passenger car-door on his side. Mai jumped in and he placed the puppy next to her before closing the door. He usually cared about muddy paws, but not this time.

"Did you see that?" he asked her, winking and slamming his door shut. "Do I know animals or what? Looking like Sasquatch works every time."

She tilted her head. "Except when it doesn't."

"What do you mean?" He paused and stared at her. "Are you saying *you* had something to do with their retreat?"

She pointed at herself. "Sculptor like Mom. Remember?"

Admitting she had almost forgotten to use her sculpting gift wouldn't have had the effect she was going for. Since her Dad hadn't witnessed her bravery and skills when she had helped defeat the king on Athanasia, she wanted to show off a little.

"Confidence over fear," he said, reciting a family motto. "You wear it well. I'm proud of you."

She smiled. Her Dad was good at figuring out the meaning *in between* the words. He nailed it. She wanted her Dad to be proud of her—to recognize she was growing up and could handle tough situations.

"Thanks, Dad." She was also curious about why he thought the coyotes acted so viciously; after all, he was a community ecologist. "Do you think the coyotes are sick? Or were just feeling threatened?"

"Sick. Animal control needs to come out and take a look. We don't want a rabies outbreak or anyone getting hurt."

With windshield wipers swishing the water from side to side, he put the SUV in reverse and started backing out of the driveway.

"Aren't we waiting for Mom?" she asked.

"Traveler. Remember?"

She smiled. Her Dad was funny, too.

Reaching for the puppy in the backseat, Gabby suddenly froze.

"Stop!" she yelled.

Her Dad slammed on the brakes and everyone jolted.

"What is it?" he asked.

"Mom's stone." Her lungs tightened. She could barely breathe. "The words are…fading. Something bad is happening, Dad."

"Quick. Try and whisper into your Mom's mind. Try to find out what's going on."

Gabby's heart felt like it had come loose and was inching up her throat. She tried to swallow. Pressing her back against the seat, she closed her eyes and concentrated.

After a quick glimpse of the President, her sight went dark.

She had lost the connection.

"Anything?" her Dad asked.

"Mom was with President Unger. Then everything blacked out."

"Read her stone again. What do you see?"

Gabby answered with a scream.

7

LYKOS HAD EARNED his coveted position as the male alpha of Skotadi's largest, fiercest wolfpack: the Night Stalkers. He wore the scars on his neck and haunches to prove it, though now, his thick black fur concealed them. Together with Accalia—his mate and female alpha, they ruled a colony of 22 adults and eight pups. Ruled, with a short leash.

Mostly because Lykos was keenly aware of the odds.

If he had been able to oust Accalia's first mate, what would stop others from challenging *him?* Maybe a drifter would seek to claim Lykos's position and territory. Or worse, a greedy member of his own pack might usurp his authority when he least expected it.

He released a growl at the prospect of another challenging him.

Beside him, his beta tucked his tail, lowered his head, and whimpered in submission.

Standing tall and holding his tail high, Lykos sauntered away toward the seven-foot-high dirt mound from which he would communicate. The moon shined brightly in the night sky, dotted with constellations of various animals. Musty breezes, perfumed by the river's moss and algae, rustled his fur and caused the ferns to sway.

Sloshing over slick rocks, the Tume River gurgled behind him.

The castle carved within the canyon's wall towered above them in the distance. The fortress still functioned, as if waiting for its king's return.

At the base of the mound, Lykos lifted his leg and urinated, displaying his authority and marking his rustic dais.

After nursing the pups, Accalia would join him.

Lykos needed to think before gathering his pack. The balance of the universe was already shifting, and he could not afford a misstep. Not if he wanted to impress Filtiarn, their female ruler whose throne was located on Besto Polus—the planet where all animals originated.

To be sure, he possessed aspirations beyond Skotadi. And being overthrown as the alpha of his pack, for any reason, would kill his chances to advance to elevated positions someday soon. Not to mention, it would destroy his ultimate dream of becoming King of the Animals.

Lykos had every reason to entertain lofty ambitions. If the Turning Point was truly upon them and the animals would crown their king, certainly *his* head could sport a crown better than any other. He was smart, cunning, and adaptable. And unstoppable.

Two truths affirmed Lykos's time to rule was nearing. First, since age affected one's longevity, Filtiarn was going to die before him; she was three years his senior. A simple law of nature was at play. And second, he was born to be royalty. He had inherited a legacy of powerful alphas, their authority increasing with each generation. Destiny was a complicated natural law; but nevertheless, it represented an irrefutable truth, as far as he was concerned.

Born larger, stronger, and more audacious than any of his siblings, he had dispersed from his natal pack after one year—a full 12 months before required. No one really wanted him around anyway. They yelped and whimpered that flames flickered in his fiery eyes before something bad happened, like the time a wildfire ravaged part of his parents' territory.

A tall tale that worked to his benefit.

After the rumor had circulated, no one in his natal pack ever locked eyes with him, not even his father. Which in Lykos's book, mirrored behaviors of subordination. Feeling elevated in stature, he left his pack to discover just how dominant he might be.

Lykos knew exactly where he'd test his readiness to rule.

As a youth in his natal pack, he had lost track of his position while patrolling. He drifted near the High Cliff territory, a 20-mile radius around King Zagan's castle. Scent markings of urine and scat, deposited every five feet, defined the territory's border. The warnings left no room for misinterpretation.

He remembered stopping dead in his tracks at the boundary.

Standing atop a boulder spotlighted by a moon's ray was Accalia, the most beautiful silvery she-wolf he had ever laid eyes on. Rings of black fur outlined her yellow eyes which glowed in the moonlight. Lykos's heart had raced.

Her mature mate stood beside her, willing to defend his territory and Accalia. The display did not discourage or intimidate Lykos.

Rising from that encounter was the next step in his destiny, as soon as he was ready: fighting to the death to claim his entitlement as alpha of the High Cliff pack, known as the Night Stalkers. When he was victorious, he and Accalia would become the dominant pair—the only breeding couple among members.

Lykos attacked his goals until they bowed to his authority, or in the case of Accalia's former mate, died while resisting.

That was three years ago.

Raising his nose, he sniffed. Accalia approached from the thicket. She joined him on top of his raised throne, nuzzling his fur. He had everything he needed to begin.

"Manaluul, ambochon," he barked, followed by an elongated howl. *"Manal-uuuuul."*

The message spread with a series of yips and calls. Every member, young and old, gathered around the mound's base. Protectors of the pack patrolled the periphery, monitoring the vulnerable.

"Since Creation," Lykos started, "we have forgone our natural instincts to hunt and ingest meat—from every species—in order to exist harmoniously with others." He gazed at his mate and she bobbed her head in agreement. "Instead of raw meat, we have feasted on spirulina—the blue-green algae growing in the Tume, as well as grains grown in Lampsi. But now, Filtiarn has issued a decree to our kind. We are to usher in a shift in society, in the universe. A shift that will be fully explained to us in time."

With the mention of Filtiarn, the wolves bowed to demonstrate their servitude.

"She commands us with the highest of honors," Lykos continued.

"We are to hunt and slay Montaro, the leader of the largest deer herd in Skotadi, in Athanasia for that matter. The directive will be fulfilled immediately after this gathering."

The pack began to whisper, most likely because many knew and respected Montaro.

"Fahaneegui!" Lykos growled, ordering silence. "Are there any among you who dare to voice their cowardly murmurings into words? For all to hear?"

A young male stepped forward, sporting white fur. "Why not harvest an old buck or a sickly fawn, Father? Must we start with the strongest, most admired soul among deer?"

Lykos scowled at Accalia. His son was bold enough to protest, yet embarrassingly timid. To think, he had suggested killing the weakest! What great feat was that? And why had Accalia never appraised him of this one's cowardice? Only brazen wolves were worthy of passing on Lykos's genealogy.

Raising his ears and baring his fangs and teeth, he released a pheromone that ordered his personal guards to eliminate the threat. On the spot. Definitely, no questions asked.

His beta Gunnolf led two guards toward the white wolf. Others backed away. To his credit, his son never begged or took his eyes off him. There was something powerful to his display of defiance, which meant his order to end his son's life was prudent. Perhaps the white wolf was no coward at all.

When Lykos nodded, Accalia stood stoic.

In a cloud of dust and snarls, it was easier to predict the outcome than to pinpoint the final wound which delivered the death sentence. When his guards backed away, his son lay lifeless, blood matting his fur. The wolves dragged his carcass into the forest to fertilize the soil.

"Are there any other questions?" Lykos snarled.

Only the crickets and cicadas dared to respond.

He ended the meeting and gathered his male and female warriors at the base of the mound.

After sharing his strategies for the kill, his hunters barked and yelped in agreement.

Leading his team, Lykos trotted and then cantered toward the field where a scout had reported Montaro was grazing with several does. Through a series of telepathic communiqués and pheromone releases, his hunting pack knew where to split into two groups. One broke left. His group traveled right. Both would form a half-circle behind the buck before forcing him into a trap by the river.

Once Lykos's hunters were in position, Montaro snorted and pawed the ground with his hoof, letting the wolves know that he was aware of their presence. That he had arrived in the pasture first and had not yet finished his meal. On a planet where animals peacefully shared habitats, this display was standard fare. However, in shifting times where species were about to divide into groups classified as either predator or prey, the hesitation carried the ultimate price.

Lykos released a locator call, requesting a response from his hunters. The howls and barks combined to form an ominous chorus in the night, one understood by Montaro. The 14-point buck dashed toward the river as his does scattered. A frightened female nearly collided with Lykos, but he let her pass. Montaro was the only quarry on the menu.

After two miles of sprinting, a dozen wolves funneled Montaro into The Cascades where the Tume River rushed over slippery steps of rock, forming tiny waterfalls and eventually dumping into a deep plunge pool.

Clearly, Montaro had lost his prowess for a counteroffensive. Harmony had dulled competencies with the exception of one: fleeing.

Lykos hoped Montaro would break a leg on the algae and moss-covered rocks. No such luck. The buck (all 230 pounds of him) leapt into the deep pool and frantically swam for the graveled shore, no doubt thinking he had experienced a close call. Little did he know that Gunnolf and his two prized warriors were waiting to finish him, hiding in the thicket.

During the ambush, Montaro gored the brown wolf, sending one of his massive crown tines deep within the wolf's stomach. The one named Channing cried out in pain.

A pity. The male wolf had showed great promise, but he would not see tomorrow.

Angered, Gunnolf snapped Montaro's hind leg with his jaws.

Exhausted, injured beyond repair, and surrounded by Lykos's hunters, Montaro relinquished the battle. The buck lay on his side, breathing rapidly. Wanting the end to come swiftly.

Lykos placed his front paws on the fallen Montaro, as if elevating himself on a podium.

"Hear me, soldiers," he said. "We must keep his heart beating for as long as possible. We are to puncture his carotid artery and drink from it."

"Like *vampires?*" one asked.

"What about the meat?" another inquired.

"Silence!" Lykos growled. "Only after we ingest his blood, draining all of it, will we feast on the meat. But only then."

Montaro's screams spread across the valley and echoed off the canyon walls.

Indeed, The Turning Point had begun.

8

Friday, July 12, 2041
The White House Executive Residence: Washington, D.C.

RUBY'S SENSES DULLED after she felt the tranquilizer dart embed in her back. Vervain: a debilitating sedative to vampires. A small dosage now circulated in her bloodstream.

Traveling from the scene was no longer an option.

Before she was completely powerless, she sculpted pressure on her skin to pop out the needle. The dart fell to the floor, empty.

In desperation, she attempted to whisper into Clay's mind, since whispering required the least amount of telepathic energy. But instead of cognitively warning him of her predicament, an image of two advancing coyotes flashed inside her brain. Her heartrate spiked, which only spread the vervain more quickly. The frightening vision blipped to nothing. Nothing, but a dark void.

Stripped of her gifts, she was at the mercy of the President and the two criminals whose heartbeats and scents she had detected and recognized: Emory Bradshaw and Vladimir Volkov.

Although she was scared—terrified, if she was honest, she couldn't advertise it. Her vulnerability was bad enough. Showing fear would only empower her enemies, giving them a green light to further harm her.

Maybe Ruby could outsmart them like she had Zagan.

Encouraging them to talk might buy her time to formulate an escape plan.

"Fraternizing with lowlifes like the mad scientist and the Russian

30

troll?" she asked the POTUS, intentionally keeping her back toward Emory and Vladimir, as if they were harmless scum. "Your wife's body isn't even cold, and you're already consorting with riffraff?"

"What does the Good Book say? *'An eye for an eye,'* that's it. You'll soon see," the President said, "that I always collect on outstanding debts in the same manner in which the asset was taken from me."

"I didn't cause Irene's cancer, Will," she retorted. "And I didn't manipulate her genomes into a hideous hybrid either. You and Emory bear that sinful burden."

"Still lecturing and judging those who are above your station?" Emory asked. "Hasn't anyone, besides me, ever told the high-and-mighty vampire warrior to shut the fuck up? To do as you're told by those with more power and brain java than yourself?"

Turning from the POTUS, she glared with narrowed eyes at her former best friend. Bile raced up her throat, burning the membranes of her esophagus, only she no longer had the ability to heal herself.

Emory was her height, slender, and equally muscular. She had always regarded him as a spectacular specimen of male beauty, with blemish-free skin that reminded her of brown silk.

But now, Emory Dixon Bradshaw repulsed her.

At 36, he hadn't changed a bit, not even after nine years in the penitentiary. With black hair cut close to his scalp, he still sported a diamond stud on the side of his left nostril. Gone was his white lab coat, replaced by a snug red T-shirt and blue jeans.

Vladimir Volkov held out his arms, palms up. "Such a pity we must resort to hostility so quickly. Especially in the presence of the...deceased. Can we not find common ground, my friends? After so many years?"

"That depends," Ruby answered. "Tell me why you're here. What you want from me...*this* time."

"Ahh," Vladimir cooed. "So you have guessed we are not at the White House to enjoy a cup of Russian tea. Always such a clever American woman." He chuckled until he coughed.

Although Emory had barely changed over the last decade, the former Russian President looked vastly different. His white hair was short compared to the long greasy strands he once gathered in a ponytail. In fact, the man known as "the troll" had become gaunt, probably from a lack of vodka, caviar, and black bread in prison. Loose skin made him look haggard and elderly.

His blue eyes, however, could still slice through someone's skin like a laser. Ruby suspected his mind was every bit as lethal as when he had dodged the Navy SEALs during their rescue mission at his private Moscow prison—the one holding her and Clay captive.

"No one has to tell *you* anything," Emory admonished. "We only injected you with a light dosage of vervain, so you'd know who was behind the long slumber you're about to endure. Maybe you'll dream of my face. Or Vlad's. God knows boredom will haunt you since the drug suppresses your ability to telepathically communicate. Which means no one will find you. Ever."

Ruby tried to entice veins to rise from her skin, as a warning of her ominous strength. No veins responded. In fact, she felt very tired, a rarity since vampires didn't sleep. Fisting her hands, she blinked rapidly to try and wake her senses. But her body felt heavy, like someone had draped a wet blanket over her.

Stepping back, she moved toward a wall to eliminate blind spots.

"Why have you done this to me?" she asked the POTUS.

"You're a scientist," he gloated. "Don't you remember? Every action has an equal and opposite reaction. When you sentenced Irene to death, refusing to heal her from cancer when you had the chance, I sentenced you...to life. Even if you aren't conscious, you'll still be alive, by undead standards. An existence that doesn't extend beyond serving as a blood bank. That's how I'll reap my revenge." He brushed his hands together as if cleaning them of dirt. "I don't even know where they're taking you. And frankly, I don't give a damn."

"Haven't we been down this road before?" Ruby asked. "By this time, the government should've figured out that stealing my blood is an old, tired plot that never leads to a happy ending."

She yawned as her body tried to replenish its oxygen. The sedative had fully circulated.

"Girlfriend," Emory said, smiling. "I'm a 'try, try again' sort of guy. Can't blame a genius for his obsession to aim higher."

Her mouth opened to respond, but Vladimir had already fired another dart. Its tip penetrated her abdomen, burning her skin at the point of entry.

THE TURNING POINT

The dosage was higher.
Feeling her body slip from consciousness, she could do nothing.
No time for an escape plan. No ability to connect with anyone.
She had forgotten what it felt like to be a victim.
Blackness enveloped her as she slumped to the floor.

9

FILTIARN QUIVERED, CAUSING the flies on her thick reddish coat to scatter. The day had been hot and humid during her rest, typical for the small lush planet during the summer months. Rain would fall as the sun dipped behind Royal Ridge, cooling off the environment; it always did.

Filtiarn was born with a unique fiery coat, setting her apart at birth. Genetically related to Earth's timber wolves and Skotadi's Night Stalkers, she was massive in size, measuring three-and-a-half feet from the ground to her shoulder. One-hundred and forty-pounds of towering female intimidation, and she was proud of it.

At the age of seven, the time to initiate The Turning Point had arrived. After all, Filtiarn had no intention of remaining Lord of the Wolves when King of the Animals was in the offering. Almost every living being (with the exception of humans) knew that after The Tether fulfilled the prophesies, the animals would crown their king.

Some male members of her pack had questioned her interpretation of The Book of Immortality, after Zagan had traveled to the planet and read the scriptures. *Since Filtiarn is female,* the challengers had asserted, *how could she rise to be king?*

In Filtiarn's opinion, the ability to expose one's erection did not qualify an individual as king. Furthermore, seeds were worthless without a womb in which to grow.

The male carcasses of these narrow-minded wolves now fertilized

34

the clover and soybean fields. However, their penises had been sun-dried, given to the female pups as chews, called bully sticks, to strengthen their teeth. Filtiarn appreciated the irony.

Before the evening rains arrived, she would share her vision with representatives selected to report back to every animal species in the universe. While she delivered her decree, her Adalwolves would patrol the outskirts of the crowd. These warriors, 200 strong, would stop deserters and break up skirmishes. Coyotes, dogs, and foxes belonging to her Mukessi (her personal pack of spies) would scatter themselves among the crowd, listening for dissenters.

As animals arrived, Filtiarn climbed the steep rise leading to the flat plateau of Royal Ridge, a grassy acre overlooking the valley below. She gracefully leapt over rocks and boulders, crisscrossing as she navigated the butte. Following her was her Vala, 20 females chosen as her inner circle, her most trusted guards.

At the top, she made her way to the weathered boulder that jutted out from the even ground and provided a level platform. She urinated at the edge of the grass, signifying that no other wolf or animal could cross over to the rock that symbolized her throne. Her Vala took their places behind her, on the plateau.

Sitting, she inhaled the breeze, scenting the elk, bison, chimpanzees, and lions. Rabbits and varmints appeared nervous, with no place to hide. Hawks and eagles, even vultures, circled overhead.

When all had gathered in the valley, Filtiarn stood. The wind rustled her coat as the dipping sun cast orange light on her pedestal. She hoped her fur resembled flickering flames.

"Bibamitad an'orchlizaah," she howled. *"Hencoh irneg; hencoh rehebüg."*

Starting her speech with *animals of the universe: hear one; hear all* quieted the crowd. All eyes, large and small, focused on her.

"Since Creation," she began, "those who stand on two legs and lack fur, feathers, or scales have used, manipulated, and abused animals. But today...today marks the genesis of The Turning Point. Animals of the universe will unite to gain dominion over those who claim authority over us: the vampire and human uprights!

"Do we stand united?" Filtiarn howled.

"United we stand!" roared the crowd in growls and roars and squawks and squeals.

"Vampires believe they are superior because some can whisper inside the minds of others," she said. "Do they not know that *every* animal species in the universe has this telepathic ability? How dare they consider us nothing more than vessels to quench their thirst.

"Do we stand united?"

"United we stand!"

"And humans…they experiment on us, harvest what they desire, and discard the rest. Some keep us locked in zoos or have us perform tricks in circuses. Others treat us, even dress us, like children and call us pets. Or abuse us," she hissed. "Do they not know our value extends beyond their selfish pleasures?

"Do we stand united?"

"United we stand!"

"Animals of the universe: the time is ripe for us to crown our king, for we have witnessed and learned about the prophesies of The Tether. And these prophesies have come to pass. Which means society is ready for a shift. A shift, elevating animals from servants to rulers of the universe. But many may wonder…why today? Why *now?*

"Hear one; hear all," Filtiarn continued. "The alpha of a wolfpack on Earth's Siberia, near Cape Chelyuskin, has warned me that humans are preparing to conduct a horrific experiment, one that will bastardize the genes of wolves. There is no purpose that could justify this blasphemous act. Hear one; hear all: other experiments will follow if we do not stop the uprights. Animals must rebel!

"Do we stand united?"

"United we stand!" the crowds cheered again.

This time, animals also pounded on the ground. Horses stomped their hooves. Bears swatted at the underbrush. Turkeys used talons to scratch the dirt. Chimpanzees jumped up and down while hooting and screaming.

"The rebellion will be fought on Athanasia and Earth, where the uprights live," she said. "Therefore, our warriors must be protected. This is why, dear subjects, earlier today, I ordered the Night Stalkers in Skotadi to slay Montaro the Great. And Lykos, alpha of the pack, has whispered to me that the deed has been done."

The crowd collectively gasped, as she had suspected they would. Montaro was, after all, a legend whom every offspring learned about.

He was fearless, proud, and adaptable; qualities admired by species both great and small.

"Fahaneegui!" she howled, commanding silence.

Her Adalwolves and Vala repeated the order. Only her Mukessi spies remained quiet to appear as part of the crowd.

A hush swept across the crowd with a cool gust.

"The Turning Point required Montaro's sacrifice," Filtiarn continued. "His death will not be the last, for more sacrifices will be needed. You see, does in his herd confessed that The Tether herself had fed and healed Montaro when she first visited the upright Zagan. Which means her blood had fortified the buck with the protective shield of self-preservation. When harvested, the Night Stalkers drank Montaro's blood, spreading this protection amongst the warriors. The Tether named Ruby will not be able to carbonize those who have ingested her blood. Without question, Montaro's sacrifice will magnify his legacy. All will learn of his selfless heroics.

"Do we stand united?"

The crowd shifted nervously, seeming unsure.

A Mukessi shouted, "United we stand!"

"Do we stand together in this cause?" Filtiarn repeated.

"United we stand!" the crowd finally bellowed.

"As we speak," she continued, "a plan is in place to spread this protection to animal warriors on Earth. And if you are asked to sacrifice, to give your life for this purpose, what will you say? *Take me?* Or, *take my neighbor?*"

"Take *me!*" the animals shouted.

"When I have proven that I am worthy to be King of the Animals, what will you say? *Crown her? Or, crown another?*"

The Mukessi scanned the crowds, observing reactions.

"Crown *her!*" they cheered in unison, as thunder rumbled in the distance like a drumroll.

10

AS CLAY DROVE to the White House from Annapolis, he couldn't shake the desperation of his daughter's scream. The panic, the helplessness of it. He was Dad, the man supposed to protect his daughter from ever needing to cry out like that.

His palms sweated as he gripped the steering wheel.

At least Gabby had seen President Unger in her brief vision, confirming Ruby had arrived at her destination. Which meant Clay was heading to the right place to find out what the hell was going on.

He had to move quickly. Had to prevent his wife's lifeline stone from fading altogether.

Worry churned in his stomach.

Ruby always saved others. And now she was in some sort of jeopardy. Jeopardy, despite being in the company of the most protected political leader in the country, federation, and world.

Every fiber of his being was on edge.

After he and Gabby had left the construction site, he drove his daughter and dogs to Margo and Tomas's waterfront home. From Cedar Lane, their best friends lived only 15 minutes away. In fact, the dogs had been staying there since the housefire.

Margo and Tomas welcomed having their Goddaughter over for a few hours while Clay investigated Ruby's whereabouts. Last minute never mattered between the closest of friends. Anyway, Gabby could hang out with Reese and keep her mind occupied.

Once his daughter and pups had entered the house, Margo and Tomas came outside, closing the front door behind them. Clay filled them in on what he knew.

Before he turned to leave for the White House, Margo mentioned a news alert on a developing story: unprovoked animal attacks. Apparently, sporadic attacks had occurred hours earlier, across the globe. *Be cautious, not alarmed,* the report had stated, since the incidences seemed unrelated, involving a variety of species. The alert was more of a heads up; an advisement to "keep eyes to the sky" sort of thing. Health organizations such as the CDC and WHO were looking into the matter.

Margo wasn't sure if he had heard, which he hadn't. She hoped the alert might have something to do with Ruby's delayed return, like maybe she was helping respond to the strange anomaly.

Helping? Maybe. But why hadn't she communicated with him? Certainly, animal attacks wouldn't cause *her* life to be at risk. His wife was a vampire who could whisper, heal, sculpt, travel, and carbonize. Even read the future when she searched for it. Ruby was an unstoppable immortal warrior. The One and Only. The Tether.

Except when vervain was involved.

Will Unger had used the sedative on Ruby before, during her arrest for the murder of Paige Jasper, his wife's scalping partner. Of course, Ruby was 100-percent innocent.

Clay had never forgotten the President's betrayal.

He tightened his grip on the steering wheel. His anger simmered.

July 12th had started with such promise. First off, Ruby and Solange had returned the victims of Zagan's cullings to Earth. Thanks to them, happy reunions were taking place in countless homes in the United States, Canada, and Europe. He knew their joy because Ruby and Gabby had also come back to him and the dogs.

Late afternoon, however, had taken a terrible turn.

Ruby was in trouble. His daughter, traumatized.

He also wondered if the aggression displayed by the coyotes on Cedar Lane related to the odd animal behaviors sweeping the globe.

Was there a blood moon? A blue moon? Or some freakish lunar event wreaking havoc on the world?

At least the traffic on the Beltway was light.

He sent a verbal videoface request to the Secretary of Defense, who answered on the first ping.

"Please tell me Ruby has returned," Eyes said, without waiting for Clay's greeting.

Clay updated him on everything.

"Damn it," the Secretary snapped. "She wasn't supposed to get anywhere near the White House without backup. Thought I had made that crystal clear."

"I tried to tell her. Even attempted to go along, but she refused. Insisted she could handle whatever was happening to the First Lady by herself. Alone."

Clay paused, realizing he should've protested a lot harder.

"Wait," Eyes said, like he was remembering something. "Doesn't she have an embedded locator chip? A government tracker? I remember we activated yours and hers for the Moscow prison rescue. That would be an easy way to find her."

"Got them surgically removed eight years ago," Clay said. "Ruby doesn't exactly trust government oversight. Listen, I'm on my way to the White House now. Can you meet me there? Maybe contact Insley to have him join us?"

"Affirmative. I'll activate my SAPs and use Marine One. The POTUS has the chopper reserved for tonight anyway, for a lift to Andrews Air Force Base. After his national address, he's heading to Camp David for some R&R. Media will think his ride arrived early."

"SAPs?"

"Added the unit to Homeland Security's terrorism division," Eyes explained. "SAPs are suspicious activity personnel—more like special ops: military first-responders who've trained with the SEALs. As we speak, our SAPs are on high alert status. We've been monitoring Bradshaw and Volkov after their release from prison last night. I was on the fence before you reached out, but now I've decided. An unannounced sweep of the White House is warranted and well within our jurisdiction."

"You think Emory and Vladimir might be *there?*" Clay asked, his voice trembling.

"Both went through security at 1630 hours, less than two hours ago. POTUS *invited* them. Relax, though. The scumbags were unarmed at entry."

"Why didn't you tell me?"

"We had no clue Ruby was even back, let alone in the President's private quarters," Eyes admitted. "When she travels the way she does, security is bypassed. And none of the POTUS's security detail in the Executive Residence have raised an alarm."

Clay banged the steering wheel. The day's downhill slide persisted.

"Stay focused," Eyes said. "Your ETA?"

Taillights began to blink red. Blinking turned to a steady glow.

"Shit," Clay said, tapping the break to release cruise control. "Need a second…"

In the distance, he saw the rotating lights of two firetrucks. Up ahead, vehicles were turned every which way on the Beltway.

"An accident," he said to Eyes, glancing at the windshield display. The car map projected a solid red line on the Beltway, for the next three miles. "Traffic is funneling into one lane on the shoulder. My ETA just got fifteen minutes longer. Should arrive at six-thirty."

Clay's heart jolted.

He stomped on the brakes.

Something had cannoned into his windshield.

Involuntarily, he closed his eyes. His right hand sprung from the steering wheel to his face, as if to deflect whatever had struck the glass, in case the object busted through.

His SUV skidded and turned sideward on the asphalt. The computer system kicked in to override his reaction, countering to prevent a rollover.

Burnt rubber assaulted his nostrils.

Cars screeched behind him, swerving. Horns, blaring.

"What's happening?" Eyes asked.

His SUV stopped, pressing his chest firmly against the seat belt. His neck jerked forward before slamming into the headrest. At least the air bag hadn't deployed.

Relieved no one had rear-ended him, he deeply inhaled.

Electronic images on his windshield flickered before fading off.

On the passenger side was a hole in the windshield's glass, measuring the circumference of a softball. Stress fractures bled from the crater like bloody rays around a hollow sun. Several white feathers had snagged in the cracks, now fluttering in the breeze.

A dead carcass lay on his passenger seat.

"A seagull hit my SUV," Clay said, dumbfounded. "Seriously. The bird literally crashed into my windshield like a dive bomber, penetrating the glass. It's dead. On my seat."

"These animals attacks are getting out of hand. Are you okay?"

"Yeah." He swallowed, trying to push his heart back into place. "Yeah, I'm fine."

"Display your emergency light. Get to the White House ASAP. Meet you there."

The Secretary of Defense disconnected.

After tossing the dead seagull out the lowered passenger window, Clay reached into the glovebox for his domed light. Attaching the fixture on its dash mount, he turned on the bright blue light, making the bulb rotate. While his intermittent siren bleeped, he maneuvered his SUV on the grass beyond the road's shoulder.

As he inched forward, making his way toward the main cluster of vehicles blocking traffic, he finally saw what had caused the accident.

Seagulls. A freaking squadron of seagulls.

Some still twitched on the roadway, their necks, wings, and bodies twisted and broken from impact. Pools of blood formed beneath them. Beaks opened and closed as they gasped for their last breaths.

The original mishap involved five cars. They probably collided after the bird kamikazes bombarded them. One car was missing a headlight, while another looked like an accordion with steam rising from its engine block. All the vehicles sported dents, as if an outraged giant had repeatedly sucker punched them. Windshields were either cracked or caved in. Seagull blood and entrails littered every surface.

On the pavement, EMTs and paramedics attended to victims. Blood trickled from their faces. Shirts and shorts resembled crimson tie-dye. Some wore neck braces.

In comparison, Clay had fared well.

Firefighters stood poised with hoses in hand, ready to prevent the pileup from turning into a bird barbecue.

Clay instructed his vehicle to lower the driver side window.

"I'm heading to another emergency," he told a firefighter. "Need anything? Or are you under control?"

"We've got it," she said. "Thanks."

Beyond the crash site, he sped, unhindered for the rest of his drive to the White House. Air rushed in through the gaping hole in his windshield, emitting a strange whistle.

An imaginary clock ticked in his head. *Tick, tock. Tick, tock.*

Time wasn't slowing down, waiting for his arrival. Pressure inside his brain increased with each passing tick.

Clay arrived at 1600 Pennsylvania Avenue five-minutes before his GPS had predicted.

After showing his credentials at the White House's security gate, Clay drove up the driveway. He hugged the pavement on the right side because a larger vehicle was leaving.

The driver looked familiar.

Behind the wheel of a black, unmarked utility van—with no back windows, was Austin Tomb, the White House's go-to medical examiner. A man whom Clay had always pegged as a slime ball opportunist, especially after his autopsy of Paige Jasper, Ruby's murdered scalping partner from D.C.'s Nationals Park Stadium.

Austin raised his eyebrows and smirked as he drove past.

In the distance, Clay heard the thwacking hum of Marine One's approach.

11

Friday, July 12, 2041
The Gonzalez Residence: Annapolis, Maryland

GABBY WANTED TIME by herself. Any other day, she would've gladly fished for crabs with Reese, off his parents' dock on Whitehall Creek. But ever since she discovered she could whisper and sculpt, her Mom had harped on and on that gifts came with responsibilities.

Today, she had to prove she understood what that meant.

Anyway, Reese was her best friend. He just "got" her. So he gave her space to concentrate while he played with the puppy and his own dogs, Uno and Dos—two-year-old French Bulldogs.

She smiled, just a little. Un and Deux should've been their names.

Gabby settled into an overstuffed chair in the library. Mai had followed her, plopping down on a fancy throw rug by her feet, glad to escape the outside humidity. The lowering sun cast an orange spotlight on a packed bookshelf, making the gold lettering on the book spines shine like glitter. They had to be classics.

Books were even better than pizza and chocolate chip cookies because their goodness lasted forever. Someday, maybe she'd become an author. Maybe even a bestseller.

Decked out in long white fur, Yona strutted into the room like she was showing off to Mai. The cat's nickname was short for Gruñona, which meant grumpy in Spanish. She really wasn't a cranky cat. Her flattened face and frown only made her look like a big old sourpuss. Thankfully, Yona was more of a snuggle muffin. And when Gabby visited the Gonzalez family, the cat liked hanging out with her.

Jumping on Gabby's lap, Yona circled a few times. She curled into a tight ball and purred before Gabby even stroked her coat.

Gabby closed her eyes. Leaning her head back, she supported her neck on the chair's cushiony headrest. She let her mind drift toward her Mom's, floating in the space-like darkness, hoping to spark a connection. Finding her Mom was all that mattered.

A burst of light flashed in Gabby's mind and her heart pumped double-time. She always saw a blaze of light before being able to see through someone else's eyes.

This time, though, she still saw darkness.

Except her ears. She heard a steady roar, like from big engines.

Wake up, Mom, she shouted into her Mom's mind, thinking her Mom had to be unconscious. Why else would Gabby see darkness?

Please, Mom. Wake up!

Only the engines answered with their non-stop hum.

Damn it. Open your eyes.

Not even cursing made a difference. Her Mom wasn't answering.

Gabby wiped away tears. She didn't know what to do.

On the drive over to Aunt Margo and Uncle Tomas's house, Gabby had asked her Dad if she could whisper to Queen Liora or to Princess Solange. He told her no. *Absolutely not.* The planets were supposed to be separate. And anyway, he had the resources of the U.S. government on his side. He had asked her to trust him.

Her Dad never mentioned not whispering inside *his* mind.

Maybe she could stowaway in his brain. See and hear what was happening at the White House. Who knows? Her Dad might even find her Mom there.

If only she was getting that feeling.

Somehow, Gabby understood her Mom wasn't at the White House anymore. Which meant her Dad needed to find clues to figure out where she'd gone. Two sets of eyes and ears were better than one. And she wasn't breaking any rules. Not really.

Concentrating, Gabby stretched her mind toward her Dad's.

Easy to find, he was beside Uncle Eyes (that's what she called him) and Mr. Insley. They were following two people in the Secret Service, walking up a staircase—the one covered with a red-carpet runner, heading to the second floor. President Unger lived on that floor. She knew because she'd been there with her Mom and Dad, before the First Lady got sick with cancer.

After the Secret Service opened the door to the Treaty Room, her Dad and his friends walked inside and waited. Her Dad kept pacing back and forth, chewing on his bottom lip. She recognized the look: impatience. Things weren't happening fast enough.

Gabby hung out in his mind as her Dad waited.

While her "sight" stayed at the White House, her hand stroked Yona's soft fur.

At last the door flew open and the President stormed in. He was tall, with a giraffe's neck. And he usually smiled a lot. Except for now. Now, he scowled, scrunching his face and making his lips curl down. Talk about sourpuss! Only his expression wasn't like Yona's. *His* looked intentional.

"What the hell's the meaning of this?" President Unger snapped, his cheeks turning red.

Uncle Eyes raised his hands like he was stopping traffic. "Hold on, Will. Let me explain what's going on."

"Better be fucking good or your head's going to roll."

"Bradshaw and Volkov were allowed entry into the White House," Uncle Eyes started. "Let's face it, terrorists have never made the guest list before. The Department of Defense has every right to ensure that they have not compromised your security or the security of this nation. That's why I've authorized a surprise sweep of the entire campus. Goes without saying our citizens would want assurances that we have taken every precaution. Of course, they might also be interested in understanding your affiliation with convicted war criminals."

"You could've videofaced me," the President snapped. "Instead, you ordered this dog and pony show when the answer is straightforward and bland, certainly lacking the excitement of some imagined espionage scheme. You'll see. I plan to mention their visit in my address to the nation tonight."

"I'm here now," Uncle Eyes said. "Why'd they visit you, Will?"

"To personally thank me for their pardons. Simple as that. In my opinion, serving nine years of their sentences was sufficient. Why not save taxpayers and release them? Besides, after the public hears what

I have to say, I doubt they'll care about Bradshaw and Volkov."

She could feel her Dad's body temperature rise. He was angry.

"What are their plans from here on out?" Uncle Eyes asked.

"You want me to do *your* job?" The President tilted his head. "Why the hell would I care anyway? They've done their time. They're free men. I've got more important issues." He glared at her Dad and Mr. Insley and nodded in their direction. "Why the sidekicks? Surely you don't need a community ecologist and his bodyguard to help cover your ass or give you courage to face me."

Her Dad cleared his throat. "At your request, Sir, my wife came here to help you. Something to do with your wife and an episode she was having. I'm worried because Ruby hasn't returned."

The President paused, bringing his finger to the side of his mouth and rubbing, as if he had an itch. "No surprise that every time I reach out to your wife, she neglects to show up." He coughed, like clearing his throat. "Helping me has never been Ruby's strength. Or priority."

"What?" her Dad asked, sounding somewhere between annoyed and panicked.

Gabby had planned to stay hidden in her Dad's thoughts, since he definitely wouldn't appreciate her eavesdropping. But before she could stop herself, she whispered to him.

He's lying, Dad, she cognitively shouted. *I saw him talking to Mom!*

She was about to leave her Dad's mind and whisper into the President's when she, along with everybody else, heard a knock on the Treaty Room door.

"How hard is it to get some damn privacy in this zoo?" President Unger snarled, as he flung open the door.

Her Dad was about to defend her Mom, but Uncle Eyes raised his hand as if to ask him to wait a minute.

Two men dressed in camouflage and black combat boots, wearing holsters with pistols and knives, walked into the room. They saluted the President before talking to Uncle Eyes.

"Mr. Secretary," the muscular one said, "the sweep is complete. The White House and premises are secure. However, no signs of the First Lady or Mrs. Spencer."

The President rolled his eyes. "Looking for terrorists? Right." He huffed. "I told you Ruby wasn't here. She never showed up."

Uncle Eyes ignored him. "Anything out of place or unusual?" he asked the muscular one.

"Not really, Sir," he answered, shifting his eyes to his partner.

"Be more definitive, SO Keyser," Eyes said. "That's an order."

"The master bathroom smelled strongly of bleach, Sir. Like it had been recently sanitized. And the door to the bathroom was…missing. Also, the housekeeping staff stripped the sheets from the master bed two days ahead of schedule. They disposed of all the linens, pillows, and bed coverings, placing them in the incinerator as instructed. The order has already been carried out."

Everyone looked at the President.

"That's right, gentlemen," President Unger said, sounding snarky. "Death isn't very neat and tidy. While you've been looking for the most powerful vampire in all the universe—an immortal who can defend herself better than all our military forces combined, I've had to say goodbye to my beloved, human wife. My precious Irene passed away in her sleep last night. Her body succumbed to the aftermath of cancer, after fighting a courageous battle."

No one spoke, but her Dad gasped.

The First Lady was…*dead?* For real?

Gabby's heart thumped in her chest.

Could she have made a mistake about her Mom being with President Unger? Truth was, she hadn't had her gifts long enough to know if she could mess up. What if she saw a snippet of the past and had mistaken it for the present? How would she know?

Laughing interrupted her concentration.

The connection to her Dad blipped off.

Opening her eyes, she turned her head toward a window in the library. The sounds were coming from outside.

Mai whined, tilting her head to the cackles, caws, and squawks.

"It's okay, Mai," she said. "I just want to see what's going on."

Rising from the chair, she cradled Yona in her arms like a baby, making sure her forearms and hands supported the cat's back. Gabby walked to the window. To her amazement, the sounds weren't laughter. Everywhere she looked, she saw seagulls swooping, circling, and fluttering, like someone shook a snow globe and sent them in motion. Loose feathers fell to the ground in no hurry.

Surprised by a burst of movement, Gabby quickly stepped back.

One bird flapped wildly on the other side of the window, squawking and screaming. Keeping its beak wide open, its tongue straightened with each cry. Wings fanned against the glass while talons scratched the surface, sending chills down Gabby's spine.

The bird freaked her out. Should she be scared? And what about Reese and Zoe? Uno and Dos? Were they okay?

She heard a growl, feeling the vibration in her arms.

Yona. Yona must be upset, too.

Mai started to bark.

Glancing at the cat, Gabby tried to read the kitty's expression. Yona narrowed her eyes. Her lips quivered. She hissed.

As Gabby started to tell the cat that everything would be okay, two front paws slammed against her cheeks. Sharp nails dug into her skin and violently yanked downward.

The pain burned. Gabby's face was on fire.

Yona scrambled from her arms, leaping to the floor and bolting from the room.

Gabby dropped to her knees. With her palms and fingers, she felt her cheeks. Long scratches were much deeper than she'd imagined. And they hurt like crazy.

When she lowered her hands, they were bright red and dripping.

Blood splatted onto the hardwood floors.

Mai rushed to her and began licking her hands clean. Then Mai moved to her cheeks, lapping her wounds with her tongue.

"It's okay, Mai. My blood is gifted," Gabby said. "My cuts will heal, remember?"

The outside grew quiet.

Sounds of laughter faded in the distance.

12

RUBY TRIED TO open her eyelids, but they wouldn't budge. At least her body was beginning to adjust to the vervain in her bloodstream. Probably because she had stopped her heart from beating and circulating the poison.

Instead of being entombed within a dark void of nothingness, she was able to reactivate her senses, providing a pseudo consciousness, albeit, still lacking the ability to physically interact with her environment. Hearing, smelling, and feeling pressure on her skin, however, felt like a miracle. One she'd put to good use.

A stiff wind whistled to her left, beyond a window, no doubt.

She acutely listened for birds or crickets chirping. For tree leaves rustling or branches rattling. For human voices or footsteps. Or the hum of engines. Even tunes on a radio.

Nothing else made a sound outside, except for the wind. Occasionally, a gust blasted sand against the window. Or was the spray from tiny bits of hail bouncing off the glass?

Taking a shallow breath through her nose, she made sure her chest didn't rise. The sweetness of flowers and grass was undetectable. Nothing smelled like summer. It was as if every living thing had slipped into a deep, wintry slumber.

Inside where she lay, clues to her whereabouts were scant at best. The sterile odor of a disinfectant lingered, but it was dissipating quickly. Probably because she detected a low hum above her, like an exhaust fan running on low.

An hour passed.

Although she'd also regained her ability to measure the passage of time, she had no clue how long the blank void of her initial vervain coma had lasted.

The wind rested for a moment, long enough for her to hear howling in the distance. *Howling?* From a wolf? A coyote?

Maybe her eardrums had played a trick.

She'd never know because the gale resumed with a fury, crashing over the doleful cry like a smothering wave.

How would she ever be able to piece together enough facts about her location to identify where Emory and Vladimir had taken her? Then again, who could she tell if she knew? Vervain prevented her from mustering the brain energy to traverse time and space in order to whisper with Clay or Gabby or her vampire friends on Athanasia.

The best she could hope for was building a greater tolerance to the vervain dosage, thus strengthening her mental competencies even more. In time, perhaps Gabby and her friends might be able to cognitively contact *her.* In fact, her daughter had briefly reached her while Ruby was on the airplane, though Ruby couldn't whisper back since the vervain continued to concentrate in her bloodstream.

However, what happened once might happen again.

If someone *could* whisper to her, maybe they'd offer advice. Strategize on how she might shed the paralysis immobilizing her body. Help find out where she was or how she could escape. Learn what abhorrent experiment her blood was being used for this time.

Reality crept in. Wishful thinking might pass the time, but it wasn't going to change her circumstances.

Ruby had been kidnapped again. Betrayed *again.*

At least the sting of betrayal felt a little less venomous, a little less shocking, like when a copperhead snake bit someone for the second time. Repeat victims learned what to expect.

A heaviness rolled over her, slowing her thoughts like someone had poured molasses over them. Spurred by a burst of emotion, she had carelessly let her heart beat.

Concentrate, she told herself, fighting the drug's ability to push her down to the bottomless pit of nothingness once more. She needed to stay in control, relaxed and calm, in order to analyze her situation. To regain her strength.

Stifling the electrical impulses in her right atrium, she prevented her heart from taking additional beats. The muscle returned to its dormant state.

Refocusing on the information available around her, she noticed darkness beyond her closed eyelids. Which meant neither daylight nor electricity were illuminating the room. Most likely, it was nighttime. That, or the window in her space had blackout shades.

She'd monitor the presence or absence of sunlight as time passed.

Lying flat, she could feel the coldness of metal underneath her, ruling out a bed and ruling *in* an operating table. She was fairly certain a thin cotton sheet covered her naked body.

A slight burning in both crooks of her forearms suggested someone had inserted IV needles there: one to administer the vervain and the other to extract her blood.

Could she move?

Fingers first. She attempted to wiggle them. Didn't happen.

Toes? Nothing.

Pressure clasped around her wrists and ankles. A strap pressed across her chest. Restraints, no doubt. Very snug restraints.

A switch clicked.

Her heart almost jolted into action.

Bright fluorescent light seeped through her eyelids.

Breathe lightly, she coached herself. *Keep your heart still.*

Differentiating footsteps and hearing the *bu-bumps* of heartbeats, she calculated two people had entered the room. She recognized their scents: Emory Bradshaw and Vladimir Volkov. They were alone.

She wanted to leap from the table and tear into their throats; drain them of life. Or rip out their hearts as they pleaded for mercy. Basically, she wanted them dead.

Forced to abandon her family—leaving them vulnerable, was a nightmare. She'd make them pay.

Since acting on her desires wasn't currently an option, she'd have to choose self-restraint to survive. Any emotional spike might give her captors a physical clue that her body was acclimating to the poison. If they suspected as much, they'd up her dosage and she'd fall back into the rabbit hole.

"Remember," Emory said, "no mention of where we are—not the area, not the climate, not anything. Because the vampire bitch can communicate telepathically. And there's no failproof way of knowing how effectively the vervain reduces her cognitive abilities. Can't chance it."

"My friend," Vladimir said. "Should we not consider an EEG to measure her brain's activity? Would this not help us to determine the appropriate…how do you say…dosage? After all, restricting her brain's functions is most desirable. Correct?"

Emory's footsteps stopped.

Ruby dreaded his answer.

"Is there a Ph.D. after your name, Volkov?" Emory snapped.

"Ahh, your point is good. Very good." Vladimir laughed. "Though I think president and supreme leader have never appeared before *your* name. Perhaps you should not forget that all of Mother Russia once bowed to my iron rule. Important to remember. Yes?"

If Ruby could've rolled her eyes, she would've. Male felons always wanted to see who could pee the farthest.

"Lucky for you, troll-man," Emory countered, pouring on his annoying sarcasm, "this decision doesn't require brain java or bowing. See, if we don't mention where we are out loud—or offer any hints to our locale, it won't matter if she cognitively chit-chats to the entire world. Because one thing she's not is a GPS beacon; a surgeon removed her locator chip long ago. And with the POTUS's blessing, we've disappeared off the grid. So why, mister *supreme leader,* would we disregard the efficacy of good old common the-fuck sense? If we agree to keep our pie-holes shut, there's no need for an electroencephalography of Ruby's brain. Capisce?"

Ruby heard Vladimir's familiar Russian *umph.*

"Her blood," the Russian said, changing the subject. "How much do you need?"

Ruby felt Emory lift her right arm, probably to examine the needle. Deep inside, she cringed at his touch. At her helplessness to govern her own body.

"Doctor Genius is in the house," he answered. "So why don't you let me do the science? You stick to the wolves. By the way, how many subjects have been inventoried?"

"Twelve." Vladimir sighed. "Most unfortunate. The storm may delay today's hunt."

Wolves. The howling was from *wolves*.

Her brain calculated over 30 countries that had free-roaming wolf populations including Russia, China, and Canada. Clearly, she was no longer in Washington D.C. or the Mid-Atlantic region of the U.S.

"What the fuck?" Em barked. "I say don't provide *any* location markers. And you blabber that we're in a region where we can hunt wolves? I simply asked how many we had. I could've ordered them from countless vendors who procure wildlife for my experiments. Guess supreme leaders rely on others for common sense."

Vladimir huffed. "Many countries have wolf populations."

"Ruby's a vampire. Nine years ago, she found your sorry ass in a hideaway compound in the Western Caucasus, didn't she? Like I said: keep everything relating to location to yourself. Got it?"

"Such a pity you lack charm! Not surprising, then, that you are without a lover."

"Science is my jam." Emory released her arm. "But if by 'lover' you're referring to sex, well, I get *that* whenever, wherever, however, and with whomever I want, boyfriend. Come to think of it: I've never done a troll before."

Emory brushed against her as he moved toward her head.

Vladimir cleared his throat. "I do not…how do you say…swing in your direction."

"*Swing?* What century are you from? And just so you know: the direction of in-and-out is gender neutral. Every opening works the same. Trust me."

Emory lifted her right eyelid and shined a light over her pupil.

Ruby forced her pupil not to constrict. She did the same when he tested her left eye.

"Good," Emory said. "The pupillary examination shows her eyes are nonreactive, probably from Anoxia. Basically, her body's shut down from a lack of oxygen."

He pressed his fingers into her neck, to find her pulse, no doubt.

"Which makes sense," he continued, "since she's not breathing and has no pulse. I think the drug's working just fine."

"Is she dead?" Vladimir asked, sounding worried. "This vervain drug...have we given her too much, then?"

Emory removed his fingers from her skin. "Does she *look* dead?"

Ruby heard Vladimir's footsteps approach the operating table. *"Hmm.* I believe the vampire warrior appears the same as she always has. Only sleeping."

"Probably why she's an *immortal,* asshole." He placed his hand on her hair and stroked it. "The only way to truly kill this cunt is to rip out her heart or decapitate her. And then burn the body parts. To make sure Humpty Dumpty can't be put back together again."

His warm breath tickled the skin on her cheek. If only she could wake at that moment, she'd scratch out his eyes.

"But for now, dearest Ruby," Emory continued, speaking directly to her, "I need your precious blood. See, I've already made progress from my little mishap involving the First Lady. Even though I'd succeeded in lateral gene transfer to a human, I failed to consider genetic prepotency. Who knew the naked mole rat would be genetically dominant? Pretty much a shocker."

Part of his chest touched hers.

Ruby urged herself not to breathe or jumpstart her heart.

"I'm going to build a new kind of army by engineering a wolf hybrid, using your superhuman blood, of course. The beasts will be exponentially bigger, stronger, and smarter than any wolf species. Best of all, they'll have internal chips embedded by their optic nerve. Once activated, their eyes glow red.

"When I press a button on a remote, the chip will function like a shock collar. They'll have to obey me and the troll. And girlfriend, we'll be up and running very soon.

"Let's face it," Emory continued, "zombies are too stupid to make good soldiers. Not to mention, they multiply like the plague. And vampires, well, you all are just too freaking hard to control."

Emory raised his chest from hers. "Make yourself useful troll-man. Hand me that dental mouth gag from the instrument table."

She could hear Vladimir's feet shuffle across the room before returning to the bedside.

"This tool...what is its purpose?" Vladimir asked.

"To prop open her mouth," he answered, shoving the cold

apparatus between her lips. "POTUS mentioned Ruby is equipped with glands which store venom. Venom that can turn humans into vampires. Seems like I should study some of that immortal mojo. Never know when it might come in handy. I mean, I've come to realize that a brain like mine should be around forever, don't you think?"

Her heart beat once before she regained control. Bile threatened to race up her throat.

Emory clamped the device open, stretching her mouth until it was uncomfortable.

"Sweet Mother of Jesus," he cheered. "Look at those plump glands behind her top incisors."

Emory briefly paused. "Quit standing around with your mouth hanging open. Hand me an empty syringe from over there."

Ruby begged herself not to move.

13

EM LOOKED FORWARD to sawing off the bitch's head when he completed the project. Even unconscious, Ruby looked regal and unafraid. High and mighty. Like she was above him. *Not.*

He glanced at the blackout shades. Even though the storm had darkened the skies at noon and was howling like it might devour the walls of the laboratory, he was impressed that he had thought to block natural light from the room.

Might be easy for a vampire, even one drugged into a coma, to zero in on regions which experienced 18 hours of daylight in July.

Of course, no way of knowing if the blabber-mouth troll would spill those beans as well. Clearly, Em had failed to anticipate the need for a muzzle. Maybe the troll's suggestion to use an EEG wasn't a bad idea after all. Just to gauge Ruby's awareness.

Vladimir handed him an empty syringe.

If the POTUS had just given Em his Sanguivorous Cocci in the first place, he wouldn't have needed to extract the venom from Ruby's glands. After all, nine years ago, he had engineered the universal SUC serum to turn any willing or unwilling human into an immortal bloodsucker. Regrettably, the President worried that procuring the serum might raise suspicions, given a special ops team guarded the SUC in the White House bunker, 24/7.

At least as a consolation prize, the POTUS had shared his knowledge of her glands.

Em pierced one gland with the needle and began extracting clear venom from its sac.

"Might become a vampire myself," he whispered, steadily pulling the plunger flange to draw venom into the barrel. "So I can kick your ass. Picture the thrill: cable multivision broadcasts our modern-day Thunderdome on pay per view. The world tunes in. The crowd chants: *two vamps enter, one vamp leaves.* I'll conveniently drug you with vervain, mind you, but that'll be our little secret."

When the syringe's barrel was full, he withdrew the needle.

"Here. Put this on the instrument table," Em ordered, turning from Ruby and placing the syringe in Vladimir's hand. "Exchange it for the empty one. You can never have too much of a good thing." He chuckled. "Who knows? Maybe you'll even want some, boyfriend. A vampire troll? Now that would rock the immortal world!"

The makeshift lab shuddered from a gust. Probably registered 60 miles-per-hour plus. The fluorescent lights blinked.

Siberia was a ruthless mother fucker, even in the summer.

Vladimir scuffed his boot soles over the tiles—an annoying sound. At the very least, vamp mojo would boost the troll's energy. The man had really thinned since his pudgy days as a well-fed dictator. Yet, despite his lighter physique, he still took his good-old damn time.

After the Russian handed him the empty syringe, Em turned back toward Ruby. A shock reflex overwhelmed him. His fingers released the needle, carelessly dropping it to the floor.

His heart leapt from his chest to his throat, blocking his airway.

Ruby's skin had become a patchwork of purple veins. A defensive response. Meaning, she could hear him. She wasn't as comatose as he'd thought. Which sure as hell meant, the bitch was pretending.

Why did she always challenge him? Always try to one-up him?

She could never just let things play out smoothly.

A microburst of anger engulfed his brain.

No doubt norepinephrine saturated the neurotransmitters in his amygdala. Translation? He was royally pissed off. Years of hating her mushroomed into a swell of molten lava, ready to spew.

His fingers trembled before fisting. Then he pummeled her face.

Raw emotion consumed him.

All that mattered was purging his hatred, displacing his rage onto the person who had inspired it.

Each punch signified something. The fact that she'd graduated second in his class at JHU—too close for comfort. The fact that she'd studied off *his* genius. The fact that everything came easily for her. The doting parents. The white house with the picket fence of privilege. The perfect husband. The cooing baby. The immortal gifts.

Hands wrapped around Em's chest, trying to pull him away.

The bitch had more coming.

Twisting his body and shoving his elbow into Vladimir's ribcage, he knocked the troll to the floor. Em resumed his assault, gritting his teeth. Sweat beaded on his forehead. Rage fueled his fists.

Ruby's face resembled raw meat. Her eyelids looked like blood blisters. Her lips, still jacked open by the dental mouth gag, had morphed into water balloons.

The vervain did its job stalling her healing magic.

His lungs burned from the exertion.

If he hadn't been out of breath, he would've kept going.

He wiped his bloodied hands on his lab coat, across his chest, unintentionally smearing blood on his embroidered name. Some of the blood belonged to his knuckles.

Bending over, he retrieved the fallen syringe.

Inhaling and exhaling, he invited calmness to return.

A bout of violence was as cleansing as sex. If he had been a smoker, he would've lit a cigarette right then and there.

Reaching out his left hand to Vladimir, Em helped him to his feet.

"Remind me to remain on your...how do you say...good side," the troll said, stating the double-duh obvious.

"You really need reminding, old man?"

The troll shook his head, looking horrified at the ground hamburger meat that now defined the face of the universe's precious *one and only*.

"Bring me some vervain serum from the fridge," Em ordered, yanking out Ruby's dental device.

Vladimir finally upped his tempo, returning with the drug.

The large vial felt cold in Em's hand.

"Time to give the bitch more poison," he said.

14

Thursday, July 18, 2041
Building #4 of the Polar Station: Cape Chelyuskin, Siberia

RUBY'S BODY ACCLIMATED to the increased vervain dosage, though like before, she had no way of calculating how many hours, days, weeks, or months she'd been out cold. Or how much blood Emory had drained from her. But at least she had re-emerged into a semiconscious state, climbing back from the dark abyss and feeling the strongest since her capture.

The wind had settled from her last awakening.

A dull ache underscored her face's swelling, reminding her of Emory's assault—a cold-blooded battering while she lay defenseless.

How had their relationship deteriorated to such hatred?

Before his cult-like obsession with dark science, she'd felt nothing but admiration for him.

Emory had always been smarter, rising to the deserved pedestal of "genius." Not only that, he was relentlessly driven, always advancing, never resting; forging forward like someone might overtake him if he coasted for a moment. His determination had paid off, too. In college, he had racked up degrees and accolades, earning professional validation as *the* top microbiologist and immunologist in the world.

With sincerity, Ruby had celebrated his well-earned celebrity.

That was the beginning of the end, she supposed. Because Emory had misinterpreted her pride in him as a right to make decisions for her, like a king claiming dominion over a subject. His arrogance corrupted his thoughts into believing that turning her vampire—

making her stronger, smarter, and invincible—would have no effect on his power play over her.

Underestimating her independence was a huge miscalculation.

Not to mention, she had inherited a legacy during her blood transfusion as a baby in utero. He had no way of knowing that turning her vampire would someday activate extraordinary gifts, elevating *her* as the most formidable immortal in the universe.

Needless to say, Emory offered no reciprocal hugs or handshakes when the public had lauded Ruby as The One and Only. He hosted no festive celebrations when the vampires bestowed upon her the role as The Tether, protector *of* and bond *between* all living things.

Her stomach grumbled.

How long had it been since she'd had sustenance?

The real question was…how long could she survive without it?

Confirming she was alone, Ruby deeply inhaled, inflating her lungs with air. As a protection in times of famine, the sacs of her bronchi still delivered oxygen into her circulatory system, though the process was hardly a substitute for fresh blood. She repeated the breathing regiment over and over, attempting to regain more strength while easing her hunger.

She activated her heart. Breathing was pointless without pushing oxygen to her organs. If the effects of vervain spiked, so be it. She didn't have a choice.

After minutes of breathing, she felt stronger. Relieved, too, since she hadn't noticed a resurgence of the drug's detrimental effects.

Maybe now her fingers could wiggle. She concentrated, but nothing happened. Nevertheless, she was making progress.

The lab's temperature suddenly plummeted.

Icy cold enveloped her, as if someone had plunged her into the Arctic Ocean. Temperature extremes didn't impact her survivability, but they did cause subtle reactions. Goosebumps formed on her skin, causing the hair on her arms to stiffen. With each exhale, she imagined a billow of white mist streaming from her mouth.

A switch clicked on. She heard it. Saw the fluorescent light through her closed eyelids.

She stopped breathing and froze, listening for any sounds.

Every indicator pointed to an empty room.

Was this one of Emory's tricks? To provoke a reaction?

"Most ironic we find ourselves neutralized," a male voice said.

She still couldn't hear a heartbeat.

"The most powerful have been rendered weak," he continued. "And once again, balance eludes us. For the pendulum has oscillated from one extreme to the other."

Her own heart raced out of control, as if the jaws of death were snapping at her heels.

The voice sounded familiar, though it projected an unfamiliar hollowness, like the words had been spoken in an unfurnished room with high ceilings.

"Considering your lack of mobility," the ominous voice added, "it appears as though your competencies have depreciated more severely than my own. Which I find most surprising."

The words wafted *within* the room where she lay.

"The racing of your heart suggests you recognize your husband's timbre," he purred.

Zagan?

Had he resurrected? Was he involved in her kidnapping?

"No need to panic, dearest wife," Zagan cooed, his voice dripping with sarcasm. "I have not come to consummate our matrimonial vows while you lay powerless. In truth, death delivered me from my love-struck delirium over your pretentious display of affection. Most assuredly, one cannot misinterpret the message conveyed when a vital organ has been hand-plucked from its chest cavity. The experience is quite sobering, indeed."

Ruby didn't know what to do. She hadn't been able to defend herself against Emory's violence. How would she ever shield herself from Zagan? Especially if he had regained his immortality and gifts?

Drugged, she couldn't read her lifeline stone. But did she really need to? Clearly, her life was coming to an end.

"Face me, Queen of Peace, or I shall abandon this laboratory and visit your precious Annapolis. To destroy your mayfly coven, of course. Only, in your absence, Clayton and Gabriella will be unable to thwart my efforts. You shall fail them if you remain afraid and hiding in this chamber."

How could she stop him when she couldn't move?

Panic irritated nerve endings, crackling like lit fuses of dynamite.

"Ahh. Darkened veins reveal my threat has touched a sour chord," Zagan taunted. "Yet, you remain cowering within your corpse.

"Although vervain prevents you from accessing your gifts," he continued, "could it be that you have forgotten, Lady Spencer? Forgotten that vampires can mimic physical death? And in death, your spirit may rise as a ghost? Believe me, this awareness comes from personal experience."

Zagan sparked a memory.

When her human body had died at Margo and Tomas's home nine years ago—while she was transitioning into a vampire, her spirit had lifted from her body and floated, light as a feather, as Clay laid beside her crying. But she *hadn't* passed over. She had hovered in a space between life and death, looking down at her own body as her soul drifted overhead.

As an immortal, she could arrest her vital systems, as Zagan implied. Already undead by definition, mimicking death would be easy, especially since she had regained control of her internal functions. She had no clue how long her spirit could separate from her body, but she had to try. Had to stop Zagan from leaving to harm her family.

"I grow bored." Zagan sighed. "Annapolis, it is then."

Ruby stopped everything. Her heartrate and circulatory system. Her respiration. And finally, her brain synapses. Everything flatlined.

Time temporarily paused.

"Are you aware you are drifting toward a vent?" Zagan asked.

Of course, she wasn't, though she vaguely remembered hearing the low hum of an exhaust fan. She'd been right in her identification because now she was inching closer, floating higher and higher toward the ceiling duct and honeycomb vent cover. Behind the opening, the fan's blades were spinning, whirring as they rotated around and around.

"Either kill me or help me," she snapped, irritated that the fan was about to shred her into confetti, scattering her into the outside world, wherever that was.

"Imagine yourself standing on these tiles beside me," he said. "In fact, the process is even simpler than sculpting or traveling."

She pictured herself standing next to Zagan, whose image was transparent like a hologram. In a nanosecond, her mental vision morphed into reality. No longer floating like a feather in an updraft, she stood by her nemesis.

"You're a...*ghost?*" she asked.

"Does the inflection in your voice indicate a question that requires an answer? Or do you merely wish to state the obvious?"

Ignoring him, she raised her hands to touch her face.

"Set worry aside, Lady Spencer," he said, almost sounding concerned. "Your ghostly form is absent the injuries marring your physical face, as you do not picture yourself as disfigured. Likewise, the gaping hole in my chest is gone."

Ruby glanced at her corpse on the operating table. Cuffs and straps restrained her body. Swollen and bruised, her face was a tapestry of horrific cuts, abrasions, and dried blood. Vervain was blocking her ability to heal. If she hadn't known the body was hers, she wouldn't have recognized herself.

Feeling emotions rise, she turned away and focused on Zagan. Except for his cloud-like appearance, his face hadn't changed a bit. His green eyes still glowed, his white hair remained short and spiked, and his pearl-white skin reflected an opalescent shimmer. He wore familiar black leather pants which hugged his legs. Different was his cherry red tunic.

"No longer wearing green or black?" Ruby asked, seeing no harm in exchanging banter. If as ghosts, they were somehow going to duel to the death, why not delay the inevitable for a minute?

Besides, if she was honest, she had missed him.

"Atea convinced me to embrace colors of the rainbow," he said, smiling. "Apparently, red compliments my green eyes. I believe she was accurate."

How Ruby missed Atea, her and Clay's New Zealand tour guide.

Forced to become Zagan's personal procurer of blood, Atea Patel had ingested one of the sacred berries from The Tree of Awareness, in a selfless sacrifice to help Ruby. In turn, when the King of Darkness drank Atea's blood at the wedding, he became mortal again, allowing Solange and Ruby to remove his heart. Allowing his goodness to be set free at his death.

"When did Atea tell you that?" Ruby asked. "Before your death? After? You haven't tried to harm her again, have you?"

"Certainly not," he said. "When I discovered I could drift from my corpse as a ghost, my first visit was to Atea in Kaitaia. Without evil corrupting my demeanor, I thought it best to apologize for my unsightly behavior. Nearly draining her at our wedding was far from chivalrous." He cleared his throat, as if nervous. "Did Atea advise you on wardrobe as well? Suggesting you embrace a *relaxed* appearance? A natural style, perhaps?"

Ruby hadn't given any thought, none whatsoever, to what she was wearing in her ghostly form. Glancing down, she almost choked. Not even her cloudy transparency could conceal her nakedness. She was nude, bare. Exposed!

When Zagan reminded her that a simple thought could change her reality, she pictured underwear, jeans, boots, and a navy sweatshirt. She was instantly clothed.

"You know we're not actually married, right?" she asked, skipping over her embarrassing wardrobe blunder.

His lips formed a half smile. "My death clearly nullified our marriage transaction."

Odd, but she didn't sense any vibes that he had come to end her life. He was different.

"Okay, good," she said. "So how *is* Atea?"

"She is most concerned about your wellbeing," he answered. "With good reason, I see. After six days, authorities have failed to unearth any clues regarding your whereabouts. Atea urged me to find you. She would not stop blabbering until I promised to do so."

"Does this mean you *don't* plan on killing me?"

"I do not share the goal of your captors. I only provoked you to encourage your determination." He raised his eyebrows and tilted his head forward. "Threatening your family has always spawned predictable results, Lady Spencer."

Relief quickly yielded to her curiosity.

"You said six days. Does that mean it's July 18th?"

He nodded.

Another relief. Six days was way better than six weeks or six months. Especially when the two people she loved more than anything were human. Well, Gabby was *mostly* human.

"Do you think," she said, sounding out of breath from excitement, "that I could travel like you? As a ghost? Like maybe I could visit Clay and Gabby and tell them I'm alive?"

"I can think of no reason why you would be restricted, though one could hardly consider me an expert. However, in the short time I have been a ghost, I have found my new competencies easily learned and requiring few prerequisites. As a manifestation, I am able to leave one place and appear in another with a mere thought. I need no location markers or coordinates to define my intended destination, as was the case traveling through time and space as a vampire. Now, I only think of an individual or place before I arrive."

"Let me try," she said, feeling jittery. "I'll be quick, so wait here."

"A dead man never rushes."

Closing her eyes, Ruby pictured Clay: his olive skin. Dark, wavy hair. Blue eyes like the Mediterranean. The dimple on his chin. His high cheek bones. And the crooked smile he reserved for her.

She opened her eyes, expecting to see her husband. To wrap her arms around him. To feel his breath on her neck.

Instead, Zagan's ghost stood before her with narrowed eyes.

"Perhaps it is more of an acquired skill than I believed," he said. "Try a simpler skill, such as drifting through that door."

With her thoughts guiding her actions, Ruby's ghost glided across the tiles. But four feet from the door, she felt a strong pull, like a rubber-band was around her waist and suddenly grew taut. She couldn't budge any further.

"Could vervain be affecting you?" Zagan asked. "Preventing you from distancing your body? Though, I suppose…yes," he nodded. "True death would break the drug's influence."

"Not funny." She rolled her eyes. "Can ghosts move things?"

Zagan appeared to be concentrating. With a whirl, the blackout shade recoiled until the bottom edge snapped loudly against the rod at the top of the window.

"I am attempting to master this skill, though it requires much energy." He smiled, revealing his bold teeth. "Did you not notice, Lady Spencer, that I had turned on the light?"

Ruby ignored his question and raced to the window. Her exhales frosted the glass.

Outside was flat land, leading to dark blue water, like a bay. Dense nimbostratus clouds formed a thick ceiling of dark gray, as if the skies were about to let loose. At the base of various shrubs and mounds of grasses were white crystals. Was that a dusting of sleet? In July?

"Let me think. Let me think," she said, starting to tire. "Do you know where we are?"

"I do not."

"Will you help me find out? Please, Zagan?"

Hearing voices, she noticed they grew louder with each step.

Zagan switched off the light.

"Quickly," he whispered. "Return to your body. Do not worry."

As Zagan's ghost vanished into thin air, Ruby started her heart. Like a vacuum, her body sucked her back into its shell.

The door opened. The light switch turned on. Footsteps entered.

"It's an iceberg in here," Emory said, pausing his march into the room. "Wait. How in the fuck did that blind open?"

"Relax, my friend," Vladimir answered. "Our subject has not moved." His footsteps shuffled to the window. "Faulty blinds do this sometimes. I suspect my beloved Russia did not manufacture this one. Perhaps the U.S. did?"

Ruby heard the elongated zip of someone lowering the blind which softly clicking into place.

Almost immediately, the shade whizzed upwards again, smacking against the rod.

She had no doubt Zagan was playing tricks.

"Crazy shit happened at breakfast, too," Emory said. "All I've got to say is in five short days, we'll be wrapping up training. And Ruby Spencer will be out of my life forever."

15

THE SONGBIRDS PERFORMED a spirited concert in the lush trees beyond Liora's hydrangea and peony garden. In the surrounding woods that bordered the queen's massive estate, the sounds of celebration abounded, led by thrushes, orioles, finches, and tanagers. After all, The Tether had fulfilled the prophesies; not to mention, Liora had wed the love of her immortal life.

As she sat on a wooden bench in the garden, with Draven beside her, her brown skin shimmered in the sunlight. Several bees were busily cleaning their wings on her arms while floral breezes perfumed the air. She inhaled the sweetness and smiled.

Her heart was full, as she had always longed it would be.

For 2.8 mega-annum, she had loved Draven in the shadows, fearful Zagan would discover their bond and destroy him. Except for stolen moments shared in The Cottage of Shadows—hidden in the middle realm within the dense Gray Forest, their relationship had been limited to cognitive whispers. Though sometimes, she had traveled as a cerebral stowaway within Solange's mind, able to see Draven through her assistant's eyes.

Liora would never forget the first time she met her true love. Their encounter happened at The Gathering, 210,000 years after Creation, when all vampires assembled in The Shadowlands to cast their final votes on establishing the realms, enacting the laws, and choosing their monarchs.

A celebrity swordsman revered by all of Athanasia, the Vampire Council had tasked Draven with placing Liora's golden crown on her head, for Lampsians had chosen her as their Queen of Light, ruler of Lampsi—the realm perpetually brightened by the sun.

As Draven had walked onto the stage, his wolf companion broke from his heel, cantered to her ceremonial throne, and leapt onto her lap. The silvery wolf licked her face, with tail wagging, as the gathered crowd cheered at the spectacle.

Apologies, Queen, he had whispered into her mind while bowing before her. *For my wolf has a habit of acting on how my heart feels.*

Their love connection grew stronger from that moment forward.

Not the passage of time, not even the curse separating vampires into realms according to their tolerance of ultraviolet rays, could suppress Liora and Draven's love. Nor the death culling by Zagan, Skotadi's evil King of Darkness. Or the fact that her nemesis had snatched Draven from his home in The Shadowlands to make him serve as Henchman in the realm of unending darkness.

Separation and fear could not break their everlasting bond.

Now, being able to openly gaze into her mate's sapphire eyes, touch his muscular gray body, and glide her hands along his long pewter braid, without fear, were sensations that hitched her breath. And to feel the softness of his lips on hers, yielding and commanding at all the right times, made her heart race and her thighs warm.

Since her marriage to Draven two weeks ago, Liora and her mate had spent every second in their master chamber: in the bed, on the rug, in each chair, on the balcony, in the bath. Lovemaking left no time for glimpsing into the future or whispering into the minds of her allies.

After several mega-annum serving as steward of the prophesies, she did not feel guilty. In truth, she and Draven had earned some "alone time," as Ruby called it.

In fact, Liora and her mate would still be in their bedchamber if Solange had not whispered to her as she awakened. With troubling news, Solange had urged the queen to put aside her brief hiatus to receive her at the castle.

As agreed, Liora's assistant would arrive at Kaliméra to personally deliver her concerns. Although Liora could have whispered into

Solange's mind to learn the news, she honored her friend's wishes to avoid unwelcomed cognitive intrusions.

Liora had dressed in a simple white-linen gown, the fabric matching Draven's untucked tunic. Of course, Draven was not without his sword or knives; he had tucked them in a scabbard or sheath and belted them around his gray leather pants.

In the queen's favorite garden, they waited for Solange.

Draven locked eyes with her. "If only we were to understand the lyrics of the songbirds. For surely, they are wondering why we have chosen to sit and gaze at flowers, occasionally touching lips, when far more interesting activities could engage us."

The birds in the trees grew silent.

Only breezes rustling through the leaves and the steady hum of lawn sprinklers made noise.

"You see, Queen," he continued, winking. "They are curious, in wait for your answer."

Tilting her head, she listened, trying to make sense of their pause.

"Are you alarmed by their absence of song?" he asked.

"They only quiet during our rest."

He chuckled. "That explains it then. For we have not rested, and now they grow weary."

"Perhaps you are right." She touched his cheek.

As her mate lowered his lips to touch hers, she felt a sharp prick on her forearm. A honeybee had stung her. And another followed. And then one more.

"Ouch!" She shook her arms, launching the insects into the air.

Her skin healed instantly. Still, why would her bees inflict pain?

"Let us greet Solange in the solarium," she said, standing, as she did not want to swat at her bees. "I must admit, I am feeling a bit of dread. Something is off balance and I need to stretch my mind to learn what the cause might be."

Draven rose and latched his arm with hers. He walked by her side, heading toward the castle. "I believe a wolf would be a valuable companion for us. Wolves often detect discord before our senses. And I have always appreciated a faithful wolf to aid with security."

"We shall make it so," she said, smiling. "One of your choosing."

Suddenly, Draven freed his arm, pivoting while drawing his sword.

She ducked, as a reflex, without knowing why.

Moving with precision and speed, her mate slashed the air above her. A hawk dropped by her feet, absent its head. Nerve endings caused the wings to flap and talons to twitch, since the bird's body did not yet know that Draven had swiftly delivered death.

"I concur. Something is amiss, Queen," he said, lowering his bloodied sword into its scabbard. He lifted her into his arms and raced toward the castle, barging through the front door and slamming it behind him. He placed her on her feet.

Liora did not need his protection, of course. Nor would she scold him for his chivalry. After all, Draven was a warrior, a protector, and she would not discourage him from his natural instincts and talents.

They walked into the sunlit solarium.

She would sit in her favorite wingback chair and stretch her mind to the future and past. Whatever it took to understand why the insects and animals were unsettled and aggressive. Her heartrate accelerated, unsure of what she might learn. At what she had missed while consumed with her thirst for Draven.

As she approached her chair by the paneled floor-to-ceiling windows, loud bangs stopped her in her tracks. Jolted her heart.

Two eagles crashed into side-by-side panels, leaving gaping holes and deep vein-like cracks in the glass. The massive birds lay dead and bloody on the wood floors.

Draven drew his sword in his right hand and a knife in the other.

"What is happening?" she asked.

Regardless of her intention, the King of Swords and Shadows did not have time to attempt an answer. Two wolves crashed through the broken windows, spraying glass shards into the room like a shower of glimmering rain. The beasts raised their upper lips above their jaws, exposing snow-white fangs which dripped with drool. The fur on their withers was raised. They crouched, ready to attack.

"Stand back," Draven ordered, his voice deeper than usual. Bending his knees, he slightly rocked back and forth to enhance agility. "Two wolves are no match for me and my blades."

Like her mate, Liora was not a sculptor or a traveler. As well, both lacked the ability to communicate with animals. Therefore, she did not hesitate to follow Draven's firm suggestion.

71

Two more wolves hurtled through the now glassless window.

"I shall occupy these beasts," he said softly, no longer boasting their defeat. "Slowly backstep through the doorway and close it from the other side. Barricade yourself upstairs. In the master chamber. And summon Solange immediately."

The brown wolf howled. Others answered from outside the castle.

She and Draven were clearly outnumbered. Worse, their lifeline stones flashed into her mind, revealing fading words—those representing their futures.

Liora was about to announce she would not abandon him. That she would stand by his side and fight until death. Separation was no longer palatable, for they would be mates in this life and the next. As long as they were together, she could handle anything.

Commotion interrupted her intended words.

A swirl of dust formed between them, rotating faster and faster.

Solange, thanks be to HIM (their Human/Immortal Maker), materialized before them. As Solange placed her palm on Draven's shoulder, her assistant reached for Liora's hand. Liora lunged toward her. Their fingers interlocked as the wolves leapt to pounce.

As soon as she, Draven, and Solange were touching, a vibration swept over her being. Tiny particles of dust lifted from each of their bodies, as they began their journey across time and space.

They materialized inside The Cottage of Shadows.

A wolf formed in the flesh as well.

The beast must have leapt on Draven as Solange traveled them to a safe location.

Her mate did not hesitate. With a flat-footed pirouette, he spun, brandishing his sword and thrusting the blade's tip into the throat of the she-wolf. The beast yelped before choking on its own blood and dropping onto the floor of the den, absent life.

Draven returned his sword to its scabbard and picked up the wolf's carcass. As he turned to take the beast outside and into the woods, Liora could see despair narrowing his eyes. Her mate had great respect and admiration for wolves, regarding them as companions. Never foes.

As for Liora, she also did not wish to see any living thing perish. She loved all creatures and cherished the harmony they had enjoyed since Creation, living side-by-side in balance.

The bee stings, hawk attack, eagle assault, and wolf onslaught were blatant acts of imbalance. There *had* to be an explanation.

"Do you know why the animals are hostile?" she asked Solange.

"Regrettably, I do not, my queen. I can only tell you that similar attacks have been reported in other realms on Athanasia, as well as on Earth."

"In other realms? Before *this day?*"

"Yes, within the last week," Solange answered. "The buck named Montaro, the one formerly reserved for Zagan himself, was found slaughtered on the Tume's embankment near Castle on High Cliff. Drained of blood and torn to shreds by...wolves. The castle's marshal of stables came across the slain stag. As well, the marshal discovered Gabriella's pony named Tenebrous in his stall, gutted by vultures."

"I must learn what has fueled this bloodshed," Liora said.

She studied Solange for the first time since her assistant had rescued them. The Shadowlander wore black leather pants and a blush blouse, which were unusual choices. Solange preferred gowns. In addition, her pewter hair commonly flowed down the length of her back, but she had pulled it into a braid. And the gray skin under her silvery eyes appeared puffy, as though she had tried to scrub her skin to remove crimson stains.

"Have you been crying?" Liora asked her.

Solange nodded. "Worse troubles fester."

"Speak of them now."

"The Tether has vanished against her will."

Liora grabbed the back of a chair positioned near the fireplace. She needed to steady herself as guilt saturated her bloodstream. For while she had been frolicking with her mate, Ruby had needed her.

"I must whisper to her," Liora said. "Find out where she is."

"Whispering is not possible," Solange answered. "She has been poisoned with vervain."

Draven returned to the den, not knowing of their conversation.

"Do not fear," he said, regarding their weary faces. "I will learn why the wolves have grown angry. We shall correct this imbalance."

"Other misfortunes require attention, King," Liora said. "Ruby is missing. Taken."

Draven's eyes widened.

"Then we will devote every energy into finding her," he said.

"Please. Let me finish," Solange begged. "Ruby has already been found, though her exact location is not yet known."

Liora tilted her head in confusion. *"Found?* By whom?"

Solange locked eyes with her.

Time paused without a breath.

"By...Zagan."

16

ZAGAN PACED BACK and forth in the office of mayfly Emory Bradshaw, waiting for the villain's return. As a ghost, Zagan could not feel the sensation of his boot soles touching the tiled floor. Nor did they make a sound. In truth, his modified existence was peculiar, though he had no intentions of complaining, as he did not wish to jeopardize his second chance—an opportunity to use his unparalleled assets to benefit…others. A foreign concept, indeed.

He examined the space. The scientist's office was unimpressive, not at all like Zagan's High Cliff study. There was no roaring fireplace. No large slate table or oriental rugs. No lit sconces with flickering wicks that formed dancing shadows on massive stone walls. No open balcony carved within the rock, allowing him to gaze at twinkling lanterns in the valley below. And no bats fluttering about.

How the king loved his magnificent fortress. Most assuredly, after he helped rescue Ruby, he would return to drifting down beloved hallways and in and out of favored chambers within his castle.

The scientist's workroom was no larger than a wardrobe chamber. It contained a child-like wooden desk, a filled bookcase, and several file cabinets. Mayflies loved their paperwork, perhaps because their insufficient brains did not have the capacity to retain information over time. Although his heart longed to relearn compassion and empathy, at present, he still found this mayfly shortcoming pathetic.

Honesty was a virtue, was it not?

A spherical model of the Earth was perched on the desk. Was it possible that the mayfly (the one whom humans considered a genius) could not remember his own planet?

Just below the window facing flat, barren land and an unknown body of water, a sill jutted out, adorned with a row of hideous potted plants. Vervain. He recognized the toothed leaves and clusters of tiny five-petaled blossoms the color of lilac.

How he loathed the herb's effect on his kind.

He blew a white mist of air, the temperature of dry ice, across the sill. The plants instantly froze, becoming brittle, ready to shatter with the slightest disturbance.

Rustling the papers on the desk with another exhale, he studied each sheet, finding no indication of their location. Apparently, the scientist could remember that small fact.

Zagan would frighten the information from the mayfly. The act of haunting would undoubtedly bring the king immeasurable pleasure. Remind him of the power he had once wielded when he made those around him tremble and quake.

He could not resist a smile.

Since there was nothing else to do until the scientist arrived, Zagan became invisible to conserve energy. Besides, an invisible haunting would be more effective. When one intended to spawn terror, being beautiful—even in ghost form—was a curse.

He sat in the wooden chair that swiveled and rolled on wheels with casters. The chair squeaked when his energy lowered onto the seat bottom, as if the rudimentary mechanisms required oil.

While waiting, Zagan gave thought to his encounter with Solange, which occurred the mornight of July 19th. He harbored no ill will against his former true love, despite the fact that she had ripped his heart from his chest. In truth, she had served the prophesies *first,* which he could hardly criticize. What eased the pain of her betrayal was that before his death, she had proclaimed her love for him.

At least, that is how Zagan chose to remember his final moments.

Though Solange lived at Kaliméra with Liora and now *King* Draven, she had been staying at The Cottage of Shadows since Zagan's death, no doubt giving the recently wedded lovebirds their privacy.

Fortunately, Zagan did not need to confirm her location prior to finding her; all he did was think of her. Absent effort, he appeared by her bedside as her silvery eyes opened.

While his ghostly heart sputtered in her presence, Solange screamed. And as she started to turn to dust to escape him, he pleaded with her to listen. Urged her to hear the grim news he had come to deliver. News of Ruby's kidnapping and condition.

Solange had ceased her travel and re-formed into the flesh, for she had been unaware of the unfortunate events involving The Tether. In fact, her first inquiry was why Gabriella had not whispered to her. Had not sought her help and assistance.

Zagan explained he had been visiting the child for several days and had gained her trust. After Gabriella approved of his plans to rescue her mother, he promised to contact Solange as soon as he believed The Tether's whereabouts were in reach of discovery. He had explained to the child that in war, troops which gathered prematurely could alert the enemy. Not even Gabriella was to tell her father until the rescue ploy was ready to be embarked upon.

Solange concurred with his plan.

Without waver, he had every intention of saving Ruby. A good deed, he hoped, which would be pleasing to HIM. And to Solange, if he was *completely* honest.

The wind rattled the window in the scientist's office, causing several frozen vervain stems to crumble like dust.

By now, Zagan thought, Solange would have whispered to Gabriella to arrange for a meeting in the hotel suite where the Spencers were staying. The gathering would take place that evening, in their time zone. He, Solange, Liora, Draven, Clayton, and the child would set the plan into motion.

Releasing energy to spin the globe attached to a bronze pedestal, Zagan watched the Earthly landmarks blur as the sphere whirred with each revolution.

All Zagan needed to learn was Ruby's precise location. Then, Solange would be able to travel his team to the facility where the villains were keeping Ruby comatose, like Sleeping Beauty.

When the doorknob turned, he had been deep in thought. He startled. His energy leapt from the chair, sending the wheels spinning.

The empty chair slammed into the bookshelf.

The door slowly creaked open, as if the mayfly named Emory had heard the commotion and was cautious.

The scientist did not immediately cross over the threshold. Instead, he stood, scanning the office interior from one wall to the other. A white mist marked each of Emory's exhales.

"What. The hell. *Now?*" he snarled, gritting his teeth while finally entering the room. "I am so over this God-forsaken freezer box." He massaged his cropped hair with his fingers. "Remember your mission," he mumbled out loud to himself.

Emory flipped a switch on a portable heater on the floor. Retrieving his chair, he rolled it back into place. He turned on the desk lamp and sat, looking at his scattered papers.

"I swear," he said, picking up a letter opener that resembled a small dagger, "if that Russian troll rummages through my papers one more time, I'm going to slice off his hands and gouge out his eyes." He drove the blade tip of the opener into the desk's wood surface.

Zagan caused the desk lamp to flicker before its bulb blew.

"That's just fucking wonderful," Emory snapped, standing up.

The king sent the chair rolling backwards again. It slammed into the bookshelf. Several large science books jolted off the shelf, violently striking the floor below. With the commotion, the vervain plants crumbled to dust.

Emory's eyes narrowed; his mouth slightly opened.

To add to the effects, Zagan sent several sheets of paper flying off the desktop.

The Russian named Vladimir arrived at the doorway.

"Turn on the light switch, Einstein," Emory said.

The man obeyed.

Flickering like a strobe, the bulb blew on the overhead light.

"Only a troll would take-up shop in Cape Chelyuskin, without even a mention—not a peep—that the Polar Station was freaking haunted. To mimic our dead friend Ox: *Well, ain't that something.*"

Zagan smiled. Mayflies were so predictable.

17

CLAY STRUGGLED WITH the decision he was about to make. As the sun lowered beneath the horizon, graying the natural light in his hotel's living room, he rubbed his temples. Sitting by himself on the couch, he felt frustration smolder inside him.

Ruby was the most powerful being in the universe. Where was she? Why hadn't she reached out to him? Was she drugged?

Grabbing the antacid bottle from the coffee table, he twisted the lid and shook out four pills, two more than the recommended dosage. Popping them into his mouth, he swigged water from his glass and swallowed hard, hoping to neutralize the acid which threatened to corrode his stomach lining.

Ruby had vanished eight days ago.

He still wasn't any closer to finding her.

President Unger had gone back to Camp David after the three-day farewell to the First Lady, which had started with the public paying their respects as she lay in repose and ended with her burial and a day of mourning.

Although Clay believed the President knew much more than he was saying, Irene Unger's passing meant the POTUS was well insulated. And 100-percent unavailable.

Eyes was doing his best to utilize resources on Clay and Ruby's behalf, both in the U.S. and overseas. But with a state funeral which included world leaders as guests, security assets weren't available.

He and Eyes had no doubt that if they located Emory and Vladimir, they'd find Ruby. But the trail was crumb free and icy cold.

That was only half of it.

Animal attacks were now escalating across the globe, spreading like a rabid infection. To deepen the mystery, blood samples from a cross-section of animals involved in attacks appeared normal. To date, scientists hadn't discovered any pathogens or anomalies.

Clay was getting calls right and left. After all, he was *the* community ecologist on the Special Warfare Council, which now had an emergency meeting on the books for the upcoming Wednesday. Along with the POTUS, CDC and WHO directors would attend.

On the "home" front, Gabby had become withdrawn.

Despite his efforts, she spent more and more time in her hotel bedroom, wanting to be alone. Sometimes he heard her talking to herself. Worry for his daughter was only increasing.

Desperation influenced his decision.

Clay believed that Athanasia and Earth should remain separate, as the planets had always been before Zagan's greed for human blood sparked an intergalactic cataclysm. But given Ruby's disappearance and Clay's lack of finding her, the agreed upon severance between the planets might need tweaking. Temporarily, at least.

Ruby was The Tether, an indispensable force in the universe; though to him and Gabby, she was so much more.

Bottomline, he was willing to take a selfish risk, though he hated the thought of getting his nine-year-old daughter involved as a liaison. What other choice did he have? The longer Ruby was missing, the less likely he would find her. And Gabby was having no luck reaching Ruby by attempting to whisper inside her mind. The situation was dire.

"Hey, Dad," Gabby said, startling him when she walked into the room. "Can we talk?"

"I wanted to speak with you, too." Clay patted the couch cushion.

"You first," she said, biting her lower lip as she sat beside him.

"Sure. I was wondering…" He paused and deeply inhaled, feeling nervous and a bit hypocritical. "I'm aware that I forbade you to contact any vampires, but I was wondering if we might make an exception. Like allowing you to whisper to Liora or Solange? I mean, even though we're pretty sure Mom hasn't left Earth, we could use some superhuman help to find her. And the vampire named Solange is a traveler, right?"

Gabby's shoulders quickly lowered, as if relieved. She smiled, full on, which he hadn't seen since they'd reunited at Cedar Lane, the day his wife and daughter had returned from Athanasia.

"Actually, we can talk to Liora and Solange face-to-face," she beamed. "Tonight."

"Excuse me?"

"Don't be mad, Dad. This is what I wanted to talk to you about. We've arranged a meeting. To talk about rescuing Mom. And everybody's meeting here to get started."

"Hold on a minute," he said.

His daughter had loaded a lot of information into a few sentences and he needed to find his footing. He didn't know if he should start by scolding Gabby for disregarding his orders not to communicate with any vampires on Athanasia. But since he had just asked her to break the rule, was the correction even warranted?

"How can we rescue Mom if we don't know where she is?" he asked, deciding his wife's whereabouts trumped everything, including broken rules. Besides, his daughter's tone and energy made his heart race. She knew something. Something promising.

"Just today, King…, I mean, *we* found out," she said. "Mom's in Siberia, Dad! She's at some weather observatory place. And we're going there tonight to bring her back."

Before Clay could even allow his heart to entertain the possibility that Ruby had been found, he needed to consider the credibility of the source. And Gabby had stumbled when she had said *king,* which meant she likely wasn't referring to Draven.

"Who told you this?" he pressed.

"Don't be angry, Dad. Please."

"Tell me."

"A ghost. A ghost said so. And now, Queen Liora, King Draven, and Princess Solange are meeting here. In a few minutes."

"A…*ghost?* Come on. Really?"

"Yes. Someone who's died and come back. As a ghost."

"Spit it out. Who is this so-called ghost?" He had his suspicions.

"*Umm.* The ghost is…King Zagan. But he's good now. And he found Mom. Which is the important thing, Dad. Not the fact that you don't like him."

"Are you kidding me?" His head throbbed from pressure. "You've been talking to that sociopath? And you *believe* him?"

With flushed cheeks, Gabby stood up. "Mom and Princess Solange freed King Zagan from evil. Remember? I'm not trying to be sassy or anything, but shouldn't we focus on saving Mom?"

Keeping Gabby safe and rescuing Ruby were all that mattered. But how could he trust the King of Darkness who had been secretly conspiring with his daughter…as a ghost? The same entity who had blown him and Gabby off a cliff's edge on Great Island in New Zealand, hoping to crush them on the jagged rocks below?

Without having time to digest his daughter's announcement, clouds of dust swirled in the hotel's living room. Three vampires materialized in the flesh.

Gabby introduced them since he had never met them in person, though he could have easily identified the queen and king from Ruby's descriptions. Solange, too.

He greeted them each with a handshake.

Minutes later, the room's temperature plummeted. A billowy mist took shape: Zagan. Liora and Draven looked as uncomfortable about working alongside the arrogant bastard as Clay felt. Only Solange and Gabby seemed oblivious, as if forgiveness was no big deal.

Zagan explained how he'd found Ruby and forced Emory to reveal their location.

The rescue plan was simple. Zagan would leave ahead of them to ensure Ruby was alone. If he didn't return within five minutes, they'd know the coast was clear. Clay, Gabby, and the vampires would huddle together, allowing Solange to travel them to the Polar Station's makeshift lab where Emory was keeping Ruby. They'd unhook her from the vervain drip, release her restraints, feed her some of Liora's blood, and travel back to the hotel. Easy in, easy out.

"We're doing this *tonight?*" Clay asked, trying to wrap his head around the immediacy of the plan. Not to mention, popping in and out of Siberia wasn't exactly normal.

Everyone nodded.

"I'll get my boots and winter coat. Put yours on, too," he said, looking at Gabby.

His daughter tilted her head and smirked, as if he should know better. Then she pointed at herself. "Sculptor like Mom, remember?"

"Best not to forget from whom this rare and impressive gift originated," Zagan piped in.

"Yes, King Zagan," she said in monotone, as if they shared a dry humor between them.

His daughter's expression turned serious and her eyes hid behind her lids as they quivered. When she opened her blue eyes, she had outfitted each member of the team in black leather from head to toe. Black leather pants, boots, jackets, and full-length cloaks. Just like Zagan. And each of them wore a leather belt with two scabbards, one housing a sword and the other, a knife. She had also sculpted a loaded, nine-millimeter handgun for him.

"No weapons for you," Clay said to Gabby, shaking his head.

"But Dad…"

"You're a sculptor, *remember?* So sculpt handcuffs on the enemy if they show up. But no weapons. They're too dangerous until you've been trained."

Gabby huffed, but made her belt and scabbards disappear.

After they revisited the plan one last time, Zagan vanished.

Clay's smartwatch showed 8:00 p.m.

The group huddled together, holding hands as they waited for the five-minute window to exhaust itself.

Pounding, Clay's heart threatened to break through his chest. He couldn't wait to see Ruby. To free her. To bring her home.

The anticipation was maddening. Nerve-racking.

What if something went wrong?

"We are to follow," Solange said softly. "Do not break the chain."

Their bodies began to vibrate until they all turned to dust.

18

RUBY'S MIND WAS drifting within vervain's dark abyss when she felt familiar lips on hers. Her heart lurched from dormancy, pumping wildly. She felt her fingers twitch. Her toes wiggle. Was she dreaming? Or had someone pulled out the vervain drip?

"Good morning, Ruby," Clay whispered, the breeze of his words touching her face. "A new day has started here. Rise and shine."

Her husband was really there!

She heard him unsnapping her restraints.

Zagan had kept his promise to pinpoint her location.

On the downside, her gut warned that they were all in jeopardy.

Concentrating on her eyelids, she slowly forced them open. Fluorescent lighting from the overhead fixtures instantly caused her to squint. As she blinked and adjusted her eyes, Clay came into focus. He was leaning over her, his mouth near hers. His blue eyes radiated relief. His smile, love. His touch, concern.

"There you are," he said, running his fingers through her hair. "My one and only."

It was so like her husband to overlook the patchwork of cuts, bruises, and swelling still disfiguring her face.

"Clay..." She was barely able to curl her lips from her injuries and the drug's heavy pull. If only she could slow down time to allow her body to recover. But she couldn't shake the dread coursing through her veins, warning her of imminent danger. "Where am I?"

"At the Polar Station on Cape Chelyuskin. In Siberia."

Ruby struggled to quell her dizziness. "We've got to leave."

"Believe me, the faster we get you home, the better," Clay said.

"I wish I wasn't...wasn't so lethargic from the vervain." She dry-swallowed. "And the lack of sustenance isn't helping."

Liora neared the operating table and lowered her bleeding wrist to Ruby's lips. Saliva seeped into her mouth in anticipation of the meal.

"Drink, Tether," Liora said, as inviting as a lullaby. "Drink and recover your strength, but do not delay, as danger is all around us."

The queen's blood rushed into Ruby's mouth and she gulped. Over and over. With each swallow, she could practically feel her cells plump like sponges. Feel her energy awaken each muscle and sharpen each brain synapse.

In her bloodstream, the vervain diluted. Maybe her facial wounds would begin to heal. Maybe her gifts would swiftly return.

"Warrior," Liora said, pulling her wrist free, "I require some of my life source to remain in my veins." Smiling, the queen licked her own wound to expedite healing.

"I'm indebted to you, Queen," Ruby said.

Clay leaned closer. "Can you sit up? Someone wants to see you."

She nodded. With his help, she rose to a sitting position.

"Mom! You're okay!"

Gabriella, her precious Gabby, stood in front of her with wide eyes. Wearing leathers, her daughter looked grownup and unafraid.

Ruby reached out and her daughter planted herself in her arms.

"I've been so worried," Gabby said. "And missed you so much."

Her daughter's face tilted upwards, her eyes finding Ruby's. How Ruby had longed to see her. To see her eyes and freckles and genuine smile. To hear her bubbly voice. Smell her familiar scent. Not just as memories inside her mind, but in the flesh. Tucked safely in her mother's arms.

"King Zagan found you," Gabby continued. "And now we can take you back home."

Clay placed his hand on Gabby's shoulder. "We have to hurry. It's not safe here."

As her daughter stepped away from the table, Ruby spotted Zagan's ghostly image near the corner—which was different, since in the recent past, he preferred being front and center.

"Thank you, Zagan. Thank you so much for keeping your word."

He nodded. "As your former husband, Lady Spencer," he added, forming a smirk, "might I be so bold as to suggest you sculpt an outfit? I would do so, but regrettably, my sculpting competencies abandoned me at death's door."

"You earned death," Draven snapped, wearing a sour expression while glaring at Zagan's ghost with bulging veins. "Or surely my brother Titus would be standing among us. No?"

Deep creases formed on Solange's forehead, since Titus had passed only 20-days earlier. At the hands of none other than the former King of Darkness.

"We do not have time to discuss old wounds," Liora said. "Not in this place."

Ruby finally processed Zagan's words and looked down at herself. The sheet had fallen to her waist, leaving her upper torso naked.

Grabbing the sheet, Clay lifted it to help cover her.

When she attempted to sculpt leathers on her body, nothing happened. Being a ghost had been easier. In the flesh, the vervain still blocked her gifts.

"I've got it, Mom," Gabby said, sculpting an outfit which matched everyone else's. She also banded her hair into a ponytail.

Ruby felt such pride over her daughter's powers and maturity.

With Clay's help, she lowered herself from the table.

"Thank you for traveling here, Solange. And for bringing my family," she said. "I'm grateful to you all for coming."

Did she hear footsteps? Ruby tilted her head to listen.

"For now," she added, feeling an overwhelming urgency, "we need to leave here."

"Knock, knock," announced a familiar voice.

A voice that caused chills to race down her spine. A voice that belonged to the fists which had pummeled her face.

Everyone turned their heads toward the doorway.

In a pristine white lab-coat, Emory Bradshaw stood, holding a remote control, flanked by two freakishly enormous wolves. One wolf was gray coated, the other black. Both sported quivering upper lips, raised above their teeth and jaws.

"Leaving so soon?" Emory taunted. "Right when our little shindig's getting started?"

A wave of nausea gripped Ruby's stomach and throat. Her meal threatened to erupt. Swallowing hard, she fought back the urge. She didn't want to vomit blood in front of her daughter.

Ruby reached for Gabby's hand and clutched it, wishing she was strong enough to conjure the energy to travel her family and friends back home. But without her gifts, she could do nothing. Instead, they needed to form a chain with Solange, the only other traveler.

Of course, nothing was ever easy.

Solange, standing by the back wall, was ten feet away from Ruby.

As a disabled vampire, the distance felt like a mile.

No doubt, Clay sensed her vulnerability.

Without hesitation, her husband moved in front of her and Gabby. As he faced Emory, he placed his hands behind him, gently nudging them to step backwards towards Solange, to increase the distance between them and the mad scientist and his snarling, oversized beasts.

Draven and Zagan were the only two who were even farther away from Solange. Floating in a corner, Zagan's location didn't matter; he was a ghost. Anyway, in a blink of an eye, he vanished into thin air.

Draven, however, was closest to the doorway.

Emory stepped into the room as his wolves flanked him. They stopped in between Draven and the rest of them.

"This may surprise you," Emory said, "but I need test subjects. Vampire? Human? Young? Ancient? Doesn't matter. Wolf venom should work regardless." He raised his hands as if delivering a sermon. "Low and behold, here you are! What's the parable say? *'Seek and you shall find. Knock, and the door shall open.'* Matthew 7:7, isn't it?"

Gabby glared at Emory with thinned lips, since this was the first time her daughter was old enough to remember being face-to-face with the man Ruby and Clay had originally chosen as her Godfather. The man who had turned her mother into a vampire.

As Ruby, Clay, and Gabby neared Liora and Solange by the back wall, Ruby felt her veins trying to push against her skin in response to the combination of stress and anger. If only everyone was touching.

Draven remained in the most vulnerable position.

The blackout shade recoiled; its bottom edge raced upwards and slammed loudly against the rod at the top of the window. Dark gray skies were beyond the glass. The IV stand, the one which had delivered Ruby's vervain drip, violently toppled over onto the floor tiles. A glass jar filled with cotton balls flew across the room.

Emory leaned to the side, without moving his feet, to avoid the projectile. The wolves had no response at all. The jar shattered against the wall nearest the door.

Zagan's commotion created a distraction, allowing Draven to slip his knife from its sheath.

"Is this any way to treat your host?" Emory asked, pulling a dart pistol from his lab coat pocket and aiming the barrel at Draven.

"Drop it," Clay ordered, having grabbed his own nine-millimeter from its holster. Her husband pointed his weapon at Emory.

Shifting his eyes from Draven's knife to Clay's handgun, the mad scientist acknowledged the double threat with a smirk, seeming to welcome the standoff.

Still clutching Gabby's hand, Ruby took several more steps back to distance her daughter from the escalating confrontation. Panic ignited her senses. As brief cognitive flashes overpowered the lingering vervain, she saw glimpses of what was about to happen.

Ruby hollered, "No, *Draaa...*"

As Draven stepped forward brandishing his blade, Emory swiveled and shot him with a dart, point blank. At the same time, the black wolf leapt onto Clay's chest, knocking him over. His back slammed onto the tiles. On impact, the nine-millimeter released from his grip and slid across the floor, out of reach.

Draven staggered. The dart had struck near his collarbone, collapsing him to the floor. His knife fell to the wayside. At first, Draven rapidly blinked, but as the vervain polluted his bloodstream, the sedative paralyzed his muscles. His eyelids locked open.

Liora attempted to rush to her mate's side. Solange held her back.

Grabbing Clay's arm, Ruby lifted him to his feet.

Everyone paused to assess the altered gameboard.

"Well," Emory finally said, snickering, "I guess we know who wants to go first as a test subject."

The mad scientist pressed a button on his handheld remote. The wolves' eyes glowed red. No doubt the device activated some sort of chip inside the beasts' brains, located near or behind the eye sockets. He pointed his discharged dart pistol at Draven and flicked it back and forth toward the door.

"Take him out," he ordered, speaking to the wolves. "Remove."

With their jaws, the beasts clamped down on each of Draven's shoulders. Barely conscious, the King of Swords and Shadows moaned through frozen lips.

As the wolves dragged Draven from the lab, he managed to release the sound of one word: *"Go!"*

"Ruby's not going anywhere, boyfriend," Emory cooed, looking smug as he raised the dart gun and aimed it at her. "This pistol chambers two rounds."

"I'm going to kill you," Ruby seethed. "Rid the universe of you."

The trigger clicked.

Emory had fired the other dart.

19

RUBY WAS RELIEVED the vervain dart was a nanosecond too late, arriving at its intended destination after Solange had already converted Ruby to dust.

A heartbeat later, Ruby materialized in the flesh, alongside Clay, Gabby, Liora, and Solange. In ghost form, Zagan manifested himself next to them.

Two miles from the lab, they stood in a field of sandy soil and sparse brownish grasses, located south of the Polar Station. Looking back at the compound in the distance, she counted eight structures comprising the research base, each building a different size. Plumes of smoke rose from a dozen chimneys.

North of the Polar Station was a cobalt blue body of water—the convergence of the Laptev and Kara Seas. Looking south was a small dense forest of Siberian stone pines, thriving farther north than the tree's preferred climate. And to the right and left as far as her eyes could see was endless lowland, flat and barren.

The blustery wind whipped and flapped their full-length black cloaks like sails in a hard luff. The temperature was just under freezing, slightly below normal for summer in Siberia. The cloudy skies were shades of pewter and slate, with fast moving layers. By her calculations, coupled with the dropping barometric pressure, freezing rain or sleet was imminent.

"Should we travel someplace warm and dry while we develop a

game plan?" Clay asked her. "Coldness doesn't deter vampires, but I'm worried the conditions aren't great for Gabby."

"Finding warmth and shelter are wise," Liora agreed, "as I do not wish for Gabriella to be uncomfortable. However, I shall remain here. I will not travel far from my mate."

"I'm not cold, Dad. I swear."

Ruby hid her eyes behind her lids and when she opened them, Gabby wore a parka, ski pants, and earmuffs.

"Will that work?" Ruby asked her daughter.

"I guess so. Thank you." Gabby's lips curled downward.

"You're still frowning. Do you need anything else?"

"No. It's just that back in the lab, I should've done more," she said. "Like sculpting something to protect King Draven. I didn't think fast enough. I'm sorry."

Ruby embraced her daughter. "Please don't think like that. You're amazing. Dad and I are so proud of you. There was very little any of us could've done."

"Do not worry, Gabriella, for we will free King Draven," Solange said. "And always remember, if you had not agreed to work with King Zagan as you did, we might not have found your mother."

"That's very true," Ruby agreed.

"Ditto on all points." Clay joined her and Gabby in a family group hug. "For the nine days that Mom was held captive, you've been our one and only sculptor. Look at all you've accomplished! We couldn't have prepared for this rescue without your gifts."

Her husband turned his head, glancing at Zagan's ghost. "Hey. Didn't mean to minimize your role in all this."

"You are a mayfly." Zagan sighed. "I shall forgive your lack of thoughtful utterances."

As she, Clay, and Gabby pulled away from their embrace, her husband rolled his eyes.

Touching his shoulder, Ruby shook her head, hoping he'd refrain from responding. She had other concerns and the clock was ticking.

"Liora?" she asked. "Are you seeing something?"

The queen had slightly turned away from the group. She looked frozen with her chin raised toward the sky.

"I cannot penetrate Draven's mind," Liora explained.

"Don't forget," Ruby said, "vervain consumes energy required for our gifts. That's why no one could whisper with me once vervain saturated my circulatory system."

"What shall we do then?" Liora's eyebrows tightened. "We must save him and soon, or his lifeline stone will continue to fade."

"I suggest," Solange said, "that I travel Ruby and her coven back to their hotel. The Tether needs to heal and restore her powers. When I return, Zagan, Liora, and I will travel to the laboratory and free Draven. With our combined competencies, the three of us will skirt harm while rescuing the king."

Ruby ran her hands over her face to assess her wounds, not that their status made any difference in her decision. She was relieved, however, that her face was healing. It meant the effects of vervain continued to weaken.

"Nonsense," Ruby countered, using a sharper tone than intended. "I'm fine. Really. We have a saying in our country: *united we stand; divided we fall.* Each of our gifts will guarantee Draven's rescue. We're all in this together."

Both Clay and Zagan opened their mouths and said, *"I…"*

Clay raised his eyebrows in a question, as if wondering what Zagan was about to say and *why* Zagan thought it was appropriate to be the first to respond to her comment.

"I," Zagan repeated, failing to relinquish his turn, "agree with Lady Spencer. Risking her own safety is consistent with her responsibilities as protector of the universe. Not to mention, our mission requires her competencies. As well, having another sculptor like Gabriella is essential. But please, Clayton, forgive me if I have overstepped. You were saying?"

Clay cleared his throat. *"I*…was about to agree with my wife. And to recommend we don't waste time. We need to plan our offensive."

"Imagine! Wisdom dribbles forth from the mayfly." Zagan smirked. "May I also suggest that I assist by gathering information on Draven's confinement, prior to our offensive? Knowing the number of guards and wolves securing his position will ensure victory over the course of our rescue campaign."

"Shouldn't someone go with you, King Z?" Gabby asked.

"One cannot kill the dead, child, though your concern would

surely touch my heart if the organ had remained beating in my chest."

Solange's gaze quickly dropped to the ground. Ruby understood since she shared in the princess's guilt over removing Zagan's heart.

Sleet streaked across the landscape, horizontal to the ground. Streams of white mist marked their exhales.

Zagan's strategy received unanimous approval. After he returned, they'd use the information he'd gleaned to initiate a fail-proof attack.

Nodding at Solange, the ghostly king disappeared.

"We have a few minutes before Zagan returns." Ruby looked at her daughter. "Want to sculpt a fire?"

"Won't the wind blow it out?"

"Let's think this through. How might you block the wind, keep our position hidden, and enjoy the warmth of a campfire?"

Gabby concentrated.

To develop as a critical thinker, her daughter had to practice reacting to problems multidimensionally—from every angle. Because during a crisis, there was no time to think. Problem solving complex situations had to become as quick as a reflex.

"Umm," Gabby started, as hair pulled loose from her ponytail and swirled around her face. "Maybe I could make a tall rectangular-box like a chimney? The tippy top could be open so the smoke escapes in the clouds. The sides would be like a two-way mirror. We could see outside, but no one could see inside."

"Now we're talking," Ruby said. "Use sleet for the structure itself. Make the mirror from a thin layer of aluminum found in our cloak buttons. And collect flames and wood from the Polar Station."

Gabby hid her eyes behind her lids. They quivered as her daughter cognitively gathered her materials and formulated the vision. When Gabby's eyes opened, she had sculpted her solutions into reality.

A campfire blazed and heated their shelter. They were warm, protected from the elements, and camouflaged.

"Great job," Ruby said, admiring her daughter's craftsmanship.

Liora paced. "Zagan's delay concerns me."

"I know it feels long," Clay said, "but he's only been gone ten minutes. Max."

As they waited for Zagan's return, Ruby stared into the flames and let her mind drift with the crackle of burning logs.

Ruby's thoughts turned to Emory's most recent attempts to bastardize the genomes of humans and animals in order to bioengineer a new species. His disregard for life and the natural order of Creation was demonic, especially his abuse of animals.

No doubt the mad scientist had created a super wolf "soldier" in another attempt to take over the world. He was the *real* bloodsucker among them, stealing blood for his own heinous causes.

Ruby would not allow him to live. Not this time.

He would die. On this day. In this place. Before his plans progressed any further.

Fueled by her thoughts, flames suddenly raged 20-feet high, as if she had thrown gasoline on their campfire.

Everyone jumped back.

Ruby felt the veins in her neck bulge and pulse.

Placing her hands on her face, she ran her fingers over her skin. Her healing was complete. Her gifts had returned.

Soon, very soon, Emory would feel the full brunt of them.

20

IN ANOTHER LAB room, two wolves released the immortal at Em's feet, as if they had retrieved the winning football from the Super Bowl. Maybe he should've stuffed one of his pockets with dog treats to reward their efforts.

"My, my, my," Em said softly.

What an NFL team might do with a specimen the likes of Draven on its roster. The gray wonder looked to be six-foot-four, probably weighing 230 pounds, comprised mostly of testosterone-fed muscle. As a vampire, his stamina had to register off the charts.

If Em wasn't careful, he might give himself a boner.

He heard footsteps and looked up. A female in a white lab coat swaggered in, followed by two armed guards outfitted in fatigues.

"Who are you?" he asked the woman, who was brown skinned like him and dressed like a scientist, holding a clipboard.

"I am Mela. Vlad sent for me to assist you in your...experiments."

Em felt an eye roll coming on.

"Why would the troll send for *you?* Specifically?" he pressed.

"I specialize in cellular integrity," she answered, sounding American, only with precise articulation. "With genetically enhanced hybrids, we want to prevent marked delays in apoptosis—the naturally occurring death of cells." She smiled and raised her eyebrows. "We would not want to grow a wolf Godzilla, now would we?"

Having her onboard might be an asset. He could use more brain java at his disposal. Anyway, her point had merit.

"Where do you practice in the States? New York City? Los Angeles? Chicago?"

"Most scientists do not make assumptions," she said, frowning.

"Lucky for me, my genius elevates me far above 'most.' In fact, if there was a throne in genetics, yours truly would be sitting on it," he snarked. "So you're not African American?"

"Must all persons of color be of *your* race? From *your* country?"

Em tilted his head and ran his eyes over her slender body. "Just tell me who you are," he barked, his mood shifting. "And where the fuck you come from. Nix the not-so-subtle innuendo that I'm racially and ethnically insensitive."

"I am Dr. Gemela Pérez, a medical professor and researcher at the University of Barcelona." She locked eyes with him as she hugged herself across her chest, rubbing her hands along her biceps as if to fight a chill. "And yes, Spain has brown and black citizens."

"Good to know, *Spaniard,*" he said, his voice a counter jab. "In the future, if you're hoping for morning coffee, arrive an hour earlier. We begin at eight, sharp. Now why don't you start impressing me with your grit by grabbing this subject's feet." Em nodded to the guards. "You goons grab his sides. We'll lift him on three."

As they placed Draven on the table, Vladimir shuffled into the lab.

"Big surprise," Em said to the troll. "A day late and a dollar short. What kind of operation do you think we're running here?"

"A dollar?" Vladimir questioned. "My friend, greater leverage can be achieved trafficking more *interesting* assets. Yes?" He stared at the vampire. "So perhaps you might share how you wagered and won this most prized lottery?"

Em strapped Draven to the table, explaining what had transpired.

"Have you considered," Vladimir said, "that our opponents might abandon this comrade now that Ruby is free? If I led their campaign, I would consider him an acceptable sacrifice."

"Guess that's why you're a troll and not The Tether, old man," Em growled. "No way would Ruby goodie-two-shoes leave anyone behind. Here, let me show you."

He had synchronized his smartwatch with the remote devices

controlling the super wolves.

Holding out his left wrist parallel to the floor, he rotated the image on the face of his smartwatch so he could read it. After verbally telling his device to project, Em displayed the image on a blank wall in the lab. Using his watch's touchscreen to navigate within the program, he advanced the pages, stopping on the screen that listed each of his wolf subjects by number. To the left of each ID was a vitality indicator: a green beating heart.

"Check this out," Em said, touching the number link of one wolf.

A menu page projected, offering several options: Access Video Cache, Display Live Camera Feed, Send Impulse Command, Deliver Verbal Command, Select Warfare Maneuver, Detonate Subject, and Cruise Ship Greenlight.

"How do you acquire such technology?" Vladimir asked, looking genuinely impressed.

"Blow the right people and generosity comes." Em smiled at his clever play on words.

Mela rolled her eyes, refusing to have a little fun. The two Russian guards were blank faced. No brainer, they had to be former Kremlin robots. Sense of humor: zero.

"I do not understand this…*Cruise Ship Greenlight,*" the troll said. "What does this option mean?"

"Don't worry about it," Em snapped. "Your remote won't include that option anyway. But what you *need* to know is that the chips implanted in our wolf subjects are our old friends—Remote Electronic Detonators or REDs, only remarkably advanced. Right now, I've stationed ten wolves in what you call The Pines: the six acres of forest about two miles south of the station. Watch this."

He touched "Display Live Camera Feed" on his watch.

Live video started to roll. The Polar Station appeared in the distance, as seen by the wolf Em was accessing via its RED chip. Barely detectable, he spotted the slight glitch in the landscape, resembling a ripple on the projection.

Em knew exactly what was causing the imperfection.

"I see only barren lowland," Vladimir said. "Perhaps my theory of abandonment is accurate after all. Yes?"

"You're too easy to fool."

Em touched the back arrow on his watch's screen and pressed the cache button. A still picture appeared on the wall, showing an empty field. To rewind the video, he used the digital slider on the footage scale. At the right time marker, he released the slider and hit play.

Everyone in the lab watched as the vampires, humans, and ghost huddled together in the sleet. The bratty kid did that freakish eye twitching thing. And when her eyes opened from the trance, some sort of camouflaged structure hid the group.

"I stand corrected, my friend," Vladimir said.

"Wonders never cease."

"You have a plan then?"

Em rolled his eyes, like when *didn't* he have a plan?

"Mela, you and the guards stay here with these wolves. Keep your vervain darts close in case the vamps show up. Don't hesitate to shoot them." Em glanced at the gray hunk of maleness sprawled out on the table. "Prepare this subject for genetic infusion, but don't proceed until I return." He moved toward the door. "Troll-man, you're coming with me."

A file cabinet in the lab began to rumble and shudder. Suddenly, a drawer opened and slammed closed. Each drawer followed suit, functioning independently. Books stacked on top of the cabinet vibrated off the edge, falling and crashing onto the floor.

The wolves crouched and growled.

"Believe me," Em said, walking out with the troll by his side, "I'm going to find a way to send that ghost back to its hell hole. For eternity."

21

Sunday, July 21, 2041
A field near the Polar Station: Cape Chelyuskin, Siberia

DESPITE THE PROTECTION of the camouflaged tower and the calm of a crackling campfire, Ruby's senses were on high alert. Enormous hybrid wolves hid in the forest. Their red eyes glowed from strategic positions under the darkened canopy of dense pines.

No doubt, the wolves were monitoring their prey. Waiting for a signal to attack.

Ruby stretched her mind toward the trees. She heard whispers exchanged between the beasts, only she couldn't decipher their meaning. Instead, she tried to identify how many heartbeats she heard, but the rhythms were too similar, too overlapping to differentiate. Suffice to say, the number of wolves constituted a pack.

"Will they try to attack us?" Gabby asked.

Ruby realized her daughter had also assessed their surroundings. Perhaps she was too frightened to also seek a glimpse of the future. A future which Ruby determined was uncertain, at best. Especially for Clay and Gabby who were the most physically vulnerable.

"As long as our lifeline stones are not blank," Liora said, without answering Gabby's question directly, "victory is within our reach."

"I hate to mention this," Clay said, looking at Ruby with a creased forehead. "Mostly because what the wolves have become isn't their fault. But if we're faced with a life or death situation, can you carbonize them?"

She shook her head. "Whatever genetic cocktail Emory used to enhance these wolves, it included my blood. So reducing them to ashes is off the table. Turns out, the protective shield of self-preservation can be a paradox."

Out of the blue, her daughter screamed. High pitched and frantic.

Gabby flailed her arms at an attacking…an attacking *hawk?*

Ruby could feel veins bulge and pulse in her neck.

The bird's talons clasped strands of her daughter's hair, yanking them from her scalp. Releasing its catch, the hawk stretched its emptied talons and swooped for more.

Ruby's predator instincts exploded into action. Clearly, vervain no longer impeded her gifts. With a sweep of her hand, she carbonized the bird. Its ashes rose with the campfire's smoke, swirling toward the gray, sleeting sky.

While they had been talking, the hawk must have entered through the opening at the top of the flue-like structure. In fact, a kettle of hawks circled overhead.

Hiding her eyes behind her lids, Ruby focused.

When she opened them, a makeshift chimney cap appeared, preventing other birds from entering.

"Are you all right?" Clay asked their daughter, examining her.

Relieved, Ruby could see and smell that Gabby wasn't bleeding.

"Why would a hawk try to hurt us?" Ruby asked.

"Animal attacks are occurring on Earth and Athanasia," Liora answered. "The reason is not yet known."

"I had to travel the queen and king to safety," Solange added. "Birds and wolves breached their castle to inflict harm."

"Strange," Ruby said. "Was that the first attack? At Kaliméra?"

"No," Liora answered. "The first took place in Skotadi. According to Solange, the buck Montaro, Zagan's personal stag, was devoured. Drained of his blood as well."

Ruby remembered the magnificent buck during her inaugural visit to Zagan's Castle on High Cliff. He was the first animal she had tasted and healed, while standing beside Zagan along the Tume River. The first being, in fact, that she had ever glamoured, visually transmitting the irresistible hypnotic suggestion not to feel pain.

"Wait. *Drained* of his blood?" she asked. "How unusual."

"Apologies for sharing this news here, Gabriella," Liora said, "but the information might be important. Like Montaro, the pony named Tenebrous met a similar demise. Found in his stall, Tenebrous was also absent his blood."

Gabby gasped.

Questions nipped at Ruby's brain.

Why would Montaro and Tenebrous suffer similar fates?

Was the common denominator Zagan? Or her and Gabby?

"I'm curious. By chance, did you ever *heal* Tenebrous?" she asked her daughter.

Her nine-year-old hesitated, as if she might get in trouble.

"Gabby?" Ruby pressed.

"That was okay, wasn't it? I mean, Tenebrous had a small cut on his hock, so I used my blood to heal him."

"I totally understand," she assured her daughter. "It's just that the information suggests the deaths of Montaro and Tenebrous (two animals which carried our blood) are connected somehow. Maybe their deaths were intentional."

Ruby rubbed her temple, trying to make sense of the evidence. "Solange, do you know if the buck and pony were killed by one predator or several?"

"The marshal of stables found both carcasses. Near the buck's remains, he observed multiple wolf prints, of varying sizes. And one vulture alone, he had told me, could not have..." Solange nervously glanced at Gabby. "Could not have inflicted the extreme damage to the pony's body."

With more questioning, Ruby learned that animals of every species had attacked humans and vampires, either injuring or killing them. However, the attackers had not drained them of their blood. Only two animals had shared *that* similarity: Montaro and Tenebrous.

"Besides this hawk attack, you mentioned other attacks have occurred on Earth," Ruby said, repeating Liora's words as she tried to further digest the implications. "Right?"

"Even happened at our property," Clay piped in. "The dogs and I were nearly attacked by brazen coyotes. Who knows what would've happened if Gabby hadn't saved the day."

"The coyotes were aggressive to Mai and Zoe? Not just you?"

Although Ruby wanted to find out how their daughter thwarted the attack, another piece of the puzzle was taking shape. She couldn't risk losing her train of thought.

"I only got involved," he said, "to try and get the dogs back into the SUV. So yeah, I think initially, the coyotes' aggression was one-hundred percent directed at Mai and Zoe."

"Everyone will have to keep a careful eye on the puppy," Ruby said, finally understanding the implication. "While the dogs are staying at Margo and Tomas's, they won't be able to let Zoe outside without supervision. Not until we figure this thing out."

"Why, Mom?" Gabby asked.

"Because Zoe also has our blood in her system, remember? I healed her at birth. And you did, too, after the fire. Because the killing of Montaro and Tenebrous seems more than a coincidence. Maybe animals are angry at humans and vampires for some unknown reason. And maybe 'soldiers' are using our blood to protect themselves from being carbonized while attacking."

"How would the animals know?" Clay asked. "Know about your blood and the protective shield of self-preservation?"

"Animals communicate telepathically, over distance and time," Ruby said, "just like vampires who can whisper. The only problem is that we don't understand their language."

Gabby was quiet, staring off into the distance. She looked worried, maybe even afraid.

"What are you thinking?" Ruby asked her.

"We'd better watch Mai closely, too," Gabby said, shifting her glance to her father. "I never mentioned it, Dad, but when you dropped me off at Aunt Margo and Uncle Tomas's house, Yona scratched my face, pretty bad. She made me bleed. A lot."

"And?" Clay asked.

"Mai licked my cheeks clean."

Tears welled in Gabby's eyes and she blinked rapidly to hold them back. "And seagulls…they were watching us through the window."

22

AS THE CRICKETS chirped on the other side of the window, Mai's thoughts drifted. How she longed to live with her uprights again on Cedar Lane, once contractors rebuilt their home.

Of course, she loved the Gonzalez family, especially their son Reese who knew exactly where to tickle her—the spot that made her lips stretch and her right leg pedal uncontrollably.

Despite the family's generosity and kindness, Mai wanted to raise Zoe on the property where her pup was born. The place where Zoe was brought back to life by the family whom Mai adored more than anything or anyone. Ruby, Clay, Gabby, and Zoe—they were her pack. Or at least, until the rainbow bridge appeared someday, and it was time to cross over to The Forever Fields.

Laying on the oriental rug in Margo and Tomas's library, Mai snuggled next to Zoe as she licked her pup's ears. With eyelids closed and quivering, and young paws twitching, her puppy was dreaming. Occasionally, Zoe released a grunt while her tiny cropped tail wagged.

Mai wondered if Zoe was reliving their evening playtime which had taken place outdoors before Margo, Tomas, and Reese had left the house for movie night. On the plush lawn, a grasshopper had leapt at Zoe's unwanted attention. A playful dance had begun. Such a treat to watch her pup's improving agility, not to mention Zoe's determination to catch her insect playmate.

Ultimately, the grasshopper proved victorious, making its way onto a tree branch, out of reach. But that would change as her puppy grew in size and quickness.

In the great big world that was itching to be explored and enjoyed, there was so much Mai wanted to teach Zoe. Take the herb garden at Cedar Lane. Thank goodness the garden had survived the housefire because Mai wanted to introduce Zoe to the joys of different flavors. Some canines, those Mai had met at the dog park, had only tasted meat flavoring in their kibble or in chunks of who-knows-what from their canned dog food. Not her pup. She planned to let Zoe nibble on herbs like echinacea and mint. Basil and thyme.

She planned on showing Zoe her cozy nook in the garden, the one shaded by a dogwood tree. In that spot, Mai liked to sprawl out on the cool dirt, inhaling the different fragrances, both sweet and savory. She couldn't wait to lay there with Zoe.

In addition, Cedar Lane had a lot more sticks than the Gonzalez property. Truth was, even though Margo and Tomas owned a lot of land close to the water, their property had less trees. And dogs and trees went together like tricks and treats.

Mai's thoughts turned to the wooded parcel next to their home on Cedar Lane. She loved to sniff for different animal markings. Then again, the woods would be off limits until the coyotes started thinking for themselves.

Why most of the animals had espoused the rantings of *the* top wolf from a faraway planet was mind boggling. Though Mai had to admit, when she first cognitively heard Filtiarn's ramblings, there was an undeniable force to them, the binding strength inherent in the voice of an alpha. Quite literally, the wolf's words felt as if they were pressing on Mai's withers, forcing her to bow and cower.

Forcing her to…*obey*.

Filtiarn spoke tirelessly inside every animal's head, including Mai's, about The Turning Point when the animals would choose their king, who just so happened to be Filtiarn from her throne-ledge on Besto Polus. Society, she avowed, was on the cusp of shifting. No longer would the uprights (vampires and humans) rule the planets. Simply put: they had abused the animals for far too long. According to Filtiarn, the reign of the uprights would end with an animal rebellion, one led by the self-appointed she-wolf monarch.

Mai refused to join a flawed cause.

However, she couldn't deny that injustices riddled the universe, many directed at the animals. Take the ever-expanding urban sprawl on Earth. Uprights were gobbling up natural animal habitats in the wild. Animal preserves and parks had all but vanished.

Sadly, science and medicine still preferred using animals for testing instead of proven alternatives.

World leaders even targeted animals with bioweapons in their tireless attempts for domination. Not to mention that some uprights raised animals (including those surviving the F8 bacteria) for nothing more than food. Raised in inhumane conditions and then processed within a slaughterhouse, the cruelest ending imaginable.

She shuddered.

Ironically, most states had banned hunting, which allowed animals to live freely and inspired skills and mutual appreciation from both the hunter and the hunted. A cruel irony, to be sure.

Sometimes, injustices even occurred in the privacy of homes, like when angry uprights abused their pets.

Even though Mai lived with wonderful uprights who loved and respected her and Zoe, she was game to advocate for those less fortunate. However, she was firmly against the practice of grouping uprights together as one, as if all were equally guilty.

That would be an injustice in and of itself. And fighting injustice with more injustice was hypocritical and flawed.

Besides, shouldn't a societal correction start with negotiations? Why was Filtiarn leaping straight to war? Unless, perhaps, war served her *personal* agenda. Her desire to be king, for example.

Fortunately, Mai wasn't prone to conforming to ideals without questioning. She had a mind of her own to discern the truth.

If any other animal tried to hurt her uprights, there would be hell to pay, one way or another.

Yona was living that reality, now quarantined in her crate.

After the cat had scratched Gabby, Mai kept a close eye on the feline who announced, quite proudly, that she was all-in when it came to the animal rebellion.

Whatever happened to cats being independent thinkers?

Since Gabby healed quickly from Yona's attack, there was no

evidence to implicate the feline as one of Filtiarn's rebels. And Gabby had never mentioned the incident to Margo or Tomas. Or even to her parents.

Yona didn't hide her intentions for long. She exposed her true colors a few days later when she decided to attack her own human: young Reese. An assault that had left Mai feeling partially responsible.

Regrettably, duty had called the morning of Reese's attack. Mai had gone outside through the pet door to do her business. Halfway through her tinkle, she heard the boy scream. Storming back inside, Mai found Yona biting and attacking poor Reese.

Using her jaws, Mai yanked the cat from bleeding Reese, slamming the feline to the floor. The crazed rebel hissed and ran off to hide under the guestroom bed.

Maybe Yona had forgotten that Reese didn't heal like Gabby did. Because the evidence didn't vanish on *his* skin. In fact, Reese had to go to the hospital for shots. And when Yona finally strutted from the bedroom as if nothing had happened, Tomas captured and isolated her inside her crate until the family figured out what to do, given the government's recommendations regarding pets who attack.

At least the family's dogs were reasonable. Uno and Dos had questions about the rebellion and were receptive to hearing Mai's point of view. So far, they were resisting Filtiarn's ridiculous commands. Clearly, French Bulldogs had a nose for bull.

The memory of tinkling during Reese's attack, sparked a new urge. The clock in the library chimed nine times. The Gonzalezes wouldn't return for another hour and Mai couldn't wait until then to relieve her full bladder. Ever since she had given birth to Zoe, "things" had gotten quite loose in the tinkle zone. She couldn't imagine what it would have been like had she birthed a normal litter of six pups.

She rose from the rug and stretched.

Zoe woke and asked where she was going.

I have to tinkle, she cognitively whispered to her pup. *You stay put and I'll be right back. And if that wretched cat makes a sound, ignore her.*

Leaving the library, Mai walked toward the pet door. As she passed the cat's crate, Yona purred. Was that a smirk raising the cat's whiskers? The feline must be losing her mind.

In the kitchen, the French Bulldogs remained still, comfortably sprawled on a rug. Only their eyebrows raised as Mai sauntered by.

Once outside, squawking caught Mai's attention. She glanced behind her. Although it was nighttime, spotlights lit the back of the house. Curiously, the roof was black and jittery, blanketed with…with *ravens*. She couldn't guess how many birds had perched on the shingles, as the roof was massive, with different levels and angles. One fact was evident: ravens were obviously hearty birds, with their population on the rebound.

Mai sniffed the grass for a spot to do her business. She found the perfect location near some aromatic rabbit pellets.

When she finished tinkling, she scratched at the grass with her back paws, alternating from right to left. Cleanliness was important. Soon, Zoe would be ready for that lesson.

On her way back to the pet door, the coolness of the night felt wonderful. She wondered what fun activities the next day would bring. Would Reese throw a ball into the creek for her to fetch? Would Margo and Tomas take her and Zoe on the boat? Or to the dog park? Maybe her pack would even stop by to visit.

A stab of pain interrupted Mai's pleasant thoughts.

Her heart accelerated at the surprise. At the sharpness of the hurt. She yelped.

Then another stab, followed by another.

Mai looked up. The ravens had taken flight from the roof. They were swarming above her like a twisting black cloud. Birds dove. Attacked. Used their beaks to pierce her skin.

Five, seven, nine penetrations. She was losing count.

Using her jaws, she snapped at a bird, catching it midflight. Mai clamped down on the raven, feeling its neck vertebrae crack before she released its carcass.

Do you need help, Mom? Zoe whispered inside her head.

No, she answered, trying to sound calm but firm. *Stay inside. I'll be a minute. Please don't interrupt me during my business.*

At that moment, her pup's safety was the only thing that mattered.

Maybe Uno and Dos would come to her rescue.

Surely, they were hearing the commotion.

Birds dive-bombed Mai's legs, knocking her down. She hit the ground hard, falling onto her side, flat on the grass.

Before she could think of a defensive move, ravens covered her from head to tail. The birds stabbed her with their beaks. Pulled at her fur. Tore open her skin.

The ravens intended on *killing* her.

Instinctively, she knew she'd never get to see her home on Cedar Lane again. She'd never get to introduce her pup to the herbs or the cool spot under the dogwood tree. Or watch Zoe grow to maturity and have pups of her own. She'd never get to snuggle with Gabby or Ruby or Clay—her precious, loving uprights.

Mai's breathing weakened when the ravens opened her gut and yanked at her innards.

They drank her blood, though she couldn't fathom why.

Perhaps her brain had misfired. Before shutting down for good.

Oh, what a wonderful life she had lived.

And as her heart sputtered, she saw an image form in the near distance. It was beautiful, with lush trees on either side and a ray of light shining on its planks.

Mai recognized the vision: her rainbow bridge.

Her passage to The Forever Fields.

Where there would be no more pain.

23

Sunday, July 21, 2041
A field near the Polar Station: Cape Chelyuskin, Siberia

ZAGAN'S GHOSTLY SELF materialized beside the flickering campfire, having extracted sufficient information from the laboratory where the villains held Draven captive.

As King of Skotadi for 2.8 mega-annum, Zagan had successfully eliminated countless threats. His victories far exceeded any who stood beside him. Was it presumptive, then, to expect his associates to heed his advisements?

Upon his arrival, he immediately glanced at Solange to gauge her reaction to his return. Her furrowed brow relaxed in his presence, as if relieved that his surveillance had not compromised his safety. This modest gesture warmed his soul.

"What of Draven?" Liora spoke with urgency.

"Vervain renders him unconscious," he answered. "Yet, Draven remains himself. Though I must warn you, Liora, there are plans to inject him with genetically enhanced wolf venom. They work to prepare his body for the infusion."

The queen wept. "I should have never left his side."

"Who are *they*, specifically?" Ruby asked him.

Zagan described those in the laboratory with Draven. There were two mayfly guards (one male, one female)—both flesh skinned, armed with an arsenal of weaponry and wearing brown fatigues. Joining them was a scientist: a brown-skinned female, also a mayfly. She wore a white lab coat. Two augmented wolves (one gray, one black) were also in the room. Each wolf stood four-foot-high from front paws to withers. Electronic chips, embedded above their optic nerves, made their eyes glow red. Handheld devices remotely controlled the wolves.

"What about Emory and Vladimir?" Ruby inquired.

"They were in the laboratory until they departed to gather a patrol. I followed them and listened to their hushed exchange," Zagan explained. "They wish to battle with us here. In this field. They know the walls of this reflective ice structure have camouflaged us. And the wolves deployed in the forest behind us will assist with their offensive." He returned his gaze to the queen. "Ease your worries, Queen. Those with Draven were instructed to wait for the lead scientist, Emory, to return before commencing the infusion."

"That settles it," Solange announced. "As the patrol arrives at our campfire, we shall all travel to the laboratory. The three humans and two wolves guarding Draven are no match for our collective competencies. Odds are heavily weighted in our favor.

"We will free Draven," the princess continued, "and travel back to our homes before the human patrol and wolves in the field return to the laboratory to confront us."

"I would not advise this strategy," Zagan countered, wishing disagreement with his former mate had not been a necessity. Nothing would have pleased him more than to utter agreement with Solange. However, because he had remained invisible and followed the villains as they rallied a mayfly posse, he had heard their revised plans.

"Why not?" Clay asked him.

"Better to defeat the enemy on the ground in which we stand, without hesitation," Zagan answered. "For postponing the battle may furnish them with additional opportunities. The risks in delaying a confrontation are not acceptable."

"Additional opportunities?" Ruby repeated. "What risks, outside of the obvious, are you referring to as…unacceptable?"

Zagan reminded himself that honesty was a virtue. "They wish…," he started, thinking he felt a lump in his throat. "Rather, they *intend* to capture Gabriella as another test subject."

Masking the truth would have served no one. And Zagan refused to increase risks to the child. In truth, he had grown quite fond of

Gabriella. A bond had formed, and he would do everything in his ghostly power to protect her.

Ruby's eyes widened. "She's only a child. And she's human."

The Tether instinctively placed her arms around Gabriella, pulling her offspring close.

"A remarkably *gifted* child," Zagan responded. "The mad scientist does not wish to rely on technology to control his canid army. Rather, he will attempt to create two specialized hybrids by transferring DNA from his enhanced wolf venom to both Gabriella and Draven. His hope is that one of the hybrids (human or vampire) will be able to speak the language of beasts."

"Even if I could talk to the animals," Gabriella protested, "I'd never help Wicked Doctor Evil. Not ever."

"*Ahh,* I admire your tenacity," Zagan said, feeling pride. "But they plan to inflict unpleasant persuasions, those designed to change your mind. The evil mayflies will use your parents in unthinkable ways. As well, they will destroy the rest of us, though I fail to understand how they could terminate a ghost who is already dead."

"My gifts have returned," Ruby said. "I'll travel Gabby back home now. To ensure her safety."

"In time, the battle would only be relocated," Zagan cautioned. "And is it not the case that your country's president wishes to sacrifice you? Back in Annapolis, you would face two battles instead of one." He tried to groom the spikes in his hair, but in his ghostly state, the habit yielded no satisfaction once again. "Have you sought to read the stones, Lady Spencer?"

Ruby's eyelids closed and quivered.

Her eyes opened. "Our lifeline stones fade in the near future. We're all at risk. But there's good news, too, because Emory and Vladimir's stones become completely blank. The Russian's stone fades first. So I agree with Zagan. The battle has to be now. Right here. With all of us using our gifts to defeat the enemy." She turned to Liora. "Are you seeing the same thing?"

The queen nodded.

From a distance, the hum of old, gas-powered engines was carried with the wind. Zagan smelled the carbon monoxide, sulfur dioxide, and nitrogen oxide from spewing exhaust.

A moment later, his eyes focused on a single-file line of all-terrain vehicles racing across the field, heading toward their structure, leaving a rising trail of smoke and sandy soil behind them.

Zagan counted eight vehicles. Emory and Vladimir each drove one. They were in the middle of the line. The other six drivers were guards, armed with dart rifles.

"Mom," Gabriella said, pointing behind them. "Look." Ten red-eyed wolves had emerged from the forest. "We're surrounded."

24

WILLIAM UNGER DABBED sweat from his forehead using a handkerchief embroidered with the Presidential seal, as he sat behind the Resolute desk in the Oval Office. If only his precious Irene could have been by his side advising him. She'd know precisely what mood he should project for his live, 9:00 p.m. address to the nation. Was the appropriate emotion…sadness? Concern? Confidence? Should his tie have been bold red or calming blue? Should he display his Bible, opened on his desk, as if God was guiding him toward wisdom? Or should he close the Good Book, like it was important, but the POTUS was ultimately the one in charge?

In truth, Will felt little emotional connection to the public, to his constituents. Irene—his Sweet Tea—had always been the bridge to helping him empathize with others. Now she was gone. After only nine days without her influence, the President's authentic self was already becoming unbridled.

To hell with building bridges. After all, emotions looked the same, whether they were genuine or simply good acting.

Keeping that in mind, he had decided to combine his two options: the real and the fabricated. On the genuine side, he had selected a purple tie; the one stuffed in the back of his dresser drawer with a sales tag still attached. He had also shelved the Bible out of sight. Where was Mr. Miracles when Will had needed help saving the First Lady?

And emotions? Irritation was the only one that felt natural, but that's where he'd employ good-old Hollywood acting.

"Sir," a videographer said, holding up three fingers. "You're live in three, two, one."

Will straightened his shoulders, gazing into the camera lens.

"Good evening and God Bless America," he started. "First, let me thank you again, from the bottom of my heart, for your kindness and goodwill over the loss of my beloved Irene. Your uplifting words and prayers have sustained me through unspeakable grief. In our highest highs and lowest lows, we stand united as family.

"Regrettably, global crises do not pause for family heartbreak."

Irene would've approved of his opening words, and he fought hard to suppress a smile.

"Despite our best attempts to recover our declining animal populations, another unprecedented phenomenon is evolving. Animal *attacks* are escalating across the world, including on the mainland of our lower forty-eight. The attacks against humankind appear to be random and unprovoked, carried out by species from all animal classifications, though the highest concentrations have occurred in the mammal, bird, fish, and insect groups.

"The World Health Organization and the Centers for Disease Control," he continued, "have tested affected species. Scientists have been unable to find a pathogen associated with these violent attacks. Again, there were no bioweapons, such as F8, or suspicious microorganisms present in the animals' bloodstreams or cerebral matter. In fact, scientists could not identify any commonalities responsible for their aggressive behavior. At this time, the cause for these attacks remains unknown."

A bead of sweat raced down his chest. Thank God his black suit jacket would conceal the wet blotches that were undoubtedly forming on his white dress shirt. The Oval Office felt like a hundred degrees.

"To date," he said, "aggregate records indicate that worldwide, five-hundred people have perished from these perplexing and unimaginable attacks, God rest their souls. Animals injured another four thousand. And trends suggest an increase in incidences, rather than a decline. Therefore, we are taking the following actions to ensure the safety of our American citizens, as well as our allies."

He neared the end of his speech. Then he'd have a stiff drink because he planned to enact his next steps, a path he'd already put into motion. For now, though, he needed to stay focused. He blinked hard to return his thoughts to the present.

"Sir?" the videographer murmured.

"I'm sorry," Will said, looking to the camera and intentionally creasing his forehead. "Even one loss of life is unfathomable. My heart aches from these impacts." He shook his head. "Five-hundred lives lost—eighty in the U.S. Such a shock."

Irene would have been proud of his recovery.

"As I was saying, governments in the Federation of Independent Nations are taking the following precautions. Effective immediately, the World Association of Zoos and Aquariums has ordered the closure of all zoos, aquariums, and animal parks.

"Pet owners," he continued, "must crate their animals and muzzle them when they need to relieve themselves on the grounds associated with the pet owner's residency. Jurisdictions have closed public places to pets (whether leashed, muzzled, or otherwise), including neighborhood streets, walkways, and parks. Domesticated stray or feral animals will be collected by Animal Control and euthanized, whether displaying identification or not."

He glanced down at his desk before raising his eyes to gaze at the camera lens, as if his words were difficult to say aloud.

"If your pet shows signs of aggression, please contact the number running on the bottom ticker of your multivision screen. Animal Control will come to your home to collect the affected animal. Do not, I repeat, *do not* transport the animal to your veterinary office for treatment, as there is no treatment available at this time.

"In addition," he said, "we are implementing a nationwide curfew, beginning on Monday, July twenty-second. The curfew will be in effect from six o'clock each evening until seven o'clock each morning, in your respective time zone. May I suggest that you use tomorrow to get your homes in order.

"Finally," he concluded, "The Special Warfare Council will meet regularly with members of the World Health Organization, Centers for Disease Control, World Association of Zoos and Aquariums, and the National Institutes of Health, beginning July twenty-fourth. Until then, I will be monitoring this crisis from Camp David, providing updates to the nation as warranted. Stay safe, stay vigilant, and God Bless the United States of America. Goodnight to one and all."

The red light on the camera blipped off.

Usually, Will liked to chat with the videographer, thanking her for a job well done. This time, he ordered her from the room, demanding she give him a minute before disassembling the camera equipment.

Alone, he massaged his temples.

The country needed a vampire to address the crisis, though he didn't regret, not for one minute, turning Ruby over to Emory and Vladimir…for God knows what. Quite frankly, he didn't give a shit.

What he did care about was the void.

Will no longer had a vampire to fix things.

The public might perceive *doing nothing* as culpable negligence. Certainly not a legacy he wished to leave for himself. After all, he still had two years remaining in his second term.

That's why he had derived a solution. A zero-sum gain: lose a vampire; gain a vampire. Simple math.

Good thing, the government had stored Emory Bradshaw's universal vampire serum in the White House bunker. A quarter mile beneath him.

As Commander in Chief, good thing Will had exchanged members of the special ops team guarding the Sanguivorous Cocci. Exchanged them with hand-picked operatives. Operatives who wouldn't question his need for a serum sample, though he possessed the required order to cover his ass. Just in case.

And good thing, his next move was a mere four hours away.

25

Sunday, July 21, 2041
A field near the Polar Station: Cape Chelyuskin, Siberia

RUBY CLENCHED HER fists as the all-terrain vehicles approached the north side of their sculpted refuge, traveling in single file.

About four yards from the ice structure, the ATVs broke formation and turned in alternating directions—the first going right, the next left—until all the vehicles formed a half-circle, leaving space in between one another.

Having emerged from the woods on the southern side of the ice tower, the wolves completed fortification of the perimeter.

Enemies surrounded Ruby, her family, and friends.

Each ATV driver wore a black, knitted balaclava mask. Ruby, however, didn't need to see faces to recognize the two ring leaders in the middle of the group. Their scent smelled particularly putrid.

She glanced at her daughter. *Stay close to Dad and me. Understood?* Ruby cognitively whispered. *And I'll explain how you can help. Okay?* She delivered a half-smile, as if everything was under control. *I love you.*

Gabby nodded.

Ruby stole a quick glance at her husband.

Clay bobbed his head, meaning he was ready for anything.

"Come out, come out…wherever you are," Emory teased. "By the way, I should let you know: if you decide to pixie dust your way to the lab, you'll find an equal battle there. Also, trying to carbonize any of us or our remotes won't work. We've sipped your precious blood. And smeared the remotes with it."

All the drivers shut off their ATV engines.

A brisk wind whistled around the ice structure. Burning logs crackled in the campfire as the charcoal skies of mid-morning continued to spit sleet.

The six guards accompanying the mad scientist and Vladimir brandished double-barreled dart rifles, equipped with laser range finders. A harness with elastic straps secured the firearms onto each guard's chest, allowing the soldier to be hands free or to quickly mount the weapon. Ruby sniffed beyond the sculpted ice walls. With a trigger pull, pressurized carbon dioxide would deploy the darts. The concentrated vervain filled the chamber of each projectile.

She compared arsenals. The enemy's included six human guards brandishing dart rifles, two human ring leaders with remotes, and ten wolf hybrids. They were challenging three vampires, two humans, and one ghost.

Sculpting firearms might bolster her team's defense, but Ruby was fairly certain that Liora and Solange had never used guns before. And clearly, discharged bullets from multiple shooters would place Gabby and Clay at greater risk.

In Ruby's estimation, as long as the vampires could avoid getting drugged and incapacitated, their physical assault on their opponents would result in victory.

The wolves were the only unknown.

"After all these years of being besties," Emory said, "you're going to give me the silent treatment? And hide behind that ridiculous ice chimney?" He looked at the guard parked to his right. "Show them."

The guard held up a large portable blowtorch.

"All my guards have one," Emory said. "A steel structure would've been wiser, girlfriend. Because in Siberia, I think they know a thing or two about ice." He rolled his eyes, as if her intelligence was beneath him.

"Zagan," Ruby said softly, since she couldn't mentally whisper inside a ghost's brain. "Help Clay protect Gabby, no matter what."

"I shall not disappoint, Lady Spencer."

Here's the plan, chronologically, Ruby whispered into the minds of Clay, Gabby, Liora, and Solange. *Gabby, you'll start by sculpting our shelter and campfire into dust. At the same time, I'll disable the triggers on their dart rifles. Just remember, I can only destroy one at a time. Liora, keep the wolves at bay. After Gabby destroys our ice tower, she'll sculpt an ice fence to help Liora keep the wolves from advancing. I'll work to deactivate each chip implanted behind the wolves' eyes, rendering the remotes useless.*

Ruby sculpted an iron kite-shield reminiscent of the high medieval period, handing it to Solange. *Solange, intercept any projectiles fired, in case I don't destroy the weapons fast enough. And Clay, work with Zagan to protect Gabby. After we neutralize the enemy, we'll kill all who don't flee, including any wolves if we have to. But Emory and Vladimir will die, regardless. Then we'll travel to the lab and rescue Draven.*

While Ruby whispered orders, two guards had begun torching an opening on the west wall of the ice structure.

"Let's do this," she said.

Her daughter sculpted their shelter into oblivion. The wind whisked away the remnants and lingering smoke. Energy from the transformation blasted the two guards onto their backs. On impact, their torches violently bounced from their hands. Wearing shock on their faces, they used the heels of their combat boots to push their bodies away from the explosion.

Triggers on the dart rifles were easy to disable; the hard part was making each inoperable before one of the guards tried to fire.

Six, five, four, three…

A guard on the far right raised his dart rifle and took aim.

Two, one—done.

Ruby exhaled relief, having finished the job before the guards could discharge their weapons.

"What the hell?" the guard mounting the rifle said, baffled the trigger wouldn't budge.

"Stop!" Emory shouted, pulling off his balaclava. "You should know something else before you continue with your annoying magic show." He raised his remote. "See, my gadget has its own techno wizardry that is aimed at targets far, far away."

With drool dripping from their raised lips, the trained wolves crouched and growled, like they anticipated receiving an attack command from the brandished remote control.

Ruby lifted her hand, urging her team to put a temporary stop on their plans. She needed to understand Emory's threat because he was hinting that higher stakes were at play, beyond their battleground. Pressing her mind toward his, she read his immediate thoughts.

Her heart accelerated, causing Liora to return a worried glance.

"So now you know," Emory said. "If you don't hand over my Godchild and let us leave in peace, unharmed, then I'll press this button on my remote labeled *Cruise Ship Greenlight.* Since you read minds, Ruby, why don't you tell your loyal clan what'll happen?"

"He has forty criminal operatives on a small cruise ship off Key West, Florida," she said. "If he presses that button, his thugs will abandon the ship on its lifeboats and activate explosives to destroy the vessel and everyone on it."

"Are a thousand lives *small* to you now?" he taunted.

Veins rose on her skin. She wanted to rip out his throat.

The wolves snarled and yapped.

Liora moved into position to defend against a wolf attack in case Gabby's ice fence didn't hold.

"Covered my bases," Emory said. "Impressive, right?"

During his blathering, Ruby tried to recalculate their options. She had to consider the new information.

In her peripheral vision, she noticed Solange's forward movement, which snapped Ruby back into the present. Carrying the shield, the princess was whizzing toward Vladimir like a tornado. That's when Ruby identified the problem, albeit a nanosecond too late.

The Russian had withdrawn a hidden dart pistol.

A red dot was dancing wildly on Gabby's chest.

Solange was like an angry bull charging a matador. Her shield struck Vladimir on his left side. Thrown from his ATV, Vladimir crashed onto the ground. His pistol released from his clutch.

Lifting the ATV with her left hand, Solange raised Vladimir's vehicle in the air and tossed it 20-feet away. Landing on its side, the ATV rolled away like tumbleweed.

Emory remained mounted on his all-terrain, unmoved by his comrade's vulnerability.

Lowering her shield, Solange leapt onto the troll, her purple veins in full bloom. With lightning speed, she clasped his gray hair and yanked his head to the side, exposing the skin on his neck. She prepared to pierce his carotid artery.

A guard leapt off his ATV, clasping a dart in his right hand. His intentions to stab Solange with the needle were clear.

Ruby was going to break his arms before he ever got the chance.

Unexpectedly, Clay began to move.

Why was *he* moving?

While racing toward Solange in a whirlwind, Ruby turned her head to analyze her husband's sideward motion. He was moving toward Gabby as if he planned to step in front of her. And Zagan's ghost appeared to be doing the same.

They had noticed something Ruby hadn't.

She quickly scanned the scene while still in motion.

Emory had retrieved *his* dart pistol. He aimed the barrel at Gabby.

In a nanosecond, Ruby searched her mind for possible outcomes.

Clay's stone had erased to a blank surface.

How could that be? Vervain had no detrimental effect on humans.

Could the dart's payload be something else? Like wolf venom?

Ruby's brief delay was costly.

A guard stabbed Solange in the back with a vervain dart. She slumped into unconsciousness on the ground beside Vladimir.

Zagan used his ghostly energies to blow Emory off his ATV, but the mad scientist had already fired his pistol.

The dart was in route for Gabby's torso.

As Ruby changed directions, racing back toward Gabby and Clay, her eyes focused on the spiraling dart. She attempted to carbonize the projectile, but it didn't turn to ashes, meaning Emory must've also smeared her blood on the dart or included it in the serum.

The projectile kept spinning toward her family.

She witnessed the horror playing out as if in slow motion.

Leaping into the air, she hoped to deflect the dart's trajectory.

"No!" Ruby screamed midflight, terrified.

She stretched her fingers, nearly dislocating her knuckles from their joints and her shoulder from its socket.

The dart spun out of reach.

Blocking Gabby, her husband took a direct hit.

Clay fell to the ground, wailing in agony.

26

GABBY DROPPED TO her knees beside her Dad who was lying on the ground, gritting his teeth, foaming from the mouth, and scratching his chest like something, something really *bad* was itching to burst out. His eyes darted around in his sockets. His skin was gray.

Gabby's heart pounded in her chest.

What had Wicked Doctor Evil shot her Dad with?

"Mom!" she hollered. "Mom! Dad needs you!"

Her mother didn't answer. Looking up, Gabby saw why. Everything seemed out of control. Every. Single. Thing.

The huge wolves were inching closer, growling and licking their lips. Queen Liora had pulled her sword from its sheath. Even in the sleet, the raised blade glimmered, warning them. But the wolves didn't care. Their oversized paws kept advancing toward the see-through ice fence she had sculpted.

Wicked Doctor E had gotten up from the ground where King Zagan had blown him off his ATV. He still held the dart pistol in his right hand. Clutching his stupid remote in his other hand, he shouted at his goons to grab the humans. Namely, her and her Dad.

Her parents had not raised Gabby to hate. But she had to confess: she flat-out hated Wicked Doctor E. If it meant protecting her family and friends, she might have to sculpt something to hurt him. But what if he ended up pressing the button on the remote? The one that would kill innocent people on that cruise ship in Florida?

Terrified, she felt like throwing up. She didn't want to hurt anyone. Or be the reason someone got hurt. She was only nine, not even a teenager. And kids weren't supposed to think of hurting or killing other people. Not ever.

Straight ahead, the guard who had stabbed Princess Solange with a vervain dart picked up the princess and hurled her over his shoulder, kicking her fallen shield out of the way. Solange's limbs and long braided ponytail swung like a rag doll's as he walked to his ATV.

Mister Vladimir got on his feet again, wobbling.

Two yards from Gabby, her Mom stood without moving, facing away from her. Her mother's black cloak flapped wildly in the wind like a superhero's. Only, she wasn't *doing* anything.

Why wasn't her Mom sculpting something to save the day?

Gabby glanced down at her Dad again. He was twitching, his arms and legs jerking as they rose and fell back to the ground in freaky movements. His lips were blue. Eyelids, frozen open. She even saw a strange wave of light make his irises glow.

Her last meal soured her tongue and she swallowed hard.

"Wake up, Dad," she pleaded, shaking his shoulder. "Please!"

The twitching continued.

She whispered inside her mother's thoughts, *Mom! Hurry!*

Gabby felt desperate, clueless about what to do. Maybe she should feed her blood to her Dad. To heal him. Maybe she could sculpt a cut on her wrist since that's where vampires liked to bleed when they wanted to heal others.

Movement pulled her focus from her Dad's face.

Finally, her Mom was in full-blown warrior mode. With skin patchworked in pulsing purple veins, her mother briefly glanced at her, as if saying she'd be right there.

Everything started to happen at lightning speed.

Her mother raised her hands and Princess Solange's body lifted from the guard's shoulder, breaking free from his grasp and whizzing through the air toward Gabby. The princess gently landed on the ground next to her Dad.

Gabby channeled the wolves' fur, sculpting two pillows—one under her Dad's head and one under Princess Solange's. Probably a dumb thing to do, but how was she supposed to know what to sculpt? Somethings, like more guns, might put everyone at risk. Or interfere with her Mom's plans. Pillows seemed like a safe bet.

Her Mom released a strong, non-stop exhale from her mouth as she moved her neck from left to right, kind of like a leaf blower. The stream of air was powerful enough to topple the ice fence and send the wolves sliding backwards, as if their nails couldn't get a grip on a slippery surface. Yipping and yapping like babies, the wolves tumbled back several yards. Served them right.

Hiding the green of her eyes behind her lids, her Mom was clearly reading the future to decide her next move. When she focused again, a clear ice-dome formed over them. The see-through igloo was much smaller and more compact than Gabby's camouflaged tower. The dome's circular base seemed buried below the surface.

Smart thinking since the wolves were dead set on eating them.

All Gabby's brain wanted to do was freeze. Pretend none of it was happening. And make silly pillows which made no difference at all.

Standing, Mister Vladimir pulled a bullet-shooting pistol from his jacket. She recognized the difference between one loaded with darts. His pistol had a magazine that snapped into the handle. Aiming the handgun at the dome, he fired, like maybe the round would shatter the ice. Her Mom was way smarter than that.

A spark jumped where the bullet struck the thick ice before ricocheting off. The dome wasn't damaged.

Her Dad had stopped moving. His eyes were still open, but he hardly blinked. His chest barely rose and fell.

She rubbed her hand over her Dad's forehead. It felt icy cold.

"Mom will help in a minute," she said. "Don't leave us, Dad."

As Gabby wiped tears from her eyes, Doctor E shouted at the wolves. He fumbled with his remote, working his fingers on the buttons and screaming into the device.

A second later, the wolves surrounded the dome and began digging like they smelled juicy bones for the picking. They were trying to burrow beneath the ice so they could squeeze themselves under; so they could enter and attack.

In between the wolves, Wicked Doctor E's guards filled in around the dome. Lighting their torches, they began melting the ice.

The remote suddenly flew from Doctor E's hands and smashed

against the dome, shattering into a bazillion pieces. *That* act of brilliance had to have come from King Z. Destroying the remote probably saved those people on the ship.

The wolves kept digging since Mister Vladimir had a remote, too.

In what seemed like forever, her Mom finally knelt on the other side of her Dad who wasn't blinking anymore. Clasping his hand, her mother concentrated. No doubt she was whispering into his mind, reliving events so she could decide what was wrong with him.

"I can't get a good read. Everything inside is unsettled and fluid." Her Mom looked frightened. "Did he say anything to you?"

"No. He was in too much pain."

Tears spilled over Gabby's lower lashes again, even though she had willed herself not to cry. Willed herself to act 13 instead of nine.

"Dad's heart is beating, right?" Gabby asked her Mom.

"The wolves will breach the dome any second," Liora warned. "I shall defend until I am no longer able. But may I suggest you sculpt another barrier? Soon?"

"Your Dad was injected with wolf venom. Has to be it. Nothing else makes sense," her Mom said, ignoring the queen's call for help. "I have no clue what it's doing to him. Only..." Her Mom began to blink rapidly. "Only..."

"What Mom? Tell me."

"Only, I can no longer see his lifeline." Reaching across her Dad's body, her Mom placed her hand on Gabby's shoulder. "His stone is blank, even though his heart's still beating."

Red tears sped down her Mom's cheeks, leaving bloody trails.

"Stop it!" Gabby cried, not holding back. "You can do something. I know you can. You're The Tether!"

Snarling echoed off the clear walls of the dome igloo.

From the *inside*.

27

LYKOS AND HIS wolf hunters concealed themselves on the rocky side of the Tume River. The time was before midnight, though on Athanasia, the amount of light or darkness in each realm remained constant. In The Shadowlands, that meant charcoal light blanketed the territory regardless of the hour.

His Skotadi Night Stalkers hid on either side of a split canyon, overlooking a ravine which marked the grassy entrance and stony exit to a well-established river crossing. The water to his left, carving a deep passageway through Gray Forest, still foamed and swirled after its journey over a waterfall 120 paces upstream.

According to Lykos's scout, 15 deer would be crossing the river, swimming through the pooled water to trek to a grazing pasture beyond the canyon and dense pines to his right. However, the rogue herd, including does and fawns, would never again enjoy full bellies.

Four nights ago, the Lord of the Wolves woke Lykos with a telepathic communiqué. The alpha of the Night Stalkers had been sleeping in his den beside Accalia and his pups.

Filtiarn's personal spies, called the Mukessi, had informed her that a small community of deer on Athanasia had defected from Skotadi to The Shadowlands. They were traveling during the late hours, feeding at midnight, and bedding down for the rest of the 24-hour cycle, hoping to avoid detection.

Apparently, the herd had denounced Filtiarn's aspirations to rise as King of the Animals, in addition to dismissing her declaration that The Turning Point was upon them.

Knowing Lykos's outwardly devotion to Filtiarn, the herd fled his authority for safer grounds.

Lykos had, indeed, worried about a misstep on his pathway to elevated power. Alas, this present oversight justified his concerns.

How had he *not* known of this herd's cowardly exodus from his own region? Of course, he was not surprised that there were defectors adjacent to his High Cliff territory; after all, Lykos's pack had slayed the great, beloved Montaro. Undoubtedly, some of Montaro's kind would flee to avoid further persecution.

What surprised him was that *his* spies—wolves from nearby, weaker packs—had not reported the illegal migration. Wolves were keen to every detail, every movement.

Had their dereliction of duty been intentional? Were they sabotaging Lykos's efforts to rise in stature?

A cleansing of his spies was in order *after* he showed Filtiarn that he could correct the herd's disobedience with swift brutality.

After righting the wrong, perhaps Filtiarn would name *him* Hand of the King at her coronation. As Hand, he would hold the second highest position over all the animals on all three planets. Not only would he serve as her most trusted advisor, privy to all happenings in the universe, he might claim the throne for himself, as King of the Animals, when the opportunity presented itself.

Or perhaps, was *forced*.

First things first.

Now was the time to demonstrate his loyalty and ability to lead.

Lykos had ordered 17 wolves from his pack to help execute the mission. Only three females, including Accalia who was still nursing his pups, remained behind in their community. Along with Mahli, the male omega—the weakest Night Stalker. Thankfully, Lykos was not worried about the safety of the four wolves left behind. Nursing or not, Accalia could defeat any intruder (wolf or otherwise).

His hunters had followed the Tume River into The Shadowlands. They steered clear of the Prison of the Unruly. Wolves would deliver justice to the vampire uprights, those imprisoned for being the worst of the worst, another time in the future.

Prior to their second cycle of rest, Lykos's pack had stopped to feed on the river's spirulina, followed by bedding down two miles from where they would annihilate their foe. Keeping their distance from the site was essential. Because if deer scented wolf on their worn trail to the pasture, they would become skittish. Avoiding the battlefield meant the pack's presence would remain undetected.

His wolves' rest had been sufficient.

Hours ago, his hunters had risen and trekked to the canyon, taking positions on and behind both sides of the parted rock walls. Some wolves hid in convex caves naturally formed on the canyon's face.

The breeze funneled across the river toward them, ensuring they would not be prematurely winded. Perfect hunting conditions heightened the pack's confidence.

Nevertheless, Lykos would have preferred to chase the herd until it tired, picking off members one by one, as each slowed from exhaustion. Unfortunately, the risk was too great. They needed the slaughter to be contained within the forest shadows, invisible from prying eyes. Word spreading about retaliation against defectors might boomerang against the cause—a misstep he could not afford.

A distance from the river crossing, a twig softly cracked.

Moments later, the first matriarchal doe appeared in the charcoal light, rotating her ears to the front and back, listening for unusual sounds. Her nose twitched to assess odd scents.

Lykos had instructed his pack to be patient, to let all the herd cross the river. The wolves were to hold their positions in wait for the dom, the dominant buck, who would traverse the waterway last. The thought disgusted Lykos. What coward would allow his weakest members to face an enemy first? In his opinion, there were other, more honorable ways to preserve genealogy.

As alpha of the Night Stalkers, he had announced his rightful claim to take down the dom himself.

The herd swam across the river, shaking moisture from their tawny fur as their cloven hooves imprinted on the muddy and pebbled shore.

Just beyond the water, the herd waited for their leader on a dry and rocky riverbed.

At last the dom—equipped with a thick and irregular 11-point rack—stepped up to the water's edge. While flagging his tail, he aggressively raised his nose to the gray sky peeking through the tree canopy. He snorted before violently stomping his fore foot, launching divots of grass into the air.

Lykos held his breath. The dom sensed danger.

As if impatient for her midnight meal, the matriarchal doe vocalized encouragement. Although the buck hesitated a moment longer, he leapt into the water and swam across to the shore.

All 15 deer remained squeezed between the canyon walls.

The attack plan was simple.

As soon as four members of his wolfpack moved to block the canyon's exit and another four prevented retreat back across the river, they would execute the perfect hunting tactic: encirclement. No way out. Allowing him and his eight offensive warriors to kill each member of the herd.

After they fulfilled the deed, his wolves would feast to restore their energy. They would dispose of the remains in the river.

Lykos released a pheromone, signaling the beginning of the attack.

As his wolves carried out their instructions, he emerged from behind the canyon wall nearest the river.

The dom was still facing forward, watching the ambush unfold.

Lykos crouched while inching forward, remaining undetected. When he reached striking distance, he sprang toward the dom. Lykos's mouth was wide open, brandishing his fangs.

Connecting with the buck's right rear-leg, below the shank, Lykos applied brute force and ripped through ligaments, penetrating the bone. With a sharp twist of his neck, he fractured the long pastern.

The dom released a shrilled bawl, falling on his side.

With the buck's other legs thrashing wildly, Lykos had to back off his quarry to ensure that the alpha's next strike was on target.

As the dom kicked in protest, Lykos clasped onto his right front leg, puncturing the beast's skin with his teeth. As he readied himself to snap the bone, the buck twisted his head and nearly penetrated the alpha's fur with one of his crown tines.

The strike tossed Lykos backwards. Regrettably, he yelped, which only angered him more. With a vengeance, he righted himself and lunged. He tore at the buck's right front-leg again. This time, Lykos nearly severed the dom's cannon bone.

Desperate bleats and groans echoed off the canyon walls as his warriors assassinated the other defectors.

Even though Lykos's attack incapacitated the dom, the buck was far from dead.

Almost getting gored infuriated Lykos. Made his blood boil. He wanted the buck to see his executioner, eye to eye. Seizing the fallen beast by the nose, head-on, Lykos clamped down on the dom's snout, crushing his victim's mouth shut while driving its nose down the wolf's throat. Not that the dom deserved a quick death, but as alpha, Lykos needed to see if any of his hunters required help.

Victory, after all, was a collaborative endeavor.

As oxygen depleted, the stag's eyes darted within their sockets. The beast surely knew suffocation was inevitable, though his body protested. With one final kick of his left hind leg, the dom could no longer claim his title. Death was all that remained.

That and providing a hearty meal far tastier than spirulina.

Lykos scanned the killing zone. Carcasses littered the rock bed and blood seeped like a red river. His hunters had slayed the entire herd, save for one. A fawn.

"Why do you hesitate?" he growled at his warrior. "Break its neck this minute!"

The wolf lowered his head in submission; yet, his mouth spoke instead of following orders. "But Lykos, this male fawn has pledged his allegiance to you and Filtiarn. He vows to bend his knees to you. He accepts The Turning Point."

"And you wish mercy for him?"

"I do, if you choose to bestow it."

Lykos sauntered over to the freckled fawn.

"Young one, do you believe, as all animals do, that when the time comes to mate, that your offspring will inherit your traits?"

"I guess I do," the fawn said, his voice quivering with uncertainty.

"Of course you do," assured Lykos. "Your parents believed the same. And do you know the trait which dominated their thoughts as mature adults?"

The fawn's eyes grew wide, perhaps recognizing the trap.

"The trait of resisting authority," Lykos answered. "Unfortunately, individual thinking threatens the new order—a time when all animals must join as one to usurp the unlawful domination of the uprights."

Without warning, Lykos stretched forward and sank his teeth into the fawn's neck, crushing his windpipe. After a few twitches, the fawn slumped to his death.

Lykos gazed at his pack with narrowed eyes.

"Do we stand united?" he asked them, mimicking Filtiarn.

"United we stand!" they recited in chorus.

"And when it is *my* time to rise to power, perhaps as high as the crown itself, what will you say? Crown Lykos? Or crown another?"

Even though confusion marked their expressions, his pack knew exactly how to respond.

"Crown Lykos!"

"Then let us feast as one."

28

Sunday, July 21, 2041
A field near the Polar Station: Cape Chelyuskin, Siberia

KNEELING BESIDE HER husband, Ruby placed her hand on his forehead. Temperature: 53-degrees and falling. Respiration: lungs experiencing pleural effusion, or fluid building in the cavities. Cardio: congestive heart failure. Brain activity: sputtering synapses. Cognitive language: incomprehensible. Consciousness: comatose.

At 11:00 a.m. Krasnoyarsk Time, Clay, her forever love, was minutes, if not seconds, from dying in front of her and Gabby. A feeling of desperation and doom tightened around her throat because she feared she couldn't save him.

Ruby moved his cloak aside, yanked out the dart which had delivered its deadly payload, and ripped open his leather shirt, exposing his chest. The needle's prick resembled a black bullseye. Onyx veins bulged and throbbed around the point of impact like Medusa's wiggling, snake-infested hair. The dark veins were growing, consuming, and spreading the bioengineered wolf venom.

Sculpting her incisors into fangs, Ruby bit her wrist, opening the faucet to her healing blood.

Gabby locked eyes with her, tears running down her face. "It should have been me, Mom. The dart was meant for *me*, not Dad."

"Thank God it wasn't you," she said, as she placed her bleeding wrist against Clay's parted lips. "Your life is worth any sacrifice. Dad and I have always felt this way, from the moment you were born. Let's just pray I can heal him."

Gabby delivered a weak smile. "Your blood always works, Mom."

As her crimson life-source flowed, commotion behind them drew her attention.

A gray wolf had entered the dome through a trench it had dug.

Liora brandished her sword, slashing in perfect countermoves as she defended the rest of them from attack. The queen's advantage would be short lived. Another wolf began to squeeze underneath the breach. Spinning her body in a pirouette, Liora connected her blade edge with the first wolf's neck, cleanly slicing through vertebrae. The severed head dropped to the ground and rolled until it crashed against the ice dome wall, splattering blood. A second later, the headless body slumped onto the sleet covered grass.

Lying next to Clay, Solange's eyelids quivered, as if trying to open.

"Another wolf is through," Liora warned, her sword pointed at the new intruder. "One more follows. Sculpting, please?"

Zagan's ghost couldn't help them inside the structure. He was outside, causing invisible havoc to the assailants and other wolves.

Ruby's eyes rolled behind her lids and she channeled the gas from the ATV tanks, coating the ice surface on the exterior of the dome. Using flames from the guard's torches, she set the surface ablaze. Instantly, the wolves and guards retreated, jumping back in panic. Some rolled on the ground to extinguish the flames which had transferred to their fur or clothing.

Liora battled the second wolf which had invaded their sanctuary. She thrust her blade into its brown chest, causing it to yelp and fall lifeless to the ground.

An additional wolf, the one halfway through the trench, rushed inside the dome to escape the flames. Ruby applied sculpting to deploy one of her knives, sending it soaring across the dome's interior. Her blade embedded into the wolf's black fur, between ribs above the sternum, penetrating the beast's heart. The wolf was dead before it dropped.

Fire continued to rage on the exterior walls of the ice dome.

Ruby turned her attention back to Clay and Gabby. Purple veins marked her daughter's neck like a vampire's.

"He's not healing, Mom," Gabby said.

Her daughter's words were accurate. Clay's body temperature now registered 42-degrees. No human could survive that temperature. Not for very long anyway. She sculpted thick blankets to cover his body.

"Clay!" Ruby shouted. "Wake up!"

To her surprise, his blue eyes flickered open. A strange wave of light raced over them.

With great relief, her mind registered his lifeline stone, only it was weak and threatened to extinguish again. Despite his plummeting body temperature, maybe her blood was working. Maybe he only needed a little more time.

"I'm not going to make it, Ruby," he whispered out loud, barely able to exhale the words. "I'm so cold." His eyes shifted from her to Gabby and back. "Take care of each other. You'll always be the loves of my life." He wheezed with a shallow inhale.

Liora rushed over, returning her bloodied sword into its sheath.

"Give him your venom," the queen advised. "For I know you see his death, as I do. Turning him vampire is your only hope."

"I've...I've never used my venom before."

"*Will* the glands behind your incisors to open. Nature will take care of the rest. As long as his heart beats, the venom will course through his veins. In three days' time, he will awake as an immortal."

Clay lost consciousness.

Ruby locked eyes with the queen. "What about the wolf venom in his veins? Will it impact the transformation process?"

"My sight cannot see the answer."

"Do it, Mom!" Gabby pleaded. "Hurry!"

Ruby had no other choice. Clay was slipping away with every passing second. Focusing her mind on her venom glands, she pictured them opening and coating her incisors. Sure enough, a brassy, metallic taste assaulted her taste-buds. Turning her husband's neck, she lowered her head and opened her mouth. She pierced his icy skin until her incisors punctured his carotid artery and she released her vampire venom into his bloodstream.

Clay's heart instantly stopped beating, like it had frozen still.

"This can't be!" Ruby cried. "What happened?"

"Move," Liora ordered. In a whirl of motion, she straddled Clay's chest, applying compressions with immortal strength.

Sobs raced from Ruby's throat. She couldn't deny what her vision revealed inside her mind. Clay's lifeline stone was blank: blank in the present, blank in the future. Her friend, her partner, her husband, her lover, the father of her child, would not live to see another moment. Would never again embrace them, assure them, make them laugh.

His essence would exist in memory only.

Stopping compressions, Liora must have read his empty stone.

"Boo-hoo-hoo," Emory chided while clapping, standing on the other side of the fading flames, now nearly extinguished on the ice dome's exterior. "Has Clay left us? Scared to…death…of his nemesis? Don't you think it's time to give us what we want, girlfriend? To handover my precious Godchild?"

Ruby growled and grew two rows of teeth resembling a great white shark. Her skin erupted in angry, pulsing veins—she could feel them. Her eyes radiated revenge.

With a sweep of her hand, the dome shattered, dispersing a cloud of icy fragments with the wind. Thrusting her hands downward, she transferred a blast of energy into the ground and forced waves of shifting shale and upturned dirt toward her enemies, like a rolling earthquake. Everything in the waves' violent path toppled over: wolves, guards, Emory and Vladimir, and the ATVs.

With a force she had never before unleashed, she raised Emory off the ground. He dropped his dart pistol as she reeled him in. Curling her fingers around the air, she transferred the effort onto Emory's neck, as his legs dangled above the brownish grass. His eyes bulged, threatening to pop from their sockets. His hands raised and thrashed at his neck, as if his pathetic display could stop the strangulation.

About to ignite an explosion inside his brain, she heard a tiny voice behind her.

"Mom! It's Dad. He's opened his eyes!"

29

Sunday, July 21, 2041
A field near the Polar Station: Cape Chelyuskin, Siberia

GABBY GASPED WHEN her Dad breathed, after being dead. And when he opened his eyes, she blinked to make sure her mind wasn't playing tricks.

Her Mom ignored her call for help. Probably because she was busy strangling Wicked Doctor E with her mind.

Everyone else was occupied, too. Like a lioness, Queen Liora paced back and forth, warning the drooling wolves to stay back or taste her sword. The guards on the ground tried to get up. King Z made sure they didn't. And Princess Solange, unconscious from the vervain, lay on the ground beside her Dad.

Which meant, Gabby was the only one who could help her Dad.

His eyes went from staring blankly to searching.

"I'm here, Dad," she said. "Right beside you."

Raising his hand, he clutched her arm. "Your Mom?"

His voice sounded raspy and weak.

"She's busy fighting Doctor E," she told him. "Should I get her?"

"No. No. As long as she's okay, let her fight."

Waves of shivers took over her Dad's body. He shook and chattered his teeth so hard that she worried he would crack them or bite his tongue. Every now and then, a streak of light or energy or electricity raced across his pupils and the blue of his eyes.

Something weird was happening inside his body.

The shaking worsened, causing her Dad's blanket to fall to the side. His cloak opened even more, showing his bare chest. Black veins looked like wiggle worms moving in dirt. Only the worms were getting longer and thicker by the second, beginning to fill in. His chest seemed bigger, too, like he had gulped a huge breath but never let it out.

"Mom!" Gabby hollered. "Dad needs you!"

"It's all right," he said. "Let her be. I just need a minute."

Gabby's Mom had her back toward her. Her Mom's right arm was raised, and her fingers curled like she was clutching air. Gabby knew she was transferring energy onto Wicked Doctor E's neck. Raised five feet above the ground in front of her Mom, the mad scientist floated, still thrashing and pawing at his neck.

Touching her Dad's icy skin, Gabby felt a strong vibration, reminding her of when she'd place her hand on the hood of their car or SUV to feel the humming motor.

"Are you okay?" she asked him.

"I've felt better." He smiled, just barely, "Not sure what's happening, but maybe you'd better move away from me."

Gabby had enough.

No way was she going to stand by and watch her Dad die for the *second* time. Heat consumed her. She couldn't see her veins bulging under her skin, but she imagined how they looked on her neck: ugly and angry.

"Mom!" she roared like God from the sky.

Gabby surprised herself. Who knew her voice could sound like a loud rumble of thunder?

Her Mom finally turned her head, while keeping Wicked Doctor E in place, hovering over the ground. She and her Mom locked eyes.

"Dad's *life* is more important than Doctor E's death," Gabby shouted. "Help us!"

She hoped she wouldn't get in trouble for being snarky.

Thankfully, her Mom popped out of her trance and released the mad scientist who crashed to the ground. He gasped for air and massaged his neck like a wimpy baby.

Racing to them, her Mom knelt by her Dad's side and ran her fingers across his forehead.

"You've come back to us," her Mom said, sounding over-the-moon relieved. She placed her hand in his hair. "I love you so much."

"Wish I could help." He grimaced. "But I'm not feeling well."

"Focus on resting," her Mom said. "Your skin's still so cold. And dark veins keep growing. I don't know how to stop them, Clay." She sculpted another thick wool blanket around him.

"Mind if I interrupt your heartwarming family huddle?" Wicked Doctor E asked, standing up from where he had fallen. He brushed off his pants and jacket. Coughing, he continued rubbing his neck. "You should have killed me when you had the chance, girlfriend."

"Mom?" Gabby asked.

Her Mom's eyes locked on the source of Gabby's question.

A red-light beam danced around Gabby's chest, mostly where her heart was. Mister Vladimir had recovered from Princess Solange's attack and was holding his own dart gun, pointing it in her direction.

"Liora," her Mom said calmly. "Keep an eye on Clay and Gabby."

Standing, her Mom sculpted Solange's shield to lift off the ground and whip across the field until her hand grabbed the handle. She stood in front of the red beam, blocking Gabby from it.

Wicked Doctor E grabbed the wolf remote that Mister Vladimir had stuffed into his jacket pocket.

"For once," her Mom said to the mad scientist, "we agree on something. I should have snapped your neck. Vampires, however, only make a mistake once."

"Come on!" he said. "Just give us the brat. I bet little miss wonderful will be able to talk with the animals when she becomes a hybrid. These remotes, you know, have shortcomings."

Wicked Doctor E started to grab his neck again.

His face turned purple.

This time, her Mom was going to finish him off.

Mister Vladimir yanked the remote from Doctor E's hand like it was a game of hot potato where each person had to pass it back and forth before getting burned.

Something overhead distracted Gabby.

A drone. One that hadn't made a sound flew above them spraying a white mist. Some of the spray whipped away with the wind. Some made it to the ground.

Her Mom dropped the shield first, before her body slumped and fell unconscious.

Liora toppled onto the grass. Her sword slipped from her hand.

Vervain.

Suddenly, a strong wind kicked up, blasting the guards, Doctor E, and Mister Vladimir. The force knocked them onto the ground again. Mister Vladimir dropped his dart gun.

King Z was doing his thing.

Gabby looked at her Mom—her arms and legs looked twisted after she had fallen. She seemed so vulnerable, so...*dead*.

"No!" Gabby yelled, starting to run toward her Mom.

Out of nowhere, her Dad leapt onto his feet. The blankets fell away. Grabbing Gabby's arm, he pulled her behind him.

Another drone appeared overhead.

No more sculpting stupid things like pillows.

Gabby's eyes hid behind her lids and when they refocused, the drone exploded into a bazillion pieces.

Wicked Doctor E took advantage of the distraction by grabbing *back* the remote from Mister Vladimir. When Doctor E pressed a few buttons, the wolves began to advance on Gabby and her Dad. The wolves' eyes glowed red like devil dogs, the kind of dogs shown in horror movies her parents *didn't* allow her to watch.

Another wave of anger raised Gabby's body temperature. Her ski parka and pants made her feel like she was a marshmallow over a campfire. Hiding her eyes behind her lids again, she gathered pressure in the atmosphere and began strangling Doctor E herself.

She didn't *want* to strangle him, but she had to. Because during the last two fights, she hadn't done anything but watch. Like when Doctor E captured King Draven, she watched. When wolf venom poisoned her Dad who *died* (for a little while anyway), she watched. When the first drone dumped vervain, she watched.

No more watching.

Doctor E grabbed at his neck while glaring at her.

Stalking toward them with raised lips, the wolves were in attack mode, calling first dibs on their juicy meal.

Standing behind her Dad, she noticed his earlier vibration was visible now. His whole body hummed and shivered uncontrollably.

"Dad!" she cried, taking her mind off the mad scientist's neck.

"Don't move," he ordered, his voice sounding stronger.

His whole body trembled, and she worried he might combust like the drone. A tornado of black dust swallowed him. She no longer saw his body.

The wolves broke into a gallop.

Gabby stepped back, not knowing what to do.

Without her Dad, she and King Z would be alone.

When the cloak of dust disappeared, a massive wolf emerged.

A *wolf* in the place of her Dad.

Her heart pounded in her chest.

Should she be afraid? Relieved?

Her Dad's wolf fur was thick and black, except for a blaze of white on his head. He growled, showing the largest fangs she had ever seen. In fact, his body was huge, way bigger than Wicked Doctor E's pack of super wolves.

Big enough, in fact, that the wolves rushing toward them tried to stop, digging their claws into the ground and pedaling backwards like they had changed their minds.

Her Dad turned his head to look at her. His yellow eyes narrowed, and she understood his expression; he wanted her to stay put.

Doctor E cursed, dropping the f-bomb.

Turning, he leapt onto the only ATV which hadn't toppled over during the earthquake her Mom had caused. He jumped on, started the engine, and sped off toward the Polar Station, taking the wolf remote with him.

Mister Vladimir gave his Russian *umph*.

"Americans," he said, standing up. "At the first sign of trouble, they run off with their tails between their legs."

Her Dad faced off with the wolfpack.

He seemed to communicate with them, like through brain whispers. After a few seconds, half the wolves took positions on her Dad's left side, half on his right. Together and very quietly, they inched toward Mister Vladimir.

When Mister Vladimir turned around, after looking at Doctor E drive away, his eyes widened.

The wolves were only 10 feet from him.

Gabby's heart thumped hard, not knowing what was about to

happen, though it didn't look good for Mister Vladimir.

"Do something," he yelled to his guards who still couldn't get their footing thanks to King Z.

The guards didn't have any working weapons anyway.

The super wolves stopped, and her Dad stepped even closer to Mister Vladimir.

"I finally appreciate the problem with remotes," Mister Vladimir said, his voice shaking. "When you do not have one, control is no longer yours to claim."

Her Dad slammed his front paws onto Mister Vladimir's chest, dropping him to the ground. He clamped down on his neck with his fangs and ripped through Mister Vladimir's windpipe, pulling away a mouthful of bloody, stringy flesh.

Gabby was about to throw up.

Looking away, she didn't want to see Mister Vladimir drown in his blood even though she wanted him to die.

When she heard the guards scream, she covered her earmuffs with her hands.

30

CLAY WAS DUMBFOUNDED about what the hell had happened to him. One minute he felt the prick of a dart's needle in his chest and the next, an arctic freeze raced through his arteries and veins. Forget his fears about morphing into some freakish wolf-hybrid who could mentally converse with the animals. After the dart struck him, his most pressing worry was turning into a block of ice.

Thank God his interception had spared Gabby.

Albeit vaguely, he remembered Ruby had tried to heal him with her blood, to no avail. As a last resort, she bit him. The heat of her venom began thawing his blood, warming him back into the living.

Clay had anticipated drifting into three days of painful unconsciousness, as the vampire venom broke down his human life before rewiring it into an immortal.

Instead, he woke up soon after, feeling rather normal-*ish*. Had the wolf venom from the dart counteracted his transformation? Perhaps shortening or negating the process of turning vampire?

But when the troll threatened his daughter again, Clay's insides ignited into liquid fire. An inferno ready to torch any danger.

An explosive response had overwhelmed him, and he thought he had combusted like a grenade—his body blasting into tiny bits of burnt flesh. Only he hadn't.

To Clay's astonishment, he had emerged from the dust cloud on all fours. His vision was beyond sharp; his hearing, impeccable; his sense of smell, flawless. His stomach, grumbling.

When he glared down into the eyes of an approaching wolf, he saw his reflection and initially denied reality. But as soon as he *understood* the wolf's telepathic voice, in addition to the voices of the other wolves, Clay accepted that the experiment Emory and Vladimir had wanted to conduct on Gabby, they had conducted on *him*.

Coupled with multiple enhancements from Ruby, no doubt.

At the time, his mind wasn't keen on contemplating his new beastly self, let alone the ramifications of his transformation. Instincts overpowered his thoughts. Protection of his offspring, thirst, fury, and…*dominance* if he was honest, were his only motivations.

He merely asked the wolves one question to get them to switch sides: did they want an upright's device to control them or the laws of nature? Their answer was predictable since nature always trumped anything uprights imposed.

After the initial consensus, Clay offered each wolf a more provocative option: join him, challenge him, or run like hell.

Without hesitation, the wolves bowed to his authority. After all, they sensed they couldn't defeat him. And they were right.

Gross as it sounded, ripping Vladimir apart and tasting his blood wasn't unpleasant at all, though hints of garlic and vodka seasoned the Russian's flesh.

Clay invited the wolves to join him in devouring the carcass. He also granted permission to kill the six guards who brandished blowtorches as if super wolves were scared of a little flame.

He was relieved that Gabby had turned away, covering her ears.

As the pack tore limb from body, flesh from bone, Clay cognitively whispered with the wolves back at the lab, giving them orders. They accepted his authority, vowing to obey.

Feasting on humans, even those evil to the core, should have given Clay pause. But he felt no empathy, no remorse, no compassion for the humans devoted to Emory Bradshaw and his twisted self-serving perversions.

Animals were not pawns in a game.

Not for anyone. Not for any cause.

In truth, ridding the world of the wicked impostors and their cronies felt natural. Like fate fulfilled. Balance restored.

When Clay's demeanor calmed, he felt a familiar chill return to his blood. In a split second, he was naked on the frigid ground, back in human form, with sleet pelting his icy flesh.

No longer a threat, the wolves withdrew into the forest.

Gabby raced to him, but Clay held her off, trying to cover his body. Thankfully, she sculpted an outfit on him: another leather shirt and pants, combat boots, a black cloak, and his arsenal of weapons.

Clothed, he embraced his daughter who immediately fired a plethora of questions at him. Questions that he was asking himself. Questions with answers that eluded him.

One part of him wanted to know how his unexpected transformation would affect his daily life. Had his shift to wolf form and back been a one-time phenomenon? Or would shifting be a frequent occurrence? How much *human* remained in him?

Another side of him wanted to calculate various strategies to rescue Draven and defeat his captors, to ensure that his team of family and friends survived the mission.

His animalistic side wanted to affirm the wolves in the lab had followed orders. Had obeyed *him*.

All sides wanted to attend to his unconscious wife.

Taking his daughter's hand, he led her to where Ruby's body lay sprawled on the ground. He knelt beside his wife. A few feet away, Zagan's ghost hovered over Solange. Liora was two yards past them, also lying unconscious on clusters of grass.

"When I dream of returning to my immortal life," Zagan said to him, "I imagine myself destroying all the vervain plants on your planet. Every single one."

"What a nightmare," Clay said. "I mean, the part where you return to immortal life. Spare us from the hideous thought."

"Dad...," Gabby whined, indicating he was being rude.

"Look behind you, Clayton," Zagan urged. "The blood and gore discoloring the landscape appear far more nightmarish than my wish to annihilate a...toxic weed. Who has more civility now?"

Zagan's point was valid, but Clay would never admit it out loud.

A tinge of shame soured his ballooning sense of self-confidence.

Gabby's blue eyes hid behind her lids. When she opened them, the grotesque remains of the guards turned into sculpted dust which disappeared in the wind. The landscape was once again barren, sparse, and free from evidence implicating him and the wolfpack of tearing seven individuals into edible pieces.

Ruby moaned and her eyes fluttered open.

He caressed her face and smiled. "There you are."

"What happened? Is Gabby okay? You?"

Smiling, he nodded. He was beginning to feel mostly human again.

Solange and Liora regained consciousness. They sat up, rubbing their temples, probably trying to dispel the sedative's cognitive fog.

Clay shared what had transpired after the drone had delivered its vervain payload.

"I don't get it," he said to his wife, as he ended his summary. "How could I morph into a super wolf and *return* to human form?"

"Let me think," she said, as he helped her stand. "Using lateral gene transfer, Emory infused the First Lady's genetic composition with naked mole rat DNA. He had programmed both genomes (hers and the creature's) to intertwine, permanently transforming Irene into a hybrid, with a unique genome.

"And the super wolves," she continued, as she paced, "were created using the same process. Emory infused them with my blood and DNA so they could transform into hybrids." She rubbed her forehead as if encouraging the facts to surface. "Only remember, with the wolves, he admitted he had learned to control genetic prepotency—meaning he was able to control which original genome dominated when it combined with the other. Clearly, his hybrids are more wolf than vampire."

"But I'm *shifting* from one species to another," Clay said.

She reached for his hand. "The answers have to be on the *inside*. Back when you were unconscious on the ice, I couldn't get a read on what was happening internally. But now that your transformation is complete, maybe I'll be able to see the truth."

As he clasped her hand, a cold gust raced across the field.

Her green eyes hid behind her lids and she assessed his condition.

Her eyes refocused. "You're amazing. Really."

"What did you see?"

"The wolf venom from the dart was meant to rewire you into a human/wolf hybrid, similar to the mythological Lycan. But then I delivered vampire venom into your bloodstream. That's the differential. Because when I examined your genetic composition, I found three *independent* sets of DNA coding: human, vampire, and wolf. All the genomes have remained separate, as if my venom halted them from intertwining. Which makes sense since vampire venom stops time within the body.

"In terms of vampirism," she added, "you must've inherited my ability to sculpt or shift into an animal. Which in your case, is a wolf, bioengineered to be superior to the nth degree.

"You're not a super wolf, Clay," she stated. "You're a *shifter.*"

He closed his eyes and shook his head in disbelief. "Nothing is ever simple or easy."

"Right now," Ruby said, "we've got to focus on one more battle ahead. The fight to free Draven."

"Okay. So maybe *some* things are easy," Clay said.

"Easy?" Liora questioned. "Are you saying that my mate is no longer in danger?"

"Before I morphed back into human form, I whispered with the wolves inside the lab where Draven was being held captive."

"Was?" Solange asked him.

"Draven's still unconscious; but by now, I suspect his captors are deceased."

"Explain." Ruby tilted her head.

"There were two wolves in the lab. I ordered them to kill Emory, his scientist sidekick, and any guards they found."

"And you think the two wolves were successful?" she asked.

"They *are* super wolves," he answered, hoping not to sound as defensive as he felt. "Why don't you read Emory's lifeline stone? What does it show?"

Her eyes quivered as her pupils hid behind her lids.

Refocusing, her expression was unreadable.

Silence lingered.

"His stone," she said softly. "It's blank."

31

QUIET SWADDLED DRAVEN as he lay sedated on top of an operating table within the laboratory. The only sounds belonged to his beating heart.

And to that of another's.

Minutes earlier, sounds of gnashing teeth and shredded lives had echoed off the walls. Minus his sight, some of the commotion was difficult to discern. As he lay in a semiconscious state, unable to move from vervain poisoning, he had little else to do except to replay the events in his mind. Perhaps clarity would ripen.

As a seasoned fighter, Draven understood that every inevitable battle encompassed a turning point of sorts: a precise nanosecond when something or someone altered the energy on the battlefield, signaling the onset of warfare.

Perhaps one side wheeled a Trojan Horse behind enemy lines. Or fired a cannon. Released an arrow. Pulled a sword from its scabbard. Or unintentionally quivered.

The energy's source was inconsequential.

The true significance was that negotiations were no longer an option. The battle had begun: the point of no return.

When the scientist named Emory had returned to the laboratory, Draven suspected the nanosecond had revealed itself. Racing heartbeats and erratic breathing confirmed the change in energy. Those in the chamber could undoubtedly taste the impending danger.

He did not require his sight to predict an imminent confrontation.

"You have bruises on your neck, Sir," a female guard had said, for both guards consistently addressed others using *sir* or *ma'am.*

"Bravo. You're observant," Emory responded. "You've earned a bloody star."

"Where is Vladimir?" the female scientist named Mela asked.

"He's getting a bite," he answered, sounding sarcastic. "Now hand me that vial of Ruby's vampire venom. Quickly."

"Have plans changed?" Mela inquired.

"While you're at it," Emory said, "give me that IV bag of wolf venom. Because all hell is about to break loose. How's that for changed plans? So yeah, I'll need to place both venoms in the guarded refrigerator. For safe keeping."

The male guard chuckled nervously, as if trying to dilute the tension. "Beware: that soldier makes you recite the password, Sir."

"Think…*move out of my way or die* will motivate him?"

No one answered.

Footsteps brushed over the floor, moving closer to Draven. Above his left shoulder, he heard the disassembly of the device that was intended to inject him with wolf serum.

"Sir, what should we do?" the female guard asked.

"Thought that'd be obvious, girlfriend, but let me spell it out for you: make sure no one takes the prisoner. Oh, and try to survive." Draven heard something whiz across the chamber. "Take my vervain dart pistol. Use it. And here, I don't need these anymore."

Draven could not detect what items the mad scientist had handed over or to whom.

"I'll be back," Emory said. "Wouldn't want to miss the fun."

Footsteps faded down the hallway.

Draven had listened intently to assess those remaining in the laboratory chamber. He heard three human heartbeats, as well as the heartbeats of two wolves. In addition, he recognized the swift glide and click of a bolt-action rifle positioning a round in its chamber.

"Something doesn't feel right," Mela whispered.

Perhaps she had been more of a warrior than she had given herself credit for.

"No arguments here, Ma'am," the male guard agreed.

Quiet infiltrated the laboratory for nearly a minute.

No one spoke, though he heard multiple footsteps.

Chaos erupted.

Growling, snarling, and guttural yipping assaulted Draven's ears.

The wolves were attacking!

Someone discharged a round, yet nothing indicated the bullet had found its target.

Draven wondered if the wolves would rip him apart while he lay paralyzed and defenseless. But he was not afraid. If death was his fate, he vowed to picture his beloved Liora until his last breath.

Sounds of screaming, crying, and moaning bounced off the walls.

Soon after, sounds of ripping, shredding, gnawing, chewing, and lapping replaced human utterances. Draven's mind pictured the feast, though he wished not to do so.

Down the hallway, a similar attack was underway.

Draven, however, remained whole.

The aroma of warm blood rose like a thick, sweetened steam. Saliva flooded his mouth as a reflexive response, though he was most certainly absent hunger.

The soft padding of paws entered and left the laboratory several times. He had lost count.

One wolf remained.

Its heartbeat was thumping near the foot of his table.

Draven was relieved. If the wolf had meant to harm him, the beast would have done so.

32

RUBY HAD ACQUIRED a strong stomach since becoming a vampire. After all, her own survival depended on drinking blood. Seeing guts, torn off limbs, and severed heads were all part of being a warrior bioengineered to annihilate zombies. Getting queasy was pointless. But when their group traveled into the lab where Emory and Vladimir held Draven captive, she instantly gagged.

Gabby vomited on the floor.

"Please take her into the hallway, Solange," Ruby said, feeling bits of flesh, swimming in blood, squish beneath her boots. "If there's any trouble still lurking, even a hint, travel her back to our hotel. We just need a minute to wake Draven and deconstruct this scene."

Zagan drifted beside Solange and Gabby as they exited the lab.

Ruby eyed the bones, guts, hair, and fingers littering the floor.

A massacre had occurred. Only, the human remains were unrecognizable. The wolves had severed skulls from necks. Arms and legs, from torsos. The little bit of raw "meat" that remained on dismembered skeletons was skinless.

Joining larger chunks, pieces of shredded flesh and fabric sloshed around in crimson puddles which were still on the move, combining with others to make larger pools. More like a bloody sea of chum.

Under her skin, veins plumped and raised.

Clay rubbed her back, offering his support.

In contrast to her reaction, her husband didn't seem affected by the gruesome sight. Or surprised by the extent of the carnage.

Liora also seemed oblivious.

The moment they materialized in the lab, the queen darted for her mate, ignoring the gore and the gray super wolf lying on the floor by the end of the raised operating table, as if protecting his master. Splattered in blood, the wolf licked his stained legs and paws.

Liora yanked the vervain IV from Draven's skin, dropping the needle once inserted into his right arm. Biting her wrist, she lowered her wound onto Draven's mouth. Moments later, his lips began to move as the queen's blood diluted the drug's effects.

He opened his eyes, withdrawing his mouth from Liora's wrist.

"Much gratitude, my queen." With Liora's help, Draven sat up. "How fortunate that vampires are accustomed to eternity, or I might have grown impatient." He smiled, revealing his bold white teeth. "I thought perhaps I was to remain among the stench and viscera."

Liora planted a deep kiss on her mate.

"What have I always told you?" Draven added, when the kiss was over. "Your lips heal all wounds of the heart and flesh. Ha! I have already forgotten the delay in my rescue."

The wolf hadn't moved from his spot on the floor, though he continued to survey his surroundings as he cleaned his fur. His eyes observed, his ears twitched.

Ruby would deal with the hybrid later. Right now, she needed answers. Besides, Clay didn't seem alarmed by the wolf's presence.

"Tell us what happened, Draven," she said.

Draven recounted what he'd heard, with precise detail.

The wolves had followed Clay's orders. With a vengeance.

Ruby squatted to get a closer look at a severed brown-skinned finger. Her heart raced. Perhaps the finger had belonged to Emory. She touched the skin. As Ruby closed her eyes and concentrated, she whispered with the cells, channeling the echoes of the life which still lingered within the flesh. Her vision blurred.

With a flash of light, Ruby opened her eyes in the immediate past.

The finger didn't belong to Emory, rather, to the female scientist.

The last moments of the woman's life were beyond horrific.

A wolf—the one with solid black fur—had stood on Gemela Pérez's chest as she lay helpless on the floor. He ravaged her face and

151

throat first. Ruby could feel the beast's teeth tear away flesh and bone. She could feel Mela's terror and blinding pain.

Ruby broke the cognitive connection. The images were repulsive. The feelings, excruciating.

Clay sniffed. "Not Emory's finger. Right?"

"The female scientist's." Her husband's internal transformation had obviously resulted in an enhanced olfactory system. "I can scent Emory, though. Even in this mess. Can you?"

"Yeah," Clay said, "but nothing on the floor is identifiable. Who knows if he's part of this human stew." Bending down, he picked up a blood-soaked strip of white fabric. "Wait. Here's something."

The fabric swatch included half of Emory's embroidered name from his lab coat: Bradshaw.

"You and Liora should read his lifeline stone again," Clay suggested. "To be sure."

Liora hid her golden eyes behind her lids.

Ruby also searched the present and future. "His stone is still void of light. It's blank."

The queen affirmed the same.

They couldn't misinterpret Emory Bradshaw's death.

Lifeline stones flawlessly revealed the truth.

Yet, she wanted more evidence. A splinter of doubt burrowed deeper into her thoughts, suggesting a lack of closure, though there was nothing logical about her uncertainty.

More likely, regret was unsettling her.

Ruby had loathed her nemesis to the core. Her dislike was painfully personal. After all, Emory had betrayed her more times than she wished to remember.

She'd never forget that Emory had stolen her unique human blood and melded it with ZOM-B to create a freakish vampire serum. Initially, he had administered the serum to unwilling test subjects. Every would-be vampire died a ghastly death. After the mad scientist hypothesized that Ruby was the *only* person who could survive an infusion, he gave the green light to Lieutenant Colonel Quinton Oxford to kidnap Gabby in order to draw Ruby out into the open.

Of course, Ruby didn't hesitate, rushing to the Annapolis Docks to rescue her daughter. A place where Ox, the embittered ex-Marine, was waiting. The government had tasked Ox with injecting Emory's serum into her.

Thankfully, Ruby killed him, shooting him point blank with his own infantry rifle. Even now, she couldn't help smiling at Ox's shock. He never saw it coming.

Ox's death, however, hadn't deterred Emory. Not one bit.

While Ruby recovered from the ordeal at Margo and Tomas's home, Emory visited her, pretending to offer support. Instead, he paralyzed her with the drug called SUX before injecting her with his hybrid serum. The serum that stopped her human heart. That turned her into a vampire. That changed her life forever.

Even after Emory had turned her, his wretched manipulations continued. He threatened to withhold sustenance unless she accepted her role as the government's vampire warrior against zombies.

Not even prison stopped Emory from practicing his twisted dark science. He managed to hook President Unger into needing him to cure the First Lady of cancer. In typical fashion, the mad scientist neglected to fully disclose the physical and mental costs of his so-called miracle "cure."

Unintentionally, Clay had become his most recent test subject.

Now, Emory had changed her husband forever.

Ruby could never, would never, forgive Emory Bradshaw.

Without question, *she* should've delivered Emory's death, though there was some irony, some poetic justice that the creatures he had bioengineered had ripped him to shreds.

Still. She had dreamt of watching Emory's life dim from his eyes. Of hearing his heartbeat sputter and thump for the very last time. She had earned the opportunity to be his executioner. And now, if she was 100-percent honest, she felt robbed. Like he was smirking at her from Hell, knowing she'd never have the satisfaction.

Without a doubt, if Clay and Gabby hadn't needed her, she would've finished him off when she was strangling him in the field near The Pines. Would've snapped his neck right then and there.

Ruby hated every fiber in Emory's body. Every strand of hair. Every single...bone.

"What's left to do?" Clay asked.

"I've thought of something," she said. "The wolves didn't ingest everything. There should be four skulls in this blood pond, right? Let's count them to confirm the number of dead."

Using their boots, they sloshed around in the slurry, pushing aside remnants of clothing.

They found three skulls; none were recognizable.

"This can't be," Ruby said, her heart starting to pound. "Only three people were here during the attack. Where's the fourth?"

She heard a whisper in her mind.

We have discovered a skull and bloodied bones in a room down the hallway, not far from the laboratory, Solange cognitively told her.

Ruby felt a wave of relief sweep over her.

"Never mind," she said. "Solange found parts of a fourth body. Including a skull. Which means everyone's accounted for."

Clay bent down and retrieved a remote covered in blood.

The wolf whimpered.

"Don't worry, Boris," Clay said, crushing the device with his hand. As he opened his fist, tiny pieces of plastic dropped into the pool of blood on the floor. "You're free of this awful contraption."

"Boris?" Ruby asked, trying not to look overly shocked or concerned by her husband's incredible strength.

She understood from her own transformation that when others treated her "normally," it helped minimize her anxiety regarding the enormity of the changes.

"I spoke with this gray, super wolf earlier," he said, "when we were in the field. Numerically, he was test subject ten sixty-four, but he prefers to be called by his real name."

33

Sunday, July 21, 2041
Building #4 of the Polar Station: Cape Chelyuskin, Siberia

NOT EVEN ETERNITY had prepared Liora for the overwhelming feeling of relief when she had stood before her mate, as he lay on the operating table in the laboratory. Witnessing the rise and fall of his chest felt like Pythia the Oracle and their Human/Immortal Maker had answered her desperate prayers for intervention.

When her beloved Draven opened his eyes and their lips touched, Liora felt as though her heart might burst from the sheer force of love's rising tide.

It was only after Draven had recounted what he had heard during his sedation that Liora noticed the hellacious conditions splattered on the laboratory walls. As well, she grew aware of the butchery beneath her boots. A contradictory crimson palette surrounded them: one of sweet perfume to the nose while unabashedly harsh to the eyes.

Liora swallowed to discourage her throat muscles from reacting.

The wolves in the laboratory had unleashed severe retribution, beyond the penalty of death.

Curiously, the gray wolf named Boris had remained, lying on the floor, at the foot of the table where Draven was now sitting—in wait for the vervain to dilute in his bloodstream. She gazed at the beast's straw-colored eyes, wondering what he was thinking, but knowing whispering into his mind would be pointless.

No vampire, not even The Tether, could decipher his language.

The beast stood and shook his body as if his coat contained

155

moisture. Gazing at Clayton, Boris bowed while lowering his tail.

Clayton nodded.

Sauntering toward Draven, the monstrous wolf nuzzled against her mate's legs which were dangling from the tabletop.

"Ahh," Draven said. "The faithful one who remained by my side to protect me amid the carnage. No?"

Boris rubbed his face against Draven's leather pants. Her mate responded by patting and scratching the wolf's oversized head.

"Gratitude for your assistance, friend," he said, smiling.

The wolf groaned with apparent pleasure.

Liora looked at Clayton. "Can you communicate with this animal? Do you know what this…*Boris* is thinking?"

"I sense he's at ease. That he's comfortable. But I can't hear his thoughts. I'm guessing I've got to be in wolf form to do that."

The gray wolf vocalized what sounded like contentment, somewhere between a whine and a whimper.

"Now that Emory and Vladimir are dead," Ruby said, "why don't we head home? This place conjures up bad memories. I'd like to put Siberia and the Polar Station behind us."

"Before we travel back," Clayton said, "Let's return to The Pines so I can speak with the wolfpack. A better understanding of what's going on with the animals will be helpful. Especially if we hope to quell animal attacks on our planets."

"I propose we travel to the forest together," Solange said, appearing at the laboratory door while keeping Gabriella behind her, blocking her view of the carnage. "My skin prickles from the negative energy here. Gabriella feels it, too. Echoes of evil linger."

Zagan drifted into the laboratory. "I suspect my pulse would also quicken with uneasiness if only…"

"We know, already," The Tether snapped. *"If only* you had a heart. You're such a broken record." She rolled her eyes. "Anyway, I have plans for this compound. So let's do this. Gabby, please close your eyes and let Solange guide you to me."

Solange led Gabriella to her mother while Draven stood. Liora clasped her mate's hand to help steady him.

Death's stench had begun to pollute the air, begun to spoil sweet into sour. Blood on the cinderblock walls had darkened and dried.

Like everyone else, Liora was eager to leave the Polar Station. She longed to return to Kaliméra with Draven.

As they gathered in a circle to hold hands, the wolf nudged against her mate's leg.

"Boris has bonded with you, Draven," Clayton said.

Liora could also see their connection.

"My mate is the King of Swords and Shadows," she added, "but perhaps he should have been coronated King of the Wolves."

Draven chuckled. "Nay. Wolves are playful with members of their pack," he said, while locking eyes with Clayton. "Yet, they tremble and bow to their king."

34

FILTIARN PERCHED ON the weathered boulder which jutted out from Royal Ridge like a thick branch. Lying with her front paws draped over the edge, she gazed at the moonlit valley below. Just past midnight, the fireflies were tiring of their flickering nighttime dance.

A fragrant breeze raced across the pastures from the west. Inhaling, she detected the bouquet of summer (mint and mosses near the Reniraby River) intermingled with the scents emitted by her inner circle of female guards.

Half of her Vala were behind her on the plateau, hidden in the darkest shadows of the butte's crown. The other half strategically stood on the boulders leading up to her throne.

Her Vala's protection did not quell her troubled musings.

Filtiarn had not expected her rise as King of the Animals to proceed without challenges, for every shift in power had to be earned in the animal kingdom. She had *not*, however, anticipated that the alpha of the Night Stalkers planned to usurp her authority in the near future to seek the crown for himself!

If her heart had been weak, this revelation might have broken her.

The disclosure, however, barely caused a sputter.

While Lykos believed only inferior canines were members of her Mukessi spies, he was mistaken. Filtiarn had not earned her position as Lord of the Wolves by having a trusting heart. Quite the opposite was true: *distrust* was at the root of every ruler who sought longevity.

Yes, wolves were also among her most cunning of spies.

Quite cleverly, when she ordered Lykos to destroy the rogue herd which had defected to The Shadowlands, Filtiarn had assigned two Mukessi who were also members of the Night Stalkers. Lykos, of course, was not aware of their affiliation outside of the wolfpack.

In addition, both wolf spies were unknown to one another; that way, she could judge the authenticity of their individual reports.

Both had spoken of the same blasphemy.

Lykos hoped Filtiarn would name him Hand of the King. As such, he would gain her trust while he sought to *dethrone* her!

She growled from her royal ledge.

Worse, Lykos was not the only usurper.

In Siberia, a Mukessi wolf had confirmed yet another anomaly in nature, propagated by the same deviant uprights responsible for the super wolves. The report asserted that a human male had been altered so he could shift into wolf form and speak the language of animals. Most disturbing was that a few had bowed to him, as if *he* had assumed the role of their king.

The thought raised her lips into a quiver.

Even more alarming was that the man-wolf kept the company of gifted vampire uprights who could travel—The Tether (his mate) among them. As well, the King of Darkness was in their company, though he existed as a ghost: a whisper of the ruler he once was, but likely just as cunning.

Filtiarn could taste the impending danger, for a man-wolf shifter (one who benefited from his bond with a vampire traveler) could bring the battle to Besto Polus.

Clayton could challenge her in a fight to the death.

Pushing back with her front paws to raise herself into a sitting position, Filtiarn lifted her snout to the starry sky, howling loud and long as the moon cast its blazing spotlight on her.

A chorus of howls erupted around her.

Filtiarn's determination was stronger than ever. Her enemies would not best her. *She* was Lord of the Wolves. Becoming King of the Animals was *her* destiny. *Her* calling. And she would never relinquish her right to the crown.

All she needed was a failproof strategy.

Perhaps she should keep Lykos blind to her awareness of his traitorous intentions? Perhaps she should use him to her advantage as he attempted to prove himself worthy to be Hand of the King?

An idea rooted.

Filtiarn would plant a seed for a confrontation between Lykos and the shifter. After all, if Clayton sought to be king, he would need a coronation. Why not have the ceremony in Athanasia? A perfect opportunity for Lykos to be present, waiting in the thicket with his warriors. Waiting to destroy the man-wolf abomination who sought the crown for himself.

With or without a direct order from Filtiarn, Lykos would be eager to attend the coronation, for if the animals crowned Clayton as their king, the Night Stalker could never be her Hand. And Lykos was far too ambitious to let that happen.

Curling her lips upwards, Filtiarn imagined the scene.

The shifter would die, ripped to shreds in front of the gathered crowds. The spectacle would cause the animals to tremble in fear.

And why not let Lykos bask in his glory for a moment's time?

The spoils of victory were the greatest among distractions.

Surely, he would not detect his own imminent slaughter.

35

RUBY CLUTCHED THE hands of her husband and daughter as their close-knit coven traveled from the grisly lab and materialized by the edge of The Pines.

Above, orange light poked through broken seams in the dark clouds. Although the sleet had stopped, the afternoon chill and blustery winds persisted. Glistening ice crystals dappled the field, now stained with bloody footprints.

Gabby squeezed Ruby's hand, looking up with a smile, no doubt assuring her and Clay that she was fine. More telling than her expression were the dark circles shading the soft skin under her eyes. The exhausting morning had left its mark. Not to mention, it was one in the morning, Eastern Standard Time.

"Workers were evacuated from the buildings, right?" Ruby asked.

She and Solange, with Zagan's help, had traveled to each of the eight buildings in the compound, warning the inhabitants to exit or die. No one had argued. They fled their workstations for the outside.

Solange nodded.

"And that gray wolf...he ran to safety. Correct?" Ruby continued, looking at her husband.

"I watched him trot away from the compound."

"Then, good riddance to the Polar Station."

Ruby hid her eyes behind her lids and began to sculpt. Gathering flammable liquids from cleaning and lab substances, as well as countless full vodka bottles, she doused the interior of each building, priming them for a fiery end. She channeled the flames from candles and fireplaces and sculpted massive fireballs which she unleashed inside each structure.

Brilliant blasts and plumes of smoke mushroomed in the sky. One by one the buildings combusted and collapsed. The ground rumbled and shuddered beneath Ruby's boots.

Embers flew upwards in the distance like launched fireflies.

Ruby looked at Solange. "Gabby and I will stay with Clay while he gets information from the wolfpack. Why don't you travel the queen and king back to Kaliméra? When we're done here, we'll meet you at the castle to discuss our next steps." She ran her hand along Gabby's ponytail. "And this young warrior is going to need to eat and rest."

"I'm fine, Mom."

"Oh, I have the perfect bedchamber for you, Gabriella," Liora cooed. "Remember the one where your mother rested after she became immortal again? After the wedding?"

Clay and Zagan glared at the queen. Her mention of *wedding* conjured up different memories for them, none of them good.

"Uneasiness remains in my veins," Solange said, ignoring the chatter. "Perhaps we should all wait together."

"Not necessary," Ruby countered. "My powers are back. Gabby's gifts are intact. And now Clay is a shifter. Besides, the threats have been neutralized." She placed her hand on her daughter's shoulder and drew her close. "Best to focus on what you'll find at Kaliméra. You may need to reclaim the estate from animals. Whatever condition it's in, when we join you, Gabby and I will restore the castle to its former glory."

"Glory may be pleasing to the eyes, Tether," Draven said, "but the castle requires fortification over beauty. The queen and I can attest, especially when crazed beasts breached the windows to attack us."

"No problem," Ruby said. "We can sculpt protections. Now off with you!" She used her hands to shoo. "Clay needs to speak with the wolves. To learn what's going on."

Reluctantly, Solange raised her palms, one to Liora and the other to Draven. They formed a small circle, joining hands.

Solange gazed at Zagan. "You *will* meet us at Kaliméra. Right?"

"To abandon you would be heartless." He winked in his ghostly form. "In all seriousness, I could not imagine parting from your side ever again."

The King of Darkness vanished, leaving everyone speechless.

"Shall we?" Solange asked, her voice slightly trembling.

"What *is* that?" Ruby asked, hearing soft padding over the ground.

A gray wolf bounded toward them in a gallop, his pink tongue dangling from the left side of his opened mouth. He stopped at Draven's side and nudged his leg.

"Boris has imprinted with you," Clay said.

Draven smiled, innocent as a child. "I believe he *has* chosen me."

"Your new wolf companion, King," Liora said.

Solange turned the four of them to dust—herself, Liora, Draven, and Boris. They disappeared as she traveled them to Kaliméra Castle.

While they had been talking, the wolfpack inched forward from the forest, exposing their enormous bodies. Their heads and tails were low in a show of respect.

"Guess I'm up," Clay said. "Hope I can remember how to shift."

"Believe in yourself," Gabby urged.

"Don't overthink," Ruby added. "Let your body take over."

Clay walked away, running his fingers through his black hair. His cloak flapped in the wind. As he approached the edge of the dense woods, the wolves retreated back into the shadowed darkness. Her husband turned his head and glanced back at them.

Wish me luck, he cognitively whispered.

Ruby's heart accelerated, stunned that he had acquired that gift.

As the forest swallowed her husband, she became overwhelmed by all that had changed. In the past, Ruby had been The One and Only. *The* one to rescue everyone else.

This time, *she* had been the one rescued. This time, a team of diverse and talented friends had saved the day. She no longer felt alone. No longer felt the burden of saving the planets all by herself. A weight had lifted. And for once, she felt relieved by the support from her friends. They were also willing to fight for justice. Even when their lives and the lives of their loved ones were at risk.

Roles had also changed, especially for her husband. As a human, Clay was strong in his own right. Nevertheless, he often admitted that he usually waited for Ruby to take charge. After all, she and she alone was The Tether, the bond between the planets: the most powerful immortal in the universe.

However, not even The Tether was capable of speaking with the animals. Sure, she could sculpt herself into any animal incarnation, but that didn't mean she could acquire their language. Or that she was actually *one* of them.

As a shifter, Clay (not her) would lead the charge against a possible animal rebellion. He could garner an amicable resolution; she was sure of it. One that would restore peace between the animals and their upright counterparts: humans and vampires.

Gabby squeezed her hand, as if feeling her mother's emotions.

Her nine-year-old daughter seemed mature beyond her years. Her experience of nearly dying when Zagan had blown her off the edge of New Zealand's Great Island had left her fearless, a young warrior. Moreover, her heart had grown, able to forgive Zagan and forge a friendship with their former nemesis.

Zagan was also transforming. He had lost his heart only to regain it. After Solange plucked the beating organ from his chest cavity, his goodness had truly been set free, as The Book of Immortality had prophesied. The former tyrant, despite his ghostly form, was proving that redemption was possible. That lost souls could be found.

Relief surged in her veins.

At last, the universe was free of Emory and Vladimir. No longer could they use dark science to manipulate nature with their sick attempts to rule the world.

"I love you," Gabby said. "And Dad, too."

"And we love *you* more than life itself."

They waited in the brisk winds. Waited for Clay to emerge from the forest and guide them toward their next moves.

36

Sunday, July 21, 2041
A field near the Polar Station: Cape Chelyuskin, Siberia

RUBY STOOD IN the field, holding her daughter's hand. The whistle of the wind whipped by them. Without speaking, she and Gabby waited for Clay to return to human form. A half hour had already passed.

I'm done, he finally whispered. *Same outfit?*

Ruby sculpted his leathers as he emerged from the woods.

"Dad!" Gabby hollered, breaking free to greet her father.

When she reached him, he lifted her. Straddling her legs around his waist, their daughter nestled her face in the crook of his neck.

Ruby outstretched her arms as they approached her. The Spencer group hug felt so good. How she adored her family.

"Scientists were right. *You* were right," Clay said, pulling back to lock eyes with her. "There isn't a pathogen or microorganism responsible for animal aggressions. Bottomline: they're angry."

"About what?"

"About how most animals are treated. Abused. Misused. Tested. Slaughtered. You name it," Clay answered. "They're fed up with being at the mercy of humans and vampires, or 'uprights' as the animals call us. Their leader believes The Turning Point is here. That the time has come to rebel and take over."

"Who is this... *leader?*" Ruby asked.

"A she-wolf named Filtiarn, Lord of the Wolves. From Besto Polus, she's commanding animals to attack uprights. Animals who

165

refuse her orders are exterminated."

"Is *that* why she had Montaro killed? And Tenebrous? Because they refused to attack?"

"No." Clay put Gabby down. "You guessed right the first time. Filtiarn is protecting hand-picked assassins from being carbonized by having them feast on animals who have your blood or Gabby's blood in their systems."

Purple veins crept up Clay's neck.

"It'll be all right." Ruby lightly squeezed his arm. "We're at the beginning of this crisis. We'll find a resolution."

In truth, she wasn't so sure.

Even though her husband could communicate with animals after shifting to wolf form and even though a team of gifted friends would help figure everything out, uncertainty gnawed at her.

She had to think. To act. One small step at a time.

"Since the rebellion is looking for animals with our blood," Ruby said, "we'd better pay a quick visit to Margo and Tomas, before heading to Kaliméra. To tell them our dogs are in grave danger."

"Yes, Mom," Gabby piped in. "Please, Dad. Please."

"If only it wasn't one in the morning in Annapolis," Clay said.

"They won't care, Dad. I know they won't."

"We won't stay long," Ruby said. "Afterwards, we need to learn more about The Turning Point. The Book of Immortality explains very little. All the scriptures say is that after the curse is broken, *balance will be restored, as it was, as it shall be, until The Turning Point, when animals will crown their King.*"

"The curse was broken when Liora and Draven wed," Clay said. "Balance was short lived because this animal rebellion has thrust the planets into escalating chaos."

"I'm curious: have the animals chosen Filtiarn as their king?"

"That's where there's some disagreement among the animals."

"How so?" Ruby asked.

"Some think there's another prospect who's better suited to negotiate with the uprights."

"Who?"

Gabby tugged on her cloak. "Don't you see? It's Dad!"

37

Sunday, July 21, 2041
Gonzalez Residence to Cedar Lane: Annapolis, Maryland

THE FULL MOON cast its spotlight on Margo and Tomas's home, as if showcased as the center of the universe. Stirred by a shifting breeze, stray black feathers danced on the lawn, twirling and skipping across the grassy carpet in no particular direction.

With his wife and daughter by his side, Clay stood twenty yards from the front door, his feet firmly planted where they had materialized after traveling from Siberia.

In addition to the feathers, he was confused by the sheets of plywood covering the windows and sliding doors on the first floor. Tomas had also clamped shut the outdoor shutters on the second and third floors.

Hurricane season was underway, but no threats had existed when he and Gabby left for the Polar Station to rescue Ruby. Hard to believe that despite the time zone differences (given Krasnoyarsk Time was 12 hours ahead), only a day on the calendar had passed.

Margo and Tomas were undoubtedly protecting their home's vulnerability from another threat.

Animal attacks.

Clay's heart accelerated.

"Aren't you going to travel us inside?" he asked, feeling impatient.

"Earth still has rules," Ruby said. "Popping in uninvited, in the middle of the night, isn't wise, even with our best friends."

"Good point." Clay raised his smartwatch. "Videoface request for

167

Margo."

"Got it, boss," Justine answered back. "I'll make sure they get up."

"I have no doubts."

He had to admit that hearing the flawless voice of his and Ruby's Digitally Enhanced Personal Ego was good. Their trusted DEPE could infiltrate any and all electronics, except in areas off the grid like Siberia and Athanasia. And probably Besto Polus.

Clay looked up to the second floor. Light seeped through closed shutters protecting the master bedroom. Clearly, Justine had intervened. And to ensure the household remained awake, their DEPE made the front doorbell chime nonstop.

Uno and Dos barked. Curiously, he didn't hear Mai or the puppy.

At least Margo and Tomas had plenty of land or the noise might've woken up neighbors, too.

Margo's face appeared on his smartwatch screen.

"We've been worried sick," Margo said, wiping her eyes which were puffy and red. "Did you find her? Please tell us you found her."

"Ruby's right here." He smiled wide. "We all are."

"Oh my God! Thank you, Jesus! We'll be right down," she said.

Despite being in human form, he heard Margo and Tomas's footsteps race down the staircase. Their son Reese joined them. Acute hearing was something he'd have to get used to.

The front door flew open and the next few minutes were a blur. Everyone was hugging and crying, relieved they were home safely. The kidnapping was behind them. Ruby had fully recovered. Emory Bradshaw and Vladimir Volkov were dead. Gone. Plans for a super wolf army, eliminated.

Without Clay noticing, Gabby must have left the foyer. When he glanced in her direction, she was standing beside the staircase with Zoe in her arms.

"Where's Mai?" Gabby asked, creases forming on her forehead.

Time seemed to pause. No one moved.

The answer to Gabby's question became painfully obvious.

Margo tried to speak. Sobs swallowed her words.

By this point, he was certain that Ruby and Gabby had cognitively whispered inside Margo's mind to discover the horrid, wretched truth. That's what he had done.

Nevertheless, Tomas painfully explained. The Gonzalez family had taken advantage of the last night before the nationwide curfew commenced. Pizza and movie night in town. And while they were out, Mai had gone outside through the doggy door.

Tomas continued to move his mouth, trying to finish the tragic story, but Clay's breaking heart kept him from listening. All he could picture were the black feathers on the lawn. A vision that seemed so innocent but was everything *but*.

"I didn't go to bed until the whole house was fortified," Tomas said, tears streaming from his eyes. "I hadn't anticipated a bird attack or any animal assault from the *outside*. I mean, Yona scratched Reese, so I should've been prepared. Should've disabled the pet door." He shook his head. "I should've prevented it. I'm so sorry. We loved Mai like she was our own."

Holding Zoe close to her chest, Gabby ran to Tomas and placed her free arm around him. "We don't blame you, Uncle Tomas."

Clay wiped tears from his cheek. His fingers were stained crimson.

Margo looked horrified. "What happened to you? Are you…"

"Another time," he said.

"Where is Mai?" Ruby asked. "Do you still have her body?"

Clay recognized his wife's look. She had an idea.

Maybe I can heal her, she whispered to him. *Depending on her injuries.*

"Can you, Mom?" Gabby asked, eavesdropping, no doubt.

"Can you…what?" Tomas started. "And yes, Mai's in the garage. We planned on burying her in the morning. We just…the night has been so devastating."

"How long has she been dead?" Ruby asked.

"We left the house at six," Tomas answered, "and returned at ten. So by now, it's been anywhere from three to seven hours."

Ruby's shoulders slouched, maybe because rigor mortis typically affected dogs in one to three hours. Maybe that made a difference.

"I need to see her," his wife said.

They walked toward the kitchen door, Tomas leading the way.

Once in the garage, Tomas partially lifted the blanket from Mai, careful to keep most of her body hidden from Gabby.

Birds had mutilated their dog, their precious family member. With her abdomen torn open, she no longer had innards. Her wounds had

169

stained what remained of her white and orange fur. However, there were no pools of blood seeping from her open wounds. The birds (probably ravens) had drained her.

Ruby knelt by their faithful companion and placed her hand on Mai's head. She was reading the echoes of their dog's life. Searching to make sense of what had happened.

No one took a breath.

Looking up, red tears streamed from his wife's eyes. "They took her heart, Clay. Her heart! And without it, I can't even try to bring her back. She's gone and…" A wave of grief prevented her from finishing. Her eyes squeezed shut. Her lips trembled.

Clay placed his hand under her elbow and raised her. Wrapping his arms around her, he drew her close, never wanting to let go. It pained him to see Ruby grieve. To see her cry.

He felt a small arm around his waist. Gabby.

His family was heartbroken.

"Let's bury her," Clay said. "Tonight."

"I picked a spot by the patch of trees near the water," Tomas said. "Mai loved trees and we thought that would be a good resting place. I'll turn on the floodlights."

"Thanks, Tomas, but I was thinking of Cedar Lane," he said. "Mai had a favorite nook in the garden, under one of our dogwood trees. And the garden survived the housefire." He looked at Ruby before glancing at Gabby. "Do you think she'd like that?"

Gabby nodded, still holding Zoe.

After sculpting a wooden urn with a nameplate, Ruby transformed Mai's body into dust. She funneled the gray particles into the urn, resembling a genie returning to its bottle, before plugging the top with a gold stopper.

Since they would travel to Kaliméra after the burial, they exchanged farewells with Tomas, Margo, and Reese. Gabby kissed Zoe goodbye and handed over the puppy to her friend.

Huddled together, with their daughter now holding the urn, they traveled to Cedar Lane, materializing under Mai's favorite dogwood.

Moonlight shone through the leafy branches of the tree. As the leaves swayed with the breeze, the patterns of light shifted on the ground. Most of the dogwood's white blooms had dropped, as they always did in late July, forming a fragrant carpet.

Ruby sculpted a burial hole in the spot where Mai loved to rest.

Solemnly, Gabby placed the urn into Mai's cradle in the ground.

"Rest in peace," Ruby said, sculpting the dirt over the grave.

"You were wise and brave, dear Mai," Clay added. "A loyal soul."

"My best friend," sniffled Gabby. "I promise to take care of Zoe, to make you proud. And I'll miss you forever and beyond."

A coyote yipped and howled, hidden somewhere in the wooded parcel adjacent to their property.

They held hands for their next destination.

Clay noticed purple veins pulsing in his wife's neck.

"Killing the innocent will stop," she said, as they turned into dust on their way to Kaliméra.

38

ZAGAN COULD NOT help but notice the disarray of the queen's castle, though he believed "grand manor" was a more suitable term.

His Castle on High Cliff was a fortress revered by all in Athanasia. Most assuredly, Kaliméra paled in comparison.

He drifted into the solarium where Liora, Draven, and Solange stood conversing, waiting for Lady Spencer and her coven to arrive. Solange briefly glanced at him, acknowledging his entrance with a smile. The other two continued to discuss the manor's ailments.

Admittedly, the disorders were plentiful.

The floor-to-ceiling window panels, those facing an expanse of grass, contained no glass. Fragments and shards littered the oak planks. Thick velvet curtains lay on the floor, torn and frayed. A wingback chair had toppled over. Bird droppings soiled intricately woven Persian rugs. Smashed vases left pink roses and peonies homeless and vulnerable to the brazen intruders who had forced their way into the manor.

The wolf named Boris did not appear affected.

Sprawled on the powder-blue loveseat, upholstered in charmeuse silk, was Draven's new pet. The gray wolf had wasted no time getting accustomed to the comforts of vampires, though he supposed the beast might have been protecting his paws from the glass shards. Nevertheless, a hint of malaise soured Zagan's impression of Boris, an uneasiness he had never felt with Draven's wolf Ozul.

Of course, when the curse was poisoning Zagan with evil, he had carbonized Ozul. A cruel act, to be sure. Now that Zagan's goodness was able to thrive, he understood that he should resist judging Draven for wanting another wolf.

Perhaps Zagan was jealous.

Indeed, he had hoped to repair his relationship with his former henchman. Yet increasingly, Draven appeared distracted by his mate and duties as King of Swords and Shadows.

Time. Everything required more of it. He did not know how long time would allow his spirit to drift from his corpse. Were ghosts everlasting or did their energy slowly fade to nothing? The thought of not existing terrified him, for he was accustomed to being immortal.

As he gazed at the massive sunroom, he acknowledged other feelings: nostalgia and sadness. He had not stepped foot in the grand manor since he had been courting Solange 2.8 mega-annum ago. Not since he had eaten the forbidden fruit from the Tree of Awareness rooted in the former microcontinent of Zealandia. Not since he had initiated the curse, only recently broken, which had prevented him and all Skotadians from being in sunlight.

Sadness weighed down his ghostly spirit. His one infraction of tasting the berries—a curiosity he had not resisted—had cost him so much. Had cost him his mate whom he had tried to destroy. Had changed and taken the lives of so many. A past he could never undo.

Ruby, Clayton, and Gabriella materialized near the tiled fireplace. After minutes of gawking tirelessly at the shambles, Ruby and her daughter began sculpting, making the debris disappear. They also installed new windows, apparently thicker and impenetrable.

If only Zagan had retained his gifts as a ghost, he would have surely taken charge. Instead, his "condition" limited him to making suggestions regarding interior design.

"Could you incorporate splashes of yellow into the décor?" he asked. "After all, Lampsi is the realm of perpetual sunlight."

Liora nodded, absent a sneer. Most unexpected.

In response, Ruby replaced the dirtied Persian floor coverings with vibrant area rugs, artfully depicting impressionistic flowers, some with yellow petals. He smiled at her flair for decorating, exchanging the dainty, teacup-style ornamentations with both tasteful and fearless applications of color.

Gabriella added similarly spirited pillows to every chair.

The sculpting session concluded with the installment of exterior bars protecting each window on the entire manor. Likewise, they strengthened the doors and sealed fireplace flues.

"Now that Kaliméra has been repaired and secured, I have other concerns that aren't easily fixed," Ruby said.

Lady Spencer shared her angst over The Book of Immortality, still protected in his library at High Cliff. Scriptures presented very little information on The Turning Point. Without direction, she said, understanding what the era truly signified would be difficult. How could they successfully counter an animal rebellion without having guidance regarding the truth? Moreover, she explained that even though her husband could speak the language of animals and some believed him to be their future king and negotiator of peace, Clayton was not a seer. He did not have sight into the future. And although Ruby *was* a seer, she could not communicate with the animals. She wondered how they could successfully calculate their next move.

The five adults chatted, their voices rising with each suggestion.

"No need to worry," Zagan announced.

Everyone ignored him. Perhaps no one heard his voice?

"Mom," Gabriella said. "King Zagan has something to say."

Voices hushed and faces turned in his direction.

"Thank you, Gabriella," Zagan said, drifting nearer to the group. "Your worry is not warranted, for Pythia wrote a sacred codicil about The Turning Point. The document is hidden in my interior cabinet room, adjacent to my master chamber, within a secret compartment."

"Why have you never mentioned it?" Liora questioned.

"As I recall, we were not on speaking terms before my death."

"Does anyone else know about this codicil?" Ruby asked. "Besides its author, I mean."

"You know...*Pythia,*" Draven said to him, using the sharpest of edges in his tone. "Our oracle whom you culled and murdered."

Liora touched her mate's arm, as if to ask for restraint.

Boris raised his head from the loveseat, appearing interested in the rising tension. He tilted his head and perked his ears.

"I have never spoken of it. Not even to my *trustworthy* henchman,"

Zagan snarled, glaring at Draven. "In my former existence, when evil corrupted me, I thought my throne might get crowded with the coronation of another king. So I hid the codicil."

"You seriously thought hiding sacred scriptures might actually prevent The Turning Point from happening?" Ruby asked.

"I recognize my flawed thinking, Lady Spencer," Zagan admitted. "History has already revealed that I was unable to prevent the coronation of my henchman, even when I possessed all my competencies. Likewise, I presume the codicil's secrecy will not avert The Turning Point. The animals will crown a king, whether I unveil the scriptures or not. Besides, the number of kings in this universe hardly seems relevant to me at this phase of my existence. Let us agree: my aspirations have changed. Why should I not help the animal's rightful king assume the throne?"

Zagan glanced at Solange, hoping she approved of his attitude.

"Your *former* henchman," Draven said, his gray skin darkening.

"Yes," Zagan countered. "I have not forgotten your betrayals which stripped you of your position and title, as you have not forgotten or forgiven mine."

"I don't mean to sound disrespectful," Gabriella said, "but shouldn't we focus on the present? King Zagan just told us about writings that could help make things clearer. Isn't that important?"

Gabriella was a remarkable child.

All the adults stared at the smallest Spencer. The bickering halted.

"Will you come with Clay and me to High Cliff?" Ruby asked him. "To examine the codicil?"

"Most certainly, Lady Spencer."

"And me, too, Mom," Gabriella said. "I want to come, too."

"You need to stay here and rest. It's like two in the morning."

"Please, Mom?" The child looked at Clayton. "Dad?"

"I am quite familiar with rest," Zagan intervened. "Believe me, resting in peace is not all it is claimed to be. And you have my pledge: I will watch over Gabriella while you read the codicil."

"There's no denying...I couldn't have been rescued without you," Ruby said to him. "But can we truly trust you? With our daughter? Because it's hard to forget you tried to kill her not too long ago."

39

THE POTUS STARED at himself in the large mirror above the double-sink vanity in the master bath. With a trembling hand, Will clutched the stolen vial of Sanguivorous Cocci. Well, he hadn't actually stolen the SUC, per se. He had obtained the legal documentation to extract a small quantity of the serum for national security purposes. Classified: *Top Secret.*

Everyone had assumed someone else in his Cabinet, team of advisors, military, Congress, or Senate knew *why* he needed to extract a SUC sample from the concrete vault in the White House bunker. And lucky for Will, distractions had kept questions at a minimum.

Distractions wholly consumed the United States (hell, the entire Federation of Independent Nations for that matter).

From his perspective, the animal crisis was a Godsend in terms of preoccupying his government. Citizens rushed to prep for the nationwide curfew. The National Guard and Military Reserve Forces deployed to major cities and towns. He recalled troops abroad to the homeland, from all branches of service.

No one gave a fuck about a nine-year-old SUC sample.

One thing the whole world *did* care about? Their *número uno* vampire warrior, their one and only Tether, who wasn't around to save the damn day.

Will rolled his eyes and leaned over the vanity, bringing his face closer to the reflective glass. At 52, he still looked handsome. His blue eyes, intense. A few gray hairs peppered the v-shaped hairline on his forehead. His exaggerated widow's peak always made him look sharp. Maybe a little dangerous. He had thought about dying the gray to match his black hair, but the aging strands added to his look, elevating his mature demeanor.

Handsome. Intense. Wise.

Good thing he was satisfied with his appearance.

He'd be 52 for eternity.

Irene, his Sweet Tea, would have to wait for his arrival at the Pearly Gates. Immortality would significantly delay his ETA.

Until then, why not enjoy himself?

He wondered if he'd look the same when he emerged from his lair on Wednesday, for his morning meeting with the Special Warfare Council. Hopefully, he wouldn't be too…thirsty.

Will smiled at his reflection. His plan was pretty much infallible.

Two people knew what he was up to: his personal physician Tina and his Senior Advisor Kenny.

Using Will's ghost banking account in Switzerland, he had already electronically wired a hefty payout to Tina. Her job? Keep his refrigerator stocked with B-positive blood bags. She also issued a medical order not to disturb the President for three days while he recovered with some R&R, since the tragic loss of the First Lady continued to have traumatizing effects. Tina was the only staff member permitted to check on him in the Executive Residence.

The public still believed he'd be at Camp David.

Between Tina and Kenny, he trusted his Senior Advisor the most. Early in Kenny's banking career, he had embezzled money. The act would've ruined him for life if Will hadn't paid back the debt and expunged his record.

Kenny was precisely the kind of confidant Will wanted. The kind who was indebted to him and never forgot it.

Lucky for Kenny, he never bit the hand that fed him.

Staffers referred to his advisor as Cutthroat Kenny, mostly behind his back. And he had bloody-well earned it.

Kenny had applied his sharp edge to substitute the members of the special ops team, those who guarded the vault containing the SUC, with hand-picked operatives loyal to him and the POTUS.

Instead of guarding the SUC, the new operatives built three prison cells in the bunker. Cells which would house three death-row inmates come tomorrow. Kenny had their records tweaked to confirm the prison had executed them.

Will's plan was to become a dairy farmer of sorts. He'd institute a feed-heal cycle like managing a cow who gave milk before returning to pasture to replenish her udders.

The inmates would keep him fortified.

When the POTUS was strong enough, he'd bleed some of his healing blood into vials. Kenny would sell them on the black market, via the dark web or through Will's international contacts—the ones who didn't shy from sordid deals that stuffed their deep pockets with American cash.

Magical Medicine. Or maybe...*Healing Hemo.*

He'd think of something catchy to market his crimson milk.

Will would be rolling in the dough.

His only regret was that he hadn't thought of the idea when his precious Sweet Tea was alive and fighting cancer. A vial of SUC should've been for her.

But Irene was gone.

So he downed the vial of vampire serum.

40

RUBY HOPED BRINGING Gabby to High Cliff was wise.

Guilt had influenced her decision. Guilt because Ruby hadn't given Gabby a choice the first time she had visited the castle. In fact, Ruby had decided on her own to uproot her nine-year-old's life, insisting Gabby accompany her to Skotadi and accept the castle as her new home. A necessity, if Ruby hoped to successfully trick the King of Darkness into thinking her marriage proposal was authentic. The alternative (leaving her daughter behind at the hotel) would have been a glaring giveaway that Ruby's proposition was a ruse, a calculated means to an end.

Zagan's death was history now.

Hard to believe "the wedding" had only been 17 days ago.

In Ruby's opinion, their daughter had earned the right to return to High Cliff, even if her bedtime had come and gone nearly twice over. Clay felt the same way. He also agreed with Zagan's assertion that Gabby was a powerful member of their coven: *remarkable,* as Zagan often described her.

Given the realities, granting and respecting Gabby's request to join them seemed logical and fair.

When she, Clay, and Gabby materialized in Zagan's master bedchamber, Zagan's ghost was drifting around the room. Wall sconces lit the space, casting restless shadows on the stone walls. A few bats darted, fluttered, and swooped around the massive chamber.

"If only I was able to sculpt a fire in the fireplace," Zagan said, "to warm the chill for Gabriella."

"Let me do it, King Z," Gabby said, sculpting roaring flames within the hearth. "There."

Their daughter walked near the raised bed and glanced upwards at the open skylight carved in the stone ceiling. "Wow! How do you get any rest? The stars are so pretty." Gabby's brows furrowed. "I'm sorry. I keep forgetting you're dead."

Clay interrupted the awkward moment. "Codicil?"

"This way." Zagan drifted through a 12-foot high mahogany door.

Ruby opened the door with her mind, leading her family into a formal sitting room that included Zagan's private collection of paintings and books. Flickering sconces lit the space. A velvet curtain, colored a deep shade of crimson, covered one wall.

"Was your staff expecting us?" she asked Zagan. "The lanterns and sconces are already lit."

"I often drift about in my beloved castle," he admitted. "I have asked my loyal staff not to treat me as a ghost." He pointed to the curtain. "Will you slide open the drape, Lady Spencer?"

Ruby glided the thick material to the left, along the curtain's track, exposing a wall of black granite. The granite included flecks of mica which sparkled like stars. Mounted on the wall were dozens of three-dimensional gold bats, flying in every direction. Different gemstones (like rubies, sapphires, citrines, and gray pearls) embellished each set of bat eyes.

The scene was reminiscent of Zagan's crown.

"Can you guess how to enter?" Zagan asked, looking pompous.

Without hesitation, Clay approached the wall, turning one of the bats. A floor-to-ceiling granite panel hissed, groaning as it moved backwards toward an inner chamber that was pitch black.

"How did you know?" Ruby asked.

"That bat was the only one with emerald eyes," Clay said, nodding toward Zagan. "Matching Mister Ego's himself."

"Perhaps you are wiser than you look," Zagan said, smirking.

They funneled into the secret chamber.

Ruby sculpted flames onto the wicks of mounted sconces, lighting the private space with a yellow glow.

A steel wall to her left had four built-in safes, each with its own dial. Directly ahead was the largest wall, formed from polished gray stone. It contained a grid of at least 100 horizontal rectangles, outlined by carved indentations, as if the wall was comprised of drawers. Only, there were no handles or knobs.

"Is the codicil in one of those safes?" Ruby asked, pointing at the steel wall.

Zagan shook his head. "Those safes previously secured artifacts known to my henchman, such as a vial of my blood, as well as the berries recovered from Great Island—the ones you dropped during our...*disagreement.* The safes were clearly the wrong choice for security, since in their betrayals, both Draven and Titus took full advantage of their easy access."

"Could we reminisce about who was *more* wrong another time?" Clay asked. "The codicil. Please?"

Zagan pointed to one specific rectangle. "A hook in the back of each drawer keeps it locked in place. Release this one's hook in your mind and the drawer will spring open. Sculpting is the only way to unlock these compartments. Indeed, until you and Gabriella inherited this rare competency, I was the only immortal who could sculpt."

Concentrating, Ruby caused the drawer to pop open.

Inside was a single sheet of thick parchment, marked with several paragraphs of inked calligraphy. Her heart accelerated. To think, Pythia had drafted the document nearly three mega-annum ago.

Ruby remembered feeling the same awe after reading The Book of Immortality in Zagan's library.

"Use my cabinet chamber to sit and examine the codicil," Zagan offered. "Perhaps I will take Gabriella to my library, to inspect that its upkeep meets with my standards."

"Is that all right, Mom? May I go?"

Ruby nodded and cognitively added, *Whisper if you need us.*

Zagan drifted from the hidden chamber and Gabby followed, until they were out of sight.

In the secret room, she and Clay sat in leather chairs and silently read the document to themselves. While glancing over the codicil for a second time, she pointed to a passage:

When the sky rains crystals,
the chosen King of the Animals
shall rise from the ground,
denying death's grip.
With eyes like the sun
and a cloak as dark as night,
the King, wearing an ivory crown,
shall speak the languages of all.

"This *is* you," Ruby said. "In Siberia."

"Only I wasn't wearing an ivory crown."

"With scriptures, you have to look deeper than the words themselves. For instance, when you shift to wolf form, the white blaze on your head is a natural crown. And when the words say *rise from the ground,* not only could they refer to physically getting up, but they could also point to your name, which means earth."

"Let's say I am the intended king," he said, pointing to the next paragraph. "Read this…"

Serving as a liaison
between the uprights and animals,
the crowned King
shall turn the masses away from rebellion,
restoring peace and balance
to the universe.

"These words don't give us any clues as to *how* I'm supposed to restore peace and balance," he said, wearing creases on his forehead.

"The Book of Immortality was just as vague when it came to my role as the *instrument of protection—for all.* It was only after I was on the right path, that the details began to reveal themselves. You have to trust that the same will happen for you."

"So how do we interpret what's next?"

"Focus on this passage." She read it aloud while directing his eyes with her finger.

THE TURNING POINT

A coronation shall be held
in a valley of shadows,
to be witnessed by animals great and small.
Before a crown of braided branches is bestowed upon its King,
the throne will be challenged.
And when the King defeats the last usurper,
the reign of harmony will begin,
enduring until the end of time.

"The coronation needs to occur in the Valley of Shade, the largest valley in The Shadowlands," Ruby explained. "For witnesses, you'll need to cognitively summon the animals on Athanasia. See? There are some clues in the codicil."

She felt veins throb with anxiety underneath her skin. "Doesn't sound like the ceremony will go off without a hitch. Instead, looks like you'll face a challenger. Maybe even more than one."

"Who do you think will challenge me?"

"Wish I knew the answer, but I don't. I can read the lifeline stones of humans and vampires, and even human-animal hybrids like Irene Unger, but *not* individuals who are one-hundred percent animal." She gazed into his eyes. "Which also means that when you're in wolf form, I can't see any etchings on your stone. It's completely blank."

Pointing to the last line of the codicil, she added, "And this is probably the most ominous line in the entire codicil: *Blood from the King of the Animals will not save innocence by itself.*"

"Yeah, bleeding is hardly ever good," Clay agreed. "But not being able to save innocence? In whatever form it encompasses? That's far worse."

41

Sunday, July 21, 2041
Castle on High Cliff: Skotadi, Athanasia

GABBY FOLLOWED THE king down a spiraling stone staircase, lit by hanging lanterns.

Her school friends would never believe how she was spending her summer. First, New Zealand. Then, Siberia. Not to mention, the vampire planet Athanasia. If that wasn't enough to impress, she could add: hanging out with a royal ghost in his gargantuan castle.

If Gabby hadn't sworn to secrecy, show-and-tell for the upcoming school year might've been interesting. But her parents constantly reminded her of the rules. *With added gifts,* her Mom would say, *come added responsibilities.* Her Dad usually piped in, *and never forget, the world's needs are more important than our individual wants.*

She was 100-percent certain curiosities didn't count as "wants."

"Just wondering," she said, interrupting the sound of her scuffing soles on the stone steps, "where's your actual body being kept?"

His ghost stopped and turned. "The dungeon. My entombment is below this very castle."

"You mean, it's something we could *see?*"

The king protested at first. After all, going to the dungeon wasn't exactly what he and her parents had agreed on. In the end, he caved. Which was what she had hoped since she'd already spent time in his library. Seeing his tomb and body? That would be super cool.

Walking down multiple staircases which never seemed to end, she began to feel out of breath.

The king finally stopped drifting after he arrived at a humongous wooden door—one reinforced with thick iron bars and decorated with a gargoyle's head, positioned right smack in the middle.

Gabby looked around, feeling goosebumps rise on her skin. Maybe her suggestion to see the king's coffin wasn't such a great idea.

"Where is everyone?" she asked.

"My staff rests during these hours," he answered. "Perhaps we should not proceed, as the dampness will chill you. As well, a few rodents may be scurrying about. I can hardly protect you, for I have found that rats are not at all intimidated by ghosts."

"No worries, King Z." Her courage was returning. "My cloak will keep me warm. And I'm a sculptor, remember?"

She sculpted a torch in her right hand and caused the heavy door to swing open. An odor of pungent dirt, like from a wet compost pile, assaulted her nostrils. Yuck.

The stone steps leading down to the dungeon were moist and slick. She had to concentrate on her footing. Beyond the stairway, she noticed a trembling black carpet, vibrating with energy. The chorus of squeaks and scratching nails on the floor gave her the creeps.

"A *few* rodents?" She had never seen so many. And they stunk.

"Numbers are relative, are they not? For this is the underground chamber of an unparalleled fortress." Across from the staircase, he pointed to a flameless torch mounted on the wall. "I recommend you ignite each cresset. After, the rats will flee back into the shadows."

Gabby did just that.

The dungeon glowed with yellow light, revealing high concrete archways which supported the vaulted ceiling and added a regal feel to the otherwise dreary surroundings. She followed King Zagan along the hardened dirt floor, walking down more long corridors.

At last, they stopped at an alcove shaped in a half-circle. Sixteen torches brightened the space. The base of the king's coffin, if she could call it that, rose about three-feet high. It was a solid pedestal of black marble or granite—she couldn't tell the difference. Someone had carved bats into the polished stone. Their eyes were emeralds that looked alive, shimmering with the light.

A glass top sealed the pedestal, reminding her of a lid for a butter dish, only giant sized. And lying on the base's flat surface was the body of the king, lying on his back, wearing a mint green tunic with gold buttons. The plaque on the base read:

Herein Rests

Zagan Glissendorf,
King of Skotadi.
His Goodness Has Been Set Free.
Vampire Creation – The Year 3,002,041

"Great resting place," Gabby said. "Did your staff build it?"

"Yes, under the direction of Solange."

"She does have a special touch." Gabby moved closer to the glass and raised her handheld torch to get a closer look at the king's corpse. "Your skin and spikey hair are so white. I mean, *really* white. Does anyone ever mention that? Or is it just me?"

"In truth, I am considering wearing a sign engraved on my forehead, reading: To all who may wonder, Skotadians are absent melanin. We are, indeed, white."

"Mom says tattoos are hard to get off, if you change your mind."

In the coffin, King Zagan's hands rested over his chest.

"What are you holding?" Gabby asked, studying the body.

"A vial of my blood. Blood that I had previously kept secured within my secret chamber, locked in a wall safe. My former henchman, Draven—once trusted like a son, had extracted my blood as a safeguard, in the event that I needed to be restored."

"Can you be restored, King Z?"

"Removal of one's head or heart prevents restoration."

"At least your head wasn't removed," Gabby said, raising her upper lip as she pictured the gross image.

"To defile such beauty would have surely constituted a crime."

"Why do you look very…*un*-dead, like you're just sleeping?"

"I was human upon my death," he explained. "Therefore, Solange had my body embalmed. My scientists drained what blood remained, replacing it with arterial preservatives—chemicals that prevent my vessels and body from decaying. My organs and skin were similarly preserved."

"Didn't the liquid leak?" she asked. "You know, from the hole where your heart was plucked out?"

"Your mother is a gifted sculptor. As the expression goes, she tied up the loose ends once she became a vampire again."

"Someday I hope to learn what you know. You're very smart."

"I am not wise regarding all matters, Gabriella."

"Like what?" she asked. "Name one thing besides not knowing how to speak with the animals."

"Consider the area of forgiveness," King Zagan said. "Forgiveness is a mystery to me. Specifically, how one can earn it from another. You see, I long to be forgiven by Solange, as I have wronged her on many fronts. For instance, I killed her mate, though I did not know that she was alive, nor that she had coupled with Titus. I regret my actions and wish I could turn back time."

"My parents always tell me to talk it out. Have you spoken with Princess Solange? Told her how your heart feels?"

His ghost shook its head.

"Then why not start there?" she asked. "Talk to her."

Gabby walked behind the coffin, between it and the curved wall, where a small, stemmed pedestal stood. She hadn't noticed it before. Like the coffin, a glass lid sealed the pedestal. Under the glass was a metal cube, the size of a music box.

"What's in there?" she asked.

"The organ of which you speak. My heart."

"Do you think it's shriveled up like a dried prune?"

"I do not believe so," Zagan answered. "My heart is being preserved in vampire blood. But enough discussion about my corpse. We must return to my living chambers or your parents may decide to remove my head after all."

"Weird, right?"

"Head removal? Is that the *weirdness* to which you refer?"

"No! That your heart wasn't destroyed. That it was saved."

She thought of Mai. If only the birds hadn't taken poor Mai's.

42

Monday, July 22, 2041
Kaliméra Castle to the Valley of Shade: Athanasia

THE SPENCER FAMILY epitomized a whirlwind which had *not* reached full velocity. Much more was unfolding at record speed. Which meant, if Ruby and her husband didn't carve out a brief moment to decompress, they might spin out of control.

Less than a half hour ago, Ruby had traveled Clay and Gabby from Castle on High Cliff to Kaliméra, after reading the codicil about The Turning Point. Gabby continued to insist she wasn't tired, but the dark circles under her eyes had only deepened.

Walking her daughter upstairs to a guest bedroom, Ruby tucked her in, kissing her forehead and encouraging her to sleep well.

She was about to close the door.

"Mom?"

Turning, she looked at her daughter. Despite the blackout curtains used to block Lampsi's perpetual sunlight, her acute vision enabled her to see every detail of Gabby's face.

"You're worried?" Ruby asked.

"You said Dad's coronation is tomorrow. Why? Why can't it be in a couple of weeks or something?"

"The animals need a leader. If they know someone is already advocating for them—negotiating on their behalf, the rebellion will stop. Lives will be saved."

"I heard you and Dad talking. At his coronation, an animal is going to challenge him for the crown. Dad will have to fight to the *death*. How is Dad supposed to know how to fight as a wolf? He's been human all his life. Can't we postpone the ceremony? Maybe Boris could teach him how to fight."

As if the wolf had heard his name, he trotted to the door, perhaps seeking an invitation to join Gabby on the bed.

"Hi, boy!" her daughter said. "Want to sleep with me?"

"You don't need any distractions, Gabby. You need your rest, especially with everything that's coming up in the next few days."

The wolf whined while looking up at Ruby.

"Sorry, Boris. Not tonight." She pointed to the stairway. "Go back down, please."

Boris lowered his head and walked toward the stairs.

"All I can say about your concerns," Ruby continued, "is that we have to have faith. As long as Dad is ready to be king and tries his hardest, we have to believe that what is meant to be, will be."

"Aren't you scared?"

"Of course. But sometimes we need to risk our own lives to save others. You've done that before."

"I know. At the wedding."

"Exactly," Ruby said. "Maybe this will help ease your mind. I'm heading back to the sunroom to talk with Dad. I'll make sure he wants to move forward with the coronation tomorrow. Or, maybe he'll tell me he needs more time. You know Dad. He's not going to do anything unless he's ready. Does that help?"

"I guess so."

"Let your mind rest with happy thoughts. Okay?" Her daughter nodded. "We've got this, sweetie. I promise. And never forget how much Dad and I love you."

"I love you, too."

Ruby closed the door and walked downstairs.

Clay, Zagan's ghost, Solange, Liora, and Draven huddled in the sunroom discussing the coronation. Boris rested by Draven's feet.

"Have a minute, Clay?" she asked, standing in the doorway.

"Sure." Leaving the group, he followed her to the outdoor breezeway. They sat on Liora's cushiony lounge chairs. Like always, the breeze carried the sweetness of blooming flowers.

"How are plans for the coronation coming along?" she asked.

"I've summoned the animals on Athanasia, so that's set," Clay answered. "In the sunroom, we were discussing options should all-hell break loose from attackers. And you're heading to the venue to do your special magic in preparation for the ceremony. Anything I'm leaving out or forgetting?"

"How about how you're feeling? I mean, you must be struggling to assimilate all the changes you've been through. Maybe I can help."

Clay reached across the gap between the two lounge chairs. They clasped hands.

"Part of me isn't sure I'm up for the job of being king," he admitted. "The rest of me is relieved."

"Can you explain? So I understand?"

"All my life," he started, "I've been more of a sidekick—the wind lifting someone *else's* wings. I'm not complaining. It's my natural tendency. The only problem has been how other people view me. How they project what they *expect* me to be.

"Even in 2041," he continued, "men who don't mind being in the background are considered weak, less manly."

"I don't see you like that at all," Ruby said. "It takes confidence to be the person you were born to be. The man you *are* versus how others think you should be. I admire that about you."

He delivered her favorite crooked smile. "It's one of the many reasons I love you so much. You get me. Accept me for who I am."

"Is that why you're worried that you're not ready to be king? Because you're not used to taking the lead?"

"There's no blending into the crowd when you're king. No dodging the spotlight. It's a role change that I'm not experienced in."

"But you adapt quickly to change, Clay. Look at how you handled my transformation from human to vampire! I'm confident you'll adjust to the spotlight. More importantly, you'll show tremendous compassion for those whom you serve."

"I'm going to try. That's for sure."

"Tell me why you're relieved. I want to know everything."

He let go of her hand and ran his fingers through his hair, from front to back. "This is the weird part. See...when I'm in human form, I worry about not being ready for the job." He locked eyes with her. "When I'm a wolf? I have no fear. I'm all-in and I've never felt that level of confidence before. I feel like I'm whole now. Like I'm complete and can make a significant difference."

"Are you worried about having to fight a challenger?" she asked. "When you've never fought as an animal before?"

He tilted his head and raised his eyebrows, as if the notion had never entered his mind.

"Gabby and I thought maybe we were rushing things," she added." Maybe you need practice defending yourself in wolf form."

"Like I said…when I'm a wolf, instincts take over. I'm ready."

He stood from his chair and she followed suit.

"Then I'm off to the venue," she said. "You're going to like how I spruce up the stage for the ceremony. I have ideas…"

Placing his hands around her waist, he pulled her close. "No doubt I'll love them. And thanks for asking how I was feeling."

He lowered his head until his lips brushed against hers. He kissed her deeply. Butterflies took flight in her stomach, only quieting when their mouths separated.

Stepping back from their embrace, she reached up and touched his cheek. "See you when I return."

Ruby turned into dust.

A second later, she materialized on the empty stage in The Shadowlands' Valley of Shade and immediately began to sculpt.

When she opened her eyes, she stood under a pergola she had created on the platform. Eight evenly spaced wood columns supported the structure. One hundred lanterns hung overhead from the exposed rafters. The flickering lights swayed with the warm breeze, their handles squeaking against hanging hooks. Adding to the chorus, crickets sang from the grassy field.

Tomorrow, animals of every species on Athanasia would gather for Clay's coronation ceremony. At least they didn't have to worry about sweltering heat or rainy weather. Charcoal light always blanketed the Valley of Shade. And vegetation received its moisture from fog and dew (not rain), occurring during the hours of rest.

Standing on the stage in anticipation of the monumental event, she should've felt excited, especially knowing that Clay was ready.

Instead, pulsing veins rose beneath her skin and signaled just how unsettled she truly felt. She inhaled, hoping summer's vibrancy would soothe her. While she had been worrying about Clay's feelings, perhaps she had neglected her own.

The Valley of Shade was clearly an emotional trigger for recent events and insecurities.

Last time she had attended the venue, she was a bundle of raw nerves, an emotional wreck, wondering if she had made the right choice to involve Gabby in the wedding masquerade between Ruby and Zagan. Wondering if her daughter would be able to repair Ruby's hand using sculpting, while under enormous pressure to make her mother appear as if she was still a vampire.

Ruby was incapable of verbally describing the horrific feeling of helplessness once she had become human again, on a vampire planet where most citizens had become fearful puppets of a crazed and cursed king. The feelings still festered.

If Ruby, Solange, and Atea's plan to destroy Zagan had failed, protecting Gabby would have been impossible.

The awful unpredictability of placing friends at risk hadn't faded either. Feelings of sorrow and guilt still lingered. After all, Titus had sacrificed himself to keep Solange's identity a secret. And Zagan had nearly killed Atea and Jasmine during the faux wedding ceremony.

Ruby needed to remain focused on the eventual outcome. On the victory. Because accepting help from a gifted team of friends, those willing to join the fight against evil, had overwhelmingly *worked*.

Together, they had stopped human cullings. Restored Zagan's soul. Broke the curse affecting the realms.

Why did she doubt success *this* time?

She thought the "shared responsibility" of working within a team had permanently lightened the full weight of being The Tether. Returning to the Valley of Shade, however, proved she wasn't quite there. The burden still felt heavy. And conflicted.

When *she* was in control, she knew what to do, how to feel. And in every situation where she wasn't, her insecurities crept back. Would evil take over the universe? Would her family get hurt or killed?

How would she ever learn to fully trust that *others* could do what *she* was accustomed to doing…by herself?

Ruby had no choice but to try.

After all, Zagan's most significant affliction (before they had cast out his wickedness) was his inability to trust anyone but himself. In the end, he trusted no one and no one trusted him.

Zagan was trying to repair this flaw. She had to do the same.

Tomorrow's coronation would happen despite her worries.

Besides, Clay had assured her he was willing and able to be the King of the Animals. And he was amazing, the perfect negotiator for the animals. She had to trust that Clay would defeat his challengers. Trust that he would usher in a reign of harmony.

Sculpting a mahogany throne on the stage, she was pleased with the armless bench, large enough to fit his wolf form. The bench's legs slightly bowed like a wolf's, with feet shaped like massive paws. Tight braids of lamb's wool covered the seat cushion. And the back of the throne showcased carvings including fish of the sea, beasts of the land, and birds of the sky.

Smiling, she thought of her birth name: Ruby Pearl Airily. *By earth, by sea, and by air,* her mother would say, referring to Ruby as her little superhero. Seemed like everything in Ruby's life was coming full circle. Because now, Clay would be *her* superhero.

Next to the throne, Ruby sculpted an end table to display his crown, prior to having it placed on his head. Clay had asked her not to create a crown, as several birds had volunteered.

In addition to preparing the venue, she'd officiate the ceremony, for the benefit of the vampires in the audience.

As she examined the stage, she was satisfied with her handiwork. Understated, yet majestic.

About to return to Kaliméra to report on the status of the site, she scanned the premises one last time.

That's when she saw them.

Well beyond the right side of the stage were a pair of fiery eyes, glaring at her from within Gray Forest, near the edge of the woods.

She might have missed them.

Except, the eyes glowed like flames.

43

Monday, July 22, 2041
Kaliméra Castle: Lampsi, Athanasia

SOLANGE RELAXED ON a bench in the rose garden, enjoying the sun's warmth on her gray skin.

Droplets of water sprayed upwards from the pond's fountain, glistening in the air like diamonds. With pistils stretching beyond blooming petals, flowers remained vacant despite their open invitation. Perhaps the bees, butterflies, and hummingbirds had already started their pilgrimage to the Valley of Shade.

Or perhaps, they favored Filtiarn as their monarch and would keep their distance, for now.

Despite the threat of animal attacks by loyalists to the Lord of the Wolves, Solange felt safe, given she was a traveler. As for her friends, she was also without worry. From the castle's solarium, her queen had promised to whisper if she required assistance. Not a likely scenario since Ruby and Gabriella had fortified the dwelling. In addition, Liora, Draven, Clayton, and Zagan's ghost were together, continuing to discuss moves and countermoves, should tomorrow's coronation become a battlefield.

Upstairs in the castle, Gabriella was still asleep in the late morning hour, slumbering in one of the guest chambers, exhausted from her lack of sleep. And Ruby had left to visit the venue, preparing the stage for the crowning ceremony.

Solange wanted some fresh air.

She leaned her head against the bench's backrest. How pleasing it was to rid her body of the tight leathers necessary for the Siberian climate. She preferred wearing a linen cotehardie that breathed with the breeze. Her pewter hair was loose, resting down the length of her back, unencumbered.

"Pardon me," said a familiar voice. "May I intrude?"

Her heart jolted at the unexpected visitor.

"Of course, King Zagan." Unsure of what to say, she glanced at the bench's open space beside her. "Would you care to sit?"

"The reason baffles me, but I appear to be more comfortable upright. Rest assured, if I ever gain acquaintance with another ghost, surely this will be my first question."

"Truly?" She giggled. "As for me, my first question would be regarding the nature of their shortened life and specifically, the cause of their untimely death."

Her eyes widened, realizing the awkwardness of her words, *after* they had already departed from her mouth.

"Apologies," she added quickly. "I regret my insensitivity."

"Nonsense. You have every right. In fact, the purpose of my visit just so happens to involve a frank accounting of my life and death. A less than chivalrous topic, indeed. However, would you do me the honor and grant me audience?"

She nodded, wondering what direction his accounting might take.

"First," Zagan started, "I wish to thank you for my entombment at High Cliff. Truly a resting place befitting a king, albeit, tucked in the farthest alcove of my dungeon. Nevertheless, I acknowledge your generosity, as my own legacy lacked all…nobleness."

"Gratitude accepted," she said. "Over the course of our existence, we are tested. I do not wish to fail in the competency of kindness."

"This gives me great relief," Zagan said. "Your words hold hope that you might bestow additional mercies on me. As you are aware, our Creator has tested me more than most. Regrettably, I have also accelerated in failure." He reached to clasp his spiked hair, yet his hands only managed to disturb his ghostly image. "Your forgiveness is what I seek, yet I do not know where to begin in the asking of it."

"Wherever you start, honesty is the cornerstone of absolution."

"Perhaps I should reflect on my youth," he said. "At Creation, my gifts were unparalleled, far exceeding my peers."

Solange would have rolled her eyes at his arrogance, except his recollection was true.

"As such," he continued, "I was more than capable of manipulating solutions to all my infractions, great or small. I traveled, sculpted, glamoured, healed, or carbonized my way out of everything. Long before the curse, I feared no consequences."

"Until the day we traveled to Zealandia," she said.

"Not at first, for after I stole berries from The Tree of Awareness, nothing happened. Not until I consumed them, not until I became mortal and evil took residency inside my body. Inarguably, I grew terrified, as I was absent gifts, no longer able to right my wrong. I had never known such vulnerability. Such desperation.

"When I consumed the fig from The Tree of Immortality," he continued, "I had not understood that my restoration to eternal life would require a price. That evil would lock inside me. That I had initiated a curse. My only awareness was that my skin erupted into flames. My fear, into insanity. For the first time since Creation, panic overwhelmed me. I did not want my manipulations exposed to Liora.

"My irrational mind was absorbed with needing to travel, to stop the burning. To end our disagreement. Without thinking, I did not resist temptation; I allowed my hand to turn you to ashes. And even though you escaped by traveling—a gift I was not aware you possessed, we both know your destruction, at my hand, had been more probable than not. As well, I was never more pathetic and unworthy as I was in that moment. Can you? Will you forgive me?"

"I have thought of this tragedy countless times," she admitted. "Neither of us knew what consequences would unfold if we disobeyed Pythia's warning. Faith compelled me to trust her; faith has never been enough for you."

"Your words are not entirely accurate."

She tilted her head, curious about what he meant.

"At my death," he said, "your last words were...*accept your sentence and rejoice in the forgiveness that awaits.* Do you recall my response?"

"You said...*make it so, dearest Solange.*"

A tear raced down her cheek as she pictured thrusting her hand inside Zagan's chest and removing his beating heart.

"I had faith," he said. "I did not cower, or run, or manipulate. I believed in the promise of something greater than myself."

"If only you had learned this lesson sooner, before our travels to Zealandia." She pictured the times in her youth when he had held her close, when her heart had raced. "You were always so confident, adventurous. Filled with wonder and excitement. Such a clever wit. The most handsome in all of Athanasia." She stopped her daydreaming and glared at him. "But after that day in Zealandia, when I realized you chose to preserve your manipulations over my very existence, I vowed to forget you. And Titus helped make it so. His love for me could never be denied, for at *his* death, he chose to sacrifice himself to save *me.*"

"Indeed," Zagan said. "Titus was a virtuous vampire of the highest caliber." His ghost paced for a few moments, as if attempting to gain courage. "In my weakness, I was intensely jealous of him. He loved Draven enough to break one of the strictest laws forbidding anyone from bringing sustenance into the Prison of the Unruly. And he loved his mate, whom I did not know was you, enough to risk meeting her at The Cottage of Shadows. In truth, my heart was devastated that Titus and Draven did not love *me* in equal capacity. As revealed, they did not love me at all."

"Am I to feel sorry for you?"

"No reason for the two of us to harbor pity regarding my shortcomings," he said. "Instead, I hoped to receive your forgiveness—for my failures with integrity and a lack of faith. For attempting to carbonize you, and for destroying your mate."

"Forgiveness will not cause memories to disappear or realities to be altered," she said. "Forgiveness is simply my proclamation that I will no longer allow your past wrongdoings and transgressions to harm me in the future. It signifies that *I* have found peace."

"Can you forgive me? So my treachery will no longer afflict you?"

"I am open to the consideration, but my wounds still bleed."

"Quite reasonable," Zagan said. "One final inquiry, perhaps?"

She raised her eyebrows to invite the question.

"For what reason did you preserve my heart?" he asked.

"Destroying it seemed permanent. Likewise, I was not ready."

44

Monday, July 22, 2041
Valley of Shade: The Shadowlands, Athanasia

LYKOS REMAINED HIDDEN near the forest's edge, as the upright known as The Tether had performed her wicked wizardry on the stage. His observations sickened his stomach. She and the entire lot of self-proclaimed royalty were abominations to the laws of nature, touting their magical manipulations as if they were blessings bestowed from the heavens.

The day of reckoning for the uprights dawned on the near horizon. And the day they would bend knees and bow heads to *him* was only two full moons away, by his estimation.

Yesterday, one day after he and his wolf hunters had successfully eliminated the rogue herd of defectors from Skotadi, Lykos received another telepathic communiqué from the Lord of the Wolves. Filtiarn, acknowledging him as the fiercest and most cunning alpha in all of Athanasia, ordered him and his Night Stalkers to infiltrate the crowds at tomorrow's coronation charade. His mission: to challenge and destroy the sacrilegious man-wolf who was claiming his right to the throne as King of the Animals.

Lykos raised his upper lip and growled.

Drool dripped from his fangs. Fur stiffened on his withers.

The upright shifter was nothing more than a freakish hoax, an experiment derived to seize even more authority over his kind. An abomination to the laws of nature.

Not to mention, if the animals crowned The Tether's mate,

Lykos's aspirations to become Filtiarn's Hand of the King would be obliterated, for he would rather die than serve an upright.

Filtiarn had assured him that the position as Hand was his to lose.

All the alpha needed to do was defeat the shifter named Clayton in front of the crowds, before announcing to the gathering that Filtiarn had selected him to be her Hand, to be known henceforth as Lord Lykos of The Three Realms. Effective, immediately.

Most importantly (from Filtiarn's perspective, of course), Lykos would also announce that her coronation as King of the Animals would take place on Besto Polus, in one day's time.

Before his communiqué with Filtiarn ended, she delivered further instructions in the event that he did not prove victorious over Clayton, since the challenge would be to the death. Lykos was to order his Night Stalkers to attack and kill the usurper if Lykos did not survive the battle. Clayton Spencer was to die no matter the outcome.

This was the only instruction that gave the alpha pause.

If his Night Stalkers were to destroy Clayton anyway, why would Filtiarn risk injury or death to her chosen Hand? Why not command his hunters to kill the shifter outright?

The fact that Lykos had drank remnants of The Tether's blood while feasting on Montaro meant the bewitched vampire could not carbonize him during the fight. However, the ingested second-hand blood would not prevent injury or death.

Lykos shook his head to clear it. Now was *not* the time to doubt Filtiarn. Or, let confusion distract him.

He would prove himself first.

With 24 hours until the ceremony, he and his hunters would rest in the forest adjacent to the valley. They would replenish their energy.

Accalia and his pups, accompanied by Mahli, were already journeying to the venue. Surely, he would not have his mate and next generation of hunters miss his fearless and noble rise to power.

The day of reckoning would begin with his victory.

45

Tuesday, July 23, 2041
Valley of Shade: The Shadowlands, Athanasia

RUBY SCANNED THE crowd with awe. Animals of every species on the planet stood side-by-side in the Valley of Shade, measuring two football fields wide, and six long. A variety of birds and bats flew overhead, silhouettes against the dim sky. To the right of the grassy basin were the dense pines of Gray Forest. To the stage's left, in the distance, were rolling hills.

Excitement had finally pushed her worry aside.

Clay stood under the stage's pergola, illuminated by the hanging lanterns. Turning, he locked eyes with her. Her husband was beaming. His blue eyes shimmered with energy. And he offered his crooked smile, her favorite—the one he reserved for her.

When Ruby had returned to Kaliméra yesterday, after preparing the venue, Clay reinforced his readiness to become the negotiator for the animals. His career as a community ecologist had deepened his scope of understanding between different life forms and their relationships and interactions. Hetero-specific species *could* adapt behaviorally to achieve mutualism, where all species contributed and benefitted from each other's co-existence.

Her husband believed in this future with every fiber of his being.

Moreover, Clay's long-time position on the SWC guaranteed that he would have an audience in high governmental positions, filled by politicians who could nurture this future, even if the President had become a personal adversary.

Ruby harbored no reservations in Clay's ability to lead. And now, he even looked the part.

For the occasion, she had asked Zagan to suggest what her husband should wear, since the ceremony would start while he was in human form. She was glad she had followed Zagan's fashion advice.

Standing on stage, Clay was stunningly regal in his garnet velvet tunic, trimmed with gold piping.

A flock of herons had delivered the crown made from woven twigs of white birch, with a few leaves left intact. They deposited the wreath on the end table beside the throne.

During the coronation, cardinals had asked to perch on the headpiece as Ruby placed it on Clay's head.

Gabby squeezed Ruby's hand. "Dad looks so handsome."

Ruby smiled, thinking her daughter must have read her thoughts.

"Are we ready?" Clay asked.

She glanced to her left. Draven and Liora nodded, each wearing a crown. They looked equally majestic in gold: the king in his ceremonial armor and the queen in her shimmering metallic gown. Curiously, Boris was not beside them, but the ceremony didn't require the super wolf anyway.

To her right, Solange, outfitted in a full-length silver dress, dipped her head. Zagan's ghost, wearing his formal white tunic, did the same.

An ensemble of vampire trumpeters raised their instruments.

Wearing a velvet gown matching her husband's tunic, Ruby approached the stage's edge and raised her arms overhead. The animals hushed. As she returned to her position beside her husband, the trumpets sounded.

In a swirl of black dust, Clay shifted into wolf form. His elegant clothing tore away from his massive body, the material falling in shreds by his paws.

Shifters had only existed in mythology and legend. Since Clay was the first in flesh and blood, the animals had clearly never witnessed such a spectacle. Pin-drop silence followed their gasps. If any in the crowd had harbored doubts about her husband's destiny as their leader, his physical transformation seemed to serve as enlightenment: their king stood before them.

Stillness was momentary.

About 120 yards in front of the stage, in the center of the crowd, panicked animals began to bump into one another, squealing and grunting. They pushed each other to the left or right, depending on where they'd been standing, as if a seam on the ground was tearing open. Like a wave, the rip raced forward until a grassy lane had formed, leading straight to the stage.

The codicil's prophesies had wasted no time.

A black wolf, large and lean, entered the pathway. Compared to Clay, this wolf's breadth was narrower. His height, shorter. But his eyes warned that looks could be deceiving. His eyes flickered like a roaring fire. She instantly recognized them from the day before.

The male wolf was Clay's challenger, no doubt. And her husband would have to defeat him, to the death, to claim the throne.

Her heart accelerated and she pulled Gabby closer.

Worry flooded back, drowning Ruby's excitement. It didn't help that she was blind to reading the future when it came to animals.

Which might account for her complete and utter surprise.

As the black wolf approached the stage and Clay prepared to leap onto the grass to defend his right to wear the crown, a smaller gray wolf entered the cleared lane, several yards from the platform, behind Clay's challenger.

Draven gasped, which could only mean that the wolf was Boris.

The challenger was too focused on Clay to have noticed Boris stalking him. The black wolf's first acknowledgement came swiftly, though, as Boris sunk his teeth into the wolf's hind leg, dropping the beast to the ground.

Had Clay directed Boris to attack his challenger from behind?

Analyzing the scene, her husband stopped in his tracks and remained on the stage.

From her position, Ruby couldn't see her husband's expression, not that she knew how a wolf would look if he was shocked or even pleased, in the event the wolf *had* followed his orders.

In front of the platform, the downed challenger rolled his body in a fluid countermove, recovering on all fours, though Boris had clearly injured his right hind leg. Snarling, the black wolf rushed at Boris, clamping his jowls on the gray wolf's neck. With his teeth locked on Boris's throat, the challenger forced Boris off balance. Yelping, the gray super wolf landed on his side, vulnerable.

Visibly a seasoned fighter, the black wolf pounced on Draven's Siberian wolf. He tore open Boris's abdomen. Blood gushed from the gaping wound. Innards threatened to spill onto the grass.

Draven removed his sword from its scabbard while Ruby sculpted her favorite 30-inch saber, the one with a double-edged blade.

Clay swung his massive head in their direction. His lips rose and quivered. The message was undeniable: they were to stand down.

Ruby had promised herself to work harder in the area of trust, accepting leadership from others. Accepting that there was more than one way to victory.

Clay deserved her trust.

The black wolf must have sensed his imminent victory. Like a gladiator, he raised his head as he sought encouragement from the crowd, before striking a final blow.

Unknown to the challenger, Boris was a bioengineered super wolf. A hybrid of wolf and vampire. Emory had intertwined his DNA with Ruby's. Her blood pulsed through his veins, so when the gray wolf began to heal from his injuries, Ruby *wasn't* at all surprised. Which was the opposite reaction of Clay's would-be challenger: the black wolf. He continued his efforts to stoke the crowd into making noises of celebration over Boris's impending death.

Animals closest to the fight receded, distancing themselves from the shock of what their eyes were witnessing.

The challenger probably thought the crowd feared *him*.

In truth, Boris's healing frightened the animals.

Recovered, Boris lunged upwards towards his opponent's neck— still stretched high in the air. The gray wolf tore at the challenger's throat, removing a large chunk of flesh. Stunned, the black wolf stepped back from Boris. Blood gushed from the challenger's punctured carotid artery.

Ruby heard the wolf wheeze as he inhaled his own blood. Likely, Boris had ruptured the challenger's windpipe.

The black wolf dropped to the ground; his tongue lolled from the side of his mouth. With glazed eyes, he gasped for a breath.

A breath that didn't come.

In the distance to Ruby's right, movement caught her attention. A silvery she-wolf with pups trotted into the forest, disappearing in the shadows.

When Ruby returned her gaze to where Boris had been, her heart jolted again. Twenty wolves had pushed beyond the first row of animals. As she tightened her grip on the leather hilt of her saber, Clay leapt from the stage and released a defensive growl.

Her husband glared at the new challengers. She suspected Clay was whispering inside their minds, explaining his intentions. Giving them a choice.

The massive congregation of animals stood still, wide-eyed.

Clay howled, louder and longer than she'd ever heard from a wolf.

The unexpected happened.

Each challenger bowed their head, low to the ground.

And the crowd followed suit.

46

Tuesday, July 23, 2041
Valley of Shade: The Shadowlands, Athanasia

CLAY HAD SHIFTED back to human form, wearing another sculpted velvet tunic, thanks to his wife.

Standing on the stage while holding hands with Ruby and his daughter, Clay watched the crowd of animals thin. Members of his domain were journeying back to their home realm in either Skotadi, The Shadowlands, or Lampsi.

After the ceremony's disruptions, his coronation had proceeded without a hitch. Clay was now King of the Animals which in his mind, was nothing more than a title. The hard work would be negotiating a peaceful mutualism between the animals and uprights.

His wife placed her hand on his far cheek and turned his face toward hers. "Congratulations, King. The animals are blessed to have you lead in their advocacy."

He was about to respond when their friends joined them.

Draven, with Boris trotting beside him, slapped Clay's back in a gesture of approval. "So tell me, brother," he said, sounding jovial, "did you *plan* to employ the service of my faithful wolf, since you are now his rightful king and he must bend his knee to your wishes?"

Clay locked eyes with the gray wolf who lowered his head in submission. "Actually, I didn't ask for his help. I was as surprised as you were when Boris attacked Lykos."

"Lykos?" Gabby asked.

"Yes, the challenger was named Lykos, alpha of Skotadi's Night

Stalkers, the fiercest wolfpack in all of Athanasia."

"And what of his Night Stalkers which emerged from the crowd?" Solange asked. "How did you convince them to abandon the rebellion and recognize you as their monarch?"

"I reminded them," Clay answered, "that if they genuinely sought peace and balance with the uprights, they needed a king who could speak both languages. With Filtiarn, there can only be war. So they agreed to give negotiations a try." He smiled, feeling satisfied with his first compromise. Winking, he added, "Anyway, I promised them we could always fight in the future."

Zagan cleared his throat. "May I speak with you privately, King?"

"Now?" Draven pressed. "Oh, all right. If we must."

"Not *you,*" Zagan said, rolling his green eyes.

Chuckling, Clay followed the ghost to a back corner on the stage.

Perhaps in Zagan's altered capacity, the ghost had forgotten that vampires could hear a feather land a mile away. Privacy was an illusion.

"What's on your mind, Zagan?"

"I wish to remind you that a king who never raises his sword in battle is considered weak among his soldiers, among his kind. Was it wise to allow an underling to fight on your behalf?"

"When it comes to weakness, look who's calling the kettle black."

"I do not understand your meaning."

"Consider this," Clay said. "A king who always raises his sword *outside* of battle is undeniably weak. This type of king, namely *you,* rules by instilling fear. Myself? I choose confidence over fear."

"Even so, concern compels me to remind you, Clayton: you are no longer a mayfly. Animals have their own laws and you must *do as they do* to win their hearts and minds."

"First of all, I was never a mayfly," Clay corrected. "But don't get me wrong, you make a valid point. In fact, I considered intervening when Boris advanced on my challenger."

"Why did you remain idle?" Zagan asked.

"The optics. If I had intervened, it might have looked as though Boris was being disobedient. That I already had members of my inner circle infringing on my authority, even before I had been crowned."

"Why do you think the wolf behaved so brazenly?"

"After his victory, Boris whispered to me that he was willing to risk his life to save mine. His actions were a demonstration of loyalty. He meant no disrespect."

"Did his words resonate truth?" Zagan asked.

"I have no reason to doubt him. Think about it. While we stood on the stage, Boris's guts nearly spilled onto the grass. Nevertheless, from here on out, I plan to fight my own battles. And we both know I haven't defeated *the last usurper*—a prerequisite to initiating a reign of harmony."

"Then you know, as I do, where our next destination must be."

Clay nodded. "Besto Polus. For an encounter with Filtiarn."

47

THE POTUS RODE down the private elevator, making the quarter mile descent to the bunker. His smartwatch beeped: 5:00 p.m. In case anyone approached him along the way, his senior advisor and personal physician had joined him, tasked with running interference.

After all, Will wasn't quite comfortable in his new skin.

The President's transformation from human to vampire was over before the 72 hours that Emory Bradshaw, creator of the SUC serum, had predicted. What could Will say? He was an overachiever. And good for him that the timing provided extra hours to acclimate to his voracious hunger, especially since he had scheduled the SWC meeting for tomorrow morning. What kind of message would he send if his Secret Service found the Council dead and drained while brainstorming on ways to prevent animal attacks? Oh, the irony.

Kenny and Tina had arranged for Will's visit to the bunker to satiate his thirst. He was eager for his first face-to-face with his death-row herd—three B-positive members of his retirement cash cow.

The thought of sinking his teeth into the inmates made him feel giddy. Not that he hadn't enjoyed the blood bag supply Tina had secured for him. But there was something deliciously appealing about the prospect of a beating heart pumping warm blood for *him*. And if he was 100-percent honest, the power of controlling whether someone lived or died *while* he was feasting on them, touching their skin, was intoxicating. Drool swam in his mouth.

The elevator jolted to a stop.

"Let's change your nickname," Will suggested to his advisor.

"Excuse me, Sir?"

"Cutthroat Kenny is too damn tempting, given my new appetite." Will winked, feeling more alive than when he actually had been.

"Excellent recommendation," his advisor said. The elevator door opened. "Cauterized Kenny will serve me better. Am I correct, Sir?"

"Money in the bank, Kenny."

They walked down the lit corridor toward the cellblock. After a few turns, they arrived at a thick, stainless steel door reinforced with chromium. An armed special ops soldier stood guard.

"I'll holler if I need you," Will said, bobbing his head to the side, as a directive for the soldier to move out of his way.

"Sir," the soldier responded. "I don't advise you to enter without armed backup. These shackled inmates are the worst of the worst."

Will closed his eyes and pictured a waterfall, hoping to elicit the roar of the water cascading over rocks. When Irene had entered her health-kick phase, before her cancer, she had urged him to adopt a go-to calming image that he could visualize whenever he felt stress. At that moment, stress enticed him to rip the soldier's head off.

For Christ's sake, Will was the President of the United States. The one man who could initiate a nuclear war with a few entered codes. And although the pretentious fuck standing before him had no idea that the POTUS was now a vampire, Will did not appreciate the implication that the most powerful leader on the planet was clueless about the risks of entering "said" cellblock.

The inmates were the only humans in danger.

Correction: inmates and a naive soldier.

"Move," Will ordered. "Hand over the keys and close the door behind me. If I need you or my associates, I'll call. Is that clear?"

"Crystal, Sir," the soldier answered, giving him the keys. "No disrespect intended." He punched a code into the mounted security panel, activating the door to electronically open.

Will walked into the cellblock area. The door shut behind him, clicking as it locked.

The inmates, each secured in individual cells, simultaneously rose from their bunks, yanking on the chains which attached to ankle shackles. With ultra-sensitive hearing, Will's eardrums reverberated from the clanking of metal on metal.

"Where the fuck *are* we?" the one in the middle cell asked, his eyes narrowing. "Wait. Aren't you…the goddamn…President?"

"Surprising, Hank," Will said. "You strangled…how many women? Eighteen hookers? Who would've guessed you had time to keep abreast of national politics?"

"I make time for all sorts of things. Let me show you."

"Sure. Okay."

Hank's eyes darted toward the inmate to his left, like Will's response surprised him. The POTUS also detected a spike in the inmate's heartrate. Hank was either excited or scared shitless.

The lock mechanism jiggled as Will worked the key to Hank's cell.

Once inside, the POTUS wasted no time embedding his teeth into the prisoner's neck. Given it was Will's first time, he had difficulty finding the carotid artery. To aid him, he tore away a mouthful of flesh with his teeth, spitting the meaty chunk on the concrete floor.

While Hank whimpered, Will resumed his quest to find the main pipeline. At last, blood gushed into Will's mouth like oil spewing from a tapped well.

After fantasizing about the experience for a full two hours prior, Will was disappointed. He could detect toxins from processed foods and preservatives. Chemicals soured the flavor. What the hell had the prison been feeding this guy?

Five deep swallows later, Will unlatched himself.

Hank raised his trembling hand to the gaping hole in his neck, trying to stop the blood flow. But his heart continued pumping through the breach. Blood gushed between Hank's fingers and cascaded onto his jumpsuit. *Huh.* A crimson waterfall of sorts.

Biting his own wrist, Will allowed his plum-colored blood to ooze.

"Drink some of mine and you'll heal," the POTUS said.

With tears and quivering lips, the bleeding inmate shook his head.

So. Very. Typical. When pathetic Hank became a victim himself, he was nothing more than a sniveling pussy.

If only the hookers could see Hank now.

"Die then," Will said, shrugging. "I'll replace you."

"Wait! I change my mind!" he cried, looking paler by the second.

Will raised his wrist to Hank's mouth. The inmate began suckling like a baby. With each gulp, Hank's wound healed. First, the arteries repaired themselves. And like a time-lapsed video in fast forward, new flesh and skin grew to fill and seal the wound.

"What the hell?" Hank said, touching his repaired neck.

"Kenny!" Will shouted, more like a roar to penetrate the other side of the steel door. "Tina!" he added, as he left the inmate's barred cubicle and began locking the cell door.

Both associates came running into the cellblock area.

"Are you all right, Sir?" his physician asked.

"Fine, Tina." Will wiped his bloodied lips with the heel of his hand. "But we need some dietary changes for these prisoners. And Kenny, you'll need to make that happen."

"Changes? Such as?"

Hank shifted his eyes between his two lowlife comrades.

"Only grass-fed organic beef and chicken," the POTUS said. "Organic fruits and vegetables, too. Wine's fine if it's organic."

Hank raised his eyebrows.

"Anything else, Sir?" Kenny asked.

Will didn't hesitate to speak freely since the prisoners would never see the light of day. Ever again.

"I should be ready to bleed, two vials worth, come Thursday. Start generating interest on the dark web. Establish a bidding minimum, too. Remember, my identity remains anonymous. No one is to know what I've become or connect me with my…I mean *our* business venture." Thoughts were racing through his mind at supersonic speed. "About Austin Tomb. His motorcycle accident needs to happen soon, while everyone is distracted with the animal crisis."

"Yes, Sir," Kenny said. "To recap: organic. Prepare *Healing Hemo* for launch. Austin dies. Everything's classified. Got it."

"One more thing about the menu for these cows," Will added. "I'm talking farm to table foods. No preservatives or GMOs."

His Sweet Tea had always detested the concept of GMOs.

Which made him wonder. Because like Irene in her final hours, Will had become a genetically modified organism.

48

GABBY WATCHED THE grownups as they huddled near the windows in the sunroom. They were talking about who should go to Besto Polus with her parents when they traveled to the planet to speak with the nasty she-wolf.

The one who thought *she* should be king.

Her Mom and Dad were not going to let Gabby go, so while she stared at the adults, her mind thought about something else.

Even though her hands shook, she gained courage to interrupt.

"I have a question," Gabby said loudly, waiting for heads to turn in her direction. When they did, she added, "Am I an important member of this team? This…coven?"

"Of course you are," her Mom answered first, separating herself from the group and walking toward the loveseat where Gabby sat, petting Boris who was lying across her lap. "Why would you ask?"

"When you meet with Filtiarn, safety is important, right? Well, I have a suggestion. Before I share it, I want to make sure you think I'm important. If you do, you might consider what I have to say."

Her Dad stared at her.

She could feel him trying to enter her mind.

"Have you constructed a shield to keep me out?" her Dad asked.

King Z's ghost chuckled. "A remarkable child, indeed."

Her Mom gave him a look that could kill, but that was okay, since her friend was already dead.

"Yes," Gabby answered her Dad, hoping she wouldn't get in trouble for raising a mental shield. "I don't want you to know what I'm going to suggest ahead of time. Because then you'd have extra time to think of reasons to say no."

"It's not safe for you to come with us, sweetie," her Mom said. "We have no idea if the animals on Besto Polus will try to attack us. Dad and I think you've been through enough."

"But I don't want to go."

Boris raised his head and gazed at her, whining.

"Then what is it, Gabriella?" Queen Liora asked.

"King Zagan was the second most powerful vampire," she started. "He could travel and sculpt and carbonize. And I think his gifts could help keep Mom and Dad safe on Besto Polus."

King Z looked like he understood where she was going.

Drifting toward her, he said, "My revival isn't possible, Gabriella, though the thought that you would hope for it touches me deeply. We spoke of this already. Regrettably, once someone removes a vampire's heart, the immortal cannot be resuscitated."

"Maybe," she said, shrugging. "Maybe not."

"You're asking that Zagan be brought back to…*life?*" her Mom said, not really as a question. More like the suggestion shocked her. "Impossible!"

"You didn't think so when it came to Mai, remember? You said if the birds hadn't taken her heart, you could've tried to heal her."

"I was upset," her Mom said. "But I would've tried. However, it was as much a moot point then, as it is now in Zagan's case. Without a heart, there is no trying."

"That's just it," Gabby said. "King Zagan's heart has been preserved. In vampire blood."

"*What?*" Her Mom glared at her friend. "Are you filling her head with lies? How dare you!"

"No, Mom," she said, knowing this was precisely the point in the conversation where she and the king were going to get in big trouble. "I saw it with my own eyes."

"Zagan's entombment is in the dungeon, below High Cliff," Princess Solange confirmed. "I gave oversight to its construction. And Gabriella is correct. I did not destroy Zagan's heart. I preserved it as your daughter has described."

"Hold on," her Dad said, like he was putting two and two together. "When we traveled to High Cliff a few nights ago, we agreed that you and Zagan could go to his *library* while Mom and I read the codicil." His lips were thin, which meant he was angry. "We never approved of you going to the dungeon."

"I apologize," King Z said.

"Keep quiet," her Mom snapped, veins bulging on her neck.

The exchange wasn't going like Gabby had hoped. The future was pointing to her getting grounded. For at least two weeks.

"It's not King Zagan's fault," she said. "I'm very persuasive."

"He was supposed to be the adult in the room," her Mom said, rolling her eyes. "But to your suggestion, let's say that Mai's heart *had* been intact. Her body had only been dead for several hours. Zagan's has been dead and decaying for twenty days."

Thanks to her Mom's sculpting that closed the king's torn arteries, Gabby explained, his embalmed body looked good as new.

"I don't even know how to attach a heart, Gabby," her Mom said.

"Heart surgeons *learn* how to do transplants. And you can whip through books in a minute, Mom. So why couldn't you learn?"

"This conversation makes me uncomfortable," King Draven said.

"Draven makes a valid point." Her Mom placed a hand on Gabby's shoulder. "Just because I might be able to *try* and revive Zagan, it doesn't mean I *should.*"

"I thought we were supposed to forgive people when they admitted their mistakes and changed their behavior," Gabby said. "That's what you and Dad taught me."

"This situation is more complicated." Her Mom gazed at King Z and for the first time in the conversation, she looked as though she cared for him. "At the wedding, when we considered letting Zagan live as a mortal, Liora read his lifeline stone. It indicated that if he was not destroyed, he would regain his immortality and begin culling humans again."

"Although your recollections are accurate, Ruby," the queen said, "do not forget: the pathway where Zagan *remained* alive as a human was never taken. Never fulfilled. And interference with a pathway will cause the granules of the future to shift like sand. What was being built will crumble and a new pathway will form."

"Liora!" King Draven said, as if he could not believe his ears.

"I must speak the truth," she answered him. "Even if the words are not pleasing to you."

Her Mom's eyes narrowed. Her forehead creased. "So you're saying since Zagan died, the warning suggested on his lifeline stone may no longer be accurate? Does that mean…since evil doesn't corrupt his soul anymore, Zagan might live again as the immortal Solange once knew *before* the curse?"

"The probability is strong," Queen Liora said. "If he can be resuscitated, we could certainly read his lifeline stone to affirm that his soul harbors no evil intent."

"In the name of Titus! This is nonsense," King Draven said.

"Could we vote?" Gabby asked, while the iron was still hot. "Except for me. I'll agree with what the adults decide."

"I shall refrain as well," King Z said. "Undeniably, I am biased."

"Perfect," her Dad said. "I'll start the voting with a no. A ghost is one thing. An immortal with powerful gifts is quite another. And I'm not able to forget when Zagan blew you off the cliff in New Zealand, Gabby. Someday I hope to, but not today. Or anytime soon."

Her Mom looked at her Dad as if she understood his position.

Gabby held her breath.

"Even though I'll never forget the horrors Zagan committed, I think he's changed," her Mom said. "Look at how he helped with my rescue. I'm going to vote yes, but with a caveat. Once alive, if his lifeline stone indicates he has any evil plans, I'll rip out his heart and destroy it myself. Still, I'm hopeful that won't be necessary. Because I want Zagan to have an opportunity for an honorable life. We all deserve a second chance. Of course, I have no clue whether I can even revive him."

"I agree with Ruby," Queen Liora said. "I vote that we try."

"No, no, and triple no," King Draven said, sounding grumpier.

Gabby knew the last vote would be Princess Solange's and she had already eavesdropped inside her mind.

"Okay," Gabby said. "That's two votes *yes* and two votes *no*. Which means you'll decide, Princess Solange."

The princess placed her hand on Draven's cheek. "I miss Titus every moment, as you do, brother. However, missing him and longing for him to be among us will not make my wishes come to pass."

"Titus would not approve of showing mercy to the one who destroyed him," King Draven said.

"You truly believe what your mouth has spoken?" Princess Solange asked. "For the Titus I knew was a lover, not a fighter. And in loving others, I believe he would have chosen forgiveness if one proved worthy of it."

"How can Zagan be worthy of a pardon?"

"My mate died at the hands of an immortal who was cursed with evil. We broke the curse and set Zagan's goodness free. With Zagan's death, the cost of his transgressions has already been paid in full."

"But can *you* forgive him, Solange?" King Draven asked. "Can you put aside your wounds in order that he might receive the greatest gift of all? His immortal life returned?"

King Z's ghost looked worried.

"I proclaim," the princess started, looking directly at King Zagan, "that I will no longer allow your past wrongdoings to harm me further. Be clear in your interpretation of my words: I shall never forget my wounds or put them aside, for the healing of them shall not return Titus back into my arms. Nor will their festering serve a meaningful purpose. Therefore..."

"Yes?" King Z asked, his voice shaking.

"Therefore, I extend forgiveness to you, Zagan. I vote...yes."

49

RUBY STOOD BESIDE the operating table, pulling on her sterile latex gloves. Wearing a facemask and visor and dressed in a surgical gown covered by a waterproof apron, she matched the other two scrub nurses in the OR.

Even without the extensive medical garb, no one would've recognized her, since the entire surgical team had been glamoured to disregard and forget every unusual aspect of the surgery. Which is why the humans in the room ignored Zagan's ghost, as well as Draven who stood watch by the door, dressed in black leathers, with his hand on the hilt of his sword.

As Gabby had suggested, Ruby read every medical journal available on heart transplants. Her DEPE Justine had also gained digital access to several clinical videos, providing Ruby with step-by-step demonstrations of the operation. And even though Ruby was fairly confident she could've handled the procedure on her own, why take the risk when she could compel renowned surgeons to reattach Zagan's heart for her?

Picking the right team was crucial, so she had traveled to Johns Hopkins several times over the two days prior and inserted herself, as a cognitive stowaway, into the minds of every staff member associated with the transplant center. By the time she finished assessing each candidate, she knew precisely who to handpick for the complex surgery.

Saturday was the perfect day for the procedure; the OR was like a ghost town on weekends. The scheduled 9:00 a.m. timeframe had also been intentional, since the surgery team would be fresh.

At dawn's equivalent, she had traveled to High Cliff's dungeon, bringing Draven with her. While they removed Zagan's body and heart from their entombments, Zagan's ghost had drifted back and forth as if nervously pacing.

Clay and the others had remained at Kaliméra with Gabby. Although Zagan wanted Solange to be present during the hospital procedure, those remaining at the castle needed Solange's gift of traveling in the event of an emergency.

Ruby and Draven, along with Zagan's ghost, had arrived in the OR about two hours ago. In addition to Zagan's corpse and heart, she had brought a chilled backpack stuffed with blood bags, enough for a complete transfusion. Every vampire in their coven had contributed, including Zagan, since Ruby had also added his vial of blood—the one his corpse had been clutching.

The supply didn't include venom.

Even though Zagan had died a mortal, his corpse was absent human blood. So if pure vampire blood replenished his veins and arteries, logically, the blood should restore his immortality. After all, vampirism was a blood-borne phenomenon. However, if her logic proved faulty, she could always bite him and release venom into his bloodstream. Either way, the outcome would be the same.

That is, if the surgeons could successfully reattach his heart.

Zagan's ghost drifted over the tiled floor of the OR, going from one wall to another. "What if the procedure does not work? Or if an unsuccessful attempt obstructs my ability to appear as a ghost?"

"You need to relax," Ruby said.

"Who are you talking to?" a scrub nurse asked.

"The ghost of the immortal we're going to revive."

"Oh." The man's eyes narrowed. "Sure. I guess that makes sense."

"No time for chit chatting, professionals," the transplant surgeon scolded. "Hook up the heart-lung machine. Once the heart is reattached, we'll need to start pumping out the embalming liquid, replacing it with blood."

"How long will the procedure take, Doctor?" Ruby asked.

"Barring complications," she said, "I'd estimate four hours."

A straight incision opened Zagan's sternum, exposing the damage created by Solange's hand. His pericardium was damaged. The cavity was empty where his heart had been.

"What the hell," the cardiologist said to the surgeon. "It's like this man's heart had been plucked from his chest and then the severed pulmonary veins and arteries were haphazardly cauterized. We can't suture the heart into place before we perform significant repairs. We're looking at an additional two hours, if not more."

"No time like the present, team," the transplant surgeon said, holding her hand out to a nurse. "Scalpel."

During the operation, the surgeon and cardiologist barked out their orders. After repairing the arterial and vein openings, they performed the preferred transplant method—the orthotropic procedure. Once Zagan's heart was reattached, they inserted a drainage tube into his chest, before stapling his sternum closed.

Seven hours after the surgery had begun, the heart-lung machine started to pump vampire blood into the arteries, forcing the embalming fluid out of his body through the drainage tube. When the clear liquid turned blood red, the nurses closed the drain. Zagan's circulatory system was intact once again.

With the ventilator on, Zagan's chest rose and fell.

But the heart monitor continued to display a flat line.

"The heart should start pumping by itself," the cardiologist said. "Something's wrong."

"Wrong?" Zagan's ghost asked. His hands tried to grab the spikes of his hair, but to no avail. "Perhaps I am meant to be punished for eternity for my heartless past."

Even though vampires could stop and restart their hearts at leisure, Ruby was pretty certain that a vampire, one who had been stone-cold dead, required a beating heart *first,* before any other heartrate options were available.

Ruby pulled off her facemask and visor. She needed to think and react faster than the doctors. Since electrical impulses caused the heart to beat, maybe all Zagan's heart needed was a zap of electricity, like a cardioversion. Concentrating, she gathered electricity from the overhead lights, drawing the energy out and sending it down to

Zagan's chest like a thin lightning bolt.

Sparks flew on impact.

The medical team jumped back.

With the jolt, Zagan's back lifted off the operating table before slamming down with a thud. Smoke rose from his chest.

The monitor began to spike. A pulse began to register.

Zagan's ghost had vanished.

Ruby looked at Draven and they shared a brief smile. The King of Swords and Shadows was softening toward his former boss.

In seconds, Zagan's heart was beating in a steady rhythm.

His green eyes opened.

Ruby froze. Was he really alive?

Sitting up, Zagan pulled the tubes from his throat and chest. He yanked the sticky electrode pads off his skin, tossing them.

Zagan reached for Ruby.

"Without haste, read my lifeline stone," he urged, sounding frantic. "Do you see honor? Or warnings of evil intent?"

Her eyes hid behind her eyelids as she visualized the readings of his immediate future.

"No warnings!" she said, opening her eyes and embracing him.

"Gratitude, Lady Spencer," he said. "I shall not disappoint you."

"Please," the transplant surgeon said. "The patient has undergone major surgery and needs rest. Plus, we must limit his movement, or his staples will fail."

Zagan gazed at his chest. His blood was working its magic. The staples popped out, one by one. The incision healed and became undetectable, as if the procedure had never happened.

The surgical team gasped at the spectacle.

"I am vampire," he said, smiling.

"We got that picture loud and clear." Ruby laughed. "Are you ready to travel back to Kaliméra, *vampire?*"

"Indeed. For I would very much like to hold Solange in my arms."

50

RUBY STARED AT the embers in the dwindling campfire while sitting beside her husband. As midnight approached, the moon was prominent among a celestial ceiling of stars. Blowing across the grassy glade, a steady warm breeze carried the sweetness of late blooming honeysuckle shrubs.

With a rising and setting sun, as well as the flora and fauna, Besto Polus reminded Ruby of Earth, only without humans.

She, Clay, Zagan, and Draven and his wolf had arrived on the planet at dusk. The grass was still wet from departing thunderstorms. She had sculpted a cabin-style tent, stocking it with cots and supplies.

While the site was readied, Clay had shifted into wolf form and telepathically demanded a meeting with Filtiarn the next morning. Regardless of the she-wolf's beliefs and grievances, Filtiarn could not refuse an order from the King of the Animals.

Sitting by the fire, the four of them passed around a bottle of Macallan from High Cliff's reserves. Zagan had insisted that he bring the aged single-malt scotch whiskey along on their mission, since his restored immortality required additional celebrating.

Draven took another swig of whiskey and gazed at Zagan. "At the hospital, when you rose from the table, pulling the tubes from your throat and body, did you not worry the hearts of the surgeons might fail? Mere moments after yours had restarted?"

"Indeed, I did." Zagan chuckled, the embers glowing in his eyes.

"And when the staples sprang from my skin in a most dramatic fashion, I feared their eyes might leap from their sockets, only to fall and bounce on the tiled floor!"

"Look at you two," Ruby said. "You're laughing together. You may become friends yet."

"*Ahh,* The Tether's optimism persists." Draven took another swig and passed the bottle to Clay. "Trust is a fickle conviction, is it not? Difficult to gain and easy to lose."

Clay raised the bottle. "To building trust." He took a long sip. "Now let's get some rest. Tomorrow promises to be challenging."

"My sword has been unsullied for too long," Draven said.

"*Ahh,* the warrior's thirst for blood abounds," Ruby said, rolling her eyes. "Seriously, though. Negotiations first, remember?"

Draven frowned. "Vampires may jest, but we do not forget."

"Perfect," Ruby said, standing. She extinguished the fire with her mind. "And since vampires also rest, I'll keep watch."

"No need," Clay said. "I'll guard our campsite in wolf form—to monitor the thoughts of any animals who might approach." Boris rose and sauntered over to her husband, rubbing against Clay's leg while keeping his head low, displaying submissiveness. "And perhaps your wolf, Draven, can keep me company on this beautiful night."

The temperature had dropped into the lower 60s, with moderate humidity. In moonlit darkness, the stars seemed closer, like Ruby could reach up and touch them.

Clay and Boris remained outside while she, Zagan, and Draven walked into the tall and roomy tent for the night. They each had a separate cot, topped with a plush sleeping bag to cushion the stiffness of the portable bed's canvas.

Ruby lowered herself onto the cot, lying down on her back. Wearing shorts and a T-shirt, she appreciated the silky softness of the sleeping bag against her arms and legs. The last couple of days had been taxing and she looked forward to cognitively drifting into the black void of her nighttime retreat.

As rest embraced her, she heard an elongated creak in the cot beside her, as if weight had pushed down on the canvas, causing the bed's joints to groan and squeak. She opened her eyes and saw Clay, in human form, lying on his side, facing her.

"I thought you were going to keep guard," she whispered.

"Boris offered to be on the lookout by himself, so I agreed," he said. "Truth is, I could use some good shuteye. Exhausting week."

Ruby squeezed his arm. "I love you more than life itself, King."

"You're my one and only." He smiled. "I'll love you for eternity."

God, how she adored him.

Her bond with Clay helped ease her worries about tomorrow's uncertainties. Whatever they'd face with Filtiarn and her pack of protectors, Ruby would be by her husband's side.

Four hours lapsed as she rested.

A soft shuffling interrupted the quiet.

She opened her eyes and slowly tilted her head toward the sound.

Zagan. Dressed in black leathers and his typical hooded cloak, Zagan was leaving the tent. She was beyond curious. He hadn't mentioned to anyone that he had plans to go somewhere, by himself, prior to Clay's meeting with Filtiarn.

Sculpting herself into a sparrow, she flapped her way outdoors. Perching on the tent's roof, she could see the expanse of the glade.

In the charcoal light of pre-dawn, Zagan walked down the field toward the woods, disturbing a blanket of low-lying fog. His figure grew smaller with distance. Before the edge of the tree line, he sculpted into a bat and took flight, flitting away.

Feelings of old flooded her thoughts.

Feelings that made her feel guilty and concerned at the same time.

Could the immortal who had killed and betrayed so many, truly be rid of his evil habits? Habits he had nurtured for nearly three mega-annum? Because in the past, Zagan had done *what* he wanted, *when* he wanted, having no regard for others. And leaving the tent without telling anyone *why* certainly seemed to resemble a familiar selfish past.

She hated questioning Zagan's authenticity. She loved him as she would love a troubled brother, wanting desperately for him to rise above his former self, to lead a good life of dignity. Perhaps, even, to couple with Solange and give their love another try.

As Draven had said: trust was difficult to gain and easy to lose.

Still in sparrow form, Ruby flew off the roof and circled around to re-enter the tent. And that's when she noticed.

Boris wasn't around, wasn't keeping guard.

51

Monday, July 29, 2041
The Glade: Besto Polus

BORIS HAD BEEN sitting on his haunches, keeping watch outside the tent, when his bladder had grown full. Come to think of it, he had never witnessed vampires relieving themselves. Interesting. However, that was not Boris's reality as a wolf. He had to urinate. Soon.

He trotted down the glade, toward the tree line. Not that he was shy. More like bored. He enjoyed working the stiffness out of his legs and *doing* something. Besides, he wouldn't stray far. Neglecting his duties wouldn't be wise.

As he headed for the woods, he marveled at his luck.

First off, instead of living out his life in hell frozen over (namely, Siberia), a powerful coven had accepted him. An inseparable pack that included the King of the Animals and his personal favorite: the King of Swords and Shadows. Add to those notables, The Tether, King of Skotadi, Queen of Light, and Princess Solange. Royalty was the norm. Not to mention, Gabby was intriguingly unique, in addition to giving great tickles.

Yes, Boris was part of an extraordinary coven where he was growing in favor. His mother would be proud.

Most remarkable, though, was that Boris could heal himself if injured, as long as he didn't die before his body repaired itself. And as long as he retained all his vital organs.

Hard to believe that some of the bioengineered super wolves at the Polar Station had whined like pups that they were freaks of nature. Abominations. Not knowing who or what they were. *Really?* A desire to curse gripped him, but since Clay (in wolf form) could monitor his thoughts, Boris decided to keep his internal opinions profanity-free. So to his Siberian pack of super wolves, he could only respond: They. Could. *Heal.*

Near the tree line, Boris spotted a plump rabbit. Suddenly, he felt overwhelming hunger and thirst. Peeing could wait.

Boris burst into a gallop and chased the hare who darted right and then left, constantly zig-zagging. His focus was singular, blanking out his surroundings. The hunt mesmerized him, and he experienced an abandon of thought.

Finally, when the rabbit dove into its hole, Boris snapped out of his hunting trance. He really couldn't recall how far or how long he had traveled within the woods.

His memory void had encompassed enough time that now, the first hint of dawn was dimming the stars on the animal planet.

Lifting his leg, he urinated on a tree and felt instant relief.

From the corner of his eye, he spotted a red fox. The woods were alive with temptations! And although he regretted losing the rabbit, a fox would be just as tasty.

With even more hunger egging him on, Boris's muscles trembled with excitement. He leapt into motion, expending his energy in an effort to capture his new quarry.

Once again, time had lapsed during the hunt, without him being cognizant of its passing. Because when Boris refocused on his surroundings, he realized he had lost track of where he was and how he had gotten there. He scanned the woods. The fox was gone.

Above, the sky's canvas included strokes of pink and orange.

Boris had to return to his post before his alpha noticed he was absent. Turning toward the glade, his heartrate spiked from shock.

Two mountain lions stood before him.

"Going somewhere?" the smaller female asked.

"Actually, I'm returning to my campsite," Boris answered.

"Without an introduction? How *ruuude,*" the larger female purred.

"Come now, Khuram." The smaller one sniffed the air. "We know who this is. His smell gives him away."

"Quite right, Arslan," Khuram said. "He is Boris of Siberia."

"Smell?" Boris asked. Had he rolled in something?

"Loyalists to Filtiarn," Arslan explained, "have been schooled on how to detect those who carry The Tether's blood." The lioness curled her mouth in what looked like a smile. "And with your opportune visit to our planet, this is the first time the animals on Besto Polus may...*acquire* the inherent blood-borne protections."

Boris released a pheromone. One that signaled fear.

He understood his precarious predicament. Not his strength nor his speed could save him. The lionesses would tear him to pieces. Physically, they would overpower him. They'd probably remove his organs before his body could sufficiently heal. No doubt they would gorge on his blood to gain the protective shield of self-preservation and there wasn't a thing Boris could do about it.

Unless, he outsmarted them. And Boris was extremely cunning.

"Yaaasss," Khuram hissed, stiffening her claws and scraping her right paw on the ground, leaving deep trenches in the dirt. "And who wouldn't want to be protected *and* gain healing powers during these tempestuous times?"

Under his fur, Boris felt the prickle of panic.

Somehow these mountain lions knew that if they consumed enough of his blood, they might be able to heal themselves while his blood concentrated in their systems. Which would make the King of the Animals vulnerable during his upcoming meeting with Filtiarn. Because two lionesses who could heal and avoid being carbonized were more than dangerous. They were lethal.

"What if I refuse to become your bloody cocktail?" Boris asked, stalling to think of solutions.

"Your dialect is quite strange for an animal," Khuram said.

"I'm genetically enhanced. What can I say?" Boris took a step closer to the beasts, hoping to show he wasn't afraid, even though that was the farthest from the truth. "Back to my point. I'm not interested in sharing my blood."

Arslan looked at Khuram. "Had we offered a choice to this lad?"

"I would have remembered if we had."

"Which is your priority?" Boris asked. "My blood? Or my death?"

"Your blood," Khuram answered. "But we can hardly enjoy one without the other."

"Not true." An idea formulated in his mind. "If I can pass on my blood's advantages to *you,* why couldn't I pass the advantages on to another? Perhaps to an animal a little more…appetizing?"

"Is this a riddle?" Arslan asked. "Khuram and I are not fond of riddles. We are accustomed to getting what we want, when we want it. So make your point. Quickly."

"Bring me three live sheep," Boris blurted out. "I'll bleed and you can persuade them to drink some of my blood. Afterwards, you can feast on the plump sheep instead of one lean wolf. You'll have enough blood and meat to provide for your entire pride. All will gain the benefits. I'll return to camp, and no one will know of our encounter. Which gives your pride many advantages."

Of course, his suggestion was part truth, part lie. Eating the sheep would provide the pride with protection from being carbonized. However, gaining the ability to heal was a pipe dream because drinking *second-hand* blood didn't activate self-healing.

A fact, he wouldn't mention.

"In contrast, let's consider *your* plan," Boris continued. "Killing me will leave your bellies unsatisfied while placing you and your pride in grave danger. Because if I'm found dead and dismembered, all hell will break loose. Not to mention, I'll whisper your names to the King of the Animals before my last breath."

Arslan began to pace, shaking her head. "Your words confuse me. Filtiarn told us we must drink from a body which has received blood directly from The Tether in order to acquire the power of self-healing. Does this information lack truth?"

Boris wanted to smile: *bait, hook, and reel in the catch.*

"No one wants the animals to know," he said, lying through his teeth. "The truth would make the King of the Animals and The Tether vulnerable. But the fact is: Ruby's blood is so powerful, that if consumed under *any* circumstances, even second hand, the consumer will gain the power to heal herself if injured."

"Not so *fassst,*" Khuram said. "You fought Athanasia's Lykos, alpha of the Night Stalkers. He drank Montaro's blood before the battle, yet he did not heal. He perished in the fight."

"No one can heal without a heart, and I removed *his* while it was still beating."

Wide eyed, the lionesses gasped.

Lying was getting easier. Mostly because his audience was gullible.

Thankfully, Khuram and Arslan agreed to his terms.

While Khuram left to collect the sheep, Arslan guarded Boris so he wouldn't run off before fulfilling his end of the deal.

The sun had crested over the horizon. Boris dreaded hearing Clay's voice in his head, wondering where he was and why he had neglected his night-watch duty.

His luck might change if he continued to make careless choices.

At last, Khuram and her pride returned with three sheep and Boris played his role beautifully. When Boris assured the lionesses that the sheep had consumed enough of his blood, the pride killed its quarry and began feasting.

"Misanao laa," Boris said loudly. Saying "thank you" was his way of gauging if any of the lions were paying attention to him while their bloodied jowls pulled at sheep innards or chewed on lamb meat.

None of them looked his way.

Which was a green light for his exit.

As he galloped toward the campsite, he thought about how he'd tell Clay everything. Hopefully, the king would forgive him. After all, because of Boris's clever trickery and persuasive abilities, he was able to survive in order to warn the king, an act that might negate his negligence of duty. Also because of him, the lion pride *believed* they had acquired his ability to heal which might make them reckless about their own safety. Surely Clay would appreciate this.

As he exited the woods, Boris heard his king inside his head.

Where the hell are you? Clay whispered.

52

Monday, July 29, 2041
The Glade: Besto Polus

CLAY HAD MIXED emotions about the wolf's commentary regarding his whereabouts and life-threatening encounter with two lionesses. If Boris had remained at his station, like he was supposed to (in fact, *ordered* to), he would've avoided trouble altogether. Never mind that his irresponsible actions had left everyone vulnerable while they rested inside the tent.

On the positive side, the wolf had confessed his wrongdoings without prompting. But to ensure Boris's full disclosure, Clay had exerted his power as alpha, compelling the gray wolf to divulge every detail he could recall associated with his unauthorized excursion.

Good as well, the wolf had been smart enough to make the best out of a dicey situation. True: Ruby could no longer carbonize the lion pride, which might be problematic should the lions attack. But at least they wouldn't be able to heal in addition.

Early morning should've been the calm before the storm. Despite sunny skies, turmoil was already rumbling. Thankfully, they had two hours before Filtiarn and her Vala would arrive at The Glade. Maybe the negative vibe would turn around before then.

Of course, Zagan was still MIA. Figured.

Ruby had watched Zagan walk away from their campsite and sculpt himself into a bat incarnation. For what reason, no one knew.

Instead of a well-oiled machine humming along toward a common purpose, some members of his team were acting more like individual parts, causing friction and sparks.

At least in human form, Clay could quiet his instincts that urged him to act on his anger, which is why he had shifted back to his upright body after communicating with Boris.

Clay seriously wondered if he was well-suited to be a king.

A cloud of dust swirled in a whirlwind beside the tent.

Zagan formed in the flesh, wearing his leathers and cloak, despite the summer heat.

"Good morning," he cheered, as if all was right in the universe. "A lovely day for negotiations. I, myself, am feeling rejuvenated."

"Who gave you permission to flutter off on your own?" Clay snarled. "Without a word?"

Zagan's eyebrows tensed and he glanced behind him as if Clay might be speaking to someone else. He turned back to face him, no doubt observing that there was no one else there.

"Apologies," Zagan said. "I returned to camp well before the scheduled meeting. And I was not aware that I required permission to leave. For like you, I am a king."

"We're not in Skotadi," Clay admonished. "We're in my territory. You're a member of this task force. At *my* request. At *my* direction."

Ruby touched Clay's arm and squeezed before Zagan could respond. She looked beyond him. Clay turned to see what had caught her attention in the field.

Emerging from the tree line at the edge of the woods was a massive she-wolf with a fiery red coat. Flanking her on both sides, like geese flying behind their lead, were a total of 20 gray wolves.

Filtiarn and her Vala. Two hours early.

The Lord of the Wolves was carrying something in her mouth.

"Prepare your weapons in case this doesn't go well," Clay warned.

With sculpting, his wife exchanged her shorts and T-shirt with her zombie scalping outfit. She wore a black leather halter-top with leather leggings designed to allow flexibility in her knees. Overlapping pewter disks protected her shoulders and triceps. And she wore a wide holster of sheaths, each filled with a specialized dagger. In her right hand was her favorite saber.

Already dressed for battle, Draven pulled his sword from its sheath while Boris stood at-the-ready, the hairs on his withers stiff.

Zagan sculpted two double-edged swords, one for each hand, though Clay knew from past history that Zagan preferred carbonizing and heart plucking over any weapon.

In a burst of black dust, Clay shifted into wolf form. He shook his fur to dispel any lingering fabric from what had been his clothing. He and his team advanced toward the approaching wolfpack. When each side was 10 yards apart, the opposing entourages stopped, letting their alphas close the remaining gap in distance.

Standing opposite Filtiarn, Clay identified what she was carrying in her mouth: a dead red fox. The she-wolf lowered the intact carcass onto the ground between them, before raising her head and locking eyes with him.

When Clay was in human form, he never needed or wanted to be a leader. He was more comfortable supporting others. But now that he could shift into wolf form, he became overwhelmed by the laws of nature. And in nature, he was dominant—the monarch of all species.

"This is where you bow to your king, Filtiarn," he said.

Only, she didn't lower her head.

She continued to stare into his eyes with defiance.

Cognitively, he pressed on her mind, a force only a true alpha could exert. She resisted, but the laws of nature compelled her to comply. She bowed her head and the Vala followed suit.

"You're two hours ahead of schedule," Clay said. "Explain why."

"Time on a clock is a tool for the uprights," she countered. "Animals prefer using the sun and the moon as our guides."

Clay ignored the slight and addressed the elephant in the room. "You've brought this dead fox with you...because?"

"Because he is proof you are not worthy to be our king," she snapped. "This fox was slayed by a vampire in your coven. Can you not protect your own kind?"

"Ridiculous," he barked. "And look who's making accusations. Just this morning, two lionesses named Khuram and Arslan slaughtered three sheep. Animals on this planet previously lived in harmony, until *you* incited war. Maybe you'll learn: hate and greed are difficult to contain; they spread like the plague."

"Your accusations are erroneous without evidence." Filtiarn turned to her Vala. "Have you seen or heard anything to substantiate the claims of this…" She looked back at him with disgust, as if trying to identify his species. "… of this man-wolf *shifter?*"

He heard her Vala cognitively answer that they hadn't.

"What kind of 'evidence' is this fox, anyway?" Clay asked. "You could've killed him yourself."

Filtiarn chuckled. "Wolves have fangs. This is true. But our Creator did not design our snouts to drain blood from our quarry. Simple physiology."

"This fox has been *drained* of its blood?"

Filtiarn turned her head to look at the wolves behind her. "Seems he is a genius, as well."

Her Vala giggled at the implied insult.

Clay's patience with her attitude was waning.

He pressed his will on her mind, forcing her to bow again.

"A genius," he growled, "as well as *your* king."

He studied the carcass. Marked in blood on the fox's fur, he easily spotted the two puncture wounds.

Filtiarn was correct. Most animals lapped not gulped. And fangs tore away flesh, not punctured skin for draining.

To his knowledge, only vampire bats did that.

And, of course, vampires.

"I need to confer with my team," Clay said. "Remain here."

Clay shifted into human form in front of the wolves.

Given he was so close to the Vala, they gasped.

Filtiarn snarled at her female protectors, no doubt chastising them for their uninhibited reaction.

53

RUBY WASN'T EXPECTING her husband to shift back into human form so quickly. She thought his conversation with the she-wolf would require time for negotiations—*if* the exchange was going well. Clearly, it wasn't.

Naked, he walked toward them, creases on his forehead.

He had nearly reached their group when she remembered to sculpt clothing on him, placing him in black leather pants and a sleeveless tank. Naked or clothed, his expression didn't change.

Clay's eyes locked with Zagan's. "What did you do after you left this campsite?" he asked, using an accusatory tone.

"I hunted. I have been parched since my return to the immortal."

"Cry me a river," he snapped.

"Aren't you being harsh?" Ruby asked her husband.

"The evidence suggests I'm spot-on."

Ruby whispered inside Clay's mind to understand his aggravation.

"You seriously drained a fox?" she asked Zagan. "While Clay's working to establish peace with a rival? Are you kidding me?"

"Lady Spencer, you are familiar with my dietary preferences," he defended. "I would not waste my energy on a measly morsel such as a fox. I favor larger quarry. In fact, I fed on a mature buck in the early hours of dawn. As well, I heal the source of my sustenance, thus restoring the balance between giver and receiver."

"Right," she said, her head flooding with old wounds. "Tell that to

233

Paige Jasper whom you drained at Nationals Park Stadium."

"A regrettable error," he admitted. "Evil corrupted my soul then."

"Glamour him," Clay said. "Find out if he killed the fox. Please."

"Might not do any good," she said. "He can construct cognitive shields and mirrors to control what I see. And even though I'm the only one who has the skills to unravel his handiwork, I'd need time to drill into his mind." She nodded toward the wolves. "I'm not sure our audience has the patience to wait for the answers."

"Is my word not sufficient?" Zagan asked.

"I wish it was," Ruby said. "But every time I've given you a second chance, every time I've trusted you, you've let me down. There's a pattern, Zagan. And I wonder if we can *ever* trust you. Maybe we shouldn't have brought you back in the first place."

Her words looked like they hit Zagan's chest with force. Which had been her intention.

He took several steps backwards as if to balance himself. "The words escaping your lips are cruel. You cannot mean them."

"You have a legacy of *cruel,*" Draven added. "Perhaps your callousness has chosen to outlive the curse."

"Consider the facts," she said to Zagan. "You left camp in the cloak of darkness. You admittedly hunted and fed. And now Filtiarn shows up with a dead fox—one with puncture wounds on its neck and drained of blood. The evidence points in your direction."

"Yet, others like me stand in close proximity." Zagan pinched at his chin with his index finger and thumb. "I insist that I am innocent of this malfeasance. Did no one else leave our campsite?"

"Boris strayed," Clay said. "But he's a wolf, *not* a vampire. And I have a full accounting of what he did while he was in the woods."

Zagan eyed the wolf with tensed eyebrows.

If Ruby had actually *followed* Zagan into the woods while she was in sparrow form instead of staying perched on the tent, she'd know what the King of Dark... of Skotadi had done.

Veins pressed against her skin.

While Clay was trying to prove that he was the rightful King of the Animals, that he was the one who could negotiate peace between the animals and uprights, Zagan was feeding his own chronic selfishness and lack of control.

Not only that, Zagan's behavior reminded her about the downsides of sharing *her* authority as the universe's protector, as The Tether. Perhaps too much was at stake to rely too heavily on others.

She'd have to reclaim the lead when it came to restoring balance and harmony to all three planets. This fiasco proved as much.

"If you do not believe my words," Zagan said to her, "then touch the slayed fox. Read the echoes of its last minutes. This is a competency you possess, is it not? Then you shall learn the identity of the one who ended its life."

"Could he have altered what the fox saw?" Clay asked her.

"Glamours and shields vanish with death," she answered. "Zagan's right. I should be able to see the face of the culprit who drained the fox."

"Afterwards, I will accept your apology," Zagan said.

"Shut up," she said. "If you hadn't gone off by yourself, satisfying your own individual needs, you wouldn't even be a suspect."

"Come with me," Clay said to her. "Tell me what you learn from the fox before I shift back into wolf form."

They walked toward Filtiarn.

The she-wolf raised her lips and growled as they approached. Ruby let her veins rise to the surface, as she placed her right hand on the hilt of her saber. The wolves would not intimidate her.

With the carcass in front of her, she knelt. Before touching the fox, she glanced up at her husband.

"Whatever the truth reveals," he said, "we'll deal with it."

As Ruby placed her hand on the fur, her eyes ducked behind her eyelids. The immediate past began to stream. Her heart accelerated as the vision of the fox's assailant materialized.

Standing, she glared at Filtiarn's gray wolves.

And withdrew her saber.

54

Monday, July 29, 2041
The Glade: Besto Polus

CLAY EASILY INTERPRETED his wife's defensive move when she brandished her sword. No doubt her vision had been alarming, seeming to implicate Filtiarn and her guards.

"What exactly did you see?" he asked, his adrenaline surging.

"A gray wolf," she said, sweeping her sword from left to right, pointing at the line of gray wolves comprising Filtiarn's Vala. "One of them pounced on the fox. The battle was a blur until I felt fangs embed in the fox's neck. The puncture wounds were precise, piercing the animal's artery. Clearly, a wolf had wanted to make the kill look as though a vampire had done it."

"To make me appear as an ineffectual leader," he said. "Unable to persuade vampires to live in peace with the animals."

Filtiarn raised her lips and growled. Her Vala inched closer.

"How will you respond?" Ruby asked.

"According to the codicil, I have to defeat the last usurper. Which means fighting to the death."

His wife briefly closed her eyes, as if absorbing the news.

After sheathing her saber, she hugged him. "Confidence over fear," she said softly into his ear. "Take her quickly so she doesn't suffer. And remember, I love you for eternity."

"And beyond." Clay gave her his crooked smile. Though internally, human doubts nipped at his nerves. Thank goodness that in wolf form, his fighter instincts would dominate.

As Ruby walked back toward his team, he allowed energy to consume his body. When the dust cleared, he was King of the Animals. His muscles trembled with an urge to be engaged. His mind was void of insecurities.

Raising his lips in disgust, he whispered to Filtiarn about the crime revealed in the echoes of the fox's last moments.

"Your tongue is that of a serpent's," she hissed. "You are a liar!"

Boris trotted to him.

"A coward, as well," Filtiarn said. "Must *he* fight all your battles?"

"Says the Lord of the Wolves who never travels without twenty guards," Clay growled. "And who harbors a murderer among them."

"Let me take her," Boris said.

Clay snapped at him. "This battle is mine to win or lose."

Filtiarn smirked. "And lose you shall."

The she-wolf lunged, initiating the fight.

He and Filtiarn locked jaws on each other's fur and rolled in a snarling, tumbling ball, forcing the Vala to scatter. The sounds of growling and yapping resonated throughout the valley.

Filtiarn's fighting prowess clearly offset his size advantage.

He concentrated, learning her moves and countermoves.

Without paying attention to his surroundings, he was surprised when she pushed him against a tree at the edge of the woods, momentarily pinning him. The she-wolf clasped down on his skin with her fangs and drove his side into the trunk. His body was unable to give. She used the strategic backdrop to gather more of his flesh in her jowls before ripping away a mouthful of his abdomen.

Pain scorched his nerves like hot coals.

His yelp reverberated in the pines. Birds took flight from treetops.

Panic ignited every cell in his body. He simply could not lose the battle. The animals depended on him. He was their negotiator dedicated to establishing animal rights.

Filtiarn pounced, her snapping jaws aiming for his gaping wound.

Twisting, he freed himself just before her fangs made contact.

His wound tingled as he felt his injury heal.

Locking onto each other's fur once more, they rolled into the woods, away from onlookers. Occasionally they separated, before latching on again and drifting deeper into the forest carpeted in a thick layer of pine needles.

Absorbed in the fight, Clay recoiled when his paws backed into the Reniraby River. The stones were slick with algae and he quickly lost his footing. He splashed down on his side as his brain registered his vulnerability.

Filtiarn must have registered it, too.

She forced her front paws onto his neck, driving him down into the water and wedging his head into the base of a large, ragged rock. He was stuck beneath the surface. Thrashing his legs, he tried to break loose. But the more he writhed, the more his oxygen depleted.

He opened his eyes underwater and for the first time since the fight had begun, he conceded that victory might not be his to claim.

His lungs screamed for air, urging him to breathe, to inhale.

Growing heavy from a lack of oxygen, his legs slowed.

He was King of the Animals! Why would he falter so quickly?

His body felt like dead weight and he could no longer move.

From his past, Ruby's words drifted into his mind.

You're amazing, she had told him in Siberia. *I found three independent sets of DNA coding: human, vampire, and wolf.*

Vampire. Why hadn't he thought of it before? Because breathing was optional for vampires. So was a heartbeat.

Mentally, he shut his body down. Flipped the switch to off.

Filtiarn released him, undoubtedly thinking he was dead.

He waited until she reached the shore before wiggling his head loose from the rock, this time, without panic. Thrusting himself onto his paws, he stood and raced from the river, leaping over the water like a porpoise.

The she-wolf was turning toward the disturbance when his paws slammed her body, knocking her down. He tore at her abdomen so severely, that her innards spilled onto the stony shore: liver, stomach, and the tubular piping of intestines. She wouldn't survive the injury.

"With your death," he said, "find comfort that the reign of harmony will begin in the universe."

"Fool!" she wheezed, blood seeping from her snout. "I am not the last usurper. Another one waits for the opportunity to strike."

Clasping onto Filtiarn's throat, he restricted her windpipe. Seconds later, the Lord of the Wolves was dead.

55

NOT KNOWING MADE the wait unbearable.

Ruby had speculated that the fight between Clay and Filtiarn would be brief, with her husband quickly defeating the she-wolf. Her prediction was wrong. In fact, Filtiarn had injured him shortly after the battle had begun. Thank God he had inherited the gift of healing. Still, healers could die.

Two hours had already passed. The woods were quiet.

In contrast, her mind threatened to explode.

Or was that her heart?

Draven gently touched her arm. "Push negative thoughts aside, Tether. The King of the Animals will not be defeated."

If only she could be sure.

"Permit me to locate him," Zagan said. "For I will gladly do so."

She shook her head, dislodging a tear.

"Pretty sure I could access his mind if I wanted to," she said. "I just couldn't understand him. But since I can't interfere regardless of what's happening, I'd rather be in the dark. Because the truth exists whether or not I'm informed of it in this moment."

Her words sounded like she was in control, like she was calm, but they hardly mirrored her inner turmoil. Her stomach was twisting in knots. A lump lodged in her throat.

Being idle was torture.

She pushed her thoughts to read Clay's lifeline stone, even though logically, she knew this competency didn't extend to animals. The effort yielded expected results: nothing.

Although Ruby had only begun reading lifeline stones and seeing into the future over a month ago, she had become dependent on these gifts. She'd forgotten what it was like to wait on the future to reveal itself. The practice required trust and blind faith, with a healthy dose of patience. She wasn't particularly proficient at either of them.

The Vala were lying in the glade, facing the woods where Clay and Filtiarn had entered. Some tilted their heads, as if listening intently.

Suddenly, they rose to their feet, peering into the tree line.

Boris whined. His bushy tail wagged.

"Something's happening," she said, her heart jolting into action.

I'm okay, Clay whispered to her. *Can you clothe me?*

She exhaled slowly, releasing her stress. "He's coming!" she announced, sculpting an outfit on his body.

"The king is victorious as I predicted," Draven said, winking. "Perhaps I am more of a seer than I thought."

Zagan rolled his eyes.

The Vala bowed as Clay emerged from the woods in human form, holding the slayed Filtiarn in his arms. He placed the wolf with the fiery red coat on the grass in front of them. Two wolves clamped down on her pelt with their jaws and began dragging her carcass back into the woods. The remaining wolves followed until they all disappeared among the tall pines.

Ruby raced toward her husband.

With outstretched arms, he lifted her into a spinning embrace. After a few rotations, he stopped and kissed her deeply.

"I was so worried," she said, as their lips unlocked.

"Believe me. You weren't the only one."

She ran her fingers through his hair. "You're wet."

"Long story."

Zagan, Draven, and Boris approached.

"Congratulations, brother," Draven cheered. "Let the reign of harmony commence."

"Too soon for that," Clay said. "With Filtiarn's last breath, she warned me there will be another challenger."

"Be assured, we shall assist you in any way we can," Zagan said.

"What's next?" Ruby asked her husband.

"I've called a meeting at Royal Ridge tomorrow to address animal representatives of all species. It's time to develop an Animal Bill of Rights. To make strides toward ending this rebellion." He rubbed his stomach. "Right now, though, I'm famished."

"Does your vampire side want to hunt?" she asked.

"Honestly, my human side wants an extra-cheese pizza. And maybe some warm chocolate chip cookies."

She laughed. "You'll have to settle for sandwiches. I packed some in the cooler we brought."

"I'm on it."

As Clay walked toward the tent, she glanced at Zagan, feeling nervous, coupled with a large dose of guilt.

"Would you hunt with me?" she asked him. "I'd like to talk."

"Have I ever denied you, Lady Spencer?"

56

ZAGAN SNIFFED THE summer breeze and scented the deer herd he had visited earlier that morning. How glorious he felt to be alive in the flesh, invigorated by his acute senses and partaking in the give and take of nature. Achieving balance was intoxicating.

"Take my hand. I shall travel you to our sustenance," he said.

Ruby rolled her eyes. "I can transport myself, you know."

"Chivalry is not a curse, Lady Spencer."

"I forgot: you're the king of civility," she said, emphasizing her sarcasm. Nevertheless, she extended her hand and he clasped it.

They materialized in a grassy field beside a babbling tributary of the Reniraby River. Twelve deer were grazing.

The herd's 12-point buck raised his majestic head and snorted. Recognizing Zagan, the alpha trotted over.

Zagan patted the buck's forehead, careful not to disturb the velvet still coating his thick antlers.

The beast playfully nipped at Zagan's seafoam linen tunic.

"You've always made friends easier with animals," Ruby said.

"Animals do not judge me. They anticipate the best." He raised one eyebrow. "You are witness to his trust in me."

As if agreeing, the buck bobbed his head and flickered his tail.

She lowered her eyes, clearly interpreting his implication.

"You make a valid point," she said. "In fact, I'm sorry for not trusting you. For accusing you of slaying and draining that fox. It wasn't a good moment for me and I'm sure my actions were disappointing for you. Hurtful, even. To say the least."

"Forgiveness is challenging on an empty stomach." He smirked. "Let us dine first and speak of reconciliation afterwards."

They both took turns feasting on the buck, before healing him. When Zagan patted his rump, the beast jogged back to his herd.

Zagan sculpted two wingback chairs, upholstered in red satin, angled to face each other. "Would you care to sit for our discussion?"

"Thank you," she said, lowering herself on the seat cushion. After he sat, she took a deep breath. "I feel terrible about how I treated you. I expected the worst. You clearly didn't deserve it."

He raised his hand to stop her. "Perhaps I can ease the distress of your confession while improving my own ability to verbalize empathy. If you will allow me, that is."

"Okay. Sure."

"Betrayal compromises our ability to trust," he started. "I have certainly betrayed you in the past. I took the life of your friend—the mayfly, I mean, the human named Paige. This led to your vervain poisoning and incarceration. Of course, I killed another to prove your innocence. Not to mention, I nearly destroyed your coven in a housefire. My most heinous act was blowing your husband and precious Gabriella off the cliff at Great Island. Not to mention, culling three hundred humans after I had agreed never to do so. And then there was Atea and Jasmine..."

"Please stop before I get furious again. I've gotten your point. You've betrayed me over and over and over again."

"Yes, well, honesty is a virtue, Lady Spencer. And as Draven has said: trust is fickle. Difficult to gain and easy to lose. Therefore, I do not expect the restoration of trust to come without hinderances. I believe the Earthling expression is *one step forward, two steps back.*"

"Still," she said. "Either I believe evil has been purged from your soul or I don't. I'm not usually wishy-washy."

"Have you decided which conviction you hold?"

"I think your soul *has* been restored. Truly, I do," she said. "Maybe my reaction was more about my own difficulty with trusting others." She curled one side of her lips in a half smile. "I'm working on it. Really. I promise."

"We share this common struggle, Lady Spencer. For as you are well aware, less than a month ago, I found no one better to trust than myself."

"Other than your previous murderous ways, we're similar."

"Like siblings, perhaps?"

Ruby turned serious, locking eyes with him and making his heart sputter, though not in a romantic way. Rather, as one would react to admiring a dear companion.

His heart swelled with joy. A most remarkable feeling.

"You are my closest friend, Lady Spencer," he admitted.

"Strange as it is, you're one of mine. I've learned a lot from you."

"Oh, do go on. I urge you to divulge."

Her full smile could tame a pride of starved lions.

"You taught me how to heal others for one thing," she said. "And the importance of achieving balance with nature. Before, I thought vampires were self-centered takers. But when I encountered that magnificent buck on your castle's estate…"

"The beloved Montaro."

"Yes," she continued. "When I saw how he respected you, I knew there was goodness in your heart, despite the curse. And your lab, where your minions were working on a cure for the mutated F8, also showed a different side of you. A special, caring side."

"The least I could do since I had propagated the pathogen, though admittedly, I did not anticipate that the ensuing infection would be resistant to my intentions. Turns out, nature is stronger than all of my competencies combined."

"Feeling invincible is understandable," she said. "We've been bestowed with powerful gifts. I get it. Believe me."

He needed to relay a promise that blossomed in his heart.

"I can think of no reason to ever betray you again, Lady Spencer."

She placed her hand on his knee. "That's the thing. Sometimes we're blindsided by the unexpected and we make bad choices without thinking them through. None of us are perfect."

"Yet, some of us are extremely close to perfection." He winked. "Are they not?"

She lifted her chin in laughter. "Will you forgive me then?"

"Indeed."

"Have I thanked you for saving me at the Polar Station?" Ruby asked. "I mean, *really* thanked you?"

"Returning my heart to my chest was quite explicit."

Standing, she added, "Thank you for being my dearest friend."

He hugged her. "The most loyal, Lady Spencer."

57

IN WOLF FORM, Clay trotted among the crowd of animals who had gathered in the valley after ending their pilgrimage hours earlier. As he passed representatives of every species, they stepped aside and bowed, allowing a pathway to form.

Making his way to the steep rise that led to Royal Ridge, he nodded to several members of Filtiarn's Vala. They had integrated among the masses, freed from their services and forgiven for their trickery associated with the slayed fox, even though none of them were brave enough to take responsibility.

The late morning skies were cyan blue, basked in brilliant sunlight. Birds flitted overhead, chirping and singing. A fragrant breeze, cool and refreshing, ruffled his coat.

Zagan and Draven were standing at the base of the rocky butte, accompanied by Boris.

Leaping over the boulders, Clay headed straight up the incline.

The crowd hushed.

When he reached the grassy acre on the plateau, he made eye contact with Ruby. He had asked her to be present on the sacred grounds, to show his kind that he and his wife were equal partners. That animals should only judge others, including uprights, on their behavior and *not* on their genetics.

Wearing black leathers and a cloak, she dipped her head.

He thrust his right leg forward and lowered his withers, displaying the level of respect he held for her.

The animals rumbled, as if uncertain about the gesture.

As he approached the weathered boulder symbolizing his throne, his heart raced. Now that the moment had arrived, he hoped he could handle the task. Convincing the animals that he was best suited to negotiate a truce might not be a walk in the park.

He strode onto the smooth ledge that jutted out from the plateau, nearly gasping at the sight below. A vast carpet of animals blanketed the landscape, as far as his eyes could see.

"Thank you for coming," he started.

The animals awkwardly glanced at one another.

He heard their mental whispers and one reaction surfaced: underwhelmed. Thankfully, he remembered Zagan's previous advice to *do as the animals do.*

"I am your king!" he shouted with authority.

The crowd roared and squealed and squawked.

Hooves and paws pounded the ground.

"We are on the cusp of The Turning Point," he continued. "A new era when animals will be treated with respect. When all living beings, including our kind, will be granted civil liberties."

"United we stand!" shouted the crowd, a leftover from Filtiarn's reign he suspected.

"Together, we will develop an Animal Bill of Rights, to be upheld on all three planets. This creed will serve as a compromise between animals and uprights, ensuring the freedoms and rights of our kind. Do you approve?"

"Isibid anashoor!" they shouted, which translated to "we approve."

"I will canvass animal and upright populations," Clay added, "to better understand reformations which will serve all parties and their needs. Do you approve?"

"Isibid anashoor!" the animals repeated.

From an unknown source, Clay overheard a disturbing whisper. Had an animal uttered the word...*kill?* Or was he imagining it?

"For too long..."

This time, the word *kill* or *hamalak*, was crystal clear.

As a natural reaction, Clay turned his head toward Ruby, hoping his face conveyed confusion. That's when he saw the lioness. No doubt, she had been hiding in the butte's rocky crown which towered upwards behind the plot of grass. The assassin galloped toward him, repeating the word *hamalak* in her mind.

Clay whipped his body around, 180-degrees, to face the usurper head on. Growling and brandishing his fangs, he was prepared to defend the throne.

With lightning speed, Ruby pivoted as the lioness became parallel to her position. His wife grabbed a dagger from its sheath and hurled the weapon, sending it whizzing through the air in a blur.

The knife embedded in between ribs, dropping the lioness.

Birds overhead saw the attack and relayed the event to the crowd.

Silence swept over the valley.

Clay trotted to the usurper who was still conscious, though not for long. He could hear her heart struggling. Clearly, she was suffering from internal bleeding.

"Killing your king won't bring peace to the planets," he said to her. "Joining me might."

"Never!" she hissed. "When I heal, I'll deliver war, not peace."

"Heal?" he asked, remembering the tall tale Draven's wolf had shared with two lionesses who threatened to drain him of blood. "Boris lied to save his own life so he could warn me about your intentions. In truth, only those who circulate The Tether's blood can acquire the ability to heal *themselves.* I'm sorry."

The lioness blinked rapidly, as if assessing the severity of her injury. No doubt she realized her prognosis was grave.

"Filtiarn was our rightful king," she growled.

"We both agreed to fight to the death," he said, "for the right to wear the crown. We abided by the laws of nature. And now I'm offering *you* a choice you otherwise wouldn't have. Join me? Or choose to die. Decide quickly."

"My death is imminent," she said, using a softer tone.

"I am your king," he snarled. "Choose."

"Join you," she coughed. Blood colored her tongue.

In a swirl of dust, Clay morphed to human form.

"I apologize for interfering," Ruby said. "My reflexes took over and I threw the knife without thinking."

"No worries. But will you save her?"

Ruby withdrew her dagger from the lioness's side. Without hesitation, she bit her wrist, allowing her vampire blood to flow. Kneeling beside the animal, she encouraged the beast to lap her blood until the wound healed.

After drinking, the lioness wobbled onto her paws.

Clay returned to wolf form.

"What's your name?" he asked her.

"I am called Khuram."

"Will you accompany me onto the ledge?"

"Onto the sacred throne?" she gasped, with wide eyes.

"Yes," he said, nudging Ruby to follow him as well.

Walking to the edge of the royal overlook, his wife stood to his right. Khuram, to his left.

"We are all brothers and sisters," he shouted to the crowd. "Every one of us. And we all deserve a second chance for mutual respect and peace. To live in harmony with every other living being. Let's coalesce around this purpose. Are you with me, friends?"

"United we stand!" the crowd roared in unison.

58

THE CLOSED DOOR to the Situation Room signified that the weekly Special Warfare Council meeting was already underway. The time was 10:15 a.m.

With one hand on the doorknob and the other holding her briefcase, Ruby took a deep breath, not knowing how she'd react to seeing President Unger—the man responsible for her kidnapping to Siberia. She hoped to be civil, as opposed to ripping out his throat.

She had dressed in "business professional," wearing a silk pencil-skirt with a matching navy blazer and high-heeled pumps. Maybe her attire would make her feel less like a predator.

Although she tried to push the thought from her mind, she wondered if some of the Council (those loyal to the POTUS) had come to the meeting equipped with vervain dart guns, in the event she decided to attend. At least with Clay by her side, the vampire drug wasn't the crippling threat it once was. In human or wolf form, the sedative didn't affect her husband. Which meant that even if she became unconscious, he could defend them both after transformed into the most powerful wolf in the entire universe. He could even call on other animals to help. As well as whisper to their vampire friends for assistance.

They were no longer on their own.

She glanced at Clay and their bodyguard Insley who had met them under the portico of the West Wing before they had entered the building. Having Insley accompany them during SWC meetings was more of a courtesy to the former Marine, as it kept him privy to governmental discussions, in terms of maintaining access to classified information. Not to mention, Insley was a symbolic reminder that a handful of emboldened patriots could pluck out the political weeds of corruption.

"Are we ready?" Ruby asked them.

Insley drew back one side of his unbuttoned blazer to reveal his holstered nine-millimeter handgun. "Let's get this party started."

She opened the door and they entered the room.

Eyes and Luther Pennington immediately stood, while the other Council members looked like deer in headlights.

"There you are!" Eyes said. "We need your help with this crisis."

Ruby scanned the room. The POTUS wasn't present. In his place was Vice President Olivia Jackson, who smiled warmly.

"Welcome," the VP said, pointing to the empty chairs. "Please. Take a seat. We'll bring you up to speed."

"Where's President Unger?" Ruby asked, hoping her disdain for the man hadn't soured her tone. "The POTUS usually presides over this meeting."

"Kenny?" Olivia prodded, as if she knew the answer but insisted that the President's advisor, the aggressive one called Cutthroat Kenny, delivered the information.

His eyes briefly shifted downward, and he touched his finger near his mouth. His heartrate accelerated.

All were signs of lying.

"He's under the weather," Kenny said. "Bad case of the flu."

"In July?" Clay questioned.

"Talk to his physician," he snapped. "I'm simply the messenger."

Kenny seemed a little too defensive.

Ruby would deal with him before the meeting was over.

The Vice President introduced them to the guests representing supporting organizations which included the WHO, CDC, WAZA, and NIH. She recapped the Council's progress on thwarting future animal attacks which basically amounted to keeping people sheltered inside their homes with crated and muzzled pets.

"Before we move on to new business," Olivia said, "is there

anything you all would like to contribute, in terms of understanding the origin of this phenomenon or recommending solutions?"

Ruby glanced at Clay to see if he wanted to take the lead. He nodded, urging her instead.

Omitting her kidnapping and Will Unger's role in the nightmare, she recapped the dark science experiment engineered by Emory Bradshaw and Vladimir Volkov, in their attempt to build a unique army of super wolves. She shared that both were deceased.

"I told the POTUS not to pardon those lowlifes." Luther said, pounding the table. "Terrorists can't be trusted. When will we learn?"

"The good news is they're dead now." Olivia turned her attention back to her and Clay. "Please continue."

"I've compiled a report regarding the outcome of a confrontation we had with Emory and Vladimir, before their deaths," she said, opening her briefcase and handing the one-page summary to her husband so he could distribute. "Clay was injected with Emory's bioengineered wolf serum before I tried to save him with my blood, and soon after, with vampire venom. Both venoms, along with my blood, quickly overwhelmed his bloodstream. The consequences were remarkable and extraordinary. May I direct you to read the section regarding the science of Clay's transformation?"

No one spoke.

The members seemed dumbfounded as they read the conclusions.

"Wait," Eyes said, finally breaking the silence. "You're reporting that Clay *shifts* into a wolf at will? I mean, I'm not doubting you, but the idea is hard to wrap my head around."

"Dark science has unexpected results," Ruby said. "I'm proof."

"But shifting into an...*animal?*" Luther asked.

Clay tilted his head and locked eyes with Luther. "Let's be clear. Animals are far more loyal and kinder than most humans."

"Oh. Right," he said, his face turning crimson. "I intended no disrespect. Sorry about the implication."

"Would you like to see the transformation?" Ruby asked.

"Please," Olivia encouraged.

"Justine?"

"I thought the POTUS had been clear," Kenny interrupted. "Your DEPE isn't to have access to our secure network. Not ever."

"Do you want to see Clay shifting or not?"

"Show us," Olivia said, overriding the objection.

"You called for me, Ruby?" Justine asked, using the room's surround sound system to project her voice.

"Please run the video footage of Clay transforming. The file we had discussed this morning."

"Certainly."

The lights dimmed and video of Clay standing in human form, wearing jeans and a T-shirt, began to play. The attendees gasped as a cloud of swirling particles concealed him. When the dust dissipated, a massive black wolf emerged in place of her husband.

"Bizarre," Eyes said.

After the video ended, the lights brightened.

"Why not show us in person?" Kenny questioned.

"His clothing shreds when he shifts," Olivia said, rolling her eyes at Kenny. "Seems rather obvious *why.*"

"Yes." Clay smiled. "That, and the business suit I'm wearing today happens to be one of my favorites."

"You have our undivided attention," Eyes said, putting on his figurative Secretary of Defense hat. "How will your revelation help with the animal crisis?"

"When I'm in wolf form," her husband said, "I can speak the language of all animals. So naturally, I now understand why they're rebelling and how we can address their disputes."

Detailing some of the grievances, Clay explained how an Animal Bill of Rights would serve to restore peace between the animals and uprights. Outlining his next steps, he assured the Council that the temporary ceasefire would hold as long as they made progress.

"Animal attacks have experienced a sharp decline since yesterday," the WAZA official admitted. "Now we know why."

"This is preposterous!" Kenny abruptly stood. "A man-wolf *freak* speaking to the animals? An Animal Bill of Rights? What fantasy world are you spinning? I've got real work to do."

Ruby noticed beads of sweat glistening on Kenny's forehead.

"You seem overly agitated," she said to the POTUS's Senior Advisor. "Care to share why?"

"*Uhh.* No."

She pressed her mind into Kenny's.

Talk about bizarre images.

A basement with three cells appeared in his thoughts. Each cell housed an inmate shackled to the floor by a chain. The area seemed familiar. Was the location in the White House bunker? Another vision formed of the President with a slit wrist, dripping his blood into a beaker, with his physician overseeing the collection.

What the hell was going on?

The Situation Room door slammed as Kenny stormed out.

Ruby broke her connection with his disturbing thoughts.

"Ruby," Clay said, sounding concerned. "Veins…on your neck."

"Sorry." She looked at Eyes. "Can we talk after we adjourn?"

"Absolutely."

"Let's go ahead and conclude this meeting," Olivia announced. "I've got another one in a few minutes anyway." She looked at her and Clay. "Thank you for your insights and suggestions. Game changers, for sure. I hope you'll join us next week and update the Council on your progress. And as soon as you have a finalized draft of an Animal Bill of Rights, I'll get it sponsored in Congress. We'll move on this quickly."

The Council and guests rose from their seats, funneling out of the room while chatting about the meeting's developments.

Clay, Insley and Eyes remained behind with her.

"How can I help?" Eyes asked.

"The SUC serum is kept in the White House bunker, correct?" Ruby asked him.

"Yes. In a vault. Guarded by special operatives. Why?"

"I read Kenny's thoughts," she said. "Something's not right and the POTUS is involved. We need to visit the bunker and get to the bottom of it."

"Lead the way," her husband said to Eyes.

"Not so fast," she countered. "We'll need reinforcements."

"Like what?" Clay asked.

"More like *who*," she answered. "I want Zagan to meet us in the bunker."

59

ZAGAN HAD BEEN instructing his High Cliff staff on how to display the hydrangeas, peonies, and roses he had collected at Kaliméra when Ruby whispered to him. She needed help, signifying their trust was, indeed, blossoming. The feeling warmed his heart.

After receiving coordinates and exchanging his casual tunic for more appropriate attire—namely, black leather from cloak to boot—he traveled to the White House bunker without delay, though he did not know how he might assist.

Zagan materialized in a dungeon; one rancid from decaying flesh.

The Spencers had just arrived, joined by two male mayflies (rather, two *humans*), one with fiery red hair and the other with brown.

The scene before them was unsightly.

Not even when Zagan's soul had overflowed with evil had he treated prisoners so ruthlessly. More often than not, he would kill them quickly or heal them for future use. These humans, however, had suffered, brought to the brink of death and abandoned. Their bodies lay unnaturally sprawled on the cement floor, with twisted limbs that had been broken. In the center cell, the inmate's heartbeat was weak. On either side of him, the males had already expired. Their bodies emitted gasses that were putrid.

Instead of gawking at the barbarity assaulting their senses, the red-haired human stared at *him,* his blue eyes wide with curiosity.

"Indeed," Zagan said, having read his thoughts. "My skin is pure white, absent melanin."

"I apologize," he said. "Didn't mean to be rude."

"Beauty is a magnet; I do not blame you." He turned to Ruby. "How am I able to assist?"

"We're standing in the lion's den," she answered. "This bunker is under the White House which is, in part, a residency occupied by the most influential human on Earth—the President of the United States and the leader of the Federation of Independent Nations. I asked you here to add one more layer of protection, since the President was responsible for handing me over to my kidnappers."

Zagan could feel veins throb and bulge under his skin.

"Shall I find this President and swiftly end his existence?"

"I've got another idea," Clayton said, employing obvious sarcasm. "Before assassinating the leader of the free world, how about we start by finding out what went on here?"

Ignoring Ruby's mate, Zagan used his mind to break the lock and fling open the barred door to the center cell. "I will glamour him."

"He needs healing first, but yes, glamouring him would give us insight on what happened."

Zagan bit his wrist as he entered the inmate's quarters. Kneeling, he rolled the prisoner onto his back, straightened his contorted appendages, and lifted his head off the floor.

The man moaned with delirium.

Zagan immediately noticed two puncture wounds on his neck. This man had served as sustenance for a vampire.

"Drink my blood and you shall heal," he told the prisoner.

The inmate obeyed. Within a minute, he sat up.

"Who the hell are you?" the man croaked. "You're so...*white*. Did he nearly suck the life out of you, too?"

Why were humans so obsessed with skin color? Or perhaps in Zagan's case, with the lack of it?

"Can you see your reflection in my eyes?" Zagan asked him, commencing the process of hypnotically glamouring him for the truth. "Look closely."

The inmate leaned toward him.

Zagan felt his own pupils enlarge and contract as his glamour of the prisoner took hold. "Sit on the cot and answer our questions."

Ruby entered the cell as the prisoner rose and sat on the bed.

"Give me your name," Zagan commanded. "And then tell me who is drinking your blood."

"Hank Matthews. And President Unger drinks my blood."

"The most influential mayfly is an immortal," Zagan said.

Clayton walked into the cell. "That's freaking wonderful."

Ruby glanced at her husband. "Will undoubtedly stole SUC from the vault to turn himself."

"Did President Unger ever mention *why* he had turned himself into a vampire?" Clayton asked Hank.

"He never shut up about it," the inmate answered. "He told us we were his retirement plan. That the three of us were his cash cows."

"Explain," she said.

"The POTUS bled his own blood to sell on the black market. Calls it *Healing Hemo,* or something close. Anyway, the douchebag used us to replenish himself."

"If you were one of his cash cows," Clayton said, "why did he leave you for dead and kill your sidekicks?"

"The maniac can't control himself," Hank answered. "He's got like no discipline whatsoever. And to think, he can activate nuclear war by pressing a few numbers."

"What should we do about the POTUS?" Clayton asked his mate.

"Like you said, we can't just *kill* the President of the United States. Not without a trial, conviction, and death penalty sentence. So first, we'll arrange to have him closely monitored while we're gathering evidence, under the radar, to indict him."

Lady Spencer looked at the mounted cameras on the walls. "Eyes, those are on. Can we get access to the footage they're capturing?"

The brown-haired man nodded. "Sure. I'll find the POTUS's secret control room and confiscate the recordings."

"Perfect," she said. "Before you do, can you accompany Insley to the vault? We need to confiscate the SUC supply and destroy it all."

"Good idea," Eyes agreed.

He and the one named Insley left the cellblock area.

"I'm not sure what we should do about Hank," Ruby said.

"Are you a convicted criminal?" Zagan asked the prisoner, knowing a thing or two about correctional institutions.

"Fuck yeah." Hank couldn't lie while glamoured. "Death row."

"What was your crime?" Clayton asked.

"My mother was a hooker," he said. "I hated her. I hated *them*. Strangled twenty-two whores. Not nearly enough." He chuckled. "The courts only knew about eighteen."

"When is your date of execution?" Zagan asked.

"That day came and went. The douchebag President fudged my records to make it look like I'd gotten the needle of doom. Instead, lucky me was transferred here to become his personal livestock."

Zagan whirled over to him in a blur, placing hands on both sides of the criminal's head. With a burst of energy, he snapped Hank's neck, instantly killing him. The mayfly slumped onto the cot.

"Prisoners must fulfill their sentences," he stated.

"Alrighty then," she said. "What should we do with the bodies?"

"Shouldn't we wait until Eyes confirms what evidence is on the camera footage?" Clayton asked. "Before we do anything?"

"Waiting won't matter," Lady Spencer countered. "Reading the past, I know the cameras have been capturing footage for some time. But regardless of what Eyes finds, the sooner we get rid of this mess, the better. Because in reading the future, I see that a staffer will leak Will's immortality and crimes *before* he's behind bars. The country will spiral into chaos and we've had enough already. Besides, I'll glamour Kenny to confess the truth. He clearly knows all about this."

"Your call," Clayton said. "I trust you."

With a swipe of his hand, Zagan tried to carbonize the foul-smelling inmate to the right of Hank's cell.

"Can't be done," Ruby reminded him. "SUC was propagated with my blood. SUC turned the POTUS. Since he had previously healed the prisoners, that means some of my blood coursed through their veins as well. And my blood and your blood are...related."

"Can you transform their remains into dust?" Clayton asked. "Apply sculpting as a workaround to carbonizing?"

"Absolutely." She sculpted an incinerator on the other side of the cells and opened the door with her mind. Gas powered flames roared inside. Using more sculpting, she raised Hank's body off the cot until the chain fastened to his ankle snapped. Lady Spencer floated his corpse into the furnace.

Zagan moved the other two cadavers in similar fashion.

The incinerator door slammed shut.

Ruby swiped her hand and the prison cells, along with all their contents, crumbled to particles of dust.

The human named Insley returned with a large container packed with sealed vials containing Emory's bioengineered vampire serum.

"Stand back from the incinerator," Ruby told Insley.

When the red-haired human stepped far enough away, Zagan took over. He mentally forced the furnace door to open. Gathering and manipulating the air to act as his hands, he lifted the container and blew it into the oven-like compartment. As the blood vials hissed and popped, he sculpted the door to close.

Eyes returned, holding something in his hand.

"Did you collect the recordings?" Ruby asked him.

"Most of what we need is on this computer thumb drive. No other copies exist," Eyes told her. "Good news: the recordings capture the POTUS red-handed, feeding from the inmates (whom he harbored illegally) as well as discussing his plans to sell his vampire blood on the black market."

"The bad news?" Clayton asked.

"His goons did *not* record him murdering the two inmates."

"Sons of bitches."

Zagan did not know how canines were involved in the matter.

"Remember, we have Kenny," Ruby said. "Eyes, can you use your resources to locate the supply of the POTUS's blood?"

"I'll assign our Suspicious Activity Personnel to the task," Eyes told her. "SAPs will get the job done. They always do."

"We're done here." She destroyed the incinerator using her mind.

"Don't hesitate to contact me," Eyes said.

Ruby reached for Zagan and Clayton's hands.

"I am able to travel on my own, Lady Spencer," Zagan said.

Smiling, she used his own words against him.

"Chivalry is not a curse, King Zagan."

60

SOLANGE GRIPPED HER former mate's hand as they traveled through time and space to his High Cliff estate. They each could have traveled independently, but he had asked to hold hands. She saw no reason to start their outing with a refusal.

She had accepted Zagan's invitation, in part, because she was curious about the castle—distinguished as the most magnificent, most embellished fortress in all of Athanasia. The king and his legion of workers had finished construction of High Cliff a century after he believed he had carbonized her.

Even though she could have secretly visited as a cognitive stowaway, hidden in the mind of someone physically going to the castle, she was committed to never doing so. She had vowed to stay far away from Zagan Glissendorf, King of Skotadi.

Distance between them was no longer an issue.

The other reason she had accepted Zagan's invitation was more complicated. He managed, despite their scandalous past, to pull at her heartstrings, making her smile and laugh. She enjoyed his company.

To be truthful, Solange was lonely and missed Titus. But as a logical being, missing her deceased mate would not restore his life. Did she wish to remain lonely and grieving for eternity? Would Titus have wanted her to live a solitary future?

She and Zagan arrived on a grassy patch of land beside the Tume River. The water gurgled as it raced downstream over rocks.

Nocturnal birds performed a cheery concert. And the earthy bouquet of mosses, algae, and river reeds perfumed the night air.

"A beautiful setting," she said. "Though I believed we were traveling to your castle."

"This is the best vantage point for your first introduction." He pointed behind her.

Turning, Solange gasped. The site was breathtaking.

In the distance, rising high above them, was a massive canyon. Carved within its steep rock wall was a glorious structure, with dozens of flat and angled roofs, and countless towers of different heights. Hundreds of windows glowed from flickering candlelight while the full moon cast its celestial spotlight on the fortress. Bats flitted in the sky, dipping and diving for insects.

"Such a spectacular citadel," Solange said.

Smiling, Zagan reached for her hand. "Let me acquaint you with one of my favorite chambers, second only to my library."

When they materialized in the flesh, they were standing in a dazzling, oversized study paneled from ceiling to floor in polished white marble, accented with black veining. An abundance of wall sconces, coupled with a large candle chandelier and a roaring fire in the fireplace, brightened the space like daylight.

The room showcased flower arrangements comprised of hydrangeas, peonies, and roses of every color, reminding her of Lampsi. And the far wall—the one facing out beyond the canyon— was non-existent. Instead, the study remained open to the outside. Several hanging ferns swayed with the breeze.

"This is not what I expected," she admitted, smiling. "Ruby cautioned that I might find your castle a bit dark and dreary, compared to Kaliméra. She did not wish for me to be shocked."

"Precisely why I renovated." He displayed his bold white teeth.

"You did this for me?"

"Indeed, Princess." He pointed to the French country-style vintage armchairs upholstered in fuchsia-colored silk. "Shall we sit by the fire and talk?"

Someone knocked on the mahogany door.

"Enter, Jasmine," he said, as they walked to the chairs and sat.

A Skotadian vampire with long white hair, except for an attractive cluster of pale-yellow strands, entered the room carrying a tray topped with two golden goblets. Wearing a simple gown of canary satin, the beautiful woman glided across the room.

"Your Excellency," Jasmine said, curtsying. "As you requested, I have brought you a midway snack." She outstretched her arms, moving the tray in reaching distance for Solange. "For you, Princess."

"Thank you." She clasped a chalice. "What is a *midway* snack?"

"Midway is our term for noon," Zagan answered, as he picked up his goblet. "And we prefer several small meals to large feasts during our active hours. Better for our constitutions."

Jasmine dipped her head. Leaving the study, she closed the door.

"Is this animal blood?" Solange asked.

"I enjoy a balanced relationship with a herd of deer. They furnish me with sustenance, and I feed them grains and hay, which they prefer over spirulina."

She sipped her wine. "Please tell them: their offering is delicious."

"Are you lonely, Solange?"

The question was unexpected. Her heartrate spiked.

"Why do you inquire?" she pressed, not ready to speak about the subject aloud, although the answer was already known to her lips.

"I am unsure if you will empathize, but nevertheless, I will attempt to explain." He took a sip. "When evil corrupted my soul, I remained busy concocting schemes and manipulations. Certainly, I was alone, absent friends. Yet, evil kept me occupied."

He stood and began to pace. Was he nervous?

"Now that my soul is at peace," Zagan continued. "I long for companionship, for I believe that goodwill is meant to be passed from one being to another." He swept his left hand across the room. "Consider my renovations. My heart filled with joy when I witnessed your reaction. In truth, goodness must be given to be felt."

"Spoken with eloquence," she said. "But you started by asking if I am lonely. How do your revelations relate to my own state of mind?"

"At my hands, Titus was wrongly taken from you. As you look toward the future, I am eager to learn if you are receptive to building a bond with another. Even if the union does not extend beyond filling the void of loneliness."

"I would not couple with a vampire unless love was shared."

"Your words provide relief," he said. "As I believe matters of the heart should always involve...the heart." He raised the goblet to his mouth again. This time, she noticed his hand was unsteady. "I would very much appreciate hearing the qualities you *would* require when considering a possible mate."

She was uncertain about the intent of their conversation. Was Zagan trying to gather knowledge about love in the event he decided to search for a partner in the future? Or was he attempting to direct her toward a specific point?

Pressing her mind to his, she tried to cognitively visit his thoughts. Zagan, however, had constructed a shield to prevent entry. She hoped he would not notice her attempted intrusion.

"Trust is *the* priority for true love," she said. "Because inherent in this one quality are many others such as adoration, honesty, respect, appreciation, and courage. Surely trust cannot exist by itself, for these other traits give it life.

"After trust is compatibility," she continued. "Partners must enjoy spending time together, undertaking mutual interests. Lastly, they must delight in each other's humor for laughter heals many wounds."

"Do you trust me?" He asked, stopping in front of her. "I mean, now that the curse has been broken and I have served my sentence?"

She downed the entire goblet of blood.

"Your directness is rather awkward," she said.

"Apologies. I merely wish to establish honesty—a cornerstone of trust, for in the past, I had difficulty with this competency."

Zagan pinched his chin with his index finger and thumb. "To put you at ease, I shall share emotional intimacy with you first, by revealing that I trust you completely. As well as adore, respect, and appreciate you. Moreover, I wish to display courage by always speaking the truth with you."

Her stomach felt as though she had released butterflies. Was Zagan's confession intended as an expression of...*love?*

Love for...*her?*

Unable to suppress her tongue, the truth rushed from her heart and formed into words. "I trusted you even when I should not have. And in the present, I trust you like our past never happened."

"Did you love me, Solange?"

He knelt down in front of her chair. Their eyes were level.

"Oh, yes," she said. "Even Titus knew that parts of my heart would always belong to you—my first true love. He understood that adoration could be eternal."

Zagan reached into his tunic's pocket and pulled out a velvet ring box. He opened the lid, revealing a 10-carat asscher-cut blue diamond, set in a platinum band ornamented with white diamonds.

"What is this?" she asked.

"I believe they call it a ring, Princess Solange."

"Literally, of course!" She chuckled. "But regarding the ring's intentions, figuratively speaking?"

Her heart felt as though it might burst from her chest.

She could barely swallow.

"If this ring was an offering of mere friendship, I imagine it might have measured a half-carat. Perhaps less if I am being fully transparent." He smiled. "So figuratively, let me assure you that this sizable gemstone, the rarest blue diamond in all of Athanasia, is one that symbolizes the enormity of my love for you. Will you accept this token as my future queen?"

"Are you asking to form an eternal union? That I *marry* you?"

"Indeed. For I have loved you since the day we met. And I wish to spend eternity showing you that I am finally ready to be your faithful, trustworthy, compatible, and humorous mate. If you will only accept my heart."

Tears streamed down her cheeks.

"Do you weep with happiness?" he asked, his fingers trembling. "Or should I brace myself?"

"Both."

Solange placed her hands on his cheeks and drew him toward her. His blush-colored lips were soft and luscious against hers. She opened her mouth and invited his tongue to explore. The experience was energizing and comfortably familiar, even after 2.8 mega-annum. Her inner thighs warmed with excitement. Her memories of their bodies touching, of their lovemaking, were still vivid.

Her heart raced.

Zagan pulled back. "Does this mean you agree to a matrimonial union with me? Or am I just irresistibly hot?"

"Once again, my answer is both!" She held out her left hand and he slipped the engagement ring onto her finger.

Taking her hands, he raised her from the chair as he stood. Wrapping his arms around her, they hugged.

After a minute, he lifted her chin, gazing into her eyes. "Might we marry in a couple of weeks or do you wish for a longer engagement?"

"Are days not an option?" she asked, seeing no reason to delay.

"Days would be preferred by me as well."

Her mind raced ahead. "Do you have a venue in mind? Maybe here in your castle? Perhaps at Kaliméra?"

"I was thinking of Besto Polus. The planet is quite lovely. And gathering animals, vampires, and humans for a joyous celebration will be a positive gesture, given Clayton is attempting to sow peace between the parties." He kissed her yet again. "Who shall stand as your closest friend during the ceremony?"

"Most certainly Liora. And for you?"

"The Tether."

61

Friday, August 2, 2041
The White House Executive Residence: Washington, D.C.

THE POTUS FOUND concentration difficult. Everywhere he turned, the scent of human blood was wafting in the air, tempting his taste buds and stimulating saliva in his mouth. That's why he had decided to take an overnight road trip to Camp David yesterday.

In the middle of the night, he had slipped away from the Secret Service and ran on foot—faster and with more endurance than any predator feared by humankind—to Catoctin Mountain Park in the Blue Ridge Mountains, nestled within Maryland's Frederick County.

Hunting, he had thought, might quench his voracious thirst.

In the park, Will had found a young couple asleep, camping inside their tent. He enjoyed every minute of draining them dry.

Burying the bodies and equipment was below his paygrade, but with superhuman strength, the task had only taken 15 minutes.

Human blood was so damn good. Worth every risk.

How Ruby Spencer resisted temptation was beyond him.

At least last night's hunting excursion had paid off.

Earlier that morning, Will had returned to the White House feeling more in control than when he had left.

He heard footsteps negotiating the steps leading to the Executive Residence. The walking pattern belonged to his Senior Advisor.

"Come in, Kenny," Will said, before his confidant knocked.

Kenny entered the room. "Good afternoon, Sir. Welcome back."

His advisor was giving off a strange vibe. Will detected an elevated heartrate, soured perspiration, and stale alcohol on his breath.

"What's on your mind?" Will asked him.

"Austin Tomb was killed this morning."

"Let me guess." The POTUS smiled, knowing exactly what he had planned for his greedy wannabe Cabinet member. "A motorcycle accident on the Beltway?"

"Impressive conjecture. Your press secretary has prepared your statement of condolence which will air once his wife is notified."

"Excellent." Will tilted his head, still trying to assess Kenny's odd demeanor. "Is this what has you worried? Don't waste your energy. Everyone knows Austin took his life in his own hands every time he mounted that crotch rocket. No one will suspect a thing."

"I have more news," he said. "News that is...unexpected."

"Cut to the chase," Will demanded. "Out with it."

"Have you visited the bunker since your return?"

"Why would I? There's nothing remaining of our inmates except empty shells of skin. And I won't need replacements until we see how much money my blood garners on the black market." Will stared at his advisor. "So are you looking for kudos because you cleaned up the mess in the bunker? Is that it?"

"Didn't get the opportunity, Sir."

"What the hell does that mean?"

More beads of sweat formed on his advisor's forehead.

"The bodies, and even the cells, have vanished," Kenny said.

Will felt his veins begin to pulse under the skin on his neck.

"I pay you heftily to furnish me with answers," the POTUS snapped. "What did security footage show? Who is responsible?"

"That's just it, Sir. Our captured video has been erased."

The President's heartrate accelerated.

"And the SUC? Is the serum still secure?"

"Negative," Kenny answered, his eyes cast downward as if in shame. "The supply has also disappeared."

"What the fuck! Tell me you have a lead."

"The Spencers attended the SWC meeting. I believe Ruby tried to read my mind. I left the meeting immediately, Sir."

"*Tried?* She doesn't have to be in close proximity to do that. You only needed to give her a reason to look inside."

"I'm just guessing she's behind this. With the bunker cleaned out and the SUC missing, my hypothesis is reasonable. And…"

"And what?" Will pressed.

"The Spencers want to speak with me. I've been avoiding them, but that won't work much longer. She'll just pop in like she does."

Kenny reached into his jacket pocket and pulled out a syringe loaded with…vervain.

Will hissed at the sight of it.

"The drug is my party favor if she pays me a visit," Kenny said.

"Give it to me. Now. While you're in *my* presence."

"As long as I get the syringe back."

His advisor handed over the needle. Will shuddered.

"Maybe it's time for me to take the money and run," the POTUS said, placing the syringe on the table.

"There's one more thing, Sir." Kenny took several steps back.

Will raised his eyebrows to encourage the disclosure.

"The vials of *Healing Hemo* were somehow confiscated from the Russian container ship," his advisor said softly.

Confiscated? Was he fucking kidding?

Fire ignited in Will's veins. Saliva flooded his mouth.

Perhaps Kenny's new-found incompetency sparked his reaction.

Or was it his tantalizing pulse?

Come to think of it, Kenny and his partner ate organic.

In a blur, Will whizzed over to his advisor, grabbing Kenny's hair. He yanked his head back, exposing his neck. With ferocity, Will bit Kenny's skin, deeply embedding his teeth. Closing his jaws, he tore away a large chunk of flesh.

His advisor screamed as blood spurted from his carotid artery.

Will sealed the wound with his lips and began to swallow. Even after Kenny's heart stopped, he sucked blood from the vessel until it ran dry. Letting go, the worthless body toppled onto the floor.

While feasting, Will had decided to handle his missing vials of blood, vampire-style: with stealth, swiftness, and savagery.

Ruby wouldn't see his retaliation coming.

He had gotten her once; he'd get her again. Especially as an equal.

Looking at his former advisor's gaping neck wound, he chuckled. "I guess Cutthroat Kenny was a good nickname after all."

62

AS RUBY RELAXED on the couch in their hotel suite, waiting for her husband and daughter who wanted to visit their Cedar Lane property, she reviewed her hefty to-do list in her mind.

First, she looked forward to confronting Will Unger about all of his heinous crimes. Government could only work if representatives adhered to the same laws as its citizenry.

Thankfully, Eyes and his SAPs had confiscated Will's vampire blood slated for the black market. SAPs followed the breadcrumbs. Turns out, the POTUS's advisor, Kenny Franklin, had been stashing the vials in his basement refrigerator until he found a buyer.

The blood sold quickly. Kenny had contracted a deal with a shady Russian entrepreneur who had transferred millions into Will's foreign bank account in Switzerland.

The vials had left on a container ship owned by the Moscow businessman. Of course, the SAP operatives, in conjunction with the U.S. Coast Guard, covertly boarded the vessel while it sailed toward Russia, climbing onto the deck in the stealth of night.

SAPs removed the vials without the ship's crew detecting them.

Congress was days away from legislating vampire blood as an illegal substance. When the bill passed, the Department of Justice might finagle Will's criminal indictments to include drug trafficking.

Selling vampire blood was only the tip of the iceberg.

The government had a new star witness in the case against Will

269

Unger: Dr. Tina Bixley, the President's personal physician.

Ruby had cognitively drilled into the doctor's mind. Tina knew everything, including how the POTUS drained the two death-row inmates; murdered Kenny, his deceased Senior Advisor; and ordered the killing of Austin Tomb while he was motorcycle riding on the Capital Beltway.

The key to having Tina Bixley testify in a court of law was keeping her alive. After Ruby had read her mind, she raised mental shields inside Tina's brain. The shields hid Ruby's intrusion in case the POTUS suspected cognitive "drilling" and went exploring himself.

Thankfully, Ruby's shields were so sophisticated, Will would never find them. In addition, she glamoured Tina to forget her and Ruby's encounter, a protection that would safeguard the physician against Will's suspicions or retaliation.

During the President's trial, Tina Bixley would be glamoured for the last time. Glamoured, to tell the truth and nothing but the truth.

No doubt, the walls were closing in on President Unger.

Before authorities made their move, however, they wanted an ironclad case. After all, Will was the most powerful leader on Earth.

Yesterday, the POTUS had hopped aboard Air Force One to Geneva for an impromptu FIN meeting. Ruby suspected Will had intentionally selected the location since his ghost banking account was in the same city.

Unbeknownst to the POTUS, Eyes had added a more effective security detail for the trip, given Will's new appetite. Liora had loaned the U.S. government four vampire guards from Lampsi, whom Ruby had traveled to the Pentagon for processing and green cards.

The guards' suits covered the sparkle reflected on their brown skin. Makeup foundation did the same for their faces. Each wore contacts to turn their eyes from glimmering gold to human brown.

The vampire guards had a specific mission: to ensure the POTUS only fed from his "secret" stash of blood bags which his glamoured personal physician had brought along for the trip.

If Will attempted to deviate from his meal plan, guards would inject him with vervain and fly him home.

Ruby took a deep breath.

The POTUS would get his comeuppance in less than a week.

The second item on her to-do list was organizing Zagan and Solange's wedding, which she was over-the-moon thrilled about. Their union would take place on Besto Polus in four short days. To boot, Zagan had asked her to stand for him at the wedding. The gesture was touching, reminding her of how far they'd come in their relationship—from foes to best friends. In addition, Gabby and Boris would be the his-and-her ring bearers.

She pictured the massive tent she would sculpt, illuminated by endless strings of lights and adorned with Solange's favorite flowers.

Maybe in centuries to come, when the universe had achieved harmony between all living beings, Ruby would become an event planner. She had a knack for it.

Lastly, she needed to take Gabby shopping for school supplies. The first day was August 19th. Sure, Ruby could save time and sculpt what Gabby needed, but their lives had to include *some* normalcy. As mostly human, Gabby's development depended on it.

In the near future, maybe before the new school year started, she also wanted to visit The Tree of Awareness, planted on Great Island. She wanted to measure the sapling's growth and progress.

"Ready if you are," Clay said, interrupting her daydreaming.

"Sorry. I was thinking of everything I have to do. We'll be quick?"

"That depends on your answer," he said. "Hey!" He looked at Gabby. "Stop trying to read my thoughts. I'll ask my question when the timing's right."

They turned to dust as Ruby traveled them to their construction site on Cedar Lane. Materializing on the front lawn, the three of them stood beside a dogwood tree.

Shadows drifted across the lawn every time the puffy pre-autumn clouds raced under the morning sun, blocking its rays. The warm breeze reminded her that the day would be hot.

"Wow!" Ruby said. "Our house looks finished on the outside."

Their 4,000-square foot home was a French country-style house sided in painted white brick with extra-tall windows on the first floor, complemented with black shutters. Ruby loved the arched double-door entrance which gave an Old-World charm. The second floor showcased three dormers, each with flower boxes brimming with ivy, against a sloping, hipped roof that included two chimneys.

"When can we move back, Dad?" Gabby asked. "Soon?"

Clay walked to the front door. "Let's take a look."

Once inside, Ruby noticed the contrast compared to their home's exterior. Although workers had hung drywall and installed wood floors, the spaces were incomplete. The walls still needed putty, sanding, and painting. The floors, staining and polishing. Wires stuck out from every wall and ceiling, waiting for light fixtures.

"Seems like there's a month of work that needs to be completed," Ruby said, imagining what a finished interior might look like.

"That's one option," Clay said. "Except, I got a great idea when you and Gabby repaired Liora's castle. My mind is open if you're interested in reading my thoughts."

Gabby jumped up and down. "I love your idea! Please, Mom?"

"Wait," Ruby said. "I thought we needed to live like normal humans when possible, for our daughter's sake. You know, so she learns hard work, over any other gifts, produces the best results."

"True. But is staying in a hotel suite for so long...*normal?* Do we really want Gabby starting school while she's living out of a suitcase? And shouldn't Zoe grow up here with us, instead of at Margo and Tomas's house? I mean, I'm just asking, since we have a choice."

"You're hoping I'll agree to an exception?"

"Yes," he said. "If you agree, here's what today could look like. I'd go into the woods, in wolf form, to find those unhappy coyotes. I'll ask them to share their ideas on an Animal Bill of Rights. Clearly, they have grievances. Talking with them might also mend fences.

"While I'm doing that," he continued, "you and Gabby could sculpt the finishing touches inside our home. That way, we could move back here tonight."

He ran his fingers through his hair. "What do you think?"

"I think you want pizza and chocolate chip cookies, baked at home. In our kitchen."

He delivered his crooked smile. "You know me."

63

ZAGAN'S DAYS AS a traveling ghost had furnished him with coordinates for Atea and Harper Patel's residence and avocado orchard. Their acreage was located in the farthest northern district of New Zealand's North Island, in Kaitaia's countryside.

With the wedding less than 24 hours away, Zagan had asked Solange and Ruby to help him invite special guests, in addition to traveling them to their Besto Polus venue, ahead of the ceremony. The Patel's home was the first stop since he was quite fond of the human who had once served as his procurer of blood at High Cliff.

Atea turned out to be "Team Ruby," as The Tether often boasted. Could he blame Atea? Zagan's former self was quite temperamental. Ruthless, in fact. Which was why his procurer's bravery had been so astounding. Instilling admiration if he was honest.

Zagan, Solange, and Ruby materialized beside a large shed.

The Patels had parked two motorcycles and a Scarab jet boat in front of the building. The seaworthy vessel was on its trailer, covered for the season, though winter registered a temperature of nearly 60-degrees Fahrenheit.

He heard the rumble of an engine.

"Follow me," Zagan said, turning toward a dirt road which divided the mature avocado trees into two parcels.

Rain had recently fallen from the ceiling of gray clouds, leaving mud puddles on the roadway.

He identified Atea from a distance, driving a tractor toward them. Despite the overcast day, she wore sunglasses and a plaid shirt. Her curly blonde hair rustled with the breeze. Even in the winter months, her skin was tan and weathered.

Atea recognized him as well. Several yards from them, she turned off the farm machinery, leapt from her seat, and raced toward him.

"King Z!" she cheered. "Is that you? In the flesh?" She threw her arms around his torso and hugged him. "The last time I saw you, mate, you were a bloody ghost!"

He glanced at Solange, feeling his face blush. "Do not be offended," he said to his fiancé. "The term *mate* is a Kiwi expression. One meaning *friend*. Nothing more."

Atea released him and thrust herself into Ruby's arms. "Damn glad to see you, Ruby!" She smiled widely after their embrace. "King Z obviously took my advice and rescued you."

"Thank you for encouraging him, Atea," Ruby said. "He's listening much better these days. Seriously though, I wouldn't have been saved without his help."

"He is a bit more thoughtful, isn't he?" She laughed. "But let's not let flattery inflate his ego or his head won't fit inside that teeny tiny castle. Speaking of body parts, I can't wait to hear how the king got his heart back." Atea looked at Solange. "Oh, how about an introduction? I've heard about you, but we didn't get to meet at the…wedding."

Zagan presented Solange to his human friend.

"Our visit has purpose," he explained to Atea. "My fiancé and I shall marry on this date."

"Congratulations, mate! Wait. You're getting married *today?*"

"Our matrimonial union is officially tomorrow, in Besto Polus's time zone. But since New Zealand is nearly a day ahead, designating today as our wedding day is, indeed, accurate."

"Strange, eh?" Atea commented. "With your traveling pixie dust, you can live the same day twice: the first time single, and the second as a married vamp."

"When one exists for eternity, repeating a day hardly captures one's attention. In this case, however, August tenth will be most memorable as a *married* immortal, for I will be coupled with my one true love."

Solange smiled, seeming pleased with his confession.

"You won't be needing my blood for *this* wedding, will you?" She winked. "Last time, the experience was quite draining."

"Be assured, you shall toast *with* us rather than *being* the toast."

"Bloody good to hear! Count Harper and me in, then."

Atea's wife jogged up to them. Her hair was short and spikey like his own, only black as coal.

"Howdy," Harper said. "Welcome to Doubleton Farmstead."

Zagan introduced her to Solange and Ruby.

"Your orchard is impressive," Ruby said. "Is there a story behind your farm's name?"

"Absolutely," Harper said. "See, avocado fruit grows in pairs. They're a symbol of love."

"Two fruits yield double the reward and a ton more love." Atea smiled. "Hence, the name Doubleton."

"I like it!" Ruby said. "When do you harvest this season's crop? I can see fruit hanging from branches."

"Soon. August is our wettest month. We like to pick the crop before the soil gets too wet."

"Can you afford a brief recess from your labors?" Zagan asked. "Solange and I wish for you and Harper to attend our celebration."

"Have I ever told you *no,* King Z?" Atea asked.

He tilted his head, replaying his memories. "Only once, in reference to your wardrobe. Perhaps your agreeable nature is the reason for our remarkable compatibility."

"Speaking of wardrobe," Harper said, "we don't have anything to wear. On the boat or in the orchard, we're casual. Plaid shirts and jeans aren't exactly wedding attire."

Atea rolled her eyes. "Careful what you ask for."

Zagan could not resist the implied invitation. He sculpted a three-quarter length gown, pink and ruffled, with puffy sleeves at the shoulders and an oversized bow tied in the back of her waist. He added a bonnet on Harper's head. All she needed to complete the fashion was a shepherd's hook and some bleating sheep.

Laughing, he was pleased with his sense of humor.

"Oh no, no, no!" Atea said. "Not Little Bo-Peep."

"Bugger!" Harper moaned. "I'll not be caught dead in this."

"Come on, King Z," Atea said to him. "Make us look badass."

"If I must."

He sculpted leather pants and matching jackets, both ornamented with silver studs. To complete the style, he added black boots.

"Sweet," Atea said, smiling. "You didn't forget."

"More like it, mate," Harper agreed. "I'll put the dogs inside and close up the farmhouse."

"Where are you going next?" Ruby asked him.

"To High Cliff, for my staff. Then to Kaliméra. And you?"

"I'll pick up Eyes and Insley," she said. "And the Gonzalez family. Then I'll pop by Annapolis's historical district to see if Pap—you know, Neviah Bain's son—can attend. Nothing like a wedding to heal old wounds."

Zagan smiled and placed his arm around Solange's waist.

Though he was technically dead, he was the happiest man alive.

64

RUBY WAS THRILLED over how the wedding was progressing.

Seeing the love between Zagan and Solange was heartwarming, despite being far from a fairytale. Their journey was as *real* as it got, complete with curses, separation, and heartbreak. Yet, their love for one another had prevailed for several mega-annum, finally bringing them to reconciliation and the alter.

The venue was fantastical, complemented by sunny skies, unusually low humidity for August, a comfortable breeze, and temperatures around the 80-degree mark.

Ruby had sculpted a massive tent, with opened side curtains so animals could attend. Garlands of blue hydrangeas, intertwined with strands of tiny white lights, hung in multiple swags throughout the interior. Flower arrangements of blue hydrangeas, blush roses, and white peonies, accented with Skotadi ferns, decorated tables draped in white linen.

The 1:00 p.m. exchange of vows, followed by Solange's coronation, had taken place inside the portable shelter, on a raised stage for guests to witness from their tables. Over a path of rose pedals, Gabby and Boris had flawlessly performed their duties. First, by presenting the rings to the bride and groom and second, by presenting the royal couple with their crowns.

Solange was breathtaking. Zagan had crafted his queen's off-the-shoulder gown in periwinkle blue silk. Attached to its full, flowing skirt were handmade 3D white peonies—the flower's anthers ornamented with pearls. Her necklace boasted blue and white diamonds. She wore matching earrings. With her pewter hair raised in a braided bun, loose flowing curls reached her bare shoulders.

In his formal white silk tunic and slacks, Zagan had selected a matching periwinkle cummerbund. As always, he styled his hair into short white spikes.

After Solange became Queen of Skotadi, both Zagan and Solange donned their crowns, the ones Zagan had originally shown to Ruby. Crafted in gold, the matching crown and tiara depicted bats in flight. The onyx bats, with ruby eyes, flew across three different skies, each representing a realm in Athanasia. Sapphires embellished the night skies of Skotadi; gray pearls, The Shadowlands; and citrine, the sunshine of Lampsi.

After the ceremonies, the Glissendorfs and their guests moved outside, where Ruby had sculpted a large dancing area. Of course, Zagan and all Skotadians had to wear sunglasses and plenty of sunblock to prevent excessive exposure to the ultraviolet rays.

Ruby had traveled a band to the venue, glamouring the musicians *after* they had agreed to the lucrative contract. Band members just wouldn't remember where they had played or for whom.

There were two bars outside. One serving humans; the other serving vampires.

Several filled water troughs were also available for the animals.

Ruby was dancing with Clay when she felt a tug on the skirt of her navy silk gown.

"Mom," Gabby whined, "I'm bored."

"Here, dance with your Dad."

"I've already danced with him. And with King Zagan, King Draven, and Uncle Eyes. Not to mention Boris, Uncle Tomas, and Miss Atea. I'm danced out."

"Have you met all the animals?" Clay asked.

"Patted each one. And now my feet hurt from these shoes."

"Some things aren't about you," Ruby said, using a motherly tone. "This gathering is a celebration for King Zagan and Queen Solange."

"Please don't stray off," Clay added. "Toasts to the happy couple are about to start. You might enjoy hearing them."

"But Dad, I don't drink…"

The lead singer from the band asked for everyone's attention. He announced for all guests—uprights and animals—to gather together to hear comments from close friends.

The order of the toasts had been pre-determined. Clay was first on the schedule. She was last, after Liora.

One of Zagan's staff handed Clay a flute of champagne.

Her husband wiggled his eyebrows at her as he moved toward the center of the wooden dance floor.

She could tell he was feeling a pleasant buzz from the alcohol.

The guests quieted.

"We're among close friends here," Clay said. "So I hope no one minds me admitting this. Zagan, your *second* wedding pleases me so much more than your first. And it's certainly working out better for the both of us, heart wise."

Everyone nervously glanced at one another, not knowing if they should chuckle or be in shock, since everyone knew what had happened when Ruby pretended to marry Zagan just five weeks ago.

Be nice, she whispered inside her husband's head.

"In all seriousness," Clay continued, "I'm so happy that you've been reunited with your true love. Solange is a remarkable being—so kind and forgiving. At least you'll have eternity to make things right, *this* time around." He raised his flute. "To new beginnings."

"To new beginnings," the guests repeated.

Animals added their roars and whinnies, squawks and grunts.

At least Clay had ended on a more positive note. *Slightly* more.

Draven was next.

Ruby guessed the sarcasm would continue. Maybe Clay and Draven had even agreed to roast Zagan during their comments. Which perhaps their former nemesis had earned.

The King of Swords and Shadows raised his glass. "No one can deny that Solange grabbed Zagan's heart the moment they were reunited." He winked. "May your heart continue to beat *inside* your chest, brother. Raise your glasses to beating hearts."

"To beating hearts!"

Atea approached the center of the dance floor with her champagne. "To my former boss and his gorgeous bride: I wish you…forever. Forever happy. Forever healthy. Forever laughing. Forever loving." She raised her flute. "Here's to all your forevers."

"To all your forevers," the guests cheered.

Ruby was relieved Atea had decided to give a proper toast.

"May I add," Atea said, before walking off the dance floor, "that it feels jolly good not to be served to others as the bloody cocktail!"

Zagan and Solange laughed, encouraging others to join them.

Liora was next.

If anyone could be serious, it was the Queen of Light.

"Your union reminds us that true love conquers all challenges."

The queen paused.

Guests leaned forward, eager to hear what she might add.

"With the King of Skotadi," she continued, "the list of challenges is exhaustingly long. Thanks be to HIM that Zagan has regained eternity to overcome them *all,* for his bride's sake."

Smiling, Liora raised her glass. "Love conquers all."

"Love conquers all!"

Ruby was going to take another route, since everyone before her had poked fun at the groom. She would end the toasting ceremony on a sincere and uplifting chord.

"Clay, Gabby, and I…," she started.

Ruby scanned the gathering, looking for her daughter.

Gabby wasn't among the guests.

Ruby's heart started to pound.

Her skin prickled with fear.

Veins pulsed in her neck.

65

GABBY HAD MADE up her mind; she didn't like weddings. Not one bit. Maybe because at the first wedding she'd ever attended, her Mom had fainted while holding King Zagan's beating heart in her hand. Pretty hard for a kid to erase that image from her thoughts.

She sat in the grassy field, apart from the celebration behind her. Watching butterflies flutter around was a bit more amusing than watching vampires, humans, and her shifter Dad drink, dance, and act a little too cheery.

If Reese, the only other kid at the wedding, didn't have a stomachache from eating three helpings of mashed potatoes, he could've explored some of the planet with her. Gabby's Mom had mentioned that a river was nearby and there was nothing Gabby liked better than lifting rocks and discovering what hid underneath.

Since she didn't have a playmate, she was flat out of luck.

Which meant she had nothing else to focus on except her feet. Who invented dress shoes anyway? They pinched her toes and rubbed her heels. And looked silly.

Gabby hid her eyes behind her lids. When she opened them, her shoes were gone. Instead of a blush colored gown, she wore shorts and a T-shirt.

Looking over her shoulder, she could tell no one from the wedding was watching her. Guests stood around the dance floor listening to the Glissendorfs' closest friends give toasts. Laughing a little too loudly.

When she thought about it, she knew she'd have to apologize to her parents for being whiny, and maybe even a little bratty. It wasn't *their* job to entertain her. She was nine, after all. And what her Mom had said was true: the wedding was about King Zagan and Queen Solange. Not her. She got that. She had just been feeling frustrated.

Turning back toward the glade, she saw Boris trotting toward her.

"Hi, boy!" she said. "Where have you been?"

The gray wolf nudged his huge head against her chest, and she toppled onto her back.

"Hey!" she giggled. "Be careful. I'm only human."

Boris plopped to the ground, obviously wanting a tickle.

His thick fur was warm as she ran her hands over his coat.

"I have an idea," she said. "Want to explore with me?"

The wolf leapt onto his four paws and wagged his bushy tail.

"I take that as a yes!"

After standing, she ran down the glade, away from the venue, enjoying the soft grass cushioning her sore feet. Boris ran beside her, his pink tongue lolling from his mouth.

This was way more fun than a wedding.

At the edge of the woods, Gabby stopped. Should she venture in?

Boris ran ahead, in between the tall pines. He turned to her and yapped, urging her to follow.

She couldn't resist. And why should she?

A thick carpet of pine needles and pinecone droppings covered the forest floor. She chuckled thinking about pinecones as tree turds.

On the serious side, the combination might prick her soles, so she sculpted flip-flops to protect the bottom of her feet.

Gabby felt free in the woods. She loved nature as much as her Dad. The smell of pine trees. The fresh air. The wildlife. She was more *alive* in the woods than anywhere else.

Hearing a roar up ahead, she stopped running.

"That's a waterfall," she said. "Last one there is a rotten egg."

Boris must not have liked spoiled eggs because he took off cantering, reaching their destination first.

The waterfall was small, but beautiful. Water cascaded over a high shelf of stacked rocks, crashing into a swirling pool below, sending mist into the air. When the sun touched the mist, a miniature rainbow formed. And the smell of damp soil and moss was pleasantly earthy.

Beside the riverbank was the perfect rock for tipping.

Maybe a crawfish was underneath. Or a salamander.

If she was lucky, even a slithering snake.

Kneeling, she started pushing on the large rock. It was stuck.

A chill caused goosebumps to rise on her arms.

Something had changed. Was the mist making her cold? Had the temperature dropped? Or, was she sensing danger?

Knowing the difference between a natural reaction and her gifts was still a mystery. She was still learning.

Turning, she hoped to find Boris.

Maybe *he* had picked up on possible danger.

The wolf stood only five feet away from her. His fur was stiff on his withers. With raised lips, drool dripped from his fangs and exposed gums. He was growling.

What did he see? She looked toward the waterfall again. Nothing seemed unusual. No other animals were around.

Her heart suddenly pounded in her chest. Her mouth grew dry.

At that moment, she wondered if Boris might be growling at *her*.

She looked back at him. "What's the matter, boy?"

He snarled. Muscles quivered on his shoulders and hips.

Slowly, she stood, facing him. "I don't know what's bothering you, Boris. But I'm going to have to sculpt a muzzle on you if you keep growling. Stop it. I mean it."

Gabby had no time to process.

Boris's front paws hit her chest. He knocked her onto her back.

Her mind froze. IN TERROR.

The wolf clamped down on her throat.

Pain pierced, stabbed, and burned all at once.

Tears swelled in her eyes.

Boris added pressure on her throat, like his jaws were vise grips, getting tighter and tighter.

What *happened* to him? Why was he attacking her?

Trying to gulp a breath, her attempt failed. There was no room for air. Hearing something crack, like a bone, she began to drift into a strange numbness.

Gabby tried to process.

Would her body heal fast enough?

Fast enough to…survive?

But when the wolf removed a mouthful of her throat and she choked on blood, she doubted it.

She was only nine years old. She didn't want to die.

Her thoughts sputtered but she managed to whisper, *Mom!*

Darkness swallowed her.

Or was she drowning in her own blood?

66

RUBY COGNITIVELY HEARD her daughter's frightened cry. She whispered inside Gabby's mind and saw Boris biting her throat.

Gabby's lifeline stone was fading.

Veins erupted on Ruby's entire body.

The champagne flute dropped from her hand, shattering on the dance floor.

"Clay!" she screamed. "Gabby's being attacked by Boris. She's in the woods. Near a waterfall. Follow her scent. I'll meet you there."

The crowd gasped.

Ruby wanted to travel to her daughter, but she didn't know exactly where she was. Traveling blind might not get her where she needed to be, in time.

A dust cloud enveloped her husband, as his transforming body shredded his tux. He emerged in wolf form and took off galloping, heading down the glade.

Sculpting into an eagle, Ruby took flight.

"Go with her!" She heard Solange shout. "Give me a visual sign so I can travel to you."

As Ruby gained altitude, able to follow Clay's direction from overhead, she noticed a raven furiously flapping alongside her. Zagan had joined her to help.

Thinking about Gabby, her mind exploded with fear. What if they found her too late? What if they couldn't save her?

Ruby's heart threatened to break through her breast cavity.

Looking down, the pine trees opened up by the river.

She saw their daughter.

Gabby lay on her back, not moving. With a muzzle dripping in her daughter's blood, Boris stood on her chest with his front paws. Gabby's throat bled profusely from a deep neck wound.

Ruby and Zagan dove, their wings tucked closely by their sides as they gained speed.

Arriving on the scene, Clay knocked Boris off their daughter. Biting down and tearing, he severed Boris's hind leg from his body.

The wolf yelped as blood gushed from his femoral artery.

As she and Zagan neared the ground, they sculpted into vampire form, dressed in their battle leathers. Running, as they landed.

Ruby raced to Gabby's side.

Struggling to breathe, her daughter choked on her own blood. With her mind, Ruby made an incision in the thin membrane of skin above her daughter's breastbone. She sculpted a tube and inserted it into Gabby's trachea, enabling air to flow. The procedure worked. Her daughter's lungs inflated. But she had lost so much blood that she wasn't healing quickly enough. Gabby was still in trouble.

"Oh my God!" Clay said.

Ruby turned to see what had caused her husband to morph back into human form while fighting Boris. Had he killed the wolf?

She stared in disbelief.

Were her eyes betraying her?

Laying on the ground, where Boris had previously been, was the loathsome human body of Emory Bradshaw.

She repeated Clay's words: *Oh my God!*

The mad scientist was naked and bleeding, though the skin around his severed thigh was trying to seal his stub. Healing was underway.

"Destroy him once and for all, Tether," Zagan urged, biting his wrist. "I shall complete Gabriella's recovery with my blood."

She hesitated.

"Do not worry, Lady Spencer. My blood is powerful. And Gabriella is breathing again. Her heart has regained a strong rhythm. Go quickly. Emory should die at your hands. Deliver the death sentence this criminal deserves."

As she ran toward Clay, she sculpted leathers on her husband's body. She didn't care about Emory; he'd be dead in minutes anyway.

"I can't believe it," Clay said. "Why didn't we know he was alive?"

"Not sure. Except I can't read lifeline stones for animals."

"But I could read his mind when I was in wolf form," Clay admitted. "All I ever got from his thoughts was loyalty. He fought Lykos for me, remember?"

"I guess it's easy to look brave when you know you can heal."

"His body's like mine, isn't it?" Clay asked. "He's a shifter, not a super wolf."

"Hell-*ooo,*" Emory said. "I can join this convo if you want."

"Fuck you," Clay snapped, stepping on Emory's ribcage until Ruby heard a couple of ribs snap from the pressure.

Emory screamed.

She knelt beside the mad scientist. "Tell me. How were you able to turn into a shifter?"

He spit in her face and she wiped the blood from her skin.

Clay stepped even harder on his chest, crushing a few more ribs.

Her nemesis fainted.

"I'll read his mind by touching his skin," she said to her husband. "And if you hold my hand, I'll channel what I see. We can learn about his past at the same time."

Holding hands, Emory's memories started to rewind in hyper-speed. Ruby needed to go back in time to Siberia, after the mad scientist had fled their stronghold in the field, abandoning Vladimir. Emory had driven an ATV toward the Polar Station.

What had happened next?

The images of his return to the lab in Building #4 began to play.

Ruby cognitively watched as Emory collected the vial of her vampire venom, as well as the IV bag of wolf venom. Having witnessed Clay's remarkable conversion in the field, Emory wanted the same transformation for himself.

Before he exited the lab with the venoms, he had handed his dart gun, lab coat, and wolf remote to the female scientist named Mela. That's why pieces of Emory's shredded lab coat had ended up in the horrific slurry of blood and body parts.

After Emory had walked out, he grabbed a pint of Ruby's blood from the nearby refrigerator where a guard was keeping watch.

Emory returned to his office and concocted a cocktail of wolf venom, vampire venom, and Ruby's blood before gulping it down. After minutes of convulsive shivering and unconsciousness, Emory had morphed into a gray wolf, of Clay's unique variety. Meaning, he had three independent strands of DNA: human, vampire, and wolf.

Emory was a shifter.

In wolf form, Emory had returned on the scene as the two wolves in the lab with Draven were tearing the humans to shreds, per Clay's directive. To silence all witnesses, as well as to appear as one of the super wolves, Emory ripped apart the guard who had been keeping watch over supplies in the refrigerator area. The guard, whose remains Solange had found; the guard, who brought the death toll to four, based on the number of skulls found.

Ruby had interpreted this finding as an affirmation that Emory was among the dead, since she and her friends knew nothing about another guard being present. To bolster this conclusion, she and Liora confirmed that Emory's lifeline stone was blank, not realizing it was because he was in pure animal form.

After the carnage was complete and unidentifiable pieces were all that remained of the humans, Emory returned to Draven's lab room in wolf form. He forced the other two super wolves to flee. Alone, he acted like Draven's protector, positioned on the floor near the foot of the operating table. Truth was, Emory had already formulated a plan to appear loyal to Ruby, her family, and friends.

Revenge had always been his endgame. He hated Ruby that much.

Emory's intent was to be useful and gain favor until given an opportunity to strike back, in a way that would hurt Ruby the most: killing her daughter.

His plans for revenge didn't stop there.

For the crown, Emory intended to challenge Clay in a fight to the death. His thoughts confirmed he had always wanted to rule the world. Maybe he would finally succeed as a shifter. Instead of making an army, he believed he would *be* the army.

Emory Dixon Bradshaw *was* the last usurper.

"Before you destroy him," Clay said, "could you verify that he was responsible for the fox's death? I'd like to know, without any doubt."

Ruby fast-forwarded to when Boris had left his duty at the tent, during their first visit to Besto Polus. The wolf had become obsessed with his unfamiliar, animalistic hunger.

First, he had hunted a rabbit, then a fox.

Only, he caught the fox.

Morphing into a vampire, Emory drained the animal quickly. With his genius and vampire adeptness, he had raised a cognitive shield to hide his memories, making it seem like he had lost awareness of time and place while hunting. After all, he was well aware that Clay could read his thoughts, at will, while her husband was in wolf form.

After he had raised a shield, Emory shifted back as a wolf.

Ruby had no reason to suspect the wolf was pretending to be "Boris," or super wolf subject "1064" (which turned out to be Emory's old department ID number in prison). She had no way of knowing that he had constructed a shield, so she had never thought to look for one.

Filtiarn and Zagan had *nothing* to do with the fox's demise.

"I want him awake when I deliver his death sentence," Ruby said.

"Try giving him some of your blood first."

She dripped blood into his mouth.

Emory's eyes opened.

"Thinking you can't live without me, girlfriend?" he wheezed.

"Thinking I want you to know that evil is no match for goodness," she corrected him. "Because you're about to meet our Creator who will be your judge and jury. Good luck."

She penetrated his chest cavity and wrapped her fingers around his beating heart.

His eyes grew wide before they froze open.

She plucked out his heart.

Sculpting a fire, she tossed the organ into the blaze. She picked up his body and threw it into the fire as well. The flames hissed and roared, sending a plume of smoke into the sky.

Ruby had no regrets.

"Lady Spencer," Zagan said, sounding worried. "Please come with haste."

67

CLAY FOLLOWED HIS wife as she rushed to their daughter's side.

A chill overwhelmed his body as a defensive response, warning him that he could shift into a wolf at any second. He had to resist. His daughter needed him in human form.

Clay had expected Gabby to heal. But she was far from recovery. A huge chunk of his daughter's throat was missing, exposing anatomy typically reserved for the eyes of a surgeon or a pathologist conducting an autopsy. He could identify torn suprahyoid and infrahyoid neck muscles. Emory had crushed her larynx. Blood still pulsed from her arteries, hemorrhaging with each weakened heartbeat. Her skin was ashen.

A tube protruded at the base of Gabby's throat, inserted into her trachea to allow air to bypass her ruptured windpipe, enabling oxygen to flow directly into her lungs.

His daughter was barely conscious.

"What the hell's happening?" he asked Zagan, who supported Gabby's head on his lap.

"I do not know," Zagan said. "I dripped my blood into her parted lips, yet she has not improved. Her wound festers. Without healing, her condition appears grave."

Ruby knelt beside Zagan and Gabby.

"Maybe she needs to swallow." His wife placed her hand on Gabby's head. "Swallow, sweetie. Let Zagan's blood heal you faster."

"Lady Spencer, with my urging, Gabriella has already swallowed. However, her consciousness is sinking instead of rising. I do not understand the cause of her deterioration."

With his heart pounding, Clay dropped to his knees next to Ruby. "Maybe she needs *your* blood? I mean, yours is the most powerful."

"All vampire blood has healing properties," she answered. "Our gifts are equal in this competency. So I don't get it. But we won't know for sure unless I try to heal her with mine." A tear raced down her cheek. "Because we're losing her, Clay. Her stone is fading fast."

Ruby bit her wrist until blood flowed. She placed her wound against Gabby's lips.

"Please. Try to swallow," she coaxed.

He watched as Gabby's throat muscles, the ones still intact, attempted to move the blood down her esophagus. Logically, there was no reason the mouth couldn't absorb his wife's blood.

Moments later, Gabby coughed up blood. Lots of it.

Was her body *rejecting* Ruby's blood?

Clay pulled at his hair. "What are we going to do?"

His frustration level was off the roof. Not even the King of the Animals had a clue about how to save his precious daughter's life.

Solange, Liora, and Draven materialized near them, probably seeing the smoke rise from the fire. The Queen of Light, no doubt, had been cognitively monitoring the situation.

"Vampire blood always heals humans," Liora said.

"Gabby's not one-hundred percent human. She's somewhere in between." Ruby stood and began to pace. "Do you think that might be complicating her healing?"

"Vampire blood heals immortals as well," Draven added.

"My heart aches," Solange said, "that such a tragedy would befall an innocent child such as Gabriella. There *must* be a solution."

Solange's words scratched a cognitive itch in Clay's mind.

"Repeat what you just said," he urged Zagan's bride. "Please."

"My heart aches that such a tragedy would befall an innocent child such as Gabriella."

"What are you thinking?" Ruby asked him.

More blood spurted from Gabby's mouth.

Her ashen skin grew paler.

JULIA ASH

"The word *innocent* is sparking a memory I can't quite grasp," Clay said. "But my instincts tell me it's relevant because the word keeps resonating inside my head."

"I believe," Zagan said, "that innocence is mentioned in the codicil explaining The Turning Point. Is it not?"

"You're right!" Ruby said. "Remember the last line? *Blood from the King of the Animals will not save innocence by itself.*"

"But what does that *mean?*" he asked, looking at his wife.

"Sounds like your blood can save Gabby, but just not by…*itself.*"

"Who else's then? Yours didn't work. Zagan's didn't work."

"Let me think," she said, "because now something germane is nipping at my thoughts. The words *blood* and *king* from the passage are popping out at *me*. The answer has to be inside my mind."

"Quickly, Lady Spencer," Zagan said, "for Gabriella is faltering. She is no longer conscious."

His wife's eyes hid behind her lids. No doubt, she was scouring her memory banks, searching for the answer. For a possible remedy.

"Gabriella's heart has stopped," Zagan cried. "We must take action without delay."

"Move!" Ruby yelled, stopping her mental search. Her skin had erupted in solid purple.

Clay felt as though he might combust.

Not being able to do anything produced a ticking time-bomb of pressure. They couldn't lose their daughter.

Zagan lowered Gabby's head to the ground and moved aside.

Ruby straddled their daughter and began chest compressions.

The blue of Gabby's eyes hid behind opened lids.

I'm recalling a memory, his wife whispered inside Clay's mind, while she continued applying pressure to Gabby's chest. *A memory of Neviah Bain, the psychic from Annapolis. Zagan had inserted his razor-sharp fingernail into her throat. He sliced across her skin, so deeply that I could see the vertebrae in her neck. With severed arteries, she died seconds later.*

Died? he questioned. *How will that memory help us?*

Neviah fell face-down on the floor, Ruby continued. *And when I went to cover her body, I saw a tattoo on her back. I told you about it, remember? The artwork was of a tree: The Tree of Awareness. But the inked words…they read: The Blood of Three Kings.*

Yes, Clay whispered, *that led us to Three Kings Islands off of Cape Reinga. But now you're thinking the words might refer to me, Zagan, and Draven? And our blood?*

Remember I told you that with scriptures, you have to look deeper than the literal words? Because they often connote multiple meanings. At the time, there was only one king—Zagan. But Neviah was a seer. And there are three kings, now. The codicil states your blood alone isn't enough. This may be our answer.

"I have an idea," Ruby said aloud, continuing to administer compressions. *"The Blood of Three Kings.* Each of you needs to give Gabby your blood, at the same time. Hurry!"

No one challenged her. They respected that she was usually right.

"I've never done this before," Clay admitted.

"Just bite your wrist," she said, removing Gabby's trachea tube. "You're also a vampire, which means you'll heal right away."

All three kings dripped their blood into Gabby's mouth.

Ruby provided more chest thrusts to aid in circulation.

Three thrusts. Five thrusts. Seven.

Miraculously, their daughter's heart began to beat.

Neck muscles reconnected. Her arteries repaired themselves. Her larynx became whole. New skin enclosed her throat.

Gabby was rapidly healing.

Kneeling beside his family, Clay felt relief saturate his body.

"We're here, sweetie," Ruby said to their daughter.

Gabby's lids blinked rapidly, and her blue irises returned to their normal position. A wave of energy raced across her eyes.

"Mom? Dad?" she said, sitting up.

All three of them wrapped their arms around each other in a Spencer group hug.

"Did you save me, Mom?" their daughter asked.

"Believe it or not," Ruby admitted, "my blood wasn't useful at all. This time, Dad, Zagan, and Draven saved you. Which proves we all need one another. We all have purpose."

68

RUBY MATERIALIZED WITH her husband, appearing in the hallway near the entrance to the Executive Residence. They had agreed that she wouldn't confront the President alone. Because a month ago, after insisting she tackle the First Lady's health issue all by herself, Ruby had ended up drugged and kidnapped to Siberia.

Having learned a valuable lesson about teamwork, she had no intentions of repeating her mistake of going solo.

Upon their arrival, she glamoured the Secret Service.

Remember, she whispered to Clay, *stay hidden until you hear your cue.*

Using sculpting, she unlocked and opened the door. Clay followed her as they walked toward the master suite, not making a sound. Before entering the room, she heard the POTUS's elevated heartbeat. She nodded to Clay. He knew what to do.

Ruby walked inside the bedroom as Will Unger turned to face her.

"I've been expecting you," he said.

"Bet you have. Turns out, we adhere to the same philosophy when it comes to collecting on outstanding debts. What does the Good Book say? *'An eye for an eye.'* That's it."

"Come on now," Will said, sipping his glass of whiskey. "We're friends. Aren't we?"

"That's what I call irony." She snickered. "See, a friend wouldn't have turned me over to known terrorists. Terrorists who used me as a blood bank, hoping to create an entire army of bioengineered super wolves. We are far from friends and you know it."

"As I told you then," Will started, "I had no clue why Emory and Vladimir wanted you. Nor did I give a damn. Quite frankly, if you weren't so self-righteous, acting as though you were the single most *expert* on what it means to be human, you would've saved my Irene from cancer. I wouldn't have had to resort to manipulating her DNA to try and save her. I wouldn't have needed to turn myself into a vampire to fill the void while you were…incapacitated. This situation is entirely your fault."

"Still lecturing those who are above your station?" she asked.

"Are we playing a little game of déjà vu?"

She smiled. "So you've guessed I'm not here for Russian tea?"

"Let's cut to the chase," he snapped. "How does this end? Are you here to bribe me about some ridiculous Animal Bill of Rights?"

"I thought even *you* could've figured out what comes next."

Clay appeared in the doorway brandishing a dart gun.

"*Ahh,* vervain," Will said. "How very *un*-original."

Her husband fired and the dart penetrated the President's chest.

Will removed it with lightning speed.

Clay had already fired two more rounds.

The POTUS's eyes blinked slowly. His heartrate was sluggish.

"What goes around, comes around," she reminded him. "You'll be kept in a vervain coma. Sound familiar?

"I should warn you: prepare to be bored," she continued, mimicking what her captors had said during *her* kidnapping. "You'll be kept in that state until The Tree of Awareness matures and produces fruit. Once administered the berry juice, you'll become mortal again. As a human, you'll stand trial for your high crimes, which include murder.

"By the way," she added, "the evidence has already been submitted to the Department of Justice. Something else you may not know: the House of Representatives and the Senate unanimously passed a provision for unique circumstances inherent in situations like yours. Impeachments can now be private proceedings, avoiding a lengthy process where both sides of the political aisle use the opportunity for grandstanding.

"Which brings me to the headline, Will. Both chambers of

Congress have impeached and convicted you, removing you from office. Congress has already sworn in Olivia Jackson as the fifty-first President. There's some déjà vu for you, right?"

In what looked like slow motion, Will hurled his glass at the wall. The amber colored whiskey splashed on the wallpaper. The glass shattered into fragments.

"Why are you doing this?" he sneered. "I'm one of your kind."

"Hardly," Ruby said. "That's where you're wrong. Someone's genome has nothing to do with their heart. Character and behavior reflect the true pulse of someone's spirit. Translation: we're *nothing* alike."

"Plain and simple, you're greedy, filled with contempt for others," Clay said to him, while loading more rounds in the dart gun.

"Can't we agree on a...compromise?" Will slurred.

"Sure. I'll meet you halfway." She looked at her husband. "Give this asshole two more injections, instead of four."

Clay pulled the trigger twice.

The darts embedded in Will's chest. He no longer attempted to remove them.

"Sleep well," she said.

The former President of the United States slumped to the floor. Unconscious.

69

RUBY TRAVELED HER family, including Zoe, to Three Kings Islands to check on the wellbeing of The Tree of Awareness, which at this stage, was a sapling. The tree species (*Pennantia Baylisiana*, the rarest in the universe because there was only one living sapling of its kind) was also known as The Three Kings Kaikomako.

The sapling sprouted from a root taken from the original Tree of Awareness. Like its predecessor, the sapling would eventually produce enchanted grape-like fruit that if ingested by vampires, would render them mortal.

Since Creation, the original tree had served as a symbol of great significance, believed to function as a cognitive portal, leading to unfiltered awareness...of both good *and* evil.

As prophesized, the first vampire to eat the forbidden fruit from the sacred tree would initiate a curse on himself and on Athanasia. *That* distinction had gone to Zagan, 2.8 mega-annum ago. He was the only ancient vampire who could shamefully claim: *been there, done that.*

Thank goodness, recent events had broken the curse and restored goodness within the King of Skotadi's soul. But the original tree hadn't survived the ordeal.

When the "cursed" Zagan had encountered Ruby, Clay, Gabby, and Atea on Great Island at the end of June, he had sculpted a violent earthquake which had swallowed the mature, original tree, destroying it. Luckily, Ruby had already clipped an exposed root.

Five weeks ago, while Ruby and Gabby were at High Cliff, a glamoured Clay returned to Great Island to plant the sprouted root. Since then, Atea and Harper attended to the sapling, ensuring that it remained protected, healthy, and able to thrive.

Already knowing the coordinates of the sapling, Ruby materialized with her family beside the young tree.

The day was partly sunny and blustery, not a surprise since they were standing by a cliff overlooking the North West Bay. The ocean below was raging. Angry waves crashed onto the ragged rocks, sending spray high into the winter air.

"Winter" boasted a high of 54-degrees Fahrenheit, though the temperature probably felt colder to Gabby.

Ruby had sculpted matching leather shirts and pants on everyone, including their favorite black leather cloaks. Why not? With a promise of peace on all three planets, their go-to battle outfits would become obsolete. They didn't quite fit into a suburbia lifestyle.

Of course, she'd still wear her leathers when she participated in scalping events, though scalping would likely be a thing of the past before long. President Jackson had reduced the once-a-month frequency to once every other month, since July's scalping had only culled 55 zombies nationwide. Also, the ZOM-B pathogen was much weaker. Thankfully, new zombies lacked the bloodlust which had spread the disease like wildfire.

The ZOM-B infection was finally dying off.

"I can't believe it," Clay said, snapping her back into the present.

The immature Tree of Awareness was in front of them, protected by wire mesh fencing to prevent rodents from nibbling on its leaves. Remarkably established, the sapling reached 18-inches high. Two gray trunks had grown branches boasting rounded, glossy leaves which curled upwards on their edges.

"Wow." Clay reached his fingers between the mesh and touched a leaf. "What are Atea and Harper feeding this sapling?"

"Double tons of love, no doubt!" Ruby smiled, feeling relieved. "At this rate, maybe it'll produce berries sooner than we thought."

"I've got a question," Gabby said, holding the puppy. "Remember when you rewound time for the original tree? You know, to collect its fruit? Well, can't you *speed-up* time, so the sapling could mature faster?

So it could grow berries for you to pick and eat?"

"I *could*," Ruby said. "The tough question is: should I?"

"Is that because you and Dad still have jobs to do?" Gabby asked.

"Exactly," she answered. "Dad needs to understand the animals, to advocate for them, to be their voice. And my gift of traveling can take us to all three planets. In other words, the universe needs us to remain immortal, for now." She ran her fingers over the smooth leaf. "However, knowing we have a choice in the future is reassuring."

"You also want the berries to turn President Unger human again for his trial. Right, Dad?"

"Yes. But having him asleep for a while gives the world a needed break from his evil shenanigans. A trial will be exhausting."

Dust swirled near them.

Zagan, Solange, Liora, and Draven materialized.

"Your artificially intelligent associate, Justine, informed us you were here," Zagan said, smiling.

"I hope you didn't refer to her by that label," Clay said. "She's a little sensitive about being called artificial."

"Indeed. She called me an asswipe, though I am not familiar with this Earthling term."

"You don't want to know, King Z!" Gabby giggled as she placed Zoe on the ground.

"Three Kings Islands." Draven took a 360-degree look at the 13 islands in the archipelago. "I appreciate that they now reference *us*."

"This one is clearly named after me," Zagan said.

"Oh? And what is this island called?" Draven asked.

"*Great* Island," Ruby answered, rolling her eyes.

Zagan twitched his eyebrows, looking pleased with himself.

"We decided to join you here," Liora said, ignoring Zagan's humor. "We are also interested in assessing the tree's health, especially since The Tree of Awareness, like The Tree of Immortality on Lampsi, is at the heart of our history."

"Queen? Admit to *all* of the truth," Draven urged.

"We also missed you," Liora admitted. "Peace slows down time, giving our hearts plenty of opportunity to long for your company."

"A pace, we surely prefer to that of battle," Solange clarified. "We simply need time to adjust to the altered pace."

JULIA ASH

"I'm in awe when I think about how much we've accomplished in such a short period of time," Ruby said.

"True," Liora agreed. "Not long ago, we randomly chose you while in your mother's womb, to evolve as our Tether. You have served the prophesies better than we had hoped for, than the stones had revealed in their etchings. You are the hero we needed."

Ruby laughed. *"Not long ago?* I remember when I considered thirty-six years a substantial period of time! I was thinking of what we've accomplished over the last two months. Because when circumstances got tough, we challenged ourselves. We've all emerged as heroes."

"I do not understand," Solange said. "For we *are* who we have always *been:* immortals with gifts. This has not changed since Creation. But you...you have risen to become significantly *more."*

"Oh, I'm not alone when it comes to growth," Ruby countered. "Take you, Solange. You've emerged as the hero of forgiveness, setting an example for all of us.

"And you, Liora? Without a doubt, the hero of steadfast commitment. Commitment to the prophesies, even sacrificing your personal happiness for several mega-annum.

"Draven: you're the hero of bravery. Not only were you brave enough to confiscate Zagan's blood to fulfill the prophesies (as in, creating *me*), but you've never shown an ounce of fear. Not when you were glamoured, captured, or imprisoned.

"Zagan," she continued. "You are our converted hero. Once evil, now serving good. Not only because we broke the curse, but because you've *chosen* to nurture compassion in your heart, to think of others, even after your extraordinary gifts returned.

"And Clay, you're our unexpected hero, embracing a fearless spirit of advocacy. Turns out, you're gifted in ways we'll never be.

"Remember when I was considered The One and Only?" Ruby asked. "I've learned there's no such thing. Everyone can rise as a hero if they choose to become the best they can be. Everyone plays a role; everyone has gifts, even if they aren't of the immortal variety."

"What about me, Mom? What kind of hero am I?" Gabby asked, not waiting for the answer as she looked around. "Where's Zoe?"

Ruby glanced behind her, analyzing the scene.

Zoe was chasing a low-flying songbird, oblivious to the 500-foot

300

drop over the cliff. Which the puppy was quickly approaching.

Gabby gasped.

Her daughter began to tremble. Maybe convulse was a more accurate description. Her eyes quivered and her pupils hid behind opened lids. Purple veins bulged under the skin of her neck. Her hands shook uncontrollably.

"What's happening?" Clay asked.

"Save the puppy," Ruby shouted, looking at Zagan, hoping he would travel to Zoe or sculpt a barrier to stop her. "Gabby's having some sort of a seizure…"

A cloud of dust consumed their daughter.

In a blink of an eye, Gabby was gone.

Ruby's heart was about to burst through her ribcage.

By the cliff's edge, a swirl of dust formed. Their daughter reappeared and scooped the puppy into her arms. A second later, she vanished, before materializing next to them, holding Zoe in her arms.

"You're a *traveler?*" Clay asked.

"I wasn't sure at first," she said, "but I was thinking there might be a really good chance."

"How? I mean, why?" Ruby asked.

"Well, after I got blood from *my* three kings, I started feeling different." Gabby looked at Clay. "I can even understand the animals, Dad. But I don't need to turn into one to hear them. I just wasn't paying attention to Zoe because she was having so much fun."

"That settles it, then," Ruby said. "You, Gabriella Emily Spencer, are our hero of surprise. Once the most innocent and naive, you're now the most gifted of us all."

"*Surprise?*" Zagan questioned. "I do believe, Lady Spencer, that I have known, from the beginning, just how remarkable Gabriella is."

"You did predict that one, brother!" Draven laughed.

"My mind has settled this matter," Liora said, looking at her and Clay. "We simply cannot be apart for long, as we are meant to be together. Will you construct a dwelling on Besto Polus? Perhaps in Athanasia, as well? There is plenty of acreage at Kaliméra."

"No dwelling on either planet," Clay said. "On Besto Polus, we don't want to interfere with natural habitats. But we'll visit the planet quite a bit, camping out in portable tents. Cedar Lane will remain our primary home. Anyway, with *two* travelers in the family, we should be seeing a lot of each other. We'll pop into Kaliméra and High Cliff on a regular basis. You might become sick of us!"

"Never," Solange said. "For you are as family."

"We feel the same way about each of you," Ruby said.

"I must ask you a question, Tether." Zagan sounded serious. "I am still becoming reacquainted with my heart or perhaps I would already know the answer. What should I remember most about our recent adventures together? For our time in partnership has been short, but our lessons, plentiful."

"Never forget," Ruby said, "that greed is the envy of hate. Which makes greed the most toxic of all Extinction Level Infections."

"Love is the cure, then?" Zagan asked.

"Yes, love and generosity. But we must *choose* to be healed."

Ruby felt emotion swell from her heart and overflow in tears, because she loved her friends dearly.

"And when we choose love over greed," she continued, "we'll experience our own turning point. One which will transform our lives forever. Imagine a universe where everyone makes this choice."

"Indeed, Lady Spencer. Indeed."

The End

EPILOGUE

RUBY ENJOYED SUNDAY dinner with her family, casually sitting at the kitchen island on stools. Gabby sat in between her and Clay.

Earlier, she and Gabby had made fresh pasta while Clay grilled cauliflower and asparagus, harvested from their garden. They tossed the veggies with the fettuccine, splashed on olive oil and lemon juice, sprinkled seasonings, and shaved parmesan over the top.

Ruby cherished their dinner conversations. Sure, she enjoyed making dinner, too, even though she didn't eat it. All *she* needed was her straw and insulated cup, filled with her sustenance.

Lying under Gabby's stool, Zoe clearly hoped her best friend would accidentally drop a noodle or a crumb of garlic bread.

"When do we visit Castle on High Cliff again?" Gabby asked.

Ruby raised her eyebrows. "We were just there yesterday!"

"I know, but I like King and Queen Z a lot. Too bad the Z's can't have babies. I would babysit the wee-Z."

"Alrighty then," Ruby said, stealing a wide-eyed glance with Clay. "How about a change in subject?"

"Isn't it great there's no curfew anymore?" Gabby asked. "And Zoe can chase sticks and balls in our yard again?"

The puppy thumped her tail on the floor.

"Thanks to Dad," Ruby said. "Yes, it's wonderful."

"Thanks to *us,*" he corrected. "And our friends."

Ruby raised her cup and clinked it against Clay and Gabby's.

"I heard on the news that the government picked a date for the President's trial," Gabby said. "Is that true?"

"January fifteenth of next year," Ruby answered.

"Will the berries be ready then? To turn him human again?"

"They'll be ready." She smiled. "I'll even help them along if they need it. But with Atea and Harper overlooking the tree's growth, I doubt that'll be necessary."

"What do you think will happen to him?" her daughter asked.

"The evidence is very damaging," she answered. "He could get life in prison or even the death penalty. A jury will decide."

Gabby creased her forehead. "What if President Jackson pardons him? Like President Unger pardoned Wicked Doctor E?"

"I don't think that will happen, not under President Jackson. Justice will prevail. My faith in the legal system has been restored."

"That's good," Gabby said. "Because no matter how powerful someone is, I think they should have to follow the same laws as everyone else."

"Amen to that." Clay put down his fork, looking at Gabby. "Speaking of laws, what time do you need me at school?"

"Eleven o'clock sharp."

"What are you doing again?" Ruby asked him.

"As the first Secretary of Animal Rights, Gabby's teacher invited me to read the adopted legislation to her class. And also to answer student questions."

"Like how it feels to be a wolf with fleas?" Gabby winked.

"Not funny. Classified here on Earth, remember?"

"I'm only kidding, Dad. Hey, want to read the bill now? Practicing might help for tomorrow at school."

"I have an idea," he said. "Justine?"

"Yes, boss?"

"Will you recite the Animal Bill of Rights? I'm sure you've memorized the amendments by now."

"I've been meaning to ask you," Justine said. "When will you advocate for DEPEs? The whole label of 'artificial intelligence' is insulting. Don't you think? I mean, what's *artificial* about being able to recite every known fact to humankind? Or to problem solve faster than the human brain? Just saying."

"Another time, Justine," he said. "The Animal Bill of Rights?"

"Oh, okay. Here goes."

Justine read the bill which aimed to remedy societal injustices toward the animals, incorporating amendments to the Constitution.

"Thank you, Justine," Clay said, when she had finished reading.

Their DEPE huffed. "Remember, *artificial* is insulting."

"I'll work on it."

Ruby leaned forward to lock eyes with her husband. "I'm so proud of you. Animals finally have rights. They'll be treated fairly."

Her smartwatch pinged with a videoface request from Margo.

She accepted the call because it was unusual to receive one during dinnertime hours.

"What's up, Margo?" Ruby asked. "Everything okay?"

"We want you to be the first to know. Uno birthed a litter. None of us even knew she was pregnant! Guess how many puppies?"

"Two!" Gabby cheered.

"Six. She had *six* pups. A full litter!"

"A miracle for sure," Ruby said.

The Turning Point was already delivering on its promises.

TRANSLATIONS
Animal Language to English

Page 1
Amadad ahoee = Help me

Pages 6, 8
Vonaig ahoee = Kill me

Pages 6, 8
Miangui ree = Please

Page 18
Laa-tah ayuuloza = You are in danger

Page 26
Manaluul, ambochon = Gather, wolves

Pages 27, 37
Fahaneegui = Silence

Page 35
Bibamitad an'orchlizaah = Animals of the universe

Page 35
Hencoh irneg; hencoh rehebüg = Hear one; hear all

Page 225
Misanao laa = Thank you

Page 244
Isibid anashoor = We approve

Page 244
Hamalak = Kill

PRONUNCIATIONS

ACCALIA: Ah-**cal**-lee-*ah* *(cal* rhymes with *gal)*

ATEA: **Ate**-*uh*

ATHANASIA: **Ath**-in-**ey**-zh*uh* *(Ath* rhymes with *math)*

BESTO POLUS: **Bess**-toe **Pole**-us

BORIS: **Bore**-iss

DEPE: **Deh**-pee

DRAVEN: **Dray**-vin

FILTIARN: **Fill**-tea-yarn

KALIMÉRA: **Kal**-lah-**mare**-*ah* *(Kal* rhymes with *gal)*

LAMPSI: **Lamp**-zee

LIORA: Lee-**or**-r*ah*

LYKOS: **Lie**-kohs

MAI: **My**

MEGA-ANNUM: M*eh*-**gan**-numm *(gan* rhymes with *ran)*

MONTARO: Mon-**tair**-oh

MUKESSI: Moo-**kess**-see

PYTHIA: **Pith**-thee-*ah*

RENIRABY: **Wren**-ear-a-bee

SKOTADI: **Skoh**-tay-dee

SOLANGE: Sol-**lawn**-j*uh*

VALA: **Val**-l*ah*

YONA: **Yo**-n*ah*

ZAGAN: **Zay**-gin *(gin* rhymes with *win)*

ZOE: **Zoh**-ee

THE PLANETS

ATHANASIA: *Planet of the Vampires and Animals*
Skotadi
  · The realm of perpetual darkness
  · Vampire Leader: Zagan, King of Skotadi
  · Animal Leader: Lykos, Wolf Alpha of the Night Stalkers
  · Landmarks: Castle on High Cliff and the Tume River

The Shadowlands
  · The realm of perpetual shadows (charcoal skies)
  · Vampire Leaders: Shared oversight by the King of Skotadi and Queen of Lampsi
  · Notable Natives: Draven, Titus, and Princess Solange
  · Landmarks: Valley of Shade, Prison of the Unruly, The Cottage of Shadows, Gray Forest, and the Tume River

Lampsi
  · The realm of perpetual sunshine
  · Vampire Leader: Liora, the Queen of Lampsi and Draven, the King of Swords and Shadows
  · Landmarks: Kaliméra Castle and the Tume River

BESTO POLUS: *Planet of the Animals*
  · A small planet with solar and lunar systems similar to Earth
  · Animal Leader: Filtiarn, Lord of the Wolves
  · Landmarks: The Glade, Royal Ridge, and the Reniraby River

EARTH: *Planet of the Humans, Animals, and The Tether*
  · A planet that revolves around a sun and has a rotating moon
  · Human Leader: William Unger, President of the U.S. and leader of the Federation of Independent Nations (FIN)
  · Universe's Leader: Ruby Spencer, The Tether and the one and only bioengineered vampire on Earth
  · Landmarks: The White House, The Polar Station in Siberia, sites in Annapolis, Maryland

ACKNOWLEDGMENTS

BRINGING A SERIES to its close is both rewarding and sad. Rewarding, because the characters whom I've breathed life into have reached "the end" I've been hoping for. Sad, because I know I'll miss them and their adventures.

Thank you for your support and for taking this journey with me, Ruby Spencer, and her cast of characters!

While I've immersed myself in this endeavor, my family has been incredibly supportive. Thank you to my husband Rick and our adult children Brooke, Mitch, and Stacey *(daughter-in-law)* and to our two pups: Lady Remington and Ote Coyote. My family is amazing!

I'm also in awe of the marvelous team members who have contributed to the success of each book in this series:

Dena Baker (Beta Reader)
Damonza (Cover Design)
Deborah Faroe (Beta Reader)
Jed Faroe (Beta Reader)
Kerrie Flanagan (Developmental Editor)
Martha Mitchell (Beta Reader)
Charlene Sharpe (Proofreader)
Cheryl Tomlinson (Beta Reader)

I'm deeply grateful to Dita Daub, Marie Kirkland, and Miranda Reads for reviewing my book early. Thank you! Appreciation is also extended to team members who have provided their expertise for one or more of my books: Mary Lee and Ashlynne Meiklejohn.

To all my family, friends, readers, authors, bloggers, reviewers, librarians, bookstore owners/managers, Goodreads community, social media communities, book industry experts, and local news media: prepare yourselves for a brief and sincere text-shouting session: THANK YOU SO MUCH! YOU ARE WONDERFUL :)

Until the next project…

ABOUT THE AUTHOR

JULIA ASH writes dark-fantasy and ghost fiction. The ELI Chronicles is a three-book series: THE ONE AND ONLY (2018), THE TETHER (2019) and THE TURNING POINT (2020).

Ash lives with her husband Rick and two Brittany bird-dogs on Maryland's Eastern Shore.

For a complete biography, please visit her website. And join her on social media.

Website:
https://juliaashbooks.wordpress.com

Goodreads:
Goodreads.com/julia_ash

Facebook:
Facebook.com/JuliaAsh.Books

Twitter:
@Author_JuliaAsh

Instagram:
julia.ash.books

Reviews

Please consider providing a star rating
(with or without a written review) of

The Turning Point
by Julia Ash

Vendors make it easy to give reviews
on the novel's detail page
(the online page where you purchased the book).

Authors appreciate reviews more than you know.

Thank you!

Made in the USA
Columbia, SC
09 October 2021